Copyright © 2013 Jon Maas

All rights reserved.

ISBN-13: 978-1490350011

ISBN-10: 1490350012

WgaW Reg #1688460

Library of Congress Reg # TXu 1-871-666

JON MAAS

CONTENTS

Prologue	5
Part I – The Fountain	
Balthasar	11
Adam	25
Mayfly	65
Phoe	87
A Fate Worse than Burial	103
The Compound	117
The Kidnapping	129
Part II – The Wild Zone	
Precocious Children	159
A City of Siblings	183
The Inquisition	219
The Rest Home	229
Part III – A Battle at the Edge of the World	
The Devil's Army	263
Panthers in the Snow	287
A Surgeon's Welcome	321
A Battle at the Edge of the World	343

JON MAAS

PROLOGUE

The average human being lives from 0–80, sequentially. *Spanners* don't.

These rare beings have different *lifespans* than the rest of us. Some live their lives in reverse, some live only six months, and some are immortal. There are hundreds of classes of spanners that live hundreds of different ways, and each class has a unique lifespan that gives them unique powers.

A few spanners find a way to live in normal human society, but most live in the shadows. There are some spanners that are extremely dangerous, and with the help of a *mayfly*-class spanner, an 8,000-year-old detective named Adam Parr is doing everything he can to keep them under control.

JON MAAS

PART I

THE FOUNTAIN

JON MAAS

BALTHASAR

The Florida Panhandle—Ten Years Ago

Balthasar Guzmán de Balboa was awoken at 2 a.m. by Christine, who apparently now went by the moniker *Drayne*. Balthasar's entire young crew had given themselves nicknames soon after they had joined him and though he thought it trite, he let them call themselves whatever they wished. If they fancied themselves superheroes, so be it. They believed in his goal, and no one else did.

"Cannon's been sobbing uncontrollably," said Drayne. "I tried to approach him, but he's in a rage; he tore his bed in half."

"Cannon?"

"Skyler, the *tweener*-class spanner."

Cannon is his name now, thought Balthasar. *It's fitting. His class of spanner is explosive as a cannon, and probably twice as deadly.*

"Christine," said Balthasar. "Now what—"

"*Drayne*," she corrected. "It's what I do. I take people's lifespans, like a—"

"Fine, *Drayne*," said Balthasar, humoring her. "Now why is Cannon upset?"

"I was giving him advice," she said, "and he got angry."

"What kind of advice?"

"Just advice …"

"Did you criticize his appearance?"

"No," said Drayne. "But I—"

"But what?"

"I told him he needed to bathe," she said. "He smells really bad."

Good Lord, thought Balthasar. *This is going to take some damage control.*

/***/

Balthasar followed Drayne to Cannon's room and made the sign of the cross when he saw the young boy; the room had been turned upside down, and Cannon's metal bed had indeed been ripped in two. Balthasar knew he had to be careful when approaching Cannon; their team was small and lived in an abandoned, teetering wood mansion. If Cannon went ballistic, they wouldn't be able to contain him, the boy would destroy their entire house, and their goal would be lost.

Balthasar expected this when he recruited the three spanners; they were teenagers and these setbacks were bound to happen. *Youths like these always bring problems, but there is no other way,* thought Balthasar, *because only the young can be recruited, and only the young will fight and die for this cause.*

Balthasar thought what to do with Cannon; the young brute had perhaps two hundred pounds of pure muscle on him, maybe more.

Balthasar himself was an immortal spanner, but he had no real powers, at least not anything that could control the boy. *Could Drayne lay her hands on him and take some of his life force away?* he thought. *The other spanner is fast and might be able to—*

Balthasar decided against turning his own team on one another, even temporarily, because they hadn't yet learned to control their powers. Drayne was a *scourge*-class spanner and might be able to take Cannon in a fight, but she might kill him too. She might take so much of his life away that he'd be reduced to a withered heap of bones and flesh.

"Perhaps we should leave him alone, sir," said Drayne.

She stood there tentatively and then ran her long fingers nervously through her stringy black hair. Balthasar knew her powers were deadly, but she was still a child, unsure of herself and her place in this world. She would one day grow into a beauty (albeit a pale, razor-thin and somewhat frightening one), but for now she was nothing more than a young girl looking to Balthasar for guidance.

"No, we will not leave him alone," said Balthasar. "Social isolation is devastating for his class."

Balthasar heard a noise from upstairs and saw his third and final recruit, a blur-class spanner from Namibia named *Fanuel*.

"I have some news, sir," said the blur-class spanner. "I've been into the swamps and found—"

"We have a crisis on our hands, so I'll speak with you about that after," said Balthasar. "Now, Fanuel—"

"Blur," said Fanuel. "I like to be called *Blur*."

"Blur," whispered Balthasar, nodding. "Your class name and first name are one and the same. At least remembering it will be easy. Let's talk somewhere more private, shall we?"

13

Balthasar pointed to a far corner of the mansion; it was close enough for Cannon to know that they hadn't abandoned him but far enough away that the boy wouldn't hear their words. Balthasar and Drayne walked to the far corner, and Blur waited a few moments and then zipped over there so quickly that he seemed to rematerialize.

Drayne takes lifespans away and Blur lives his life at a different frequency, thought Balthasar. *We are not without our powers.*

"Now, Cannon is a *tweener*-class spanner," said Balthasar calmly as soon as they were out of range.

His tall, thin frame blocked the moonlight and cast a faint shadow over Drayne as he spoke, and his salt-and-pepper hair was combed back perfectly. Balthasar had always taken great pride in his grooming and looked meticulous even now, lecturing a pair of teenagers at two in the morning.

"He is a tweener-class spanner," repeated Balthasar, "which means he remains stuck at one part of his lifespan for his entire life. Cannon happened to get stuck in puberty, and *that* means his testosterone is five hundred times its normal level, and rising. This gives him incredible strength, but also puts him in extremely fragile moods. Though he might not wish you ill, he could rip your head off, and mine too."

"His testosterone gives him a foul odor," said Drayne. "He smells like rotten—"

"You'll not mention his odor," interrupted Balthasar. "Nor will you mention the acne on his face, nor even his incredibly muscular physique. He's quite insecure about being different, and that insecurity manifests itself as anger. *Teenage* anger, if you will, multiplied five hundred times. So let me do the talking, and for God's sake be nice to him."

Drayne and Blur nodded quietly and then nervously held their breath, which led Balthasar to trust that they would do the right thing. To them, Cannon was less a scared adolescent and more a trapped bear, and they would proceed with caution.

They approached the door slowly and Cannon was in the corner of his destroyed room, crying. Tears flowed down his face, which was slick with acne. Balthasar got down beside the boy and tried to breathe through his mouth, but it didn't work. Cannon had the sharp, dreadful kind of body odor, one that smelled of sour, rotting meat.

Lie to him, thought Balthasar. *There is too much at stake to tell the truth.*

"Young man," said Balthasar. "You completely misinterpreted what Christine said."

"Drayne," corrected Christine. "My name's—"

Balthasar put up his thin hand to silence her.

"Drayne said I ..." Cannon's voice cracked with tears and he pounded his fist into the ground, but Balthasar spoke before the boy's emotions rose further.

"She said no such thing," said Balthasar. "She meant to say we *all* need to bathe, because we *all* smell bad."

"Really?" asked Cannon.

"Yes," said Balthasar. "This area of Florida emits a certain swamp odor, and it gets on our clothes. We all have it, all of us, and must scrub it away every day. This is our lot, our cross to bear for living in this wondrous mansion."

"Really," said Cannon, his deep voice quivering. "Because I thought—"

"Whatever it is, you thought wrong," said Balthasar with a smile. "Now, we need you. How are we to achieve our objectives without our strongest team member?"

"I don't know ..."

"We can't achieve anything without you," said Balthasar, "and it's vitally important to the group that you refrain from further outbursts. Can you do that?"

Cannon nodded.

"Good, Skyler," said Balthasar, "because I—"

"My name's Cannon."

"Of course," said Balthasar. "I'm an old man and slow to learn these things. You're quick, strong and explosive like a cannon and—"

"No," said Cannon. "I'm Cannon for a different reason."

"Oh?"

"I heard hundreds of years ago you led a ship across the ocean," said Cannon. "And that's what I want to be: the guy who fires the ship's cannons."

Balthasar smiled; Cannon was even less mature than he had thought, but this wasn't a bad thing. *He'll be loyal,* thought Balthasar, *even if he's not strong with metaphors.*

"Splendid," said Balthasar. "This mansion is our ship, and you're officially our cannoneer. Now, we're all going to take two baths a day to counteract the swamp gas; can you do the same?"

Cannon nodded, and Balthasar got up and gave Blur and Drayne a look telling them that all would be okay. He motioned for them to walk back out in the distance and then whispered again so Cannon wouldn't hear them.

"*You* don't have to take two baths a day," said Balthasar, "but pretend that you do. His spanner class places a tremendous amount of importance on *fitting in*, and he'll conform to the group's actions."

Cannon walked by them up the stairs, and his odor hit the group moments later. Drayne started to cough, and Blur disappeared into another room before getting sick.

"And put something in Cannon's bath water," whispered Balthasar. "I suggest *bleach*."

/***/

As soon as Drayne and Cannon had gone back to bed, Balthasar met with Blur and examined the boy's map of the Florida Everglades. It was quite clear where they needed to go: Blur had placed a giant *X* over one small area of the map.

"Do you think this is it?" asked Balthasar.

"I think so," said Blur. "All I brought was a metal detector, but it's unmistakable; there's something big down there. It's too deep to dive, so I didn't—"

"It's okay," said Balthasar. "You couldn't have lifted it by yourself anyway. We should bring a small crane, and perhaps a dredger."

"We could bring Cannon," said Blur.

Blur smiled excitedly at his idea, and his white teeth were visible within his dark face, even as he vibrated.

He's right, thought Balthasar. *If we got Cannon under control, the boy could swim down and bring up a sunken truck if need be.*

"Fine," said Balthasar. "We leave first thing in the morning, so be sure to rouse Cannon as soon as you awake; his class tends to sleep late."

"Of course, sir," said Blur, and in another instant he was gone.

/***/

Balthasar couldn't sleep the rest of the night, though he was neither excited nor nervous. He just wanted to soak in the moment, the moment of calm and anonymity before the momentum began. He felt like Napoleon as a second lieutenant during the French Revolution, or perhaps Alexander the Great as a teenager, being quietly tutored by Aristotle. Balthasar and his group were unknown now, but they wouldn't live in anonymity forever. They would soon find their leader in the Florida swamp, and their leader was destined to be both Napoleon and Alexander, multiplied by a thousand.

But for now, Balthasar found the moment peaceful and couldn't help but smile; their rickety mansion had no running water or even electricity, but he was enjoying the darkness. He sipped his tequila and listened as the forest creatures continued their endless song of the night; they sounded to Balthasar like an orchestra warming up before a performance.

It won't be the same after tomorrow, he thought, *but we must move forward. History waits for neither man nor immortal, and it won't wait for us.*

/***/

The next morning they were in the Florida Everglades on two rented fanboats, one driven by Balthasar and the other driven by Blur, which also carried Cannon and the dredging equipment. They drove their boats without much notice; Blur had taken sedatives to stop vibrating and took on the mien of an ordinary African American. Balthasar and Drayne looked like normal humans; Balthasar's thin, dry features had allowed him to blend in with relative anonymity his whole life, and although Drayne's pale face and dark clothing looked out of place in the Florida swamps, she looked like the average disaffected youth that Balthasar thought was becoming all too common nowadays. Even Cannon blended in somewhat. He wore heavy clothes to cover his shiny acne, and the passersby would send only a look that said *that's the biggest boy we've ever seen*. As far as the rest of the world was concerned, they were just three humans and a weightlifter out for a tour of the marshlands.

They passed the Sawgrass Plains, traveled through rivers, skimmed over Lake Okeechobee and then went down through the endless sloughs that snaked through the swamp. Blur was a skilled pilot and kept the pace up; the pills had slowed his body but not his driving. Blur kept zooming ahead of Balthasar, but Cannon seemed to be enjoying the ride so Balthasar allowed it. *We'll have to rely on Cannon to pull up the casket,* thought Balthasar. *It doesn't hurt to have the kid in a good mood.*

They traveled for two days and camped out in the open air, but the crew didn't seem to mind. They were a tough group; Balthasar had found Blur in the rough shantytown outside of Windhoek and had rescued Drayne from an Eastern European brothel, and though Cannon was temperamental, he could sleep anywhere. Balthasar gave them a speech about their goal the first night, but it wasn't needed. The kids were too young to see that far ahead and didn't really need a pep talk anyway. As far as they were concerned, there was no goal; this was their life, and sleeping in the swamp was just another evening.

An alligator had gotten onto Blur's boat on the second night and laid there until the morning, and the young man awoke with a shriek. Blur was fast, but only on land; the swamp pushed him out of his element. The fanboats were moored together, so Drayne snuck up behind the creature, ungloved her hand and put it on the alligator's tail. It thrashed, nearly knocking her over, but soon appeared to lapse into a deep sleep, and a minute later it stopped breathing. Balthasar noticed that the creature's tail had been stained a deadly necrotic white in the place that Drayne had touched him, and that stain seemed to have spread outward. Cannon pushed the creature into the water and it floated away with its stomach to the sky, and that was that.

"How close are we to our goal?" asked Balthasar.

"Two hours if you can keep up with me," said Blur, still shaken and eager to leave the swamp.

"Let's make it four," said Balthasar. "No one's after us, and Drayne will handle any more creatures that come our way. The casket's been buried for five hundred years; it can wait a little longer."

/***/

They found the area four hours later, and it took another two hours to find the exact spot. On his first trip, Blur had left a small buoy marking the point of burial, but its connecting rope had been gnawed by a creature and the orange bulb now floated adrift in the water. So they paddled their boats in a methodical way, with Blur dragging the underwater metal detector that Balthasar had made. The metal detector worked, and two hours later it beeped consistently above a patch that looked indistinguishable from any other part of the swamp. They tested it to be sure, and it beeped and stopped beeping at just the right points; they were right over a metal container that was about the size of a coffin.

"Do you sense it down there?" Balthasar asked Drayne.

"What?"

"Do you sense a life force down there?" asked Balthasar. "You haven't been trained in this yet, but your class senses sparks of life much as a shark senses blood. If anything is down there it will be extremely faint, so listen carefully."

Drayne closed her eyes, knelt and put her hands on the water. After a few moments she nodded.

"Yes," she said. "I feel something."

Balthasar nodded and then thought for a moment.

"Let's wait until nightfall," said Balthasar. "For though we're alone, we're still digging up a body, and we can't afford to gain attention. No one's around here, but too much is at stake to take any chances now."

/***/

They spent the night dredging, digging and kicking up mud, lit by the dim glow of their battery-powered work lights. Blur was still scared of the alligators, but Drayne didn't seem to mind them and Cannon didn't seem to care. The boy crashed into the water whenever the dredger needed adjustment, and if a creature dared attack him, Balthasar would feel sorry for it.

So they dug and dug, and soon their machinery hit something solid. Cannon swam down into the muck to touch it, and came up smiling.

"It's metal," he said, "and real big."

They sent down a claw to pull up the casket. They came up empty twice, but it held on the third time and Cannon guided it to just the right spot, and they brought up the box and let it dangle in the air for a moment. They had attached metal rods between the fanboats and placed the claw between them so that it would be stabilized, but the sheer weight of the casket caused both boats to angle inwards as it hung in the moonlight. The box was dull and corroded from years under the soil, but it was still solid and had maintained its shape after all this time.

"We must cover the casket and get it to our van as soon as possible," said Balthasar. "Four men carrying a body is too suspicious, even in this area."

/***/

The next day they were driving up Interstate 75 when Blur came to the front cab to alert Balthasar.

"Sir," he said. "He's moving within the coffin."

Moving, thought Balthasar. *Five centuries later, and he still has energy to move. Our leader is truly extraordinary.*

"He won't harm you," said Balthasar, "though we should still be cautious. He might be disoriented when he arises."

Balthasar put the truck in park and went in the back to be sure. Cannon was listening nervously, and Balthasar wiped mud off a section of the coffin and placed his ear against it. There was no moving, but he heard a faint whisper.

"Ayúdame. ..."

He's pleading for help, thought Balthasar, *and he's still conscious.* Balthasar took a lock from his pocket and placed it on one of the coffin's clasps, just to be sure that none of the kids would give their leader "help." After securing the lock, he stood and once again addressed the crew.

"I know you're excited for this," said Balthasar. "I am too. To you it's an arrival, to me it's a return, but for all of us it's the first step of a new era; one that requires a tremendous amount of patience. So please resist the urge to open this coffin, because he's waited too long to arrive prematurely."

/***/

They arrived at their mansion at midnight, and after checking for snooping neighbors, Cannon brought the coffin into the building. Blur went to help, but Cannon had placed the casket on his shoulder as if it were a bag of dirt, nearly a foot above Blur's head. Cannon walked into the mansion and brought the metal box downstairs, dropping it on the ground with a *thud*.

Balthasar took the lock off and motioned for Cannon to get a sledgehammer from the side of the room, and the boy grabbed it and banged the side of the coffin until it opened. They took off the top slowly to reveal their leader, or at least what was left of him: his body had atrophied severely, and he looked like a corpse. But he was intact, and judging from his shallow breaths, quivering jaw and faint moans, he was alive.

Balthasar smiled at the group and then kneeled down in front of their leader, whispering so that he could hear them.

"*You are saved,*" said Balthasar, careful to use fifteenth-century Spanish. "*I don't know if you can hear me, but you are saved. I can't imagine the horrors you experienced down there; punishment for immortal spanners is quite cruel, unfortunately.*

"*It's been some time since you disappeared at the hands of the devil Adam Parr, and I assure you that we've spent every minute since then searching for you. It took until now for technology to improve to the point where you could be located and exhumed, but you are here with us, and you are safe.*

"*Though it will take months for you to recover, you will recover. And once you're healthy, you will once again lead us.*"

Their leader made a faint wheezing sound, but Balthasar couldn't understand it.

He could be asking who, what or any number of things, thought Balthasar. *I'll answer it all. He deserves the truth.*

"I am your steward, Balthasar, whom you gave immortality five centuries ago, and these young ones are your new crew," said Balthasar. "Together we will complete the quest that you started so long ago, the one you had almost accomplished before burial prevented you from doing so."

Balthasar stood up and spoke in a louder voice, this time in English, addressing the crew more than their leader.

"Your name is Captain Juan Ponce de León," said Balthasar. "And when you are healthy, you are going to lead us to the *Fountain of Youth*."

ADAM

Kolkata, India—Ten Years Later

As he had done every night for the past 8,000 years, Adam Parr dreamt that he was buried alive. His nightmare had him clawing at a coffin's ceiling and he woke up with his hands in the air, sweating and breathing heavily. Burial was his worst fear; it was the fear of most immortal spanners. You can't kill an immortal, so if someone ever wanted one gone, they'd bury them instead. Adam's enemies had vowed to do just that, and though he was smarter than most of them, all it would take would be for one of them to get lucky once, and he'd be trapped under the ground forever.

After he calmed down, he ran his fingers through his thick brown hair and tried to remember another dream he'd had before his nightmare.

I was dreaming of blonde hair, he thought, *and of glowing orange eyes.*

He was dreaming of Phoe, his sister. She was a *phoenix*-class spanner, and their kind got reincarnated. Adam had always taken care of her in each of her lifetimes; sometimes he called her his sister, sometimes he raised her as his daughter. It didn't matter; each time she died and came back, she would always come back to him.

Until her last lifetime, thought Adam. *She didn't die like she normally did, and she didn't come back to me.*

Adam knew Phoe had to be alive; her class of spanner always came back. Always.

I can't worry about this now, he thought. *There's too much at stake.*

He shook off his thoughts and got up. He washed his face and looked in his hotel room's scratched mirror. He had a square jaw, and though his tan face was completely free of wrinkles, he felt old; he had felt old every day of his life as far back as he could remember. He rubbed a thin towel over his face and noticed that his eyes were still glowing green, so he waited a moment until they faded. Now he could face the day and walk amongst normal humans unnoticed.

/***/

Adam came down the stairs and put his keys on the concierge's table. The hotel owners were a nice old married couple named Anuj and Puja Patel, but Adam hadn't said a word to them all week.

"I trust your stay was good, Dr. Parr?" she asked.

"Yes," he said. "I'd like to keep the room for a week at least, perhaps longer. I can pay for a month in advance, but there's a chance it could be more. I'll keep my things there, but if you need more than a month—"

"Can you leave a credit card?" asked Puja.

"No," said Adam. "I don't have one."

"Do you have a bank?"

"No."

"Cellular phone?"

"No," said Adam, "I can't figure them out—"

"Really?"

"They aren't my thing," said Adam. "If you'd like me to pay for two months in advance or more, that's not a problem."

"One month is fine," said her husband Anuj from the back, in Sanskrit. *"He looks familiar. I think he's been here before."*

"He does look familiar," said Puja in their tongue. *"He's good-looking. I think he's a movie star."*

"I'm no one," said Adam in Sanskrit. *"I've just been here a few times before."*

Puja and Anuj looked at each other and laughed.

"You speak this language, Dr. Parr?" said Puja. "Impressive!"

"I've been here a few times," said Adam.

"But it's not an active language in India," said Puja. "There are only a few Sanskrit speakers left."

"There used to be quite a bit more," said Adam.

He smiled again and left the hotel, walking into the scorching Kolkata heat.

/***/

Adam hailed a three-wheeled auto rickshaw, and the taxi driver sped off with him as Adam chided himself. Speaking the near-dead language of Sanskrit was a foolish maneuver at any time, especially now; his duties were too important to do anything that would make him stand out. Still, he couldn't help it; Adam had visited Anuj Patel sixty years ago, when Adam was helped by the man's grandfather, Dinesh Patel. Dinesh was a *pandit* who spoke Sanskrit and taught the language to his son, because it was in Dinesh's nature to protect vulnerable things. He had protected Adam too after Adam had survived an execution at the hands of the Axis. The Nazis were desperate to take him alive so that they could study his powers, and German spies had spread word throughout Kolkata that anyone giving Adam up would be given more gold than they could dream of. Adam waited out the war in one of Dinesh's hidden rooms, and the man told no one and asked for nothing in return.

And Anuj is just like his grandfather was, thought Adam, *kind, generous, and trusting. Those types never end up with the gold, but they always seem to fall on the right side of history.*

"The place … where?" asked the driver in severely broken English.

"Up ahead," said Adam in Hindi. "*I'll show you.*"

As they traveled down the streets of Kolkata, Adam's thoughts drifted to all the other times he had lived in this city over the years. He had first heard of it when he traveled with Marco Polo, and had later come here to escape the Inquisition. Kolkata was hot, crowded and had so many languages that it was a miracle it stayed together. But Adam felt safe in multicultural cities like this. Areas with one language and one ruler were easier to understand perhaps, but when history turned against you, there was no safe haven. In a place like this, if someone was hunting for your kind, you only needed a short ride to wind up in an area of people who didn't care. There was always a place to hide in Kolkata.

Don't succumb to nostalgia now, thought Adam. *Your task is too important.*

"Three blocks up there, to the left," said Adam to the rickshaw driver.

The driver parked in front of the building, Adam paid him and the driver left. Adam looked up at the sign:

> MANOJ DANDEKAR TRAVEL
> WE WILL GET YOU THERE
> NO EXCEPTIONS

/***/

Manoj Dandekar sat behind the desk, a fan blowing hot air in his emotionless face. He noticed Adam come in, but pretended not to. Adam knew Manoj's kind and knew that there was only one way to make a real impression, so he took out five thousand US dollars and put it on the table. Manoj took a look at the money and then took a look at Adam, but he didn't take the stack and sat detached as if the cash were a sack of rocks.

"So, who are you?" said Manoj. "A fortune hunter? An explorer? A PhD candidate with a thesis?"

"None of those," said Adam. "I'm just a man. And I want to go to the Sentinel Islands."

"Surely you know that even I can't—"

"You can, you have, and so can others," said Adam, "but I prefer your services."

Adam put another wad of cash onto the desk, but averted his eyes from Manoj. He was angry and didn't want Manoj to notice his eyes flashing green.

/***/

In Manoj Dandekar's back office, the stone-faced Kolkata man spread out a picture of a windburnt, brown-skinned woman and a group of short black Africans.

"The Tungus live in Siberia, where temperatures can drop to fifty degrees below freezing," said Dandekar. "These Aka pygmies live behind two war zones. Through me, you can visit both. But you cannot visit the Sentinelese, Dr. Parr. It's not allowed."

"I need to see them," said Adam. "This won't get back to you."

"The Sentinelese are the last uncontacted people on earth—"

"You got an anthropologist there five years ago," said Adam. "You learned how to do it from your mentor, Sandeep Shukla, who set up trips there for a wealthy hunter. Shukla used that money to retire."

Adam had Dandekar's full attention now.

"If you mean to blackmail me, Dr. Parr—" said Dandekar.

"I have no intention of blackmailing you," said Adam. "I just know you have a price."

Dandekar thought for a moment and then spoke.

"If you've come this far I'm sure you know the risks, but I must repeat the full truth," said Dandekar. "The Sentinelese are uncontacted for a reason. They're extremely violent to outsiders and kill anyone that comes upon their shores. Fisherman have been killed just for approaching the islands."

"I know," said Adam. "I know the hunter didn't make it back, and neither did the anthropologist. That's why I'm paying half my fee up front."

"The UN has no jurisdiction there," said Dandekar. "If they're to attack you, there will be no one to save you. No one will pursue your killers because it's not illegal for them to murder you, and they *will* murder you; I guarantee this."

"I'll take my chances," said Adam. "I need passage there, which I'll pay you for. Then double that if the boat comes and picks me up again."

Dandekar looked at the money, and then sighed.

"I never ask my clients' intentions," said Dandekar, "but I question your sanity, Dr. Parr. Why are you going to the Sentinel Islands of all places? What is there?"

Adam smiled; he could do many things, but he had never learned to lie well. He thought for a moment about how to best respond to Dandekar without sounding crazy.

"I have a theory that something miraculous happened there long ago," said Adam. "And I must go there to find out for myself, firsthand."

"Sounds like you too are an anthropologist," said Dandekar. "Is that what the *Dr.* in front of your name is for?"

"I'm an anthropologist of sorts," said Adam with a smile, "but an amateur only."

"What are you going to study there, Dr. Parr?"

"Survival," said Adam, but he was no longer smiling.

/***/

The trawler was called *Malvina*; it was Russian, but the crew was Indonesian. They took their time getting to the Sentinel Islands, which was fine with Adam. He didn't want to risk being stopped by any authorities. They slept during the day but turned on their lights and dropped their nets at night, capturing tiger shrimp by the ton, and the crew crept slowly towards the islands because the shrimp haul was so good. Adam didn't mind waiting; if there was one thing he was good at, it was waiting. He had a hard time pretending that he didn't understand them, though. Manoj told the fishermen that Adam was simply a Western thrill-seeker, and if they heard him understanding their rare Indonesian dialect, it would bring attention to him. So he just sat there as they spoke about him, time and time again.

"*How long until we throw this carcass to the sharks?*" asked a young crewman.

"*We'll drop him off tomorrow,*" said the captain. "*Dandekar says we have to return in a week's time.*"

"He'll be dead as soon as he sets foot on shore," said the crewman.

"I know," said the captain, "but we get a bonus if we send our coordinates to Dandekar through GPS, one week from today. That's all we need to do."

Adam smiled to himself; Dandekar might not follow the law, but he wasn't unscrupulous.

/***/

Darkness fell and a full moon shone through a cloudless sky. Adam saw the islands in the distance; they were barely visible above the horizon. *If these oceans were to rise*, thought Adam, *it would be the end of times for these people.*

Adam also saw that the island was dotted with small bits of orange.

They have fire, thought Adam. *The Sentinelese aren't supposed to have fire, at least not yet.*

Adam sensed a presence behind him, and turned around to see the Indonesian captain carrying a shotgun.

"Whoah," said Adam, holding up his hands. "No need to—"

"This gun *for* you, not for shoot you," said the captain, pointing the gun at the island. "You take gun, shoot them. You take this."

"It's still okay," said Adam. "They won't—"

"You go now," said the captain.

"Here?"

Adam noticed that they were a few kilometers from shore. He turned around and saw the rest of the crew; they were terrified. All the lights in the trawler were off; they didn't want to be boarded by any Sentinelese in canoes.

"Closer," said Adam. "Can you get closer?"

"Now!" said the captain, offering the shotgun to Adam.

"All right, I'll go," said Adam. "You keep the shotgun."

Adam looked around again; they weren't leaving him any option but to swim. He got up on the boat's edge, but before he jumped he turned around and spoke with them in Indonesian, thickening up his accent so as not to raise suspicion.

"*Be here one week from now,*" said Adam. "*I be here. You not pick me up, you not get bonus.*"

The crew was surprised that Adam spoke their language, and he heard them chattering as he jumped into the moonlit water.

/***/

The currents battered Adam hard as he swam towards the island; he couldn't swim too well, so it took him some time to get to shore. When he finally did, he sat down and rested, sopping wet.

I wish Mayfly was here helping me, thought Adam. *Mayfly would have befriended the Indonesians, and they probably would have given us our own boat.*

Adam saw a figure in the distance; it was an islander.

Mayfly would have charmed the Sentinelese too, thought Adam. *If he were here, I wouldn't have to do what I'm about to do.*

Upon closer look, Adam noticed that it was a fisherwoman. She hadn't noticed Adam yet and was throwing a basket into the water. She was short, with brown skin and tight curled hair. Adam went up slowly to her and put his hands out so as not to surprise her.

"Hello," he said.

The Sentinelese fisherwoman did a double take and then dropped her basket. She was frozen with fear, so Adam held his hands up higher to let her know he had no weapons. He smiled, but she didn't return his smile. He grinned harder and then tried out his Sentinelese. He had no idea if it would work because he'd gained his knowledge of the language from Herodotus, a historian-class spanner who had visited these islands three hundred years ago.

"My name is Adam Parr," he said.

"Parr-uh," said the islander. *"DamPARR-uh."*

"Yes," he said. "I need to speak to your leader. The pale one."

"DamPARR-uh."

"Yes."

Adam came one step nearer to her and she let out a small scream before running towards the interior of the island.

"Wait!" he said.

A few moments later he heard talk all around him, and the chatter was in deeper voices. He couldn't make out what they were saying; the dialect hadn't changed much over the centuries, but they were speaking too fast. He sensed lights, and turned around to see that the interior of the island was covered with freshly lit campfires, sprouting up one by one.

"I mean no harm!" shouted Adam into the darkness.

There was silence, and then a few moments later Adam saw a Sentinelese warrior peeking through the bushes. He looked to the left and right and saw that two more men flanked the first man. Adam looked to the ocean; two more were coming in from the coast, and he was surrounded.

There are only five, thought Adam, *but their strategy is sound. There's no escape for me.*

The lead warrior approached Adam; he was wearing a metal conquistador helmet.

"I mean you no harm," said Adam in the native language. *"I want to speak to your leader."*

The lead warrior let out a shriek and one of his compatriots threw a spear at Adam. It landed perfectly between his legs in the sand. Adam knew it was a warning shot, so he took the spear and held it in front of him, the sharp end sticking inwards. The warriors spoke amongst themselves some more, so Adam quickly threw the spear to the ground in front of him, and then put his hands in the air again. He spoke to the lead warrior once more.

"I mean you no harm," said Adam. "I want to speak to the one who gave you that helmet."

The lead warrior approached Adam steadily, growling some more commands to his warriors.

"I need to speak to your leader," said Adam. "The one who gave you that helmet and—"

One more warrior threw a spear at Adam that went right by his head. They continued to encroach upon him, and Adam realized that he wouldn't be able to talk his way out of this. *What I need to show them doesn't take words,* thought Adam. *There's only one way to get to their leader.*

Adam smiled at them one last time, lifted his arms parallel to the ground, and then opened his hands until his empty palms faced the men, as if he were on a cross. The lead warrior motioned to one of the younger compatriots to approach Adam. The young male approached cautiously, and the lead warrior yelled one more command at him. The young warrior threw his spear, and it landed in Adam's leg. Adam screamed in agony, and after he fell to the ground he stifled his cries and got up on his knees. He held out his hands again and stared at the lead warrior. The man yelled and two more of his compatriots rushed at Adam and threw their spears. One grazed his side, and one went through his stomach. Adam was knocked back to the ground, but once again managed to stifle his yells. He got back up, sand mixing in with the blood of his open wound, and lifted his head to stare down the lead warrior once again.

The lead warrior approached Adam and kicked him to the ground. Adam was too weak to resist and fell backwards while the lead warrior straightened his metal helmet and raised his spear to the sky. He threw the spear down and it pierced Adam's chest, tearing through his heart. Adam could feel his insides filling with blood, coughed some of it out and tried to talk, but couldn't utter another word. Soon, all he knew was darkness.

/***/

Adam had a dream in his death state, which was rare. It wasn't a full dream; it was merely images of Phoe and the emotions he felt each time she ran away. He felt sad that she had left him, but it wasn't necessarily a bad feeling; he enjoyed the intensity of emotion, even in the muted tones of thoughts dreamt while his heart wasn't beating.

As his heart started to beat again and begin healing, Adam woke up to pain; he coughed up some blood before seizing and rolling over on his side. He hit the ground with a *thud*, and after a few moments, he realized what had happened. The Sentinelese had been transporting his body on a makeshift gurney when he turned over and fell to the ground.

One of them yelled, and within moments they were pointing their spears at him again. Adam brushed himself off and felt his chest wound; it was still sore, but it had mostly healed. He was covered with blood, but opened his shirt to show the natives that the laceration was repairing itself right before their eyes. He then showed his leg wound. Adam brushed off the dried blood and showed that there was nothing there but unbroken skin.

The lead warrior was aghast. He took off his conquistador's helmet and came close to Adam. Adam held up his hands to show that once again, he wasn't a threat. The lead warrior nodded and then yelled at his fellow warriors, causing them to kneel in unison.

"Stand up," said Adam. "Please—"

The warriors wouldn't stand.

"You are a god," said the lead warrior, before kneeling himself.

"I'm not a god," said Adam. "Stand up."

"You are a god!" shrieked the lead warrior.

Adam looked at the kneeling warriors and knew he had to change his tone.

"I'm not a god!" yelled Adam, making the warriors flinch. "I'm not a god, and neither is your leader, Diego. Now take me to him."

/***/

Adam had to command the warriors to walk with him. They wanted to walk behind him, in front of him or even carry him, but they didn't want to walk *with* him. They only began to treat him as a normal person after he yelled at them to do so at the top of his lungs. Still, they kept their distance and refused to look him in the eye. The young warrior who had first stuck him with his spear now patrolled the front, eager to give his life to anything or anyone that might attack Adam.

Nothing's going to take my life, thought Adam. *Not here at least.*

He and the small retinue of the warriors traveled overland and then in canoes over the bays, and then through the small strips of ocean that connected the islands, often paddling through water shallow enough to walk across. They went on foot and through the ocean, from island to island, coming across no one and seeing nothing on the horizon. The warriors sang a slow song as they went forward; Adam could only understand a few of the words, but he gathered the song was about defending their island and keeping it from harm.

The world needs more pockets like this, thought Adam. *Humanity doesn't need another city.*

They traversed the ocean a final time and headed to what seemed like the main island. The foliage was thicker, and the Sentinelese had even made a canal through the middle of it. Adam knew it was Diego's handiwork and shook his head. *Diego has brought enough of his knowledge to make himself comfortable,* thought Adam, *but not enough to make his people wonder if there's a greater world beyond this small archipelago.*

As they traveled through the center of the island, women came up to see them and immediately knelt in reverence. They commanded their children to do the same, and all but the youngest did so. The young ones stared at Adam wide-eyed and cried in horror as their mothers put a hand over their children's mouths before bowing their heads again.

They traveled through the island, and Adam saw what appeared to be a rudimentary city lit by several campfires. The boat came to a stop at the shore and a hut was in front of him, only slightly larger than the rest. The warriors exited the boat in unison and then knelt on the shore for Adam.

"Please wait," said the lead warrior.

The lead warrior entered the hut and Adam heard an animated discussion inside. He heard the man inside yelling angrily, as if he had just woken up.

"Parr-uh," said the warrior from inside the hut. "DamPARR-uh."

"DamPARR-uh?" said the other voice.

"Dam PARR-uh," said the lead warrior. "Dam."

"Adam PARR-uh," said the other man's voice as he started to laugh. "Adam PARR-uh! Adam Parr!"

Diego burst out of the hut. He was disheveled, bearded, and at least 100 pounds overweight, but other than that he hadn't aged a day since Adam saw him last.

"Adam Parr," he said. "What brings you around these parts?"

"I need to talk to you about your brother," said Adam. "Juan Ponce de León. He's up to something, and I need to know what it is."

"Juan isn't up to anything," said Diego. "I made sure that he'd never harm anyone again."

"He's back and fully recovered," said Adam. "Five hundred years after you buried him alive."

/***/

Two women brought in freshly caught fish and prepared them right in front of Adam. They cleaned their catch and put them in a basket and then basted the filets with coconut oil, salt and local fruits. They skewered the fish and then put them over the fire; the filets cooked in a matter of seconds. The women placed the meal on reeded mats and put them in front of a cross-legged Adam, Diego and a small mulatto child who appeared to be Diego's son. From the child's glowing eyes, the boy also appeared to be a spanner. Two men waved fans at Adam while he ate. The fish was some of the best he'd ever eaten, though he tried not to show it; he didn't feel comfortable eating beside two men with fans.

"Does the Sentinelese obeisance bother you, Adam?" asked Diego.

"Yes," said Adam. "We're not gods."

Diego laughed heartily at that and then started to cough. One of the women came up to him and rubbed his back; Diego soon recovered and waved her off with a smile. She went back to preparing some more fish. Diego pointed at Adam's bloodied shirt and then at Adam's skin, which was flawless.

"You plucked a spear from your own heart, only to rise again," said Diego. "What *are* you, if not a god?"

"Something else."

"Something else, Adam? Like what?"

"I don't know," said Adam. "But we're not gods. Spanners aren't gods."

Diego stared at Adam darkly, scratched his large belly with his thick fingers and then broke the silence with a small nod.

"Perhaps you're right," said Diego. "Gods have agendas. The small gods of mythology were petty, perhaps, but they *acted*. Most spanners are content to hide in the shadows, whether their life lasts a day or … *eight thousand years.*"

Diego smiled at Adam, but Adam chose not to recognize the gesture.

"But let's assume you're correct, Adam—we're *not gods*," said Diego. "You still disapprove of my lifestyle?"

Adam knew he had to get Diego's help, but still couldn't lie.

"Yes," said Adam. "It's odd that you take advantage of these people's … *simplicity.*"

"Last time you saw me, I was a *conquistador*," said Diego. "I found people like this and killed them. Would you prefer I revert to my original behavior?"

"No," said Adam. "But spanners don't do this. They hide, perhaps, but they don't—"

"This is my penance, Adam."

"Your penance?"

"Indeed," said Diego, skewering two slices of fish and eating them both at once. "As you know, I spent my natural life murdering the less advanced, and after I gained immortality I chose to protect the last pre-Colombian civilization left. I trained them to kill intruders, and here they live unsullied by modern life, more or less."

Adam smiled and then had a second bite of his meal, which was even better than the first.

"Perhaps you're right," said Adam.

"I am," said Diego. "I'm no longer a conquistador, vassal or landlord; I'm but a beekeeper to these people. I give them protection from the predatory world around them, and all I ask for is a bit of honey in return."

Adam nodded, and Diego smiled. Diego barked some commands and the warriors and women both bowed and left, leaving only Adam and the boy.

"My friends' obeisance shall bother you no more," said Diego. "Now, before we speculate as to what my brother Juan is up to, we must explain our story to my son. Would you allow it?"

"Of course," said Adam.

The child looked at his father, and the boy's eyes glowed deeply with excitement.

"This tale started years ago," said Diego, "with our first visit to the New World."

/***/

"The year was 1493," said Diego. "We were three brothers: myself, Santos and our captain, Juan Ponce de León, and we were sent by Spain to follow Christopher Columbus on his second expedition to the East Indies. We soon realized that there was land in between of course, so when we reached the islands of Hispaniola we made several colonies there, and in a few short years Juan had muscled his way to a high position: the governor of Puerto Rico.

"Years passed and we prospered, and soon rumors came of a large island to the Northwest. We didn't know at the time that this 'island' was what is now Florida, but Juan was willing to give up his governorship to travel there, so Santos and I went with him. I quickly arranged a small crew for Juan and took off to Florida with him, filled with the usual conquistador dreams of women, land and, of course, gold.

"Spain had only sent us on a mission to scout and map the territory, so we arrived with three lightly armed boats. We found a small cove that we used as a base for our operations, and then proceeded to launch small expeditions from there, mapping out the coastline and trading with the naturals. Sometimes the naturals were vicious and we had to battle them, but we spent most of our time traveling, and most of our struggle was against the elements.

"After months of expeditions, it soon became obvious that this was no island, so Juan sent one ship back with copies of the maps, and a request to scout inland. While he waited for a response, he set up missions for Santos and me to lead. He had proven himself loyal over the years and knew Spain would grant whatever he requested, so he sent us forward.

"Santos and I weren't so eager to leave the coast though; the naturals had become increasingly violent, and it soon became clear that there was no gold in this land, no matter how vast it might be. We came to Juan Ponce and he chided us.

"'*Do you not care for Spain? For God?*' he asked.

"'*We honor Spain neither by being massacred inland nor by succumbing to malarial flies,*' said Santos in response.

"I was not so politic in my complaint, of course. I brandished my knife, stuck it in Juan's desk and yelled at him. '*There is no GOLD here!*' I said. '*Why are we here if there is no gold?*'

"Juan wasn't bothered by our hostility, but he did worry about his brothers' confidence, so he asked us to wait until our crew had gone to sleep and promised to tell us the real reason he went to Florida.

"We agreed to meet in secret, and later that evening he woke us up and took us to a tent far from the camp; it was pouring rain and both the distance and the weather colluded to ensure that no prying ears would hear his plans. Juan was not alone; he had brought his steward, Balthasar.

"'*Santos, Diego and Balthasar,*' said Juan. '*I trust you three and no one else, so hear my tale. I was visited in a dream by an angel who told me that this land is filled with the gold that will help us rule the world.*'

"Santos and I were both perplexed; Juan wasn't one to speak of dreamtime visions of angels.

"'*Forgive me,*' said Juan with a laugh, '*I don't mean to speak in riddles. Let me tell you what I'm really after.*'

"Juan told us that the naturals weren't hiding any gold. '*The real gold,*' he said, '*lies within the naturals themselves.*'

"He explained that there were rumors of angels with strange powers floating around Europe, beings that we now know today to be *spanners*. But he said that there were rumors of *whole tribes* of these beings living in the New World.

"'*In Europe, these angels know to hide in the shadows,*' said Juan, '*but one of those angels visited me in a dream and told me that in the virginal territories here, they live openly. It's up to us to find a tribe of these creatures, and take their powers for ourselves.*'

"I knew it wasn't that simple to take a spanner's abilities, and so did my brother.

"'But if we find this tribe, we can't simply take their powers,' said our brother Santos. *'They have found angels in Europe and fruitlessly tried to extract their powers; it's of no use, and you should believe me because I personally oversaw the extractions.'*

"'You're right, hermano,' said Juan, *'but the angel in my dream told me that there was one creature here who is the source of these powers and can bestow abilities. This creature can give us the ultimate spanner power: eternal life. I call this angel the Fountain of Youth.'*

"'We might find this angel,' said Santos, *'but I'm not convinced we'll be able to extract its powers. I've tried in many sessions, and have come away with nothing.'*

"'Help me find the Fountain, and I will take its powers,' said Juan. *'I have many methods of persuasion at my disposal.'"*

/***/

The servant girl brought in a cup of cloud-white tea in a wooden gourd. It was one of the smoothest things Adam had ever tasted, and he asked for more.

"It's brewed from an herb that's common here, and it's available nowhere else on earth," said Diego. "The Sentinelese drink it every day of their life."

"You'd be a multimillionaire if you brought it to the world," said Adam. "You'd finally get your gold."

"The temptation arises every time the rain leaks through my hut's roof," said Diego with a smile, "but I've made my choice, and here I'll stay; *king of nowhere.*"

Adam smiled and looked into his glass of the cloud-white tea before drinking it. Diego pointed at Adam's eyes before talking to his son.

"See his eyes glow just a bit?" said Diego to the boy. "A spanner's eyes glow during times of strong emotion. Adam likes our tea, and that was enough to bring out the green in his pupils. My eyes glow and so do my brothers' eyes, but not like Adam's and not like yours. You and Adam, your eyes glow like embers."

"Why?" asked the child.

"I don't know *why* exactly," said Diego, "but it's how spanners *are*. You and Adam were *born* spanners, so your eyes glow brightly. Juan, Santos, Balthasar and I *became* spanners, so our eyes glow too, but not as strongly as yours."

Diego looked right at Adam.

"But do not underestimate my brother Juan Ponce de León, Adam," said Diego. "Though his eyes glow faintly, he's not weak."

/***/

"We sent our crew back to Puerto Rico, stating that we—the three de León brothers and Balthasar the steward—would scout alone. So we traversed inland slowly, but lightly," continued Diego. "We brought a few dogs to scare the naturals, a couple of trinkets to bribe some armies to our side, and lots of weapons. But we didn't have to use the weapons at first; the land was all but abandoned near our first landing."

"Disease," said Adam. "My brother Phage claims that he's responsible."

"Indirectly, perhaps," said Diego with a grimace, now talking to his son. "Adam's brother Phage is an immortal, but he was born without an immune system. So every disease that ever existed flourishes within him, and he spreads them wherever he goes."

Diego now looked at Adam.

"Phage spread a few plagues throughout Europe at the time," said Diego. "Perhaps some of his plagues were brought by us to the naturals, but he wasn't responsible. *He* didn't walk onto the Florida shores and bring the sicknesses to the natives; we did. *We* were responsible for the devastation that they wrought."

Diego's jaw was quivering with emotion. A woman came in to rub his back again, but he calmed himself and gently shooed her away.

"And though we didn't know what we had brought," said Diego, clenching his jaw, "we knew what we did next. We had learned enough of the various tongues to communicate with the naturals, and when we did find a village with survivors, we let them know what we were looking for. The naturals didn't have a clue as to what we were talking about, but Juan had to be sure that they weren't lying."

Diego began to choke up a little bit, but continued.

"We took the villagers, most of them delirious and weakened with various sores and pustules," said Diego. "We took these villagers and put them on wooden racks."

Diego's eyes became downcast and he stopped talking. *He's ashamed,* thought Adam, *and he hasn't thought of this for a century. But I need answers now.*

"I was on the rack during the Spanish Inquisition," said Adam. "It was horrible, but it was a dark time; a lot of people did a lot of bad things back then. They burnt my brother Geryon at the stake for sorcery, and he still hasn't recovered to this day."

"The Inquisition was brutal, to be sure," said Diego. "But we were worse. The tortures of the Inquisition were such that they wouldn't leave visible marks. And though extreme cases like your brother's immolation did occur, his agony was only meant to last a few minutes; we took hours, and sometimes days."

Diego's emotion was rising again, but he was talking and Adam decided to let him talk.

"We went from village to weakened village, tormenting the pockmarked, sore-addled naturals until we could be sure they weren't lying about their ignorance of the angels we sought. There was no Grand Inquisitor overseeing our activities, ensuring that we didn't leave a bruise, and they couldn't end their suffering by simply converting to our religion. Juan was determined to get the truth, even if he had to keep a natural alive for a week to do it.

"No one had answers, but Juan wouldn't relent. We would torture the naturals for a week and then let a few go so that they could run to the next village and spread the infection forward. We went from village to village doing this until six months had passed and untold numbers of these innocent people had been eliminated in the slowest way possible."

Diego gathered himself and then spoke grimly.

"But Juan's patience paid off," said Diego. "We finally got word from a tormented woman that there was indeed a tribe of angels living deep within Florida's central swamp. To be sure of it, Juan still went to the next village, and an old man who had no connection to the previous woman said the same thing.

"'These people do not die,' said the old man, 'and their eyes shine like stars.'

"We traveled immediately, and within a fortnight we'd found them. They spoke Arawak and must have migrated to Florida from the West Indies. They were a tribe like any other, though their eyes occasionally glowed in the night. There was not an old one amongst them, and they seemed to be content with their small lives, hidden deep within the swamp. We hid in the mud for two days to observe them; at night they had strange ceremonies where they would cut each other and then heal almost instantly, and they kept no scars.

"'These are the angels whom we seek,' said Juan. 'These are the immortals. We will take their power from them.'"

/***/

Diego took another glass of the cloud-white tea.

"I asked Juan how we could proceed," he said. "'How can we defeat angels who cannot themselves be killed?'

"Juan stood up and smiled," said Diego. "He was cruel to his captives, but to us he showed nothing but calm.

"'Indeed, angels cannot be killed,' said Juan. 'But angels can always be controlled; that is their purpose.'

"'Control an angel?' I asked. 'It can't be done.'

"'The only angel to escape control was Lucifer, and he was banished to Hell by God,' said Juan. 'Angels have been put on earth to serve us, so let's fight these immortals until they share their powers.'

"'I care not to fight a group of immortals,' I said.

"'I'd rather face an immortal army ten times than a mortal army once,' said Juan. 'The mortal army fights for their own survival, but what does the immortal army fight for? Tell me this!'

"There was a moment of silence before the steward Balthasar spoke.

"'We don't know, sir,' said Balthasar. 'Please inform us.'

"'It's not a real question,' said Juan with a smile, 'for an immortal army doesn't fight in the first place. They have no need to battle if they can just wait for their opponent to die. So they keep to themselves, tucked away in the swamp until eternity comes.'

"'But how can we get what we want?' asked Santos. 'How can we defeat them and get what we want?'

"'We can't defeat them,' said Juan, 'but we can get what we want. For though they can't be killed, they can feel pain. And the prospect of an eternity of pain places more fear in the heart of an immortal than we could possibly imagine. This is how you control an angel: through pain.'"

/***/

Diego drank more of his white tea and looked somberly at Adam. Adam motioned for Diego to go outside with him, mouthing the words *alone*, and Diego left the hut, leaving the child behind. The moon was bright enough to see Diego clearly, and Adam calmed himself before speaking.

"I understand that this is an emotional story, but your brother is a very dangerous man," said Adam. "He has come back, and I need to know what his plan is and how to *stop* him. Are you sure it's necessary to tell this dark tale in front of your child?"

"It's *beyond* necessary," said Diego.

"Why?" asked Adam.

"Because he's the *future*," said Diego. "I don't know what spanner power he has, but I do know that he *grows*. He's not like your Phoe, trapped in an infinite loop of love, fire and rebirth; he grows, and one day he'll leave this island and join the world. I need him to know the truth about what I've done."

"Immortality gives you time to do bad things," said Adam. "We've all done bad things."

"You've not done bad things, Adam," said Diego. "At times you've been misguided or fought on the wrong side, but you've not done the things I've done."

"He may grow up to hate you," said Adam.

"And I pray that he does," said Diego. "I pray that he takes in the naked truth and that, when he enters the real world, he undoes some of the damage I've inflicted. I'm immortal, yes, but I'm too broken to re-enter the world myself. Do you know that I've heard their screams every night since I left? Do you know what it's like to have a century of nightmares?"

"Yes," said Adam. "I know *precisely* what it's like."

"Then you must also understand the power of having a child who *doesn't* have those bad dreams," said Diego, "and you must realize why I'm doing everything in my power to ensure that he never does."

"All right," said Adam, nodding. "I get it."

"Then let me tell you the whole story," said Diego. "And let my son see me for the monster that I was. For only you can lead the battle against Juan when he closes in on the Fountain of Youth. And only my son can reconstruct the world after the battle is over."

"The battle?"

"There's a much larger story going on than my brother and the Fountain," said Diego. "Let me tell the whole story to both my child *and* you."

/***/

Diego sat down and sipped his white tea once more. Adam followed suit; the tea was just as good as it was the first time that he had drunk it.

"They were easy to conquer," said Diego. "They were like immortal lambs. We stabbed them through the heart and they fell to the ground; their eyes glowed for a moment, and their wounds healed over. They survived, but they stayed down, cowed in fear.

"'We have not yet found the Fountain of Youth,' Juan told us, *'but we have found the scent of its water. You have extracted truth from the naturals that has led us to this place, and you must use your skills to extract more. We extinguished the tribes of months past in days or weeks, but these angels cannot be extinguished, so we have time to learn their secrets, and we will take the time necessary to learn what we need.'*

"We annexed their village by chaining the women and children, and shackling their males into stocks," said Diego. "We took a boy who collected birds, his name was *Koriuaka,* and we taught him our language so that he could translate. He picked up our tongue quickly and gave them commands as we tormented them for days, but they wouldn't relent. None of the psychological tricks worked; they had no fear of death and no concept of honor. We cut children in front of their mothers, and neither child nor mother would give in to our torments."

"Did their class feel pain?" asked Adam.

"Undoubtedly; we could see it in their eyes. We had wrung more tears from them in a fortnight than had been wrought during our entire previous rampage. But they resisted our methods with steadfast resolve, much like you resisted your own torment during the Inquisition; do you remember that, Adam?"

"Unfortunately, yes," said Adam, "though I've tried to forget."

"We didn't know it at the time, but we were outmatched; their class doesn't respond to momentary discomforts like ordinary humans do. Perhaps they were your class specifically; I believe your immortal class is called a *tree?*"

"Yes," said Adam. "We're slow to pick up new technology, but we absorb wisdom and don't respond to physical distress."

"Indeed," said Diego. "These angels resisted our blades, and no threats would sway them. After weeks of failed intimidation, Juan tried a different method, and it worked. These Indians were highly sensitive to *claustrophobia*."

Adam's heart skipped a beat, but he tried not to show it.

"We locked them in small, dark boxes and they gave in," said Diego. "They told us the secret dwelt within one of their own—a pale girl who lived far away. She held the power of both life and death; her blood gave life and her body brought death."

"Was this the Fountain?" asked Adam.

"Indeed," said Diego. "This girl was the Fountain of Youth."

"I didn't know the Fountain of Youth was a girl, and that she also brought death," said Adam.

"The Fountain of Youth can kill, and she's more than just a girl," said Diego. "She's both life and death, power and destruction wrapped into one. They kept her in the far, far north; the cold muted her powers."

Adam drank another sip of the white tea, and Diego shook his head.

"Juan, of course, was determined to find her," said Diego. "So we increased our torment, doing things that shouldn't be done, things that would make Lucifer himself beg us to stop. They still wouldn't reveal the location; it was sacred to them, so Juan brought the claustrophobia to the next level. He had us cut off their heads, and put those heads in a box. He did this to many of the villagers and showed what he had done to young Koriuaka, who immediately started to cry.

"'*The heads of your parents are very much alive in these boxes,*' Juan told the young boy. '*The only way to cease their suffering is if you show us where the Fountain is; do you know her location?*'

"The boy nodded yes," said Diego. "And that was that. We prepared for a journey north, cutting the heads off the old and placing them in boxes, and shackling several of the young and taking them with us. We trekked north for months, hunting animals along the way and wrapping ourselves in furs as the cold set in. Our young Arawak guides wouldn't escape; they were too loyal to their elders.

"And months later, we found her, trapped in a cave with eyes glowing and skin devoid of pigment. She had great powers, but in the cold she was just another girl, so she was easy to overtake and soon she was shackled to a post, completely under our control.

"The naturals had said that her power lay in her blood, and Juan had prepared for this; he had brought great vats on our journey as well as leeches to prevent our blood from clotting. He then proceeded to sever her veins and let her blood drip into a vat. It took a week of cutting her skin to gain enough blood to fill the container, and when it was filled, Juan cut his own veins on his inner elbows and put his arms in the vat. He soaked it for an hour and soon developed a horrible fever; two days later he emerged and his eyes glowed, albeit faintly. He stabbed his own leg and it healed quickly. Despite our objections, he pierced his own heart, and that didn't kill him either. So we followed suit, cutting our veins, soaking in the vat, developing fevers and then emerging as immortals."

Adam smiled.

"Spanners are rare," said Adam, "but humans that become spanners are even rarer still. I don't think anyone would gain my powers by soaking in my blood."

"Perhaps," said Diego. "We didn't know at the time the uncommonness of what had happened to us, and if we had known the ramifications of immortality, we wouldn't have let those leeches go."

"Spanner leeches," said Adam with a smile. "I don't think I'd ever want to meet them."

"Nor would I," said Diego. "But at the time, Santos, Balthasar and I were ecstatic. We thought we had found the *Fountain of Youth*. We could live forever; what more could we want? We were excited, but Juan would have none of it.

"'*Immortality is nothing,*' said Juan. '*We have not the powers of angels; we are merely the undead. We need to spend the next few years extracting* ALL *of the Fountain's power, not stopping until everything that she has is exhausted and we become like gods, destined to rule the world.*'

"Juan was convinced that the power of the Fountain was limitless, and in retrospect, he was right," said Diego.

"A world under Juan Ponce de León would have been a dark place," said Adam.

"I had an inkling of that back then," said Diego. "I saw the look in my brother's eyes, and I knew that he was going to succeed and that bad things were going to happen. I didn't quite know what to do, so I spent the evening praying by myself, begging for guidance."

Diego looked at his son and smiled just a bit.

"I was at a loss as to what I should do, but that night the Lord answered my prayers and I was visited by an angel of my own, and he told me what we were doing was wrong," said Diego. "It was then that I grew a conscience, my son."

Diego took his son and had him look at Adam.

"God sent me an angel that night," said Diego. "An angel in the form of Adam Parr."

/***/

"I remember when I found you like it was yesterday, Diego," said Adam. "But I was only in the New World because I'd fallen afoul of

Henry the Eighth, and he'd put a price on my head. I wasn't sent by God; I was on the run, and finding you was pure luck."

"This is the fatalistic mantra that you've spouted your whole life, Adam," said Diego. "You do this to protect yourself from the harsh realities of life, perhaps? Regardless, I needed guidance that night, and you came to me. If you were sent by God, fate or luck, it didn't matter; you ran into our camp and saw that my brother's actions were wrong."

"I did," said Adam.

"Each spanner has their own unique power," said Diego to his son. "Adam is a tree-class spanner, and part of their power is that they use their vast experience to predict the future. They've seen every situation a thousand times before, so with a mere glance they can tell what has happened and what is *going to happen*. After my brothers had gone to sleep, I told Adam our tale, and his eyes flashed green with horror."

"I saw that Juan was going to take the power of the Fountain," said Adam. "I saw that he would take that power and place the entire world in his torture rack."

"He would have succeeded too," said Diego. "The world was at a vulnerable part of history, and he would have bent it to his will; I know not how, but the Fountain contains the powers of life and death; he would have used her to accomplish dark things."

"So what did you do?" asked Diego's son.

"Harsh leaders must meet their ends in harsh ways," said Diego, "and Juan was powerful and wouldn't be deterred from his goal by reason or by force; the only way to stop him was to end him. The Lord spoke to me through the angel Adam Parr, and I knew the only way to end my brother was to do a devilish act, one that I hadn't thought of until Adam came to guide me."

/***/

"Adam and I waited until the night and then freed our child guide Koriuaka, and I whispered to him in his native Arawak that we'd had a change of heart. As proof I delivered the heads of his elders, and then told him that we needed to rectify what we had done.

"So we freed the Fountain and bid her travel north, west or east; as long as it was out of our clutches. She disappeared, and the next morning my brother Juan came in, horrified.

"'Hermano,' Juan said, 'what's happened?'"

Diego took one more sip of white tea and then sighed.

"I knew Juan was going to be dangerous as soon as he realized my treachery, so I attacked him with the axe that I'd used to unshackle the Fountain. I hacked him to bits; I knew that he would survive, but blows like that would keep him out of commission for a day or two at least."

"This is where our paths parted," said Adam.

"Indeed," said Diego.

"The plan was for us to take him back to Hispaniola," said Adam. "He was to be tried for disobeying the queen's orders and would have been imprisoned back in Spain."

"He would have gotten out," said Diego.

"The Fountain would have been safely hidden by then," said Adam.

"He would have found her no matter where she hid, and you know this to be true," said Diego. "He would have escaped, and he would have found her."

Adam thought for a moment and then nodded; Diego was right.

"I know you disapprove of what I did, Adam," said Diego, "but you didn't stop me, and you didn't correct my actions after the fact."

"I didn't," said Adam, "though perhaps I should have; no man deserves that punishment."

"No man does, but you didn't interfere because you knew that it was the *only way* to protect the world from Juan's lust for power."

"Perhaps," said Adam.

"What did you do?" asked the young boy.

Diego nodded his head one more time and then looked directly at his son.

"I took his body back to the village in Florida; the journey was slow, and every night I had to chop at Juan with my axe lest he come alive and run away. When I arrived at the village, the few remaining Arawaks there healed their decapitated brethren. It was a grisly few weeks, but soon they were whole and had to decide what to do with my brother, and there was only one punishment for their kind."

"Burial," said Adam, his voice sounding hollow.

"Indeed," said Diego. "Typical capital punishment for an immortal spanner is a century, but the Arawaks punished their own much more harshly than that, and Juan's sin was so grievous that they decided to punish him indefinitely. They put him in a metal box that we had brought and put him deep in the swamp, in a place that no one would ever find. I agreed to the punishment, and I even helped dig his grave."

"And five hundred years later, he's out," said Adam, "and he's still a threat."

"He's a greater threat than ever before," said Diego, "because now my brother Juan Ponce de León is *angry*."

/***/

The child was now sleeping and Diego patted his son's head.

"His eyes glow while he rests," said Diego.

"Dreams produce an intensity of emotion not found in real life," said Adam.

The women brought in some of the raw fruit that produced the tea. It was crispy and white with hard edges, and somewhat flavorless, but still good; it was like eating warm snow. Adam took a few bites and looked darkly at Diego.

"So we didn't complete a job five hundred years ago," said Adam, "and here we are, dealing with the consequences."

"Tell me what you know of my brother," said Diego, "and I'll do what I can to help."

"Your brother has recovered completely," said Adam. "He lives in a compound with his new crew: Balthasar, his steward, a scourge-class spanner; a blur-class spanner; and a tweener named Cannon. He has quite a few humans working for him too; Balthasar leads the operation and they work under the guise of science."

"Balthasar the steward leading the operation," said Diego. "It makes sense; he did everything Juan asked him to do. Balthasar has a conscience, but his desire to do Juan's bidding overpowers it."

"He's intelligent too; Balthasar's inflicted more pain on the spanner community since then," said Adam. "He and his crew trap other spanners in their compound and do experiments on them to take their powers."

"And their compound exists in normal society?"

"Yes," said Adam. "Somehow they coexist."

"I understand how they coexist," said Diego. "A man like my brother will always fit in with society, especially with Balthasar second in command. They'll do bad things while no one's looking and pay tribute to whomever is in charge, be it gold to Spain or a patent to some financier. They probably take a spanner's power, turn it into a medicine and the world leaves them alone for it."

"Rumor has it that they have the Fountain," said Adam. "Five hundred years later, they have the Fountain."

"Like I said," said Diego, "if Juan is free, he'd find the Fountain wherever she is."

"What's he going to do with her?"

"Extract her power," said Diego, "or at least try to. That's Juan's one weakness; he can command others to do things, but can't do them himself. The Fountain's power is so arcane that he won't be able to figure her out. He and Balthasar will be able to take other spanners' powers, but not hers, or at least not soon. Right now she's just an immortal spanner who gives immortality with her blood, and nothing more."

"Her presence is deadly, or so I've heard," said Adam.

"Indeed," said Diego, "her blood brings life, but her skin brings death because she holds the power of both life and death within her. The cold controls her powers, but if she's in normal temperatures, I'd advise you to stay away from her, Adam."

"Will Juan extract her power?"

"Eventually, yes," said Diego. "With time, my brother and Balthasar will do just that."

"The power of life and death," said Adam. "What does that mean?"

"I don't quite know, and neither does Juan, but it's powerful," said Diego. "And Juan will take those powers and rule the world with them."

"Rule the world? How?"

"Most likely by taking death and turning it into a poison, a plague or something else and killing large numbers of people," said Diego. "He'll raise an army and give them the power of life until they're invincible. I don't understand quite what he's going to do, but make no mistake, he'll accomplish everything I say and more; he's capable of anything you can imagine, a thousand times over."

"How do you know this?"

Diego smiled and took another bite out of the white fruit.

"Legend," said Diego. "The immortal Arawaks have him as part of their mythos. They say that there will be a great battle for the Fountain, and the winner will control the fate of history. There hasn't been a battle yet, but their legend seems to describe a man like Juan well."

"I've heard this tale too," said Adam. "It's become spanner lore."

"Indeed," said Diego, "and legend or not, I know my brother. Given the chance, he'll turn the world into a dark place."

"If Juan is destined to take the Fountain and use her to rule the world," said Adam, "how do I prevent it?"

"There's only one way to prevent another's destiny," said Diego. "It's to take that destiny for yourself."

"So you want *me* to take the Fountain?"

"Precisely," said Diego. "Assemble a team and break into my brother's compound and take her."

"Assuming we can do that," said Adam, "what would we do with her afterwards?"

Diego thought for a moment and then nodded his head.

"You can't kill her; she's immortal," said Diego, "but you can help her reach her destiny by extracting her power for yourself."

"How?"

"There is a spanner who lives far in the north who can extract her power," said Diego. "He is the fourth member of our party—my brother, Santos de León."

Adam knew of Santos de León; every spanner did. Adam hadn't seen Santos since the day he left Diego, but the lore around Santos had permeated the spanner community, and he wasn't a benevolent figure. Legend had it that he lived in the north and did bad things to spanners; his nickname was *the Surgeon.*

"I know that Santos brings fear to the average spanner's heart," said Diego. "But he maintains that aura only so that others will leave him alone, and I assure you he detests Juan on a level far greater than you."

Adam mulled over his options, and didn't like any of them.

"Take the Fountain from Juan and bring her north to my brother Santos," said Diego. "He will extract her power and give it to you; I assure you of this."

"And then what?"

"And then you'll have it and not Juan," said Diego. "This is all I know."

Adam knew that Diego was telling the truth, but also knew that his truth was incomplete. Diego had given Adam the best option, but didn't know precisely where it would lead. *Still, Diego can be trusted and Juan must be stopped,* thought Adam. *At this point, this is all I have to stand on.*

Diego tried to get up from his sitting position, but had eaten so much of the fruit that he fell down and started to cough.

"You said when you first came to this island that *we're not gods*," said Diego. "Do you believe that?"

"Completely," said Adam.

"Well you're correct," said Diego, coughing once more. "Neither you nor I are gods; we're simply two old men hiding from the world. Are you ready to come out of hiding?"

"Yes," said Adam.

"Good," said Diego. "For though you and I admit we're not deities, my brother Juan believes himself to be one, and if he gains the power of the Fountain, that may become true. He'll grant himself strange powers and will do things that you can't even imagine."

Diego got up, coughed once more and then looked at Adam.

"I know not what the Arawaks' legend of destiny says, nor what power the Fountain truly holds. But I do know that you must take the Fountain and bring her to my brother Santos," said Diego. "For if Juan Ponce de León gains her powers, Juan *will* become a god. And he will *not* be a benevolent one."

JON MAAS

MAYFLY

The City

One of the girls had awoken. The other remained draped perpendicularly across his grey hooded jacket on the bed, still collapsed from the pills she had taken. Mayfly took care never to let his dates overdose on the drugs he brought, but she had passed out from her own stash and wasn't overdosing, so he let her sleep. The girl that had awoken was crying softly, but deeply. Mayfly took a look at her and his heart sank. Her tears weren't from pills or alcohol; her tears were real, and she was completely sober.

I met her four hours ago and she's already fallen for me, thought Mayfly. *If she had taken drugs, at least her emotions would have been subdued.*

Girls fell in love with Mayfly quickly. That was part of his spanner class's power, but he didn't enjoy it because it always left the girl hurt at the end. He'd catch their attention with his clear brown eyes, youthful face and soft smile, and being just over five feet tall with the taut musculature of a jockey, girls would find it easy to approach him. Even the tall girls would become smitten by his charms, each and every time. Once they ran their fingers through his short, brown hair and kissed him, it was done. They would love him forever, and they would inevitably end up hurt when he left. He thought the girl next to him would be an exception, but as he listened to her tears, he knew that it wouldn't be the case.

"What's wrong?" he asked.

"I've never felt a connection like I've had with you," she said. "It's just hitting me all at once, and it doesn't feel good, you know? It's just all these emotions at once—"

"It's okay," said Mayfly.

Mayfly knew this wasn't going to end well. He cared for this girl he just met, but he had cared for girls in the past and they spent the rest of their lives missing him, even after they'd only known him a few hours.

Mayfly reached in his bag and went through a half-dozen bottles until he found the one he wanted, a drug they called the *Mind-Eraser*.

"Take this," he said.

"What is it?" she asked.

"It's a cousin of GHB. It leaves you intact, but it takes away the short-term memories you have now," said Mayfly. "Tomorrow you won't remember who I am."

"But I want to remember," she said.

"No you don't," he said. "Take it and I'll tell you everything."

The girl took the pill. She curled up close to Mayfly and kissed him twice. He saw that she was fading a bit and then decided he could tell her the truth. She'd remember him as a feeling, or perhaps think of him in a dream, but she wouldn't recall enough to be heartbroken. Most importantly, she wouldn't remember the truth he was about to tell her.

"First of all, what's your name?" he asked.

"Kassandra," she said. "What's yours?"

"Technically, I don't have a name," he said with a laugh, "but I go by my class name, *Mayfly*."

"Your class name?"

"My spanner class."

"You're one of those guys with weird lifetimes, right?" she asked, her voice slurring a little more.

"Yeah," he said. "My class lives only six months. A friend of mine named Adam extended my lifespan, but it's like fixing a house of cards. You can only extend my life so long—"

"What's your power?" she asked, her eyes closing. "All of you guys have powers, right?"

"I pack a whole life in half a year," he said. "So I only sleep an hour a night, my IQ is three hundred seventy-five and I'm really good at getting people to befriend me, or in your case, fall in love with me."

"Do you love me …?"

"I do," he said. "We've only known each other a few hours, but you're a big part of my life. I'll think about you before I die."

"Don't die," said Kassandra. "Don't die …"

"If only it were that easy," said Mayfly.

There was a crash from the kitchen outside and the sounds of a man fumbling for something, most likely a weapon. Mayfly looked out of the penthouse apartment at the moonlit city below and took it in one more time. *When we're young we throw our time away so carelessly, but towards the end, we realize that every moment is precious and can never be had again.*

Mayfly listened outside for the sounds from the kitchen; whoever it was out there, it sounded like he had a knife and was frightened.

/***/

The girl passed out, and Mayfly made sure she would be okay before he left to face the person in the kitchen. Mayfly found the man standing nervously behind the granite countertop, and he felt sorry for him. The man was scared, but instead of a knife, he had a gun, and his hands shook as he pointed it at Mayfly.

"Who are you?" he asked. "And what are you doing in my house?"

Mayfly kept his hands up but took a look at the gun; it wasn't loaded. *Still,* he thought, *it's not fair to this guy. I'll give him the truth, and then have a drink with him. He looks like he needs a friend.*

"I broke into your house with two girls, and both of them are now passed out in your bedroom," said Mayfly. "I haven't stolen anything and don't plan to. I saw how well you lived and wanted a piece of it, and nothing more. I've got a few weeks left to live at most, and wanted to spend the night here."

Mayfly's eyes glowed just a bit. The man didn't notice it, but put down his gun.

"I'm sorry," said the man.

"What's your name?" asked Mayfly.

"Paul," said the man.

"Well, Paul," said Mayfly, "I'd like to be friends with you. Do you want to have a drink with me?"

"Yeah," said Paul. "Yeah."

/***/

Five minutes later, Paul was sharing some Louis XIII Cognac with Mayfly. Mayfly laughed.

"What's so funny?" asked Paul.

"A friend of mine named Adam also drinks Louis the Thirteenth," said Mayfly.

They drank heavily for the next hour, with Mayfly checking discreetly on the girls to make sure they were still okay. They were, so Mayfly told Paul a few stories, but nothing that would reveal he was a spanner. Paul told Mayfly that he hadn't had this much fun since his divorce three years ago, and got a little weepy when he thought of Mayfly dying.

"This isn't a wake, Paul," said Mayfly with a smile. "I didn't set out to make you sad tonight. I'm tired of making people miss me before I'm even gone."

"If you didn't come to make people miss you, what are your plans tonight, then?" asked Paul.

"I want to get fucked up with you Paul," said Mayfly. "More fucked up than anyone's ever been in human history."

/***/

They did three lines of cocaine to get the party started, and then Mayfly took another swig of cognac.

"Paul, you're one of my closest friends, so promise me you won't overdo it?"

"What do you mean?" asked Paul, "I haven't laughed this much since my divorce and I need—"

"I'm dying, you're not," said Mayfly. "I won't forgive myself if you get hurt. So just take it easy?"

"Sure," said Paul. "Will you?"

"I'm gonna die soon anyway," said Mayfly, "so I'm gonna do what I want."

"I don't know, man," said Paul. "You look pretty healthy, and if something were to happen to you—"

Paul started to weep again, but he held it in this time. *Emotions aside, I can't do this to Paul*, thought Mayfly. *I want to overdo it, but if the police find a dead mayfly and two young girls in Paul's room, bad things are gonna happen to him.*

Mayfly wrote down an address and handed it to Paul.

"I tell you what," said Mayfly. "If I pass out, take me to *this* doctor. No other doctor. Can you do that?"

"Sure," said Paul.

"Then let's get the party started," said Mayfly with a smile.

/***/

It took Mayfly a half-day to recover from the stomach pumping, and when he came to, Dr. Shaw looked at him with fierce eyes that glowed pale blue. Julius Shaw was a spanner and also a doctor. He worked with humans mostly, but if spanners came to him he'd treat them without revealing their secrets. He was one of the few spanners who had fully integrated himself into normal society, and he was a grumpy son-of-a-bitch.

"Are you angry?" asked Mayfly.

"Beyond angry," said Dr. Shaw.

"If you think I'm gonna give away spanner secrets to the humans I party with," said Mayfly, "I'm not. I always cover my tracks and—"

"I don't care about spanner secrets," said Dr. Shaw. "I'm angry that you're throwing your life away."

"Throwing my life away?" asked Mayfly. "I'm gonna die any day now."

"Adam extended your lifespan by a month."

"By two months," said Mayfly.

"By two months, but you've been partying. The drugs have overloaded your system, so now it's down to a month."

"I guess that's too bad," said Mayfly. "Life's short."

"No, it's not," said Dr. Shaw. "There's so much you can do, even in the brief time you have left."

"What can *I* do?" asked Mayfly. "Tell me, in the month I have left on this earth, what can *I* do?"

"You can stop taking drugs and help Adam," said Dr. Shaw. "He's hoping to stop Juan Ponce de—"

Mayfly got up and put his hands up in the air.

"Oh no," said Mayfly. "I'm not helping him fight a five-hundred-year-old psychopath."

"He needs your help," said Dr. Shaw. "He can't do it without you."

Mayfly thought about it, and then shook his head.

"Adam understands a lot," said Mayfly. "But he doesn't understand mortality. What little time I have left on this earth, I can't spend it chasing a mythical spanner who might not even exist."

"Juan Ponce de León exists, Mayfly," said Dr. Shaw. "He's back, and he's dangerous."

"All the more reason to avoid him, then," said Mayfly with a smile as he got up.

"Take care of yourself, Mayfly," said Dr. Shaw.

"I will," said Mayfly.

"No, I mean it," said Dr. Shaw, his eyes glowing with anger again. "You don't want to help Adam, that's fine. But know that Juan Ponce de León and his crew are out there now, and they're dangerous. They roam the streets, collecting spanners and doing experiments on them. If you don't want to stop them, that's your business, but next time you do drugs, make sure you don't wake up in their clutches. They love collecting spanners—especially mayflies."

/***/

Mayfly put on his grey hooded jacket, went to the liquor store, got a bottle of *Belvedere* vodka and headed out on the town. He knew Dr. Shaw's heart was in the right place, and a few months ago Mayfly would have jumped at the chance to help Adam stop Juan Ponce de León, or whoever needed stopping. But times were different now, and he had to take care of himself.

Mayfly walked through the city, taking a few gulps of the vodka, and looked upward, trying to take everything in at once. He loved every bit of the city, even the bad parts, the predatory corners and the things that could hurt you. He saw some girls at a street corner giggling, approached them and offered them some of his vodka. They agreed, but when he pulled out his bottle, it had already been emptied. The girls were already smitten with him though, and one of the girls offered to get him into a fancy club downtown called *the Atrium.*

"I can't wait to show it to you," said the girl before she kissed him. "You'll love it."

Mayfly smiled and hid the fact that he had been to the Atrium three times in the last week.

/***/

"Do you think that RV is following us?" asked Mayfly.

"I don't care," said the one of the girls.

Mayfly looked through the back window of the taxicab and saw an odd RV van following them. There was a young blond teen inside driving, and next to him was quite possibly the biggest, hairiest man he'd ever seen in his life. There was movement in the back of the RV; it was clear that it held a group.

"I don't care," said the girl again with a laugh, taking Mayfly's face and pulling it away from the back window. "I just care about you. What's your name?"

"Malachai," said Mayfly. He hated to lie but didn't want to go through his normal speech about spanners and mortality.

"Mal-kai," said the girl, her speech slurred with booze. "I just care about you, Mal-kai."

/***/

Mayfly ordered the girls shots and pounded three of them at the bar before bringing them back to the group. His girl was about ready to pass out, and he stopped her before she had another.

"But I love ... *you,* Mal-kai ...," she said before placing her head on the table.

73

"I know," he said with a smile.

Mayfly gave her a kiss on the cheek and then looked around the club. There was a commotion at the entrance; the large, hairy man was trying to get past the bouncer, but the bouncer wouldn't let him in. The blond guy tried to speak calmly, but the guard wouldn't have any of it until a girl with strikingly pink hair stepped in front and flashed a smile. After a few moments of talking, the bouncer let the group in.

Why are they after me? thought Mayfly. *They don't look like they'd be a part of Juan Ponce's crew.*

Mayfly kissed his drunk girl once more and looked at her group.

"Get her home safe and give her plenty of water, okay?"

They agreed and Mayfly went down to the main floor of the Atrium. The bartender was a former girlfriend of his and gave him a double of his favorite drink, Red Bull–Everclear with a dash of lime. When Mayfly turned around, he thought he had run into a wall, but looked up to see that it was the massive, hairy man who had followed him in the RV. Mayfly spilled the drink over the man's shirt, but the big man didn't seem to notice.

"Hey, I'm sorry, bro," said Mayfly.

"*We drink you,*" said the man. He spoke in an odd, crude dialect, like he was still getting used to the concept of language.

"What?" asked Mayfly.

"*Drink you,*" said the man.

"My large friend is trying to say he'd like you to join us for a drink," said his blond friend, stepping in. "My name's Trey."

Trey pointed at a secluded VIP corner at the back of the club. The pink-haired girl winked at Mayfly and beckoned him forward.

Trey smiled at Mayfly, and his straight blond hair dangled gently over his lightly tanned, angular face. He was dressed stylishly, with a soft-shouldered jacket complementing his tall, thin frame. Though he had the features of a young model, Trey didn't put on the airs of someone who would take pride in such things. It was as if 'being recognized' was the last thing he wanted, and he continued to stare down at Mayfly, not in an intimidating fashion, but as if he could see right through Mayfly's charm.

"Want to have a drink with us?" asked Trey.

"Sure," said Mayfly. "My name's Malachai."

"Pleased to meet you, *Mayfly*," said Trey. "We look forward to partying with you."

/***/

"My name's Cattaga," said the girl. "I'm from Alaska."

Mayfly noticed that the roots of her hair were completely white; he hadn't noticed that the first time he saw her. He also saw that Trey had two identical twin brothers, dressed in matching outfits and standing around the table, looking in different directions.

"You've met Trey," said Cattaga, pointing at Trey and his two brothers. "This is Trey Two and Trey Three."

"Pleased to meet you," said Mayfly.

"Pleased to meet *you*," said Trey 3, still looking out at the club.

The big, hairy man came to the table with a large bottle of *Belvedere* vodka in one hand and six shot glasses in another. He slammed the bottle on the table and let the shot glasses fall and roll around.

"Hope like it," said the hairy man.

"This," said Cattaga, "is *Brogg*."

Brogg seemed to be twice Mayfly's height, and perhaps three times as broad. He was built like a boulder and his large belly nearly pushed the table over as he crammed himself into his seat, but he had an underlying look of health and strength to him, as if his large frame could run for three days without stopping. His hair was long on top and his beard was almost as long, and though he was clearly a grown man, Mayfly sensed a subtle innocence in him, as if Brogg wasn't aware of the modern arts of deceit and betrayal.

Mayfly still eyed the group warily though, because they were clearly on to him. They weren't unaware like the girl who had passed out on the bed, and they weren't lonely like Paul had been. They knew him well, and they had sought him out for a reason.

Keep your guard up, this could be dangerous, thought Mayfly, *but stay, because it could also be a lot of fun.*

Mayfly took the vodka with one hand and unscrewed the cap, and then placed the shot glasses upward with his other hand. He flipped the bottle in the air and poured six shots in one motion without spilling a drop.

"To new friends," said Mayfly, holding up his shot.

Trey 1 smiled.

"I'm a bit of a lightweight, and Brogg is hard to control when drunk, so we'll limit ourselves to one shot, if that's okay," said Trey 1.

"Fine by me," said Mayfly with a smile.

Trey 1 and Cattaga clinked the shots with Mayfly. Brogg's hands were so big that he missed and ended up spilling most of his vodka.

Mayfly downed his drink with Cattaga, Brogg drank what remained in his glass, and Trey 1 paused to steel himself. Trey 1 finally took the shot, and soon after he did, his two brothers shuddered simultaneously with him, even though neither of them drank.

"Can I split the rest of the bottle with you, Mayfly?" asked Cattaga. "Just you and me."

"If you give me a kiss," said Mayfly.

"Sorry, I'm taken," said Cattaga, motioning towards the Treys.

"Lucky guy," said Mayfly. "Which one?"

"All of him," said Cattaga, before pouring two shots and downing one.

Mayfly downed his shot and smiled.

"Now," he said. "Care to tell me what this is about?"

"We need you, Mayfly," said Cattaga. "Adam sent us."

"It's been fun, guys," said Mayfly, before putting his shot glass on the table and getting up. Brogg wouldn't let him leave though.

"Just hear us out," said Trey 1.

"I don't know who you guys are," said Mayfly, "but you're not recruiting me to do whatever it is that you're doing. I got to go."

Mayfly struggled to get past Brogg, but he couldn't; the man was just too big. After a few moments, Cattaga spoke up.

"Would you like to make a bet?" she asked.

Mayfly struggled for a moment more, and then turned around and smiled.

"What kind of bet?" he asked.

"In your short time on earth, you've seen a lot," said Cattaga. "Nothing surprises you anymore. Is it safe to say that?"

"Yeah," said Mayfly.

"If I do something that shocks you," said Cattaga, "will you hear us out? You don't have to agree to anything; we just want you to hear us out."

"All right, I agree," said Mayfly. "But I gotta warn you, nothing shocks me anymore—"

Trey 2 and Trey 3 sidled up next to him in a flash. Trey 1 started talking to him, and Mayfly felt a bit of jostling from both sides. The Treys then jumped away and Trey 3 procured a small prescription bottle that Mayfly kept in his shirt. *I've seen pickpockets work in groups before*, thought Mayfly, *but not like that.*

"I don't know what you're doing," said Mayfly, "but I think you should stop—"

Cattaga opened the prescription bottle and procured the oversized pill inside.

"We know precisely what we're doing, and precisely what this is," said Cattaga. "You've built quite a reputation in your brief time here, Mayfly. And word on the street has it you're saving this pill for your last day on earth. Is that true?"

"It's none of your business," said Mayfly.

He tried to rush at Cattaga and get the pill, but Brogg held him back.

"It is my business, considering I'm about to take this pill," said Cattaga.

"You'll die," said Mayfly.

"This pill has a bit of every single illegal drug known to man," said Cattaga. "It kills you, but takes you on a ride first—"

"Please," said Mayfly. "I don't want to hurt anyone; just put the pill down."

"Agreed," said Cattaga.

Cattaga put the pill in her mouth and held it there for a moment, as if thinking. She then swallowed it with her head back, and when she looked forward, her eyes were glowing and a thin strip of green hair had started to grow underneath her white roots. She waited a few moments, time enough for the drug to start acting, and then spoke with a clear voice, unaffected.

"I think we've shocked you enough to win the bet," she said. "It's time for you to hear us out."

/***/

An hour later they were at a diner. Two of the Treys were looking out the window and Brogg was eating three rare steaks, grunting while he chewed.

"Brogg as you can tell is a *trog*-class spanner," said Cattaga. "He ages backwards along the evolutionary scale. He can't quite fit into normal society anymore, but his body gives him incredible strength and endurance."

"I'm a *single-eye*-class spanner," said Trey. "This is me and—"

"This is—" said Trey 2.

"Also me." said Trey 3.

They talked as if they were one person, and if Mayfly had closed his eyes he would have thought that only one of them had spoken.

"In my lifespan I was born with one consciousness split between three bodies," said Trey. "The world sees me as a triplet, but needless to say, I'm not."

"And you?" said Mayfly to Cattaga. "Are you immune to poison or something?"

"Hardly," said Cattaga. "I'm a *manipulator*-class spanner. I can control my lifespan on a molecular level, specifically my DNA."

Cattaga closed her eyes and concentrated. A thin strip of red hair grew from her scalp.

"Before I took your pill, I turned the saliva in my mouth into a strong acid," she said. "I denatured every last bit of the drugs before I took them down."

"Good thing you didn't kiss me," said Mayfly with a smile.

"Are you ready to hear us out?" asked Cattaga.

"I'm not on board, not even close," said Mayfly, "but this is interesting at least. Tell me what you want from me."

Trey 2 and Trey 3 continued to look out the window, but Trey 1 focused on Mayfly.

"Before we met Adam, we were just a street gang of spanners," said Trey. "Adam took us in and taught us how to hide and defend ourselves against Juan Ponce de León's crew."

"Juan's been on everyone's mind lately," said Mayfly. "He's got a compound full of spanners, filled with crazy experiments."

"He's got the Fountain now," said Trey. "Adam wants us to break into de León's compound and free her. We can't do it without you."

"Why can't you do it without me?" asked Mayfly, looking at Trey 1. "You could pick a few pockets, have Brogg bust a few walls—"

"We need *you*," said Trey. "We have powers, but they're not enough. Adam's made it clear that it'll take more than just strength and a few tricks to get the Fountain."

"Then what can I do?"

"Juan's compound relies mostly on secrecy, not modern technology, so the computer systems are a decade old," said Cattaga. "Easy for you to hack, impossible for us."

"You need more than hacking to open up a prison," said Mayfly.

"Precisely," said Trey. "After you open the locks and turn off the alarms, we'll use our powers to extract the Fountain, but we still need you for the first step. Adam's made it clear that one way or another you'll help with all the other steps too."

Mayfly sipped his coffee and then paused for a moment to think.

"What you're asking is fair," he said, "but I've got a few weeks left on this earth until my heart stops. I don't want to run the risk of being captured by Juan Ponce de León and dying in one of his cages. They love mayflies and—"

"Look—" said Trey 2.

"Out!" said Trey 1.

Trey 3 ran in front of the table and pushed everyone's head down. There was a crash as a metal trashcan filled with burning paper shattered the diner's window. It rolled towards them, but Brogg picked it up and threw it back into the street before anything else caught on fire.

Mayfly looked into the street and saw rioters, but they looked more like zombies than anything else. Their eyes glowed softly as they roved through the streets, destroying everything in their way.

"Juan's minions," said Trey 1. "I'll go up on the roof, scout for another way out and hide in the back alley with you. We've got to go through the back; it's never good to take *the populous* head-on."

/***/

The back alley was safe, but only for a few more minutes. At one end was the street where the rioters had massed, and the other way led to a dead end. It was only a matter of time before the mob traversed down and trapped them; the roving looters were already coming their way. Brogg found an empty dumpster, lifted it over his head and then put it over Cattaga, Trey and Mayfly. It was dark, but Cattaga made her arm glow and they had a little bit of light.

"Brogg can only defend against the populous for so long," said Trey.

"I've never heard of the populous," said Mayfly. "What are they?"

"A spanner class that Juan's steward Balthasar controls," said Trey. "They're a mob with one mind."

"Like you?" asked Mayfly.

"Not quite," said Trey. "They live their lifespans with a thousand consciousnesses, all mixed together and spread out evenly. You can't reason with them; there are just too many voices and thoughts floating amongst their collective psyche. Juan has Balthasar send the populous on these riots to pick up spanners and bring them back to his compound."

There was a clank and a grunt as the populous started attacking Brogg outside.

"Brogg's fighting the mob off," said Trey. "But he won't last more than a minute; we need answers."

Mayfly thought for a moment.

"We can't fight them," said Mayfly, "but can we hide from them somehow?"

"No," said Trey. "The populous see anything that's different from them and destroys it."

Mayfly thought for a moment longer.

"Then that's it," said Mayfly with a smile. "We'll join the riot. If we fight alongside them, they won't see us."

/***/

Brogg ran with the empty dumpster bin and threw it through a plate glass window. He chose to throw it through an abandoned storefront, and so far they were all fitting into the mob without hurting any innocent people. But when the police showed up with tear gas, it enraged the mob further. Whenever Mayfly eased up on the violence just a little, someone from the populous would start beating him. So Mayfly continued to fight and so did the rest of his team.

"The cops need about ten more minutes to contain everyone, so we have to make it count!" yelled Trey. "We can get arrested by the police, but we can't get dragged to Juan's compound."

Mayfly saw a small bakery that was empty and figured he could do ten minutes of damage to it without completely destroying it. He took a brick and threw it through the front door, avoiding the plate glass window at the storefront. He looked outside and saw that the rest of his gang were taking care of themselves, so he looked for a place where he could do minimal damage. *Or better yet*, he thought, *hide*.

Mayfly scanned the room and found a walk-in pantry in the back of the kitchen. *The populous will never find me there,* he thought, *and if they do, I'll hear them coming in.*

Mayfly went to the back room and opened the pantry. When he did, an old man hiding inside came out carrying a baseball bat. From the man's demeanor, Mayfly could tell it was the storeowner, and that the old man was blind.

"Easy," said Mayfly.

"Stay away," said the old man in a thick accent.

"You got it, sir," said Mayfly. "But I'm here to tell you—"

"Stay away!" said the man.

"I will, sir!" said Mayfly. "But I'm here to tell you that those aren't just rioters outside. If they see you in here, they'll—"

There was a *crash!* as the plate glass window of the main storefront shattered and smoke billowed in. One of the populous had thrown a tear gas canister through the glass, and the old man started to cough. Mayfly saw police in the streets, but he also saw ten vacant-eyed populous spanners coming in through the shattered window. He figured if he could hold them off for a minute, the police would have enough time to stop the riot, and the man would be fine.

"I'm gonna have you hide, sir," said Mayfly.

"But I—"

"Unless they're the cops, hit anyone who comes through that door," said Mayfly.

In a flash, Mayfly shoved the old man and his baseball bat into the pantry, and then bolted the heavy door behind him. Mayfly turned around and saw the ten populous spanners staring at him with dead, faintly glowing eyes.

Mayfly looked around and searched for a weapon; he only needed something that could hold them off until the cops came. One of the stools had fallen on the ground, and without taking his eyes away from the approaching populous, Mayfly put his hand on one of the metal legs and wrenched it off. He thought for a moment that he might resume destroying the store, but couldn't bear to do any more damage. He held the metal rod up like a sword and then stared at the approaching group.

"Are you ... one of ... us?" three of them said simultaneously, their eyes glowing through the haze.

"The cops outside might think so," said Mayfly. "But no, I'm not."

The populous stopped to think, and then spoke again.

"Are you a mayfly?" they asked. "We gather ... mayflies."

"That's my spanner class," said Mayfly. "But you won't be gathering me, *or my kind*, not today."

Mayfly charged at them with his pole. They were quite effective as a swarm, but in a pack of ten they were slow and easy to fight. Mayfly knew he only had a few moments before the cops showed up, but a few moments was all he would need. He just wanted to send a message to their collective consciousness that if they were ever sent to collect a mayfly again, they should think twice.

JON MAAS

PHOE

Isla del Sol, Bolivia

Kalar awoke at dawn in the meadow and had no idea how she had arrived there. She went to the shore and splashed her face with the waters of Lake Titicaca and saw her reflection in the water after she dried herself off: she had clear, soft skin, thick golden hair that fell around her face like a picture frame, and two large brown eyes. She stood up and then returned to the interior of the island, trying to piece together the night before as she walked. She couldn't quite remember what had happened; it was only a haze. As she got up to face the sunrise, a few memories came back to her; she had a feeling of great despair, sadness and then anger, but she couldn't remember any details. She remembered leaving her room to cool off outside, and then ... nothing. *Did I go to the—?* she thought, but she was interrupted by a younger sister, a girl named Fiora.

"Kalar," said Fiora. "Master Chergon's barn was burnt to cinders last night. Did the fumes make you pass out?"

"Burnt to cinders?" asked Kalar. "But it's—"

"They think Dano did it," said Fiora.

"Dano didn't do it," said Kalar. "He would never do anything like that."

"Love can drive people to do awful things," said Fiora. "We should talk to Porella right now."

"But she married Master Chergon only yesterday!" said Kalar.

"Master Chergon's sick," said Fiora, "and she's crying. We should talk to her."

/***/

Kalar reasoned that perhaps Dano *had* burnt down the barn; he was in love with Porella, and she with him. But Master Chergon took her to be his fifth wife (*his fifth!*), so that was that. Kalar didn't believe it to be true at first because Chergon was three times Porella's age, but now Kalar consoled her friend as the girl wept bitter tears.

"Dano didn't burn down the barn," said Porella. "They framed him."

"Master Chergon would never—" said Kalar.

"They framed him," said Porella.

After a brief pause, Fiora spoke.

"Porella, you should be happy you're marrying our leader; your ascent into Heaven is now—"

"I want Dano, not Heaven," said Porella, "and I don't want to marry our Master! It's not right!"

Kalar wanted to tell Porella to run away, but didn't have the courage to say it. Kalar could do nothing but repeat what she'd been taught for years.

"It's every girl's dream to marry the Master," said Kalar. "It assures your ascent into Heaven."

In response, Porella slapped Kalar's face. After a moment, she kissed Kalar on the cheek and started to cry again.

"I'm sorry," said Porella. "It's not *my* dream to marry the Master."

"I understand," said Kalar.

"You may come to understand more than you think," said Porella with a touch of sympathy and not a hint of malice. "There are rumors that the Master wants to marry you next."

Kalar's heart sank at the thought. She'd never thought that she would marry *at all*, let alone marry *the Master*. He was three times Porella's age, but *four times* hers! How could she marry a man such as their Master? He had taught them since she was young; he was to be wise and trusted, not to be married! She allowed herself to calm down, and then had a sudden thought. *This isn't the first time I've heard this rumor*, thought Kalar. Girls were teasing her about this yesterday, and it made her feel so bad that she *had to go for a walk*. It was then that she blacked out and—

"Kalar," said Porella, interrupting. "When I told you the Master was interested in you, what did you think?"

Kalar tried to come up with a lie, but couldn't think of anything to say; she had never been good at lying.

"Deep sadness," said Kalar. "That's all I thought. Deep sadness."

"Fiora, did you see it?" asked Porella.

Fiora nodded.

"What?" asked Kalar.

"Right after I told you about Chergon, your eyes flashed," said Porella. "They seemed to glow orange."

/***/

"I'll have to give the sermon," said Brother Bocephalus. "Master Chergon is feeling a little … indisposed."

Brother Bocephalus took the lectern and coughed twice; wet, deep coughs. He was built like a bear, but his voice was calm and soft, even through his wet coughs.

"I'm feeling a little under the weather myself," said Brother Bocephalus. "Something's going around."

Kalar heard a few sniffles in the audience and looked around to see that quite a few people were ill. Kalar felt fine and all her friends seemed fine, but the elders in particular looked like they all had the flu.

"But sickness is part of God's world," said Brother Bocephalus, "as is death, disparity, cruelty and suffering. In our former homes we denied God's truth, that the world was a place of *cold, hard lines*, with suffering a part of God's plan. The dark truth of our existence may be harsh to our ears, but God's reality is all around us, and we have but two options: deny it, or accept it and obey *His* rules. God didn't make humans because he needed us to love Him, because God doesn't *need* our love.

"God didn't make humans to love each other either, and His will is evidenced by nature. For if a lioness devours a deer in front of its fawns, is that evil? If the deer evades the lioness and the cat's cubs die of starvation, is that an abomination?

"Neither occurrences are wrong because they're both God's will. Reality may appear harsh to us, it may seem cruel, but it's not unjust. God made the universe simply *as it is*, and the rules that He set just *are*. We are blessed to have the only being on earth that can interpret those rules in Master Chergon, and from Master Chergon's blessed lips we will learn truth.

"The world outside our island enclave seeks only to deny the truth that Master Chergon disseminates, but we accept it and follow the Master."

Brother Bocephalus stopped speaking to get a glass of water. He coughed twice, and Kalar noticed two odd pustules were growing from his neck.

"But to some of you, truth might still not be good enough. You might ask yourself, *'Why? Why should I follow the Master?'*

"And I tell you, in the harshest of terms, that the world is coming to an end and God doesn't care what happens to you individually, for we're but a colony of ants in God's holy garden. I'll also tell you that amongst other holy truths, God has magnanimously lent Master Chergon *the path to Heaven.* There is but one road to God's firmament, and this road doesn't belong to the deserving, the good, the bad, the swift deer or the hungry lioness. This path just *is,* and only Master Chergon knows its way. And when Master Chergon goes to Heaven in the end times, it's up to us to hang on to his coattails, or stay behind and burn."

Brother Bocephalus coughed once more into his handkerchief. Kalar noticed that drops of blood had stained the cloth.

"We are all Chergon's children," said Bocephalus. "And it's our decision to follow him to Heaven or not. So do as Chergon says, for when our souls ascend to paradise, he'll not come back for those left behind; that's not God's way. It's not fair, it's not soft, and it's not warm. The truth just *is.*"

/***/

Kalar was doing her chores later that day when she noticed that one of the native Bolivians was coughing. Kalar put down her bucket and went over to the woman and noticed the same pustules that had started to grow on the other village elders. The boils didn't look nearly as bad on the woman's dark skin, and the woman wasn't coughing as badly as Bocephalus had been. Kalar didn't speak *Aymara* well, so she spoke to the woman in Spanish.

"*What is this sickness from?*" asked Kalar.

The Aymara woman thought a minute and then laughed.

"*You people think everything bad comes from God,*" said the woman. "*But this plague isn't bad, and it doesn't come from God.*"

"Where does it come from, then?" asked Kalar.

"From the Devil," said the Aymara woman, "and this plague is good. It's a blessing."

"Our people don't believe in the Devil," said Kalar. "But if we did, the Devil wouldn't bring blessings."

"The Devil was created by God to cleanse the earth of sin," said the woman. "And he'll clean this place thoroughly."

"The Devil is coming here?"

The Aymara woman laughed.

"I'm sorry if I'm speaking in riddles," she said. "But yes, the Devil has sent this plague here, and he'll manifest himself in two forms that will arrive shortly."

"Two forms?"

"Two men who appear to be demons, and though they may frighten you, they will cleanse this place and rescue you."

Kalar was trying to understand this woman. Was she delirious because of her boils? Was she simply speaking nonsense? *No*, thought Kalar. *This woman is too lucid, too direct to be speaking nonsense.*

"Please tell me," said Kalar. "What's going to happen?"

"The Devil will come in the form of two men," said the woman. "They will destroy this island and rescue you."

"Rescue me? Why?"

"Because it's not your destiny to stay here," said the woman. "It's not your destiny to marry, produce children and then die an old woman."

"What's my destiny?" asked Kalar.

"Your destiny is to burn brightly," said the Aymara woman, "and you can't burn here."

"What do you mean?"

"The Devil will save you because you are *La Paloma del Fuego*," said the Aymara woman. "And *La Paloma del Fuego* must burn to fulfill her destiny."

Paloma del Fuego, thought Kalar, *the "Dove of Fire."*

/***/

Kalar had been led by the elders to a large room to spend the night. The suite was quite luxurious; it was filled with soft pillows, an oversized bed and blankets with frilled edges. Despite the strange day, Kalar fell asleep in the silken bed quite easily.

She awoke at midnight to sharp knocks at the window; Porella was outside and she was no longer crying. Kalar looked out the window and noticed that her sister Porella was with Dano.

"We're leaving," said Porella with a smile.

"Where?" asked Kalar.

"It doesn't matter where," said Porella. "We just have to leave."

"But you can't get into Heaven without Master Chergon," said Kalar.

"I've got all the Heaven I need right here," said Porella, pointing to Dano.

"I don't understand—"

"You don't understand because you've never been in love," said Porella. "And you won't find it here, especially not with Chergon. Now come with us, please."

"I can't—"

"Come with us, Kalar," said Dano. "*I didn't burn the barn, and they wouldn't care if I did. Chergon wants all the males gone anyway; we're competition. They'll follow us for a day, but once we're off the island, they have no power. We'll be free."

"But Master—"

There was a clamoring outside and some faint coughing sounds; someone had been alerted that Porella had gone missing from Chergon's bedchambers.

"If you don't leave with us," said Porella, "you're to be married to Chergon tonight. This room you're in is a *bridal suite*. And if you marry him, you'll never escape this island."

Kalar nodded and then gritted her teeth. They were right; she had to escape. She tried to open the window further, but it wouldn't budge. She tried again with Porella and Dano's help, but the window simply wouldn't move. Dano got a rock and smashed it through the glass, but the hole was too small; the windows of the bridal suite weren't built to allow escape. Kalar tried to open the door, but it was locked.

Kalar looked around the corner and saw two adults running slowly at Porella and Dano; the two adults were covered in boils and looked quite weak. *But still*, thought Kalar, *if they catch Porella and Dano, it won't be pretty.*

"Go," said Kalar.

"But we can't—" said Porella.

"Go!" said Kalar. "I'll find you later."

Porella cried and then nodded.

"Your eyes are glowing again," said Porella. "Bright orange."

Porella kissed the glass, and then she and Dano disappeared into the night. Kalar felt sad, but soon smelled burning from behind her. She turned around and found that her bed sheets were smoldering! She ran over to get a blanket and then covered the bed. It took her a while to smother all the little embers, and when she did she heard the door behind her opening.

Kalar turned around to see Brother Bocephalus and Master Chergon's second wife, a hag named Zorchina. Both of them were covered with pustules.

"We know it was you who burned the barn, Kalar," said Brother Bocephalus. "You're a witch. We've known this since the day you just *appeared here*, with no parents to speak of."

"And we know you started this plague, child," said Zorchina. "We wanted to kill you outright, but Master Chergon in his infinite wisdom has found another way out of this."

Kalar's jaw quivered; she didn't know what to say.

"Master Chergon has been told by the Lord himself the way out of this plague," said Brother Bocephalus. "The plague will be lifted if he marries you."

"But—" said Kalar.

"This is the only way," said Brother Bocephalus. "The Master is righteous and you are filth, and because of your filth he may not last another forty-eight hours. The only way he can cleanse both you and our land of this plague is if he marries *and* impregnates you tonight."

/***/

Kalar stood by an altar hewn of native eucalyptus as they wheeled in Master Chergon. The old man was wearing an oxygen mask and seemed almost twice the size of Brother Bocephalus. He could no longer sit up, so they had bound two gurneys together and he laid there like a dying horse. Many of his boils had burst and new ones were growing to take their place; he smelled of rancid meat and Kalar couldn't help but wince when he came in.

Master Chergon had a coughing fit and his oxygen mask steamed up. While his attendants rushed to him, Zorchina whispered into Kalar's ear.

"Rest assured, love, we've given him some medication and he'll be able to *perform* upon you," said the old woman. "Do you catch my meaning?"

"No," said Kalar.

"You'll understand it tonight," said Zorchina. "It's your destiny."

Brother Bocephalus got to the front of the room and snapped his fingers. The attendants wheeled Master Chergon around and assembled in formation to start the wedding. Kalar noticed that all the exits were closed, and many of the attendants had weapons.

"Brethren and sisters," said Bocephalus. "We're here to witness something miraculous this evening; the continuation of our Master's legacy. In his magnanimity, he has agreed to bless one more of our daughters with his being, and through her our Master shall live again."

Master Chergon coughed again, and this time his oxygen mask became speckled with blood. Zorchina nodded at Bocephalus, and he put his hands on a gun by his hip before getting up to the pulpit again.

"We'll make this short," said Bocephalus. "Master Chergon, do you agree to take our daughter Kalar as one of your family, and to lead her to holiness and the afterlife?"

Chergon turned his head to look at Kalar. He stared at her body for a moment and then smiled.

"Yes …" wheezed Chergon.

"And do you, Kalar, take Master Chergon as your one and only love for eternity?" asked Bocephalus.

Kalar froze; she didn't know what to do. She couldn't say yes, but she couldn't say *no* either; she'd never disagreed with anyone in her life. *I wish to be far, far away from here; this is what I want*, thought Kalar, *and if I cannot leave, I wish to die.*

The carpet around her began to smolder and some of the guests started to yell. Brother Bocephalus ran to a corner and got a fire extinguisher and then came back to put it out. Kalar looked around; many of the guards had their own fire extinguishers and approached the carpet, but Bocephalus bid them back and extinguished it himself. There were cries of *witch*, but Bocephalus calmed them down, coughed and then resumed his place at the pulpit.

"Our daughter Kalar has strange and dark powers, but we have prepared for them," said Bocephalus, still clutching his fire extinguisher. "And this is all the more reason she must be purified by our Master in perhaps his final act."

Bocephalus nodded at a guard whose face was covered with burst pustules, now scabbed over. The guard took Kalar's legs from under her, shoved her to the ground and held her arm behind her back. He then put a gun to her head.

"You have ten seconds to say 'I do,'" said Bocephalus. "Otherwise we'll cleanse you *our* way. Now, do you, Kalar, take Master Chergon as your one and only love for eternity?"

There's no way out of this, thought Kalar. *Perhaps I should just let the guard kill me. It will be better than—*

Kalar heard a massive *BOOM!* and for a moment she thought the gun had gone off. Kalar wriggled out of the guard's grip and then turned around to see that Master Chergon's gurney had been tipped over. The old man was lying on the ground moaning, and it smelled like he had soiled himself. Kalar saw Bocephalus pointing his gun in horror, and then she looked around to see that he was facing a massive hole in the wall.

"Everybody calm!" said Bocephalus. "For though we're being attacked, we have God's prophet on our—"

There was a smaller *BOOM*, and a thin strip of air seemed to fold in upon itself for a moment. Bocephalus was pushed backwards into the altar behind him, knocking it over. Two men came through the door, both tall but one nearly two meters in height. The taller man was completely covered in dark blue clothing held together with heavy buttons. He wore thick, black gloves and had wrapped a set of wrought-iron shackles around his waist. He looked strange, but Kalar noticed that the strangest thing about him was his *mask*. It was like a welder's mask, but it looked heavy, as if it contained machinery. The mask clicked and whirred, and it sounded to Kalar as if the mask's inner gears were making the whirring, and he himself was making the clicking noises. The man made more strange clicking sounds, as if he were inspecting his surroundings, and a moment later another guard raised his weapon. In a flash, the masked man turned around and crossed his arms with great speed. There was another *BOOM*, and folded air emanated from his arms and traveled towards the guard, dislodged his weapon and blew him backwards into the wall.

The tall man's comrade stood up. He wasn't covered with a mask and would have been handsome save for the fact that it looked like he hadn't slept or bathed in weeks. His eyes were watery and had rims of blood at their edges, and his hair looked as if he had slicked it back using his own spit. His clothes were caked in dust, as if they had reached their utmost level of filth long ago, and his leather boots had more holes in them than actual leather. Kalar noticed that this grisly-looking man had a single pustule on his own neck, but seemed otherwise unaffected by the sickness.

"This island, this community, this entire place is an affront to humanity," said the unbathed man. "And I have cleansed it. For those still healthy enough to walk, if you want to live, depart this island and never come back. For the rest of you sinners, all we ask is that you give us this daughter and we'll leave you alone to die in peace."

There was a silence, and then a wheezing from Master Chergon. Brother Bocephalus knelt down and listened to Chergon's words and then spoke.

"Did the Devil send you?" asked Bocephalus.

"No," said the unbathed man. "The Devil made me, but I've seen the error in my ways, and now I serve no one else but humanity."

Master Chergon wheezed again and Brother Bocephalus spoke.

"He says that you shouldn't be here," said Bocephalus. "You're interfering with our path to Heaven."

The unbathed man knelt down in front of Chergon, poked one of Chergon's pustules until it burst, tasted the seepage and then nodded.

"I don't know if the path to Heaven exists," said the man, "but if it does, it's far, far away from this place."

/***/

After a short boat ride, they got in a car that the unbathed man had procured. Kalar looked back and saw her island fade into the distance. It was the only world she had ever known, and now it was invisible. She started to frown, but the man stopped her.

"Don't get all misty," said the man. "You're liable to start a fire."

Kalar nodded and then smiled; she had prayed for a way out of her marriage to Chergon and someone, somewhere had answered.

"What name did they give you?" asked the man.

"Kalar," she responded.

"That's not your name," he laughed. "I go by my spanner class name, so my name's *Phage*. The tall, masked man in the back, his name's Geryon. We're brothers."

Geryon made some small clicking sounds and then Phage breathed in deeply.

"We're your brothers too," he said, "but not like brothers on that island. Meaning same mom, same dad; we're related."

Kalar didn't know what to say; how could this sick man and his mute friend be her brothers?

"Don't get too overwhelmed," said Phage. "We've got a long way to go, and some bad men are after us, men a lot smarter than Brother Bocephalus and company."

Kalar couldn't tell if these men were her actual brothers. Phage resembled her somewhat, but he was smothered in dirt and could have looked like anyone on the island if she thought about it hard enough. She looked back and realized she might never figure out what Geryon looked like. The tall man sat in silence, shrouded in the darkness, his features and emotions completely obscured by his thick blue clothes and his opaque welder's mask.

"Why did you rescue me?"

Phage smiled and then nodded at Geryon, who clicked in return.

"A favor to our other brother, and he's your brother too," said Phage. "A man named Adam Parr. A group led by Juan Ponce de León is after him, and you're the one thing that Adam cares about in this world. They won't be able to get him, but they'll find a way to get you and hold you hostage, that kind of thing. Adam helped me control my sickness a few years back, so I owe him a favor, and I'm bringing you to him."

"Thank you," said Kalar.

She paused a moment and then asked Phage a question.

"What's my real name?" she asked.

Phage smiled at Geryon and then looked at her.

"Your name's Phoe," said Phage. "P-h-o-e; rhymes with *tree*."

A FATE WORSE THAN BURIAL

Adam slumped down in the chair of his living room and took a sip of his Louis XIII Cognac. *I'm not quite happy*, he thought with a slight smile, *but it does feel good to be home.*

He took a shallow draft and let it sit on his tongue for a bit. He didn't look at the bottle, but he remembered from the taste where he had been when the cognac was made. He had been working this bottle's vineyard and had probably plucked these grapes himself. It was a simple hundred-year-old bottle, nothing special, but Adam smiled again when he remembered that year, *that quiet year*. It wasn't a great vintage for grapes; it had rained a bit too much, but it had been a good time for Adam, so he smiled. He had been chased out of Scotland Yard by some particularly nasty criminals, and like he always did when the heat got too high, he disappeared, and this time he had disappeared to the vineyards of France.

The work was taxing, but he enjoyed it. No one cared who he was or where he came from; they only cared that he brought in the grapes, and of that, they didn't seem to care too deeply. All the vineyard required was that he be able to walk, lift and refrain from stealing anything.

Why did I ever leave those fields? he wondered. *I could still be there today, anonymous and working amongst migrants.*

Adam took another swig of the cognac and knew his regrets were mistaken; he couldn't have stayed in the vineyards forever. He had too many enemies, both spanner and human, and he would have been hunted down sooner or later, dragged out of the quiet fields and buried in a ditch somewhere. Cities gave him the protection he needed, and though they moved too fast for him, they also gave him plenty of places to hide.

Adam poured himself a second glass of cognac before noticing that his phone's answering machine was blinking.

He went over to the phone and tried to figure out how to get the machine to play its message. He looked over it for a good five minutes before working up the courage to push a button; he was paranoid about pressing the wrong thing and erasing the message.

Mayfly would always tease him about this. *"Adam, I know you have a problem with new technology,"* Mayfly would say, *"but you're the only one left who even HAS an answering machine, and it's not that hard. You just press 'play.'"*

Adam pressed *play* with a shaking hand and heard Mayfly's voice.

"Adam," said Mayfly on the answering machine. "I'm in prison, but I'll get out soon, so don't worry about me. I'm not going to join you on this quest; I just don't have enough time, and I hope you'll understand that. But your gang is there for you, I'm sure of that, and as always, if you really get into a jam, I'll find you. If I'm still alive, I'll find you."

Adam was disappointed that Mayfly wouldn't help him, but there was nothing he could do. He'd have a team, but they weren't as good as Mayfly. *I've never had a partner as good as him,* thought Adam, *not once in eight thousand years.*

Adam checked his wall clock; it was midnight. He'd find Cattaga, Brogg and the Treys soon, but first he had to pay a visit to a spanner who probably knew a lot more about the current situation than anyone else did. He would know about Juan Ponce de León's motives, the Fountain and just about everything else. The spanner went by the nickname *Special Ed*, and he saw *everything*.

/***/

"This place you're going is not safe, boss," said the cab driver.

Adam guessed the cab driver was from Armenia, and judging by his accent and name probably from the city of Kapan, but Adam feigned ignorance in the interest of time.

"I know it's not safe," said Adam. "But a friend of mine works there."

"He work *there*, this time?" asked the cab driver. "Guy like you no have friend in place like this, not working this time. Not safe, boss."

"You're right," said Adam. "Just drop me close; I can pay you double fare, whatever. I just need you to take me there and then wait for us."

"Then wait? Why?"

Because Ed's probably conning some guy out of his life savings and we'll need a getaway car, thought Adam.

"My friend is handicapped and we'll need a cab to get us out of there," said Adam. "Drop me close; I'll pay double fare."

"I take you, drop you, wait and pick you up," said the cab driver. "But I not need double pay. I need you not die, I need you not be killed."

Maybe there's hope for humanity after all, thought Adam with a smile, making a mental note to pay the cab driver double anyway, perhaps triple.

/***/

They drove for a half hour and the neighborhoods got worse, and to soothe his nerves the cab driver turned on the AM radio.

"This radio bother you, boss?" asked the cab driver. "It's *shock jock*. I like *shock jock*."

"Leave it on," said Adam. "I like it too."

"*We got a caller from La Loche, a town way up in Northern Saskatchewan,*" said the DJ. "*And surprise, surprise, he says spanners are real.*"

"*They're all around us,*" said the caller. "*A lot of them come up here, to Saskatchewan.*"

"*Why would beings with odd lifespans go to Saskatchewan, of all places?*"

"*I don't know,*" said the caller. "*But some of 'em live up here like animals. They have strange powers, so they hunt moose with their bare hands.*"

The radio DJ laughed a bit, and then played a sound clip from an old movie where someone was saying *"You're crazy!"* over and over again. The DJ settled down and then gained a serious tone.

"*All right,*" said the DJ. "*Let's ignore the fact that you just said spanners live in Saskatchewan and eat moose, because as we all know that's ludicrous. I'll ask you a question that I ask all the Bigfoot-hunters, ghost chasers and astral-energy looneys: If this truth is 'all around us' as you say, how come there hasn't been one video, I mean ONE video of indisputable evidence of just ONE of these spanners doing something* crazy, like getting shot and then surviving, shooting rainbows or doing whatever it is that they do?"

"They hide," said the caller.

"They hide," said the DJ, incredulous. "But with all the video cameras now, you'd think one of them and their so-called powers would be documented."

"They hide, and lately they've been disappearing," said the caller.

"Disappearing?" said the DJ. "These spanners can disappear now?"

"No, disappearing, like being killed," said the caller. "One of their own is taking them off the streets and killing them. He's trying to take their powers in the hopes of taking over the world and—"

The cab driver turned the radio off with a click.

"Sorry for nonsense," said the cab driver. "Lot of crazies out there."

"Yeah," said Adam. "There's a lot of crazies out there."

"Yes, yes," said the cab driver. "We here. Now pick up your friend and I drive around. Be fast, hurry, or you be dead."

/***/

Adam had to bribe the guard at the gate to get into the game, and after they patted him down, a man twice his size escorted him down to the main card room. The players turned around and scowled at Adam, but Ed vouched for him.

"He's ... a f-f-friend of m-mine," said Ed in a shaky voice.

The men snickered at Ed's words, but Adam's heart skipped a beat. He knew Ed was about to take all of their money; everyone underestimated "Special" Ed, even other spanners.

Ed was a *slomo*-class spanner, so named because he lived his lifespan in extreme slow motion. His body couldn't adjust to it, so to everyone else it looked and sounded like he had profound cerebral palsy. But in reality, Ed was *quick*. He noticed small differences in a person's breathing and heard microchanges in their heartbeat. So he could tell when a person was lying, and he used his powers to make a killing in the underground poker circuit. Ed could even listen to differences in the sound of card swipes to deduce what card was going to be drawn next. Unfortunately for Ed, the main rooms caught on to the fact that he always won, and soon all they all barred him permanently. So now he played in the rough edges of town for smaller stakes.

And he's still making a killing, thought Adam as he looked at Ed's chips, *but he's playing with desperate men, men who will go hungry if they lose to him.*

"Your call," said the dealer. "Player three goes all in. What do you want?"

"I'm all i ... in t-too," said Ed.

Ed pushed his chips in.

"Flip 'em," said the dealer.

The board had ace, king, ace, and Ed's opponent flipped over an ace-king hand. Ed flipped over a pair of threes, and the other man celebrated.

"Full house, aces full of kings versus aces over threes," said the dealer.

"Yeah! Yeaaaah!" said the guy playing Ed.

When the man jumped up, Adam noticed a bulge in the man's pocket; he was carrying a switchblade. *This is about to take a turn for the worse,* thought Adam, *and we need an exit strategy.*

The dealer burned a card and then turned over a three.

"Hell *no*, man," said Ed's opponent, half jokingly.

Adam put himself behind Ed's opponent just slightly, and then looked for the door. There was a clear path, but Adam saw that one of the guards was young and eager to prove himself. Adam's experience told him exactly what was going to happen. The player would pull a knife, tackle Ed, the guards would separate them, and the young guard would pull out his weapon and after a few moments, fire it. It wouldn't hit Ed, but it would hit one of the other players, and then things would start to get messy.

The dealer burned another card, and then turned over another three. *Two threes in a row,* thought Adam, *less than a one-in-two-thousand chance, and Ed knows it.*

"Four of a kind for Ed," said the dealer, "beats aces full of kings."

The other players erupted in guffaws, catcalls and head shakes.

"Now *that's* a bad beat," said one, laughing.

But the guy who lost wasn't laughing.

"You cheated," said the loser.

"I ... don't cheat," said Ed, pulling in his chips. "I see ... everyth ... th ... thing."

"No one goes all in hopin' for two threes," said the guy who lost. "Especially not some retarded motherfucker who can't even keep his eyes uncrossed."

109

There was a moment of silence, and then Ed resumed taking in his chips. The guy who lost pulled out his knife and lunged at Ed. Adam dove at the man, and then swung him around to protect himself against the guards who had all pulled out their guns. The young guard was particularly close to pulling his trigger, so Adam spoke up.

"Wait," he said. "Please, don't shoot. I'm talking especially to the kid in front of me, to my left."

After a moment, one of the older guards nodded at the kid, and the kid lowered his weapon.

"You got ten seconds to explain just what the fuck's goin' on, man," said the main guard.

"Ed's a good card player, and he's incredibly good at reading people," said Adam, not missing a beat. "I mean he's really good. I've seen this before; he wins fair and square, and people get upset. I need him to help me with my own problem, something that has nothing to do with poker, and I want to buy him off of you. Let us go, and I'll cover the losses completely, plus five hundred to the house."

The guard wavered for a bit, and then looked at the guy who lost, who thought a moment and then nodded.

"Now, how much are you out?" asked Adam.

The guard counted the money.

"Three hundred and fifty dollars," said the guard.

Ed used to play for a hundred times this much, thought Adam as he pulled a wad of bills from his pocket and placed them on the table, *and one day he's probably gonna get killed for less.*

"Count it," said Adam.

The guard counted the money, and then nodded.

"A thousand dollars and change," said the guard, looking at the man who lost. "Makes a compelling case. You cool?"

"I'm cool," said the man.

Adam let the man go and he brushed himself off. The guard looked at Ed and laughed.

"Ed, you ain't welcome here no more," said the guard before shifting his focus to Adam. "But bro, *you're* welcome here *anytime*."

/***/

The cab driver smiled at Adam and then drove away, four times the fare in his hand, plus tip. Adam and Ed stepped into the diner, sat down and then Ed ordered three espressos and a large coffee. Adam didn't know how the caffeine helped Ed calm down, but it did and soon he didn't shake as much. *Every spanner knows about Ed,* thought Adam. *He's a legend within our community. But I know he's just a guy who doesn't fit into this world and is making a living the only way he can. Judging from his two black eyes, the living is a harsh one.*

Adam thought about giving Ed some cash in exchange for the advice he was about to receive. Like Ed, Adam always had money on him, but Adam earned his living the safe way, by selling the occasional priceless bottle of cognac, saving compulsively and living frugally. He wanted to offer Ed money just to keep Ed out of the poker rooms, but thought against it. Ed had no other place than the poker rooms to go, and he always refused payment from those he considered friends. Ed never took favors and always gave his advice for free.

"You've been to visit D-Diego de León," said Ed, his voice calmed by the espresso.

"How did you know?" asked Adam with a smile.

"I see everyth-thing," said Ed. "Hear everything too."

Adam understood Ed's power; he'd watch the angle of someone's sweat drop over his brow, or listen for heartbeats to gauge someone's emotion. But Ed always seemed to go beyond that; he'd listen to you and gauge the rest of the story, or listen to someone who knew you and figure out the rest of the tale from that. Adam didn't understand how Ed knew what Adam had done, but he always knew, even when Adam hadn't told anyone.

Adam recapped the story just to be sure Ed had the details, and Ed nodded.

"It makes s-sense," said Ed. "Juan's a bad man. He tried to exterminate m-me."

"Why did he do that?" asked Adam. "It seems like he'd want your abilities."

"No one wants m-my abilities," said Ed. "I can't help him unlock the Fountain's power, so he tried to h-have me killed. I h-heard of it early and hid. He left me alone; I'm n-not his highest priority."

Ed went into a small shaking fit, calmed down and ordered two more espressos.

"What's Juan going to do?" asked Adam. "What's his plan?"

"To bring to the world the thing that he t-tried to bring me," said Ed. "Elimination."

"Elimination?"

"He wants to use the Fountain's power of life to m-make himself strong, and use the p-power of death to kill everyone else."

"If that's his plan, I believe it," said Adam. "But how? How will he *kill everyone else?*"

Ed took his coffee and put it in the center of the table. He then poured both sugar and salt in it.

"Drink it," said Ed.

Adam took a sip and shuddered at the taste.

"This coffee's not quite sweet and not quite salty; they b-balance each other out. It's a strong taste, but s-still not quite either one. Salty and sweet at once b-become their own thing."

Ed put the coffee aside, flagged down the waitress and ordered another espresso, with grits on the side.

"The F-Fountain is like that. She has the p-power of life and death within her at the same time; two entities in one. So her b-blood gives immortality and her presence can k-kill a man. But what she sh-shows now is a fraction of either of her powers, about as strong as that coffee was sweet."

The waitress brought over the coffee and the grits. Ed poured sugar into his new coffee, and then poured salt on the grits.

"Juan wants to separate the Fountain into her t-two forms," said Ed. "Pure life and pure death. Once s-separated, their power will not be counteracted, and he *will* have both powers at his disposal, un-unadulterated."

"And he'll use this power to kill people?" asked Adam.

"Y-yeah," said Ed. "Use the Fountain's power of death to make a p-poison or something, maybe kidnap your brother Phage and make a plague. Use the power of life to make an invincible army, hunt people down one by one until they're all gone. I don't know how he'll do it, but he'll do it; he's good at k-killing."

"Why? Why does he want to kill?"

"Why did he kill all those Indians five hundred years ago?" asked Ed. "Why does anyone kill? To make space for themselves, that's all. He wants to eliminate everyone on earth, make room for his empire—just *his* people, you know."

Ed sipped his coffee and then looked at Adam without shaking.

"He wanted to kill me, and he'll kill others, but it's not like he's killing the handicapped, the weak, that kind of thing," said Ed. "He wants to eliminate *everyone*, except for maybe a few thousand of his own. He wants to create a new world—a new, perfect world."

"And he'll grant the subjects in this world the power of life from the Fountain," said Adam.

"The power of g-gods, yes," said Ed, his voice beginning to quiver again. "I don't know what those powers will b-be, all I know is th-that I won't make the cut, and n-neither will you."

"I know," said Adam. "I'm one of his sworn enemies, along with his brothers."

"Sp-speaking of that, Diego told you to see the Surgeon, Santos de León?"

"He told me to steal the Fountain and then see Santos," said Adam, not bothering to wonder how Ed had heard of Diego's plan. "Can Santos be trusted?"

"Yes," said Ed, "and you h-have no other choice."

"I've heard that the Surgeon is dangerous, and I know he lives in a dangerous place."

"You're correct in both r-regards," said Ed. "But you need n-not worry about him now, because you have to steal the F-Fountain from Juan's compound first. Are you bringing Mayfly?"

"No."

"Then g-give up," said Ed. "You can't fight Juan with strength, or s-stealth, or sneaking a-around because that's his g-game. Juan's one w-weakness is technology, and his security systems are child's play for Mayfly. Without your m-mayfly though, you'll be caught and put in Juan's rack in a matter of moments."

Ed's not lying, thought Adam. *We can't do this by ourselves.*

"Understood," said Adam.

"I'm serious when I tell you to give up and h-hide," said Ed, "because Juan has something bad in store for you, worse than b-burial."

"Worse than burial?"

"I don't know what it is," said Ed, "but I felt it, just by talking to other s-spanners. Juan'll b-bury you if he gets the ch-chance, but he'll eventually dig you up and do something w-worse. I don't know what it is, but it's w-worse. So give up now and t-take care of yourself; Juan has a plan j-just for you, and he's been th-thinking about it for five h-hundred years."

THE COMPOUND

Mayfly woke at 2 a.m. feeling refreshed from his hour of sleep. He stood up and put his hands on the iron bars, looked outwards and decided to escape; he had escaped from prisons much worse than this before. Mayfly felt in his pocket for his hidden lock-pick and placed it in the jail cell lock, which unfortunately also needed a guard to hit a buzzer behind a far desk. Mayfly smiled and shook his head; he'd have to come up with a different solution, but still, he'd escaped from worse and just needed some time to think.

The police had captured twenty rioters: Mayfly, Brogg and a small fraction of the populous. The imprisoned populous became violently sick as soon as they were locked in and had to be removed; isolation was death for their kind. *They're the perfect foot soldiers,* thought Mayfly. *If they're captured, they won't reveal any secrets.*

Mayfly noticed that the guard behind the desk was a female, and what was more, she had a wedding ring on. Mayfly knew that married women who worked night shifts tended to be lonely.

Maybe I should convince her to let me out, thought Mayfly. *It'll take me a few hours to charm her, but then I could get the rest of my group out. If only I could—*

"I like your jacket, boy," said a deep voice behind him.

Mayfly turned around and saw a large, rough man with a cobweb tattoo on his face staring at back at him. The guy was hardened by at least a decade's worth of incarceration and was over twice Mayfly's size.

"Thanks," said Mayfly with a smile. "It's mine."

"I don't think so," said the man, getting up. "I want it."

"Let's wait until morning," said Mayfly. "We can talk then. I still won't give you anything, but we can talk then."

"We can do this the easy way or the hard way," said the prisoner.

Mayfly got up and stretched his arms. He knew he didn't have half this guy's strength, but Mayfly had studied judo, mixed martial arts, karate and taekwondo over the course of two days and was now an expert in each discipline. *Be careful*, thought Mayfly. *Prison fighting is different; cheating is okay here. He might have a friend or he might be carrying a shank—*

The prisoner charged, but before he got to Mayfly, huge fingers fell on top of the prisoner's head and yanked him backwards. The prisoner with the cobweb tattoo fell to the ground, and Brogg placed his big hand on the man's chest. The prisoner struggled but had no leverage; Brogg was holding him down with his full weight.

"Leave alone," said Brogg. "Friend."

The prisoner struggled for a bit, but soon realized it was no use. He didn't show weakness but nodded in defeat.

"All right," he said. "I won't bother your friend."

Brogg looked at the prisoner and then looked at Mayfly for approval. Mayfly nodded and Brogg let the prisoner go. The prisoner dusted himself off and then looked at Mayfly.

"You're lucky," said the prisoner.

"That I am," said Mayfly with a smile.

"You're lucky to be this stupid dude's bitch," said the prisoner.

In a flash Mayfly pounced at the prisoner. The prisoner steeled himself for the confrontation, but Mayfly went low and tripped the man with his foot. As the prisoner fell forward, Mayfly pulled the man's left arm behind his back and shoved it upwards. The man screamed; just a little push and his arm would be broken in two.

"We have only a little time left in this cell, you and I," said Mayfly. "Do you understand?"

The prisoner yelled in agony and Mayfly took it as a *yes*.

"And in our brief time together, if you ever call my friend *stupid* again, I'll rip your fucking head off, do you understand?"

"Yeah, just let me—"

Mayfly pushed the man's arm up and he screamed.

"A word of advice that you'd better take," said Mayfly. "I know you probably grew up hard and some bad shit led you to this point here, begging me for forgiveness. But you've got a gift of life, and of *time*, and it's a gift that many would kill for. Life's too short to be running around threatening kids for their jackets. Stop picking on the weak and *do something*. Work in the shop, write jailhouse poetry or find religion; just *do something*. Life's too short to do anything else."

The prisoner didn't say anything; he just spat.

"What's your name?" asked Mayfly.

"Spider," said the man.

"Get yourself a real name, maybe take back the one your mom gave you," said Mayfly, releasing the prisoner with a shove, "because I hate spiders."

/***/

Mayfly decided against escaping and kept watch, just in case Spider tried to shank Brogg while the caveman snored. As soon as the day began, Cattaga came to bail them out, but she didn't look like herself; her hair was darker and so was her skin. The guards opened the cell doors and escorted them out. Mayfly, Brogg and Cattaga walked to the bottom of the police building's steps and looked at the sun rising above the city. Their RV was parked by the side of the street, and one of the Treys was sleeping in the back while the other one was at the wheel.

"Thanks Cattaga," said Mayfly, with a smile. "I owe you one."

"Trey's about to owe me one too," said Cattaga.

Cattaga went back into the police building and came out with the third Trey.

"Different cell," said Trey. "I didn't have Brogg to protect me, but I was able to stay awake the whole night."

The sleeping Trey opened his eyes and looked at Mayfly, and then came out to put his arm around Cattaga.

"So here we are again, Mayfly," she said. "Are you coming with us?"

Mayfly looked at the sunset, thought for a moment, and then shook his head.

"No," he said. "I've wasted too much time already; I've got to go, do my own thing. Adam will just have to handle this by himself."

"Where are you going to go?" she asked.

"I don't know," said Mayfly. "But I'm going to have fun."

Cattaga laughed and Trey scowled.

"Two of me and Brogg will take a cab back with you, Cattaga," said Trey. "There's something I need to show Mayfly by myself."

"I'm sorry," said Mayfly. "I don't have time."

"Yes you do," said Trey, getting into the RV. "You have time for this."

/***/

Trey drove along the empty highway for an hour before he spoke.

"You like Cattaga, right?" asked Trey.

Mayfly thought for a moment and then decided to answer truthfully.

"Yes," he said. "Yes I do. I can't help it, and in the short time we have on this earth, mayflies act on their desires, so I might give her one more shot. Nothing personal."

Trey drove for a moment and then smiled.

"Fair enough," he said. "I get it; it's who you are, and quite frankly, Cattaga's charmed by you. I'm the established leader of this group, you come in all brash and full of freedom, you win her over, maybe take her away, right?"

"It's not like that," said Mayfly.

"Damn right it's not," said Trey. "There's too much at stake to worry about who likes who, or anything small like that. Even if Cattaga fell head over heels for you right now I'd still bring you on board, because what we're trying to do is more important than my own happiness, or even my life."

Mayfly thought for a moment; Trey was indeed telling the truth.

"I see your point," said Mayfly. "But whatever we accomplish, you'll be around to see it; I won't."

"You think you have nothing to live for?" asked Trey.

"Nothing here, anyway," said Mayfly.

"I disagree," said Trey.

"I like you, Trey, you're good, noble and all that," said Mayfly, "but you don't know anything about me."

"I know more about you than you think," said Trey. "And you have a lot to live for."

"Like what?" asked Mayfly.

"I'm about to show you," said Trey with a smile.

/***/

They circumnavigated the compound building for half an hour, and then climbed over two fences that had *Keep Out* signs above them. Trey led Mayfly to a grassy knoll; they knelt down and then Trey took out a pair of binoculars. He looked through them and then gave them to Mayfly.

"This is Juan's compound—at least the part that's visible to the public. Most of the experimentation and torture happens underground, out of our sight," said Trey, "but you can see a glimpse here. This is where they let the well-behaved spanners out for maybe half an hour a week, if that."

Mayfly looked through the binoculars and saw a fenced-in area and within it, a little girl with her head in her hands, crying. When another went to comfort her, the little girl showed that her face was that of an older woman, perhaps seventy.

"It's sad," said Mayfly. "I don't know what spanner class that girl is, but—"

"Look over there," said Trey. "The far corner."

Mayfly saw a pack of cute, small, pixie-thin spanners just like him; he did some quick math and realized that they made up over half the population in the yard.

"Are they …?" asked Mayfly.

"Yes," said Trey. "By and large, most of the subjects kept here are mayfly-class spanners. Juan's trying to unlock the Fountain's power, and he needs a group that breeds well and dies fast. Your class brings in a lot of data."

Mayfly took another look at his fellow mayflies. They were just like him but had a dull, vacant look in their eyes. A female was lying face down on the ground, seizing. After a few moments she stopped and laid still. Two mayflies went over to help, but there was nothing they could do; the girl was dead.

"Generations of mayflies live within these walls," said Trey, "and *die* within these walls too. Most of them have never seen the sun, not once. Some of them spend their whole lives in an experimental container; they don't even learn a language."

Mayfly shuddered at the thought.

"This is bigger than you and bigger than me," said Trey. "There are other hidden compounds just like this around the world. If you help us, we'll take down Juan's crew. And after we do that, we'll send Brogg to every last one of these places and he'll break *every* door, *every* cage and every *test tube* that contains a mayfly."

Mayfly thought for a moment, and then nodded.

"Your time is short; ours isn't much longer," said Trey. "But stick with us and you'll help free every last one of your class. I promise you that."

/***/

Mayfly and Trey drove back in silence, entered a garage and immediately parked, then took a flight of stairs down until they had reached *P4*. Trey opened up a hidden door to reveal a large storage room that the group had made habitable. Trey closed the door shut and they were locked in completely; the room was probably even soundproof. *Juan's crew might eventually find us*, thought Mayfly, *but this won't be the first place they look.*

"This is nice," said Mayfly. "How do you afford the rent?"

"I work three jobs," said Trey with a smile.

Two of the other Treys were studying a map with Cattaga and Brogg. Cattaga looked up and smiled; she hugged Trey and then gave Mayfly a slightly longer hug. After she lingered just a bit longer than she should have, he pushed her away gently.

"All right," said Mayfly. "What's the plan and how can I help?"

Cattaga smiled and showed him the map; they were stolen blueprints of Juan's compound.

"Adam wants us to steal the Fountain, and she's right *here*," said Cattaga, pointing at the most protected location.

Mayfly took a look at his team. Cattaga had the powers of stealth and disguise, the Treys had vision and Brogg looked like he was ready to rip a hole through a wall. *Brogg's dangerous but he's eager to do the right thing*, thought Mayfly. *We just need to tell him what the right thing is.*

"We need a sneak attack," said Cattaga. "We need something smart, something that can get past their computerized security."

"That I can do," said Mayfly with a smile. "But for our overall plan we might need both stealth *and* a bit of force."

"Juan has a lot of people," said Trey. "We can't take them with force."

"We're not fighting a war with them, not yet at least," said Mayfly. "We just need to give them a little punch, and then run away with the Fountain while they're stunned."

"Who's going to *punch* them?" asked Trey.

"Brogg," said Mayfly, "and you're going to help him do it."

/***/

There was a pounding at the door at midnight. Brogg growled, and one of the Treys was already opening a cabinet filled with weapons. Another Trey took a gun and hid behind the door. The third Trey disappeared for a moment and then shut the lights off. Mayfly saw that Cattaga's eyes glowed.

"I've increased the amount of rods in my eyes," whispered Cattaga. "I can see in the dark now."

"Both our back exits are clear," said Trey from the darkness. "We can escape at any time."

Something felt odd to Mayfly and he held up his hand for everyone to be quiet. He listened intently and then relaxed a bit.

"Adam, is that you?" he asked.

"Yeah it's me," said Adam.

Trey was still cautious and opened the door slowly to reveal Adam Parr, who soon had his hands up in the air. Another Trey frisked Adam, and Cattaga peered out into the darkness of the stairwell above the door.

"No one's following him," said Cattaga, "at least no one that I can see."

"Looks like you're good, Dr. Parr," said Trey. "Sorry for the treatment, but these times are tough."

"No problem, and times are worse than you think," said Adam. "Good to see you guys. And great to see you, Mayfly; I'd thought I'd lost you."

"You haven't," said Mayfly. "This world can't seem to lose me, even though it keeps telling me it will."

"All right," said Adam, now looking at Cattaga. "Now show me the plan."

/***/

"This could work," said Adam, poring over the blueprints, "but there are two flaws."

"What are those?" said Mayfly.

"The first is that *you're* rescuing the Fountain," said Adam. "She's highly dangerous, especially to your class."

"They put her in the cold," said Mayfly. "The cold mutes her powers."

"Not nearly enough," said Adam. "Once she's outside in normal temperature, she could kill you with a glance."

"I'll be fine," said Mayfly.

"No you won't," said Adam.

"*Fine*," said Mayfly. "What's the second flaw?"

"This raid takes twenty minutes too long," said Adam.

"Twenty minutes is all I need to free a few prisoners," said Mayfly.

"We don't have that time," said Adam.

"I'll stay behind," Mayfly.

"No you won't," said Adam. "Once we get the Fountain, we need to take her to the Surgeon, and he's a long way off. Juan will be on our heels and we'll need you."

"There'll be time," said Mayfly, "and if there's not, I'll *make* time."

THE KIDNAPPING

Balthasar was again awoken at 5 a.m.; someone had broken into the Fountain's cell. He rushed over to the security room to see Juan peering at the camera display and was relieved to see that it had been a false alarm, or close to it. Cannon had entered the Fountain's cell and was keeping his distance, but staring at her frozen bed. Two human guards had tried to remove him already, but he wouldn't budge.

"Our cannoneer has a crush on this young girl," said Juan, "and like most teenage crushes, he picks the unattainable flower, the one too distant to hurt him."

"I shall personally remove him myself and—" said Balthasar, but Juan held up a hand.

"No need," said Juan. "I've sent Drayne."

Balthasar saw Drayne sneaking up behind Cannon; she slowly removed her right glove and then gently put her hand on his neck. It was hard to tell what was happening through the old black-and-white security monitors, but Cannon turned pale and fell first to his knees and then to the floor, his large frame gently guided by Drayne. Drayne looked at the camera and gave a thumbs-up; the whole action had taken only a few seconds.

Juan smiled and Drayne walked outside to tell the human guards outside the room to take Cannon away. They did so and then closed the heavy frozen doors behind them. The computer monitor blinked green to show that the doors were indeed locked.

"Drayne's skill level has improved dramatically," said Juan, "she's no longer a lost whore with the powers of a scourge. She's an assassin, and she'll do what needs to be done to abet our cause. She's even begun to learn Arawak in hopes of becoming the Fountain's bodyguard."

"Of course," said Balthasar.

"Do you understand our cause, Balthasar?"

"Of course, sir," said Balthasar.

"No, I mean do you *really* understand our cause?"

"Sir?"

Juan thought for a moment and then smiled.

"Come," said Juan, "let's have a glass of wine. It's either late in the evening or early in the morning, but whatever the time, I could use a glass of wine."

/***/

Juan poured himself a chalice of Malbec and offered Balthasar one, but he refused. Juan smiled and grabbed the tequila from the cupboard, which Balthasar accepted.

"I understand you drink only this brand of tequila, which goes for a thousand dollars a bottle," said Juan. "How did you afford this before I came along, when you were destitute?"

"I helped found the distillery in southern Mexico a century ago," said Balthasar. "I visit and tell them that I'm the founder's great-grandson, and they give me free bottles."

"Marvelous," said Juan. "You're fortunate to have taken part in history for the past five centuries. My Argentinean wine and your distillery's tequila are from two fiefdoms risen and then broken off from Spain, with whole histories to themselves; histories that I've missed during my time under the earth. All I know of them now is their products."

Juan sipped his red wine and Balthasar took a taste of his tequila, savoring its clear flavor.

"Both countries' histories have been bloody, have they not?" asked Juan.

"Of course, sir," said Balthasar.

"I would expect nothing else," said Juan. "Conflict is in our nature; it's not good, it's not bad, it just *is*. I was reading of the Maori of New Zealand, the Easter Islanders, the New Guineans and their histories. A violent, warlike people, all three countries, and that's not passing judgment; the conditions of their islands could lead to nothing *but* constant conflict, blood feuds, perhaps even cannibalism. Before the Europeans came they weren't a *violent* people, so much as they were human.

"The only difference between them and us was our agricultural methods, which led to an explosion of European cities, which led to disease and advanced warfare and so on. But do you know what *really* set our desire for domination apart from the more savage islanders?"

"No, sir," said Balthasar.

"It was that our advanced agriculture allowed us to bring a priest or two along with every mission," said Juan. "A man not needed to plow the field or fight on the front lines; his only job was to sit back and *justify* what we were doing, through religion. Ask a peasant to leave home to kill strangers and he'll most likely pass, but ask him to *'join a crusade'* and he'll fight and die for you every time."

"Indeed, sir."

"Which brings an interesting question, Balthasar," said Juan. "What is your role in our mission? Is it that of the priest? Or that of the foot soldier?"

"I am a steward sir, and nothing more."

"The job of steward hasn't existed for more than a century. I ask again, if you *had to choose*, which role would fit you better, that of priest or of foot soldier?"

"Then I would choose priest, sir."

"Good," said Juan. "We're going to change the world and we need a priest, not for religious purposes, but to have someone who can prod our people to do ignoble things in the interest of attaining our goals. Are you comfortable with the ignoble, Balthasar?"

"I'm comfortable with anything that supports our cause, sir."

"Those are words, but would you actually do what needs to be done to take this world to its next evolution? Would you kill a child?"

"Sir, I—"

"That's an unfair question, I admit," said Juan with a smile. "I wouldn't want a child-killer by my side. But for argument's sake, let's say there was a button before you. If you press it, an innocent child dies, but a hundred elsewhere are saved. Would you press it?"

"I suppose, sir."

"What if the button killed a million innocent children but resulted in a lasting world peace and eliminated hunger, disease and poverty?"

"Then I would press it, sir."

Juan poured himself another glass of wine and looked out the window to watch the sun rise over the mayflies out in the yard.

"These are preposterous ethical choices, I know," said Juan, "but they are choices you *will have* to make, because we are close to unleashing the Fountain's full power. The life aspect of her being will magnify our abilities by a thousand until we're like the gods of yesteryear. The only difference between you and Apollo is that you'll be greater than he and you'll be *real*."

Balthasar didn't know what to say, so he nodded instead.

"But I don't wish to make us gods only so that we can be gods amongst mortals, with temples, worshippers and such," said Juan. "And if we only use the life power of the Fountain, that's the only outcome. A world crowded with mortals with our kind at the top; that would lead us backwards, not forwards."

Juan smiled and took another sip of his wine.

"How can we become the gods of yesteryear without falling into the traps of yesteryear?" asked Juan.

"I don't know, sir," said Balthasar. "What would you propose?"

"I hope to make a perfect society," said Juan, "and the only path away from the violence that lies within the human heart requires extensive *eradication*."

Juan took one more drink from his wine and then poured Balthasar another glass of tequila.

"Drink," he commanded, and Balthasar drank.

"Violence and depravity are in our nature, you know, and they're both unavoidable. Academics seem to cast us conquistadors as villains, but they've missed the big picture," said Juan. "Before we came, the naturals were killing and raping each other in a sort of constant equilibrium, with no end and no purpose other than instinct. The same could be said for the Maori warrior, the Guinean headhunter or the Easter Island cannibal. We did ignoble things, but our ignobility ended their equilibrium of constant warfare and cleared the path for history to proceed. I awoke five hundred years later to be greeted by Malbec, tequila and an endless array of crowded cities, but *history has proceeded* in Argentina, Mexico and countless other vassalages. How? By becoming friends with the naturals and trading with them? By being nice? No; by wiping them out when we could and having them conform when we couldn't."

Balthasar sipped his tequila and then poured another glass.

"Tell me, Balthasar, have you been to Mexico City?"

"Yes," said Balthasar. "I've been many times."

"And what do you think of it? Be honest."

"It's quite large, overpowering and—"

"It's an abomination," said Juan. "We ended the natural's equilibrium of constant war, established our cities and gave them lives of poverty, prostitution, endless garbage and crime. History happened to the city, but it didn't happen to its fullest extent. You can say the same of São Paulo, Johannesburg, Manila and everywhere else. Humanity has taken a step in the *right direction*, but we've not gone far enough, and whatever the case we have currently *stalled*. Do you agree?"

"Of course, sir," said Balthasar.

"We need a drastic measure to move this world forward, perhaps more drastic than our exodus five hundred years ago, when the overflowing population of Europe took shelter in this western land."

"Of course, sir."

"This is where the Fountain comes in, not just her *good half*, but the half that brings *death*. Death is important to humanity, and though we ignore it, *death* is the notion that allows for the new to spring up. Death makes space, and if it weren't for *death* we'd be sipping neither Malbec nor tequila, but rather sitting in some mud hut somewhere, grunting at each other. Do you agree?"

"Of course, sir."

"Perhaps death will come in the form of a *battle*. The Arawaks have a prophecy that there will be a great battle for the Fountain to decide the fate of humanity, and perhaps that will be our vehicle to bring death. Perhaps it's just another yarn from an illiterate tribe and should be ignored.

"Regardless of the legend, we're headed forward to our own destiny. Once we have separated her powers, we'll take a sip of life from the Fountain of Youth ourselves and become gods, and then take the death in its unadulterated form and work on the rest of humanity. I don't know if we will make a poison, a disease, or some sort of weapon, but we will bring death. We'll do it quickly and cleanly, putting minimal destruction on the environment."

"Sir?"

"We'll kill every single human but ten thousand children," said Juan, not missing a beat. "Ten thousand will be left, children of all ethnicities, too young to remember anything but us as their parents. These children will be our wards, and once grown, they'll be the bulk of our society. We'll bless them with the power of the Fountain's life, and they'll live the lives of gods themselves, though we will leave certain controls in place."

"Controls?"

"I haven't quite thought of the details—that will be your job," said Juan, "but we'll need strict and clear controls to ensure that in this new society, there will be no crime because we won't allow it. There will be no more war because we won't allow it. There will be no more disease and no more suffering because we *will not allow it*. We'll live in perfect harmony with our natural surroundings, because pollution, species-extinction and expansion won't be allowed."

Juan smiled for a moment and stared at Balthasar.

"Again, I know not the details," he said, "and I know not how the Fountain's bifurcated powers will abet this, but I know that it can and will happen. This new society will have powers and we will forever be its *parents*, as it were. Our children will have the freedom to fly to the moon and back if they so desire, but we will have instituted certain *controls* that allow us to stop them if our children should do *anything* to threaten our permanent utopia. Does this make sense?"

"Of course, sir."

"Good," said Juan. "We've yet to unlock the Fountain's power, but when we do, I'll need you to be just as fervent in bringing this utopia about as a Spanish priest was when he trekked into the Amazon to baptize a hundred children of the forest. You must *know* you are ultimately doing the right thing, even when the path gets arduous. You must *know* that the cost to make this society is great, and you must not waver, even when a million cry out before you. When the time comes, will you do what is right to abet the future?"

"Of course, sir."

"Good," said Juan. "For you will have to do dirty and dark things, things that will make our own past misdeeds look like child's play. When the time comes to press a button that will cause a million innocent children to suffer, you must press that button, for doing so will get us one step closer to a world where no one will ever suffer again."

/***/

Balthasar walked the halls of the compound all day, thinking about what Juan had said. Juan was known to speak of grandiose, impossible things, but Balthasar knew that those things usually came true. He had spoken of expanding the compound, and they had moved into a bunker twenty times the size of their previous estate. Juan had spoken of capturing, taming and then sending out the populous to capture other spanners, and they had done just that. Juan had spoken of recruiting human guards to work for them, and now they had an army of loyal servants who would do anything in exchange for the promise of a piece of the Fountain's power.

But he speaks of eradication, and I've not considered that, thought Balthasar.

Balthasar had done what was asked in the past, but would he be able to do it again, on a much larger scale? Balthasar thought back on all that he had witnessed while Juan had lain in the ground: the wars, the crime, the vice and the devastation. He had seen more uprisings and counter-uprisings than he had cared to remember, and looking back on his life, his memories simply held an uninterrupted sequence of violent events. *The 1910 civil war of Mexico killed a million people,* thought Balthasar. *Coup and counter-coup in endless succession, one group seized power while the other plotted to take it back.*

Balthasar thought back to the time of the Mexican Revolution and remembered foolishly escaping to Europe, only to find himself trapped in the throes of World War I, watching as men on both sides volunteered to die in the trenches by the millions. The war ended and Balthasar fled back to Mexico, the civil war not yet complete.

The conflict in Mexico never ended, thought Balthasar. *Each side's victory was just an assassin's bullet away from another coup.*

Balthasar thought back to a time fifteen years after World War II when he worked as an engineer for the Van Horn diamond mining company in the Belgian Congo. He had needed an adventure and thought he'd find one in Africa, but found only strife and bloodshed. *When they broke free of Belgium, things took a turn for the worse,* he thought. *They started a civil war and haven't ended it since. It's not their fault, of course; humanity's instinct is to reproduce and consume, and then kill all others so that they can reproduce and consume more. This has been the only story I've seen the past five hundred years, from Hispaniola to Mexico, from Europe to Africa.*

Balthasar thought of what Juan had said, of thinking of eradication as a solution to humanity's ills. It seemed counterintuitive and cruel, but what had history been, if not that? Wars never ended with a truce, because truces only set the stage for the next coup. When wars did end, they ended only with the *eradication* of which Juan spoke. When one side was completely eliminated, the peace would last; if both sides remained, the peace would only last until the losers found time to organize themselves.

There will be no more civil wars if the world population declines to ten thousand, thought Balthasar. *There will be no more coups, no more assassinations and no more violence if the world's population decreases and Juan controls those who remain. He'll be like a strict father keeping his house in order. Eradication is a part of this, and if the time comes to push the button to start the process, I have no option but to press it.*

Balthasar was also mystified by Juan's mention of a final battle, though. He had seen his share of fights over the years, of course; in fact, it was rare that he'd live a year without seeing one. But he'd never led a battle, let alone a "great battle to decide the fate of humanity." Arawak legend or not, Juan had brought it up, and what Juan mentioned would always have to be taken seriously. If he mentioned a battle, Balthasar would have to prepare for it.

But who would fight for us? thought Balthasar. *Will the populous be our army? And who would we be fighting against?*

"Sir," interrupted one of the human guards, meeting him as he walked. "Circumstances require your attention."

"Speak."

"Two spanners have volunteered themselves for commitment," said the guard.

That's odd, thought Balthasar. *In all my years I've never had a spanner voluntarily* surrender *himself to this place, let alone two.*

Balthasar nodded at the guard, and they walked towards the interrogation room to question the prospective detainees. *Juan's course is the right course,* thought Balthasar. *I'm prepared to do ignoble things and I'm prepared to bring eradication because that's what it will take to bring the world to its next state of being. If a final battle comes, I'll be prepared for that too. I'll do what needs to be done, no matter the cost.*

/***/

The two spanners were an odd pair. The first was a trog-class spanner that was built like a wrecking ball. Balthasar knew that he was strong enough to break everything in the room even though he sat calm and dull-eyed next to his blond friend. The blond boy was a shivering kid with greasy hair and a dirty face, and would have passed for a simple bed-hopping runaway were it not for the fact that his eyes glowed occasionally.

"Names?" asked Balthasar.

The trog grunted and then looked at the blond boy.

"His name is *Gurk*," said the shivering kid. "My name's Trevor."

"Class?" asked Balthasar.

"He's the caveman-class spanner, I think," said the boy. "I don't know what I am. All I know is that I want to be with my own kind."

"Why would you turn yourself in?" asked Balthasar.

"I don't want to be kicked out again," said the boy, "and I don't want to hurt anyone anymore."

"Very well," said Balthasar to the guards. "Take them to be processed, registered and analyzed. Keep an eye on both and put double security on the big one."

A trog's strength is almost that of Cannon's, thought Balthasar. *If he gets angry, bad things could happen.*

/***/

Late that evening, a female guard knocked on Balthasar's quarters.

"The trog's currently throwing a fit," said the guard. "Please tell us what to do."

Balthasar dressed quickly, putting a tie on over a buttoned silk shirt, and followed the guard to the security room. The female guard pointed to the seventh monitor, and Balthasar saw that the trog was in the process of destroying the dormitory and had turned over the desks around him and made them into a makeshift fort. Three guards had surrounded him but were too afraid to approach.

"Tell them to fire their tranquilizers," said Balthasar.

"I already have, sir," said the female guard. "No effect."

His biology has changed such that tranquilizers are useless, thought Balthasar.

"Can we kill him?" asked Balthasar. "Just shoot him and be done with it?"

"I wouldn't, sir," said the guard. "The bullets might slow him down, but he could get angry and kill our guards in retaliation."

"Then suggestions?"

"I suggest we evacuate the guards from the dormitory and lock down the heavy doors around him. He'll be contained and we can figure out what to do from there."

"Make it happen," said Balthasar. "But tell me, where is his companion, the blond youth?"

"There, sir," said the guard.

The blond kid was sitting in a corner, observing the whole situation with blank, glowing eyes.

"Lock him in too," said Balthasar. "Get our men out, and we'll proceed from there."

/***/

Outside the compound, in the RV, one of the Treys was driving and the other nodded and looked at Adam.

"We're in," said Trey. "She evacuated the room; that's our signal."

"Good," said Adam. "Cattaga's made it inside, but she'll only be able to disable the alarms on the outer doors; we'll have to do the rest."

"I'll handle it," said Mayfly.

"Our goal is to get the Fountain," said Adam. "Everything else is secondary."

Mayfly nodded without making eye contact.

/***/

Mayfly and Adam exited the RV and ran into a chain link fence. There was barbed wire on top and Adam was about to climb it, but Mayfly stopped him and then scampered up the fence himself, popping over the blades without a scratch. He stopped, took out some wire cutters from his pocket and snipped the top until Adam had a clear path. Adam then climbed the fence, taking twice the time Mayfly had taken.

Mayfly had studied the blueprints of the compound well and soon found a heavily chained door. He took out his lock pick from his pocket, and within moments all the chains fell to the floor. Mayfly opened the door to reveal a guard in the halls coming right at them. They hid around the corner, but it was no use; they had been spotted. Adam gave Mayfly a look to tell him to grab the guard and do what needed to be done, and Mayfly nodded. The guard came out and Mayfly pushed her into a prostrate position and prepared to knock her out.

"Wait!" said the guard. "It's me!"

Mayfly instinctively let her go and then smiled.

"Sorry," he said.

"It's me," said the guard to Adam, right as her eyes started to glow. "Cattaga."

/***/

They walked down the halls with Cattaga in the disguise of another woman. She had changed her DNA until her bone structure, skin and hair were different; for all intents and purposes, Cattaga was the guard she was pretending to be.

"The control room is up ahead," said Cattaga. "If anyone stops us, I'm escorting you."

Adam and Mayfly followed her into the security guard's room and when they arrived it was empty, save for the woman Cattaga had impersonated, who was now bound, gagged and tranquilized underneath the desk.

"Here we are," said Cattaga. "All the guards are busy trying to deal with Brogg, so the rest is up to you two now. We need to open the Fountain's door and then give a clear path to the exit."

Adam looked over the control board and the video monitors, and was immediately lost. He looked at Mayfly for help, but Mayfly was already moving forward with dismantling the advanced parts of the compound's security systems. Mayfly typed for five minutes uninterrupted, and then brought up a few interfaces that Adam couldn't even begin to comprehend.

"Their computer architecture is old," said Mayfly. "It'll take time, but I'll be able to get in."

Mayfly typed at the computer for a few more minutes, and the words and symbols went by the screen so fast that Adam got a headache. Adam noticed that Cattaga's eyes began to glow a bit, and she nodded; she understood everything that Mayfly typed and even gave him a bit of advice at points.

After five more minutes, Mayfly smiled.

"It's open," said Mayfly. "We'll get the Fountain, and then free the rest of the spanners here."

"I'll get the Fountain myself," said Adam. "She's dangerous."

"The cold dampens her powers," said Mayfly. "They've even given her a cold suit so she can walk outside. I'll be fine."

"Any amount of her power that leaks out could kill you," said Adam.

"You're taking me for two reasons," said Mayfly. "The first is that the Fountain might not want to go, and I can be very persuasive."

"It doesn't matter," said Adam. "You can't just—"

"The second reason is that you can't speak her language," said Mayfly, "and I became fluent in Arawak this morning."

/***/

Adam and Mayfly opened the heavy door to the Fountain's room, and frozen air spewed out from its edges. They closed the door behind them but didn't shut it; Adam wanted to conserve the cold but was afraid of getting locked in. Her room was like a walk-in freezer, and she was placed in a metal container built into the wall. The structure looked like the place that coroners stored cadavers, and it had multiple locks on it. Mayfly analyzed the locks and then opened two, and then had Adam put his hand on a sensor to open the third. They pulled the slab open and the Fountain came out with a puff of frozen air, still sleeping.

She was a strikingly beautiful girl with Indian features, but she had the platinum hair and the porcelain skin of an albino. Her eyes glowed red underneath her closed eyelids and her whole body was perfectly white, the color of milk. She was bound to her slab with chains and had a tourniquet in her mouth, but Adam pulled Mayfly back nonetheless.

"Think of her as radioactive," said Adam. "She may not mean you any harm, but—"

The Fountain awoke and started to panic; she struggled against her chains and screamed. Adam put his hands to his lips to quiet her, and she became quiet. Mayfly kept his distance, but spoke to her in Arawak until she started to nod in agreement.

Adam took the gag from her mouth. She spoke softly to Mayfly.

"She's not scared of us; she's just worried about our safety," said Mayfly. "She doesn't want to hurt anyone."

"Tell her that she can't hurt me, especially if she stays in her cold suit," said Adam. "And tell her that you're smart enough to keep your distance."

Mayfly told her this and she spoke back.

"She asks what we're doing," said Mayfly.

"Tell her we're freeing her," said Adam.

Mayfly spoke to her and she unleashed a torrent of words.

"She doesn't believe us," said Mayfly.

She's been kidnapped and put in a freezer, thought Adam. *I don't blame her for being wary.*

"I have an idea," said Adam. "Translate everything I say."

Adam came up close to her and put his hands on hers. She tried to shrink back but he held on, letting her know that it was okay.

"I give you my word that you can trust us, but that's all I can do," said Adam, giving Mayfly time to translate. "We'll attempt to free you, and I can't promise you more than that. After this we're hoping to take you north, to a man who will bring your true powers out but doesn't want to use them for his own gain. For right now though, we need to get you out of this compound. If you should choose to part ways with us as soon as you leave, there's not much we can do. But for

145

right now, if you follow us, we'll do everything in our power to free you from this room and take you as far away from this place as we can."

Adam took his hands off of hers and unshackled her wrists, and then her legs. She stood up and pointed to the cold suit in the far corner. Mayfly took it, handed it to Adam, and they placed it on her, wrapping it around her shoulders like an oversized shawl. She waited for a moment and then spoke softly to Mayfly.

"She'll go with us," he said.

"The desire for freedom is universal," said Adam. "Regardless of the circumstances, no one wants to stay in a prison."

/***/

The three of them snuck out of the room with the cold suit draped over her; it was basically a form-fitting blanket, but it was large and fit her perfectly. Mayfly crept through the halls and served as a scout; he would peek around every corner and tell them if they were good to go or not. They walked quietly, then quickly, and then hid for five minutes while a retinue of guards passed. There was one guard who wouldn't leave, so Mayfly snuck up behind him and delivered a hit that made him collapse to the ground like a bag of meat.

"It's a nonlethal trick I've learned: the one-punch knockout," said Mayfly. "There are three people on earth who can make it work every time."

"Sounds good," said Adam. "Perhaps we should—"

"Hands up!"

They looked ahead and saw three guards coming at them, all with guns. Adam couldn't lead them the other way; it led deeper into the compound and they would be trapped. The only way out was through these guards, and Adam knew that they were outmatched. Two were nervous young recruits, but one was an experienced marksman.

One of the young recruits would pull the trigger prematurely, and the experienced one would end it. Adam had to make a decision and had to make it now.

In one motion, Adam grabbed Mayfly and gave him a look and a nod; Mayfly was sharp enough to intuit Adam's plan from just that single glance. In another motion, Adam took the cold sheet off the Fountain and draped it onto Mayfly, who fell against the wall. The guards yelled as if blinded by an invisible blast, and then crumpled to the ground twenty feet away. Adam waited for them to stop moving, then in a flash took the cold cloak off Mayfly and covered the Fountain again.

"I told you she was dangerous," said Adam.

"Radioactive," said Mayfly. "A one-punch knockout."

Mayfly inspected the guards and then looked up at Adam.

"They're still alive," said Mayfly, "but other guards must have heard it."

"We need to go now," said Adam.

"But we—" said Mayfly.

"There's no time," said Adam. "We need to go."

/***/

They caught up with Trey and Brogg ten minutes later. Though Juan's guards had locked Brogg in the dormitory, he had punched the door open and then knocked the guards out. Cattaga was soon behind them, and her face had changed halfway from the guard she was impersonating back to her old self.

"One of my bodies snuck into this place and I've scouted a way out. The third is back in the car looking at a map," said Trey. "Follow me down this hallway."

"We should go this way," said Mayfly, pointing at another hallway. "It's shorter."

"That path dead-ends," said Adam.

"True," said Mayfly with a smile, "but Brogg will be able to go through it."

"I agree with Mayfly," said Trey. "Brogg can punch through anything."

/***/

They met the second Trey at the dead end, which was next to a heavy metal door. Adam knew where Mayfly had led them. *This is where Juan keeps his mayflies,* thought Adam.

Mayfly first tried to open the lock with his pick, but it was no use; the door was meant to hold mayflies *in* and couldn't be broken by one of their own. The mayflies inside had assembled near the door and were clamoring to get out. Mayfly tried a few other tricks, but none of them worked. *There's no fence to hop, no guard to charm, and no electric security system to override,* thought Adam. *This is perhaps the one door on earth that Mayfly can't open.*

Brogg started to hit it as hard as he could, but he wasn't making a dent in it. Adam held Brogg back and the mayflies started to scream from the inside. It became quiet for a moment, and Adam heard the sound of approaching guards.

"We need to go," said Adam.

"We need to free these spanners," said Mayfly.

"We have no time," said Adam.

"Keep punching, Brogg," said Mayfly.

Brogg went to punch the door again, but Adam held up his hand to stop him.

"It won't work," said Adam. "Brogg's strong, but he can't break down these doors. We'll have to come back to rescue them."

"They'll be dead by the time we return," said Mayfly. "Leave me here. I'll find a way out of this."

"If we leave you here, they'll capture you and throw you in the cell too," said Trey.

"I'll find a way out."

"No you won't, because this prison is *built* for your kind," said Cattaga. "We only have one option, which is to *leave now and come back for them later*."

Mayfly stared inside the door and Adam heard the spanners inside scream back and pound the door to be let out. Mayfly nodded at Brogg, who punched a hole in the wall of the dead end. A few more punches cleared the bricks away, and soon they were looking at the RV with Trey revving the engine and staring outwards into the night.

"I promise I'll come back here and free every one of you," said Mayfly to his brethren behind the heavy door. "Stay alive until then."

Mayfly left in a flash for the RV, and the trapped mayflies' screams increased to a high squeal. Adam caught up with him at the RV and for the first time in his life, Adam noted that his friend Mayfly had been crying.

/***/

Trey drove the RV and they sped through the night quietly, taking shortcuts and left turns wherever they could to ensure that Juan couldn't follow them. Most of the crew slept, including the Fountain. Mayfly had converted a large storage freezer into a bed and had improved the cooler so that it could run on the RV's limited electricity. He opened the freezer up with a smile and the Fountain willfully went inside; she was used to the cold and glad to be unshackled. *Mayfly worked on this freezer for twenty minutes and he's already improved it tenfold,* thought Adam. *If he had a full lifetime to work, he'd solve all of our problems. Perhaps Mayfly is the key to our future and not the Fountain.*

/***/

The next morning the crew was up and had gathered in the RV's central area.

"We're going to keep going north until we reach Santos de León," said Adam. "Juan's crew will keep at us and we have no other choice."

"I'll be sleeping at all times," said Trey, pointing to one of his selves at rest. "We won't need to stop."

"Legend has it that Santos lives in a dark place," said Cattaga. "They call it the *Wild Zone,* and it's dangerous."

"It's more dangerous than you can possibly imagine," said Adam. "The human government set out a plot of land for us to place all the spanners that couldn't hide in normal society: violent spanners, insane ones and countless others. There are no rules up there, and though the creatures of the Wild Zone won't plot against us like Juan, they're good at killing. Every bit of the land is dangerous, so keep your guard up at all times."

Brogg shuddered and Adam wondered how much the caveman had understood, and if someone with his size and strength could truly be afraid.

"I've heard of spanners going into the Wild Zone," said Cattaga. "But I've never heard of one leaving."

"That's the way it goes up here, and some of us might not make it back either," said Adam. "But we must bring the Fountain to her destiny because if Juan gets her, he'll kill us all the same. We have no recourse but to go north."

Adam heard a high-pitched howl from the distance, even over the sound of the RV's engine. He listened for the sound again, and when he heard it, he thought it was the sound of a wolf.

/***/

Balthasar had ordered one of his guards to whip him, and though the guard balked at first, Balthasar threatened to exile him from the compound if he refused. The session lasted ten minutes, and though he didn't yell, the pain was enough to cause Balthasar to pass out. He awoke, thanked the guard and then took two drafts of tequila before walking into Juan's office. Juan was drinking another glass of Malbec, and looked surprisingly upbeat considering the circumstances.

"Would you like another glass of tequila, Balthasar?" asked Juan, pouring a shot. "In addition to the two you just drank?"

Balthasar didn't bother to wonder how Juan knew he'd already had two glasses; he just nodded, drained the glass without tasting it and asked for another. Juan poured a shot, sipped his own wine and then sighed deeply.

"The Arawak legends predicted this," he said. "They alluded to a chase for the Fountain, followed by a great battle. I suppose we're about to start with the chase, do you agree?"

"Of course, sir," said Balthasar.

"The funny thing about these legends is that they don't have an end," said Juan. "I've done study; there's a chase, and then a battle for the Fountain, but no prophecy for a clear victor. All they state is that the victor will control history, whoever the victor might be. This gives me confidence; do you know why?"

"Please tell me, sir," said Balthasar.

"First of all, because the legends state that after the chase we *will* find her. I believe that they're headed to my brother Santos's place, and though I know not where he lives, we will find her. As long as the Fountain exists on Earth, she is ours. All we need is time."

"Very good, sir," said Balthasar. "Why else do these prophecies give you confidence?"

"The second bit of confidence comes from my own experience. Though the prophecy doesn't show a clear victor, I'm assured that we will win," said Juan, "because we have purpose and they do not. *We* want to change the world, and they want only the status quo. The world wants change and favors those who want it too. Do you believe this?"

"Of course, sir," said Balthasar.

"Good," said Juan, walking behind Balthasar.

Juan took a sip of his Malbec and then slapped Balthasar on the back, right where his wounds from the whipping had been. Balthasar spat out his tequila and screamed in agony, and then Juan put him in a headlock and dug his nails into Balthasar's open wounds.

"Would you like me to stop, Balthasar?"

"P-please!" yelled Balthasar.

Juan immediately stopped, allowed Balthasar to sit back in his seat, and then poured him another glass of tequila.

"I hated doing that, but I had to prove a point," said Juan. "I understand you've been flagellating yourself like a monk for this security failure, and I wanted to get it out of your system. If we're to be successful, we can't be like the humble friar, feasting on self-inflicted wounds and humility. If we're to change history, we must take our anger and project it *outward*. Do you understand?"

"Of course, sir."

Juan Ponce de León smiled at Balthasar.

"Now tell me, and be honest with no fear of being whipped again," said Juan. "Do you fear Adam?"

"No sir."

"You *should* fear him," said Juan, "because so many have underestimated him in the past and paid the price for it; he always finds a way to accomplish his goals, especially when they're antithetical to yours."

Juan thought for a moment and took another sip of wine.

"Your dogs will follow him, will they not?" asked Juan.

"They are tracking him as we speak," said Balthasar.

"Tell me about them again, Balthasar," said Juan. "These are spanner animals, these spider-dogs?"

"Spider-wolves, sir," said Balthasar.

"Of course," said Juan. "Now tell me what they can do, and how they will help us."

"They're a breed indigenous to the Wild Zone," said Balthasar. "They're wolves with the lifespan of a spider. I've been able to train them, and they're excellent at tracking and relaying messages back here. They'll find Adam even if it takes them several generations to do so."

"Splendid," said Juan. "They'll find him, but they won't kill him because he'll be able to find a way out. Adam has lived far too long to meet his end at the hands of a few dogs. Would you be able to follow them as they pursue Adam north?"

"Of course, sir."

"Good. You'll go with Cannon, Drayne and a few human guards. I've already sent our blur south to find Adam's sister Phoe," said Juan. "Our blur will bring her to us, and if you haven't found Adam by then, send the message that we have her and Adam will find you."

"Of course, sir."

Juan took one final sip of the wine and placed the glass on the table. Balthasar noticed that the bottle had been emptied, and that there were three other empty bottles beside it.

"We're approaching events, Balthasar, great events that will change the course of history," said Juan. "The events may be as small as a conversation or as large as a war, but they're coming, and it's not a matter of *if*, but *when* and *what do we do* when we reach these moments.

"You will find Adam, and when you find him you must seize the opportunity to put him away, no matter how dark your action must be. When that option comes, can I trust you to do the right thing? Can you take the whip off your own back and point it outwards? Do you believe in what we're doing so much that you would put Adam in the ground?"

"Burial, sir?"

"Yes, Balthasar; could you bury Adam alive if it would serve to eliminate him?"

Balthasar thought for a moment and then nodded.

"My goal is to find the Fountain and bring her back here," said Balthasar. "But I'll also do whatever else needs to be done."

"Then we are halfway to our destiny," said Juan with a smile, "and it's just a matter of time before the entire world is ours."

JON MAAS

PART II

THE WILD ZONE

PRECOCIOUS CHILDREN

Phoe rode the train north with Phage and Geryon, holding on for dear life at every turn. She was getting used to calling herself Phoe (*rhymes with "tree"*) and not Kalar, and had an even harder time pretending that she was a migrant. The others on top of the train looked at her pale skin with surprise, and though she had dyed her hair black, she still couldn't pass as a Bolivian emigrant. *Soy una periodista,* she learned to say with a smile. *"I'm a reporter."*

The *Train of Death* funneled countless migrants north through Mexico each year, and now Phoe was one of them. So were Phage and Geryon, and they blended in surprisingly well. Phage, though he had the high cheekbones and the narrow, aquiline nose of a European, was so disheveled that he could have been any race. He simply looked like he was about to die, and the other migrants avoided him because they didn't want to catch what he had.

They avoided Geryon because they were afraid of him. Some of the children called him *El Chupacabra* or *El Cucuy* under their breath, but the adults avoided him because they thought that this large man with a mask was a spy for the gangs who lurked at every stop.

For these reasons, Phoe had begged Phage to take them north on a more traditional route, but he insisted that they take this *Train of Death*. It was part of his penance to travel with the dispossessed, he had said, but Phoe thought that his reparations would have been better paid elsewhere. Still, she followed Phage on this dangerous journey; even death on these trains would have been better than returning home to Master Chergon in Bolivia.

"*Rama!*" yelled one of the women up front, and soon the rest of the stowaways echoed the same thing: "*branch!*"

Several tree limbs brushed over the top of the train, dislodging many of the migrants from their spots. Phoe ducked, but it hit a woman behind her squarely in the stomach, pushing her over. The tree branch eventually hit Geryon, breaking off against his big body, but the woman was gone. She had fallen off the train, perhaps landing on the ground with a few broken bones, perhaps sucked into the wheels and killed.

Phoe recovered and wept a few bitter tears at the notion that this lady's life, and at the very least her journey, had ended. Phoe had bonded with this woman, a mother of two, and knew that one way or another, her children would never see her again.

Phoe heard yelling and turned around to find that part of the train's metal roof was now glowing with heat and was burning some of the passengers. She forced herself to stop crying, and soon the others stopped yelling, and all was quiet again.

Five minutes later, the train slowed and then came to a halt. She at first thought it was because the woman had fallen off, but soon realized that it was because the train had arrived at a loading station, and nothing more. As soon as the train stopped, the migrants fled off; there were gangs lying in wait to rob them, or worse. Phoe saw several children head towards brown pools on the ground, kneel down and then lap up the dirty water like dogs.

"You can drink it too," said Phage. "Your class of spanner is highly mortal, but doesn't get hurt by sickness, bacteria, that kind of thing."

Phoe nodded, and then knelt down by the muddy water. It tasted of dirt, metal and gasoline, but it eventually slaked her thirst.

/***/

"I was born eight thousand years ago," said Phage. "Maybe earlier; that's all any of us can remember. I don't remember a childhood, and neither does Adam. As far as our memories go, we were always grown-up like this."

Geryon clicked twice and then put two more logs on the campfire, throwing them in from far away. He retreated to the darkness, clicked several times more and then disappeared.

"He's scared of the fire," said Phage, "but he isn't scared of anything else."

"What is he?" asked Phoe. "What's Geryon's spanner class?"

"No one knows for sure, but they call him a *golem*-class spanner," said Phage. "I don't know the full extent of his powers, which started to grow after he was burned at the stake. But he's got powers, don't you worry about that, and we're lucky he's on our side. There are gangs out here robbing and raping the poor and what have you, but Geryon will sense them coming from far away, and they'll regret they ever approached us."

Phoe nodded. She knew the gangs were dangerous, but felt safe with Geryon on the periphery.

"Was I with you?" she asked. "Eight thousand years ago?"

"Yeah," said Phage. "We were all together, always. Five kids total, four straight-up immortal with different nuances and powers, and you, immortal in the reincarnative sense."

Phage explained to Phoe about her class, how they're destined to fall in love, get their hearts broken and then be reborn in flames.

"You ain't fallin' in love or dyin' this lifetime, or at least not yet," said Phage. "But whenever you get upset, shit catches on fire, so watch yourself. That's why Geryon's scared of you, because of fire."

"You said he was burnt?" said Phoe.

"At the stake, for sorcery," said Phage, nodding. "He was a monk during the Inquisition, and he refused a few orders, so a fellow monk stabbed him in the heart. Geryon didn't die, so they thought he was a sorcerer from Hell, or something like that. They burned him for three days straight, and then buried him in a potter's field. Adam found him and dug him up, but Geryon wasn't right after that and ran away.

"Geryon recovered, but not fully. He ain't like Adam, regenerating and what not. He's strong, mind you, probably as strong as ten men, but he ain't pretty under that mask, and he can't see. His eyes didn't survive those flames.

"So he wandered aimlessly, probably a century or so, and then I found him, took him under my wing. We were two outcasts, angry at a world that didn't want them, but couldn't kill them either. He eventually got to working on a mask, one that amplifies sound waves. That clicking? It's what we call *echolocation*, helps him get around, and he's really good at getting around in the dark."

Phoe nodded and smiled to herself. Her old family on Chergon's island seemed normal by comparison.

"Who else?" she asked. "Who else is in our family?"

"There's me, the sicko," said Phage. "There's Samantha; she's an *allergic*-class spanner, an immortal like us, but everything can kill her: hazelnuts, soy, lettuce and a million other things. And then there's Adam; he's a tree-class immortal and real know-it-all prick too."

"You don't get along with him?" asked Phoe.

"I didn't," said Phage with a slight smile, "for a few millennia at least. I did bad things, and he did everything he could to stop me. Now I realize he was right, and he should have done more; he should have killed me when he had the chance."

"Can immortals be killed?"

"If so, Adam could find a way," said Phage with another smile. "He should have killed me eight thousand years ago and spared the world some trouble."

"I don't remember Adam, but from what you've told me, he doesn't sound like a guy who would kill his own brother," said Phoe.

Phage laughed dryly for a moment, and then became somber. He rubbed his eyes, coughed a wet cough, lit a cigarette and then looked at her, trembling slightly.

"Maybe that's the problem," said Phage. "Because I've killed a lot of people."

"How many?"

"Billions."

Phage motioned for Phoe to be quiet, looked into the darkness again and listened. There was a commotion coming from beyond the campfire, and after a few moments Phoe realized that it was the sounds of a fight, with punches thrown and landed. There were a few clicks and then a horrified shrieking; it sounded like a man was being torn in half.

"Billions with an *s*," said Phage, throwing his cigarette on the ground and standing up, "but just give me a moment. Geryon must have caught a robber, and I gotta stop him before it becomes billions plus one."

/***/

Five minutes later, Phage came back to the campfire with a dark smile on his face. The train ride had blown some of the dust off his clothes, and Phoe saw that he was wearing a leather jacket over tight jeans, and didn't walk with the limping gait of a sick man, but rather with the indifferent swagger of someone with nothing to lose. She also noticed that Phage had specks of blood on his shirt, and the stains seemed fresh.

"The aforementioned trespasser will live," said Phage, "but he won't be trespassing again any time soon."

Phage sat down, took the cigarette off the ground and swiped it across the campfire to light it. He took a few drags and continued his story. He started by explaining to Phoe about how his class of spanner was immortal but had no immune system, so viruses and bacteria flourished within them but didn't kill them.

"And we become a repository for every disease that's ever existed, and not just the ones today. I still have infections from past millennia, and if I let 'em out, there'll be trouble."

"But *billions*?" asked Phoe.

"Yep. There are other phage-class spanners around, but none have had the effect that I've had. Eight thousand years is a long time, and I started about twenty plagues before I even knew what was happening. I remember being a sick guy, walking into an area, and then everyone else would get sick. I'd stay alive and they'd die, time and time again. I don't know for sure, but I guess those twenty plagues killed a few million when all was said and done.

"Millions was just the start. After I put two and two together, I taught myself how to control the diseases within me, and things got real ugly, real fast."

Phage looked down into the fire and clenched his jaw; it seemed to Phoe as if Phage had practiced this speech countless times in his head before and finally had someone with whom to share it.

"I've known you for a lot of your lifetimes," said Phage. "Most of the time I wasn't that nice to you, and if it weren't for Adam protecting you, you'd have been in real trouble."

"What did you do to me?" asked Phoe.

"Nothing weird, nothing like that, if that's what you're getting at," said Phage with a grim look on his face.

Phoe didn't understand what he thought she was *getting at*, but could tell that he was genuine.

"I was bad to your boyfriends, mostly," said Phage. "They broke your heart, and I made sure they died for it."

"Sounds like you were trying to protect me," said Phoe.

"Nah," said Phage. "I told myself I was protecting you at first, but later on I had to admit I just liked killing them. There was a Babylonian fishmonger who was a prick to you and an Amorite who was a real sweetheart. Gave the first a variant of measles, the second a precursor to the Spanish Flu. They both got sick, and they both brought their sicknesses back to their home villages. Both times you still ended up heartbroken, and both times you ended up in flames."

Phage took another drag of his cigarette.

"You hate me for it?" asked Phage.

"I can't," said Phoe. "I don't remember any of it."

"Just as well," said Phage. "But I wasn't looking out for you, not like Adam did. You might not remember him, but he was always real nice to you, so be nice when you see him."

"I will," said Phoe.

Phage smiled a bit. He reminded Phoe of a recovered alcoholic who had come to Chergon's island. That man was deeply shamed by his past misdeeds, but maintained a perverse pride at their extent. Like him, Phage had done bad things, but they were *big* things.

"I spent the rest of my life in exile, up until a few years ago," said Phage. "Disease after disease until the number reached into the billions."

"Billions is a lot," said Phoe.

"It wasn't just diseases, at least not directly," said Phage. "Give the plague to a group of farmers and the nation falls into famine. Give a few prostitutes in an army camp a new form of syphilis, and it'll spread to the general who'll go crazy and start three wars. Believe me, you can reach billions real quick if you infect the right people."

"So why the change of heart?" asked Phoe. "Why are you doing Adam a favor?"

Phage smiled a bit, took one last drag off his cigarette and threw it to the ground, crushing it under his boot.

"Change of heart happened fifty years ago, and it's too long a tale to tell now," said Phage. "But needless to say, I wanted to stop killing people, and asked Adam for help. He and the mayfly found a substance that turns a spanner mortal. I took it; I'm gonna die at seventy, and that'll be that."

Phage looked at Phoe, and his eyes glowed red for a moment.

"I still have powers, but I'm not gonna do any more harm; I've sworn this," said Phage. "Until I die, I'm gonna do what I can to make amends for my past sins."

"What are you going to do?" asked Phoe. "What will make it right?"

"Delivering you to Adam's gonna make it right with him," said Phage. "As for the rest, I'm a killer, and that's all I know how to do. So I'm gonna spend the rest of my days smiting as many sinners as I can. No innocents, only sinners. Your island was just a start, and furthermore, I—"

Phage motioned for Phoe to be quiet and looked into the darkness. Once again there was the sound of a fight, only this time there were just the noises of punches thrown and landed; there was no shriek afterward. There was the sound of Geryon clicking, and Phage listened and seemed to understand.

"We've got to go," said Phage, yanking Phoe up.

"What's out there?"

"A spanner, out to get you," said Phage. "Geryon'll hold him off, but not for long. This guy'll be here soon and he's *fast*."

Phage threw dirt on the fire and there was no more light. Clouds had covered the moon so it was completely dark, and there was no sound except for Geryon's continued clicks. Phoe could hear the fight clearly, and it sounded like Geryon was losing.

/***/

They ran through the night towards a neighboring village, and Phage broke into a truck and hotwired it. Phoe got in the cab and saw the owner of the car run out with a rifle, cursing in Spanish. The owner kept cursing and pointing the weapon at Phage, but then suddenly stopped, dropped his gun, mouthed the word *Diablo* and made the sign of the cross across his chest. Phoe looked back and saw that Geryon had stepped into the back of the truck and was peering straight at the man.

"Translate for me," Phage said to Phoe, digging into his pocket. "Tell the man I'm gonna take his truck and give him three times its price, because I ain't a thief."

Phoe translated and Phage threw a thick wad of bills at the man, who took the money cautiously.

"Now tell him we're not gonna hurt him, but there's a kid following us who will," said Phage. "This boy is very dangerous."

Phoe translated and the man nodded, and then asked her a question.

"He wants to know who this boy is," said Phoe.

"I don't know," said Phage. "But I'd advise him to hide. If this kid comes anywhere near him, he's as good as dead. The boy ain't *el Diablo*, but he's close."

/***/

They sped overland through the desert, bouncing up and down over the gravel road. Phage had turned off the lights and Geryon seemed to be guiding him. Geryon was standing in the truck bed behind them and would occasionally crouch down into the cab and let off a few clicks into Phage's ear.

"We're headed to a safe house of sorts," said Phage to Phoe. "It wasn't on my itinerary, but plans change. If we get there, we'll be fine."

Geryon leaned into the cab and clicked a few more times.

"The guy who's after you is probably a blur-class spanner, and he's real fast," said Phage. "He's without a vehicle but he's keeping pace with us, somewhere to our left."

Phoe looked out past Phage through the window, but all she could see was darkness. They drove for a few more seconds and then *boom!* The truck shook with an incredible impact. After the truck stabilized again, Geryon poked his head into the cab again and clicked angrily.

"No!" said Phage to Geryon. "We need more time!"

Geryon clicked again and stood back up in the bed of the truck.

"The blur just hit our car because he missed," said Phage. "He's trying to steal you out of the cab. Geryon wants to fight, but we can't take him on, not out here."

Boom! The truck shook with another impact, only this time a blurry black hand crashed through the glass and grabbed at Phoe. She tried to pull the fingers off, but they were impossible to get a hold of; the hand vibrated so much that it didn't seem as if it was really there. The blur's arm was pulling her out of the window and she couldn't beat it away.

"Geryon!" yelled Phage. "Hold on to her!"

Geryon's hand reached through the cab and got a hold of Phoe's upper body, wrapping his hands around her like a seat belt. A few moments later, Phage slammed on the brakes and Phoe went flying forward. She would have smashed her head into the windshield were it not for Geryon gripping her body like a straitjacket.

The hand lost its grip and flew into the darkness. Phoe saw a dark figure go forward; Phage turned on the headlights, and then the brights. She saw a vibrating man directly ahead of them in the beams, getting up and dusting himself off.

"We're almost at the safe house, Geryon," whispered Phage. "No fighting; just stun him and we'll be okay."

The figure charged at them and accelerated much like a motorcycle would. It jumped at the glass and Phoe heard a deafening *boom* and saw a ripple of folded air hit the man square in the chest. The man went flying backwards off and to the left, and Phage hit the gas pedal.

"Geryon's sound waves can rip a hole through a wall, but he probably only got a piece of the blur," said Phage. "The safe house is a few minutes away, and your kidnapper won't be able to get in, but whoever he is, he'll be waiting for us when we get out."

/***/

The safe house wasn't inviting from the outside. It had four long, fenced walls, ten feet high and two hundred feet long, and they were electrified with rolled barbed wire on top and gunned turrets on each corner. Phage parked at the front and then got out with Geryon. A wiry old man with a shock of smooth white hair, perhaps sixty, stood behind one of the turret guns that had fire coming from its tip. When the old man pointed the gun at the truck, Geryon clicked and squealed and knelt down behind the cab.

"We come in peace," said Phage. "No need to light us up, Kerké."

"The world's greatest mass murderer and his Frankenstein brother march into our safe house, and I'm supposed to just *let them in*?" said Kerké.

Phoe listened to Kerké's voice and realized that Kerké was a woman.

"I don't blame you for being suspicious," said Phage. "But as you know, I've seen the error of my ways, and you of all people should understand the power of *rebirth*."

"Adam sent a message that you were for real, and I trust him," said Kerké. "But you still carry diseases, willing or not, and the inhabitants of this house don't have the best immune systems."

"I promise I'll do my best to keep any coughs to myself," said Phage. "And you can do what you need to do to keep me away from the *prodigies*. Hell, kill me if you feel it's necessary; I'm mortal now. But we've got a blur-class spanner out there hoping to capture our cargo, and we need to keep her safe until we can take her to Adam."

"And who would that cargo be?"

Phage motioned Phoe to get out, and when Phoe did, Kerké dropped her flamethrower immediately. Kerké smiled at Phoe and then looked at Phage.

"Never thought I'd see her with my own eyes," said Kerké.

Kerké came down from her perch and opened the door to the compound and motioned for them to drive in. She told Phage to stop and came up close to Phoe and looked at her admiringly. Kerké smiled at Phoe for a few moments, and then frowned again when she looked at Phage.

"I know the importance of what you're doing, Phage, and I know the power of this girl you've brought with you," said Kerké. "But both you and Geryon should be aware that I only have one job now: I'm sworn to protect the prodigies inside this compound. If either you or Geryon do *anything* to threaten what I'm sworn to protect, I'll torch you both in your sleep."

Phage smiled, but Geryon let out a whimper, and Phoe could tell that he was terrified.

/***/

Kerké led them to a small dormitory and they all slept well; it was the first time in days that they rested with shelter around them.

They woke up in the morning to the sound of high-pitched singing from one of the adjoining buildings.

Phoe exited her dormitory with Phage; Geryon stayed in the room because he didn't like the sun. The interior of the compound was like a small suburban community: clean, modern and a world apart from the outside. The roads were paved and lined with soft grass and little picket fences. It was like a neighborhood filled with small cottages, and each house had small doors and was colored with bright shades of red, green and pink. There were drawings on the walls— children's drawings of puppies, flowers and clouds. Phoe inspected them closer and was shocked at the skill put into each illustration; each painting was done in a different style: sometimes impressionistic, sometimes surreal and sometimes as detailed as a painting from the Renaissance. One picture of a blue pony had been made with a series of more than a million dots.

A small child burst out of one of the doors and came to hug Kerké before hiding behind her legs and staring up at Phage. Phoe couldn't quite see the boy as he peeked from behind Kerké, but the kid seemed to be smiling.

"Stay away from them, Isaac," said Kerké. "They're sick."

"She's right, bro," said Phage. "I'm feeling a little under the weather."

"With what?" said the kid.

"Common cold," said Phage.

"Which cold?" asked the kid.

Phage smiled and looked at the kid, and then looked at Kerké for approval to answer. Kerké nodded yes.

"Rhinovirus C, strain L3, came about twenty years ago," said Phage.

"Marie developed a vaccine to that," said the child, coming out from behind the Kerké's legs. "We're going to release it to the humans next year, but we'll give it to you now, if that's okay; it'll make you feel better."

Phoe noticed the kid looked odd. Though he had the body of a five year old, his face was that of an older man, perhaps forty; he even had a mustache.

/***/

Kerké took the vaccine from Marie, another child with a five-year-old face and an adult's body. This girl's face was beautiful; it was the face of a twenty-four year old, but it still looked odd on her undeveloped frame. Kerké blocked the child from coming near Phage, and then administered the vaccine to Phage's arm herself.

"Prodigy-class spanners stay young, but live until eighty years old or so," explained Phage to Phoe. "So they have a child's ability to learn and to absorb for their whole lives. They're weak in body, but their minds are just as sharp as a mayfly's. Mid-three-hundred IQs, but they live a whole life so they can get traction when they develop stuff."

"And they're known to regular humans?" asked Phoe.

"Yeah, only a small number though," said Kerké. "A few governments give them this place in exchange for developing innovations, books, philosophies, medicines, and just about everything else. A bunch of geniuses and dumb old me, who's paid to protect 'em."

Phoe thought for a moment and then looked at Kerké's leathery skin.

"What class are you?" asked Phoe.

Before Kerké could answer, another child came in.

"Our leader would like to speak with you all," said the child.

"All right," said Kerké. "But not Phage, he's sick and—"

"Our leader is particularly interested in speaking with Phage and of learning about his conversion," said the child. "We'll be speaking with you all: I understand that the golem fears the sun and remains in his room, but we'd like to speak with Phage and both phoenīcēs. Your presence is required at once."

"Then I guess we go," said Kerké, winking at Phoe.

As she winked, Kerké's eyes flashed orange.

/***/

They held the meeting like preschoolers were wont to do: sitting cross-legged in a circle. Phage was sitting far from the group like Kerké demanded, but the focus was on him. The leader of the prodigies was a child with a seventy-year-old man's face. He called himself *Mendel*.

"Please, Phage, tell me of your conversion," said Mendel.

"With all due respect, sir," said Phage. "I don't know if we have time. We've got to deliver Phoe to Adam, and there's a man out there plotting to steal her from us."

"Adam *always* has time, even now," said Mendel. "And our own Nikola's fence will deter the blur. Juan's lackey is a pest, but Kerké will deal with him upon your exit. Now, tell us of your conversion."

Phage got another nod of approval from Kerké and spoke.

"I'm not much for philosophy," said Phage. "But as you know, I've done bad things. A lot of bad things; and now I'm hoping to make amends in what time I have left on this earth."

"Do you feel bad for what you've done?" asked Mendel.

"Not really," said Phage. "But I know what's wrong and I know what's right."

"Killing people is wrong?" asked Mendel.

"Sure," said Phage.

"Why?" asked Mendel.

"I don't know," said Phage. "Just is."

"How many people have you killed?"

"Billions," said Phage. "Billions with an *s,* and furthermore—"

"If you hadn't killed those people," asked Mendel. "How many would be alive today?"

Phage thought for a moment, became nervous and reached for a cigarette in his pocket. He pulled out the pack and started banging the edge to push in the tobacco, but Kerké mouthed the words *no* and he put the cigarettes away.

"Most of them would be dead," said Phage. "Ninety percent, maybe."

"And how many would be alive a hundred years from now?" asked Mendel.

"None."

"Then why are you upset over your past misdeeds? You were like a lion on the savannah, killing prey out of instinct and only playing the role that nature provided."

Phage looked down, thought for a minute and then looked the child right in the eye.

"I didn't kill out of instinct, I killed out of *choice*, and that made it wrong," said Phage. "Death comes for us all; it'll even call on you pipsqueaks one day. Death just *is*, but I made a choice to bring it to a lot of innocent folks before their time, people that could have done something with that time."

Phage became lost in thought for a moment and then addressed the group.

"I guess that's it," said Phage. "They had time remaining in their lives, and I robbed them of it. I was a *thief*."

Mendel smiled and then looked at another boy, who smiled in return. The boy was a bit chubby, but his face showed that he was roughly the same age as Mendel.

"All crime can be considered theft, with murder being theft of a life, assault being theft of personal safety, and so on," said Mendel. "My friend Bentham has quite a bit to say in that regard.

"We've been debating you for some time, and yes, you're a thief of life as you say; but it's not that simple," said Bentham, "because you fail to recognize *intent.* Intent is inexorably bound to culpability and *wrongness*, as it were. Who is worse: the man who willingly kills a ninety year old, or a girl who slips and falls on a hidden button that launches a missile that destroys a nation? The murdering man is worse, of course, for though the girl caused more net suffering, societies must consider *intent*. Over time, forgiveness of crimes without intent leads to a healthier, more compassionate and *successful* society."

"There you go then," said Phage. "I'm an asshole."

"Not necessarily," said Mendel. "We performed an analysis where we considered humanity to be *one being*, and then saw how that being would fare with and without your plagues. Would you like to know what we found?"

"I'd like to know that very much," said Phage. "Tell me what the world would be like if I'd never been born."

"If you consider the health of humanity as the health of one being," said Mendel, "you would be the equivalent of a lingering virus. You killed billions of cells, as it were, but didn't kill the body and allowed humanity to recover completely, and effectively *stronger*. So if we ignore intent, we realize—"

"You can't ignore intent," said Phage. "You just said that."

"Intent is irrelevant in this second analysis," said Bentham, "for *intent* means nothing in terms of history. Pompeii would surely have preferred a hundred mass-murderers full of *intent* than a single volcano; but I digress. We found that your plagues have actually helped humanity in the long run. *The Black Death*, that was yours, right?"

"Yeah," said Phage. "I was traveling through China and a chick dumped me, so I infected a few fleas in her village and things got outta control."

"The Black Death was devastating for the *individual*," said Bentham, "but it wasn't a bad thing for humanity. It served to catapult Europe out of stagnation and—"

Kerké tapped Phoe on the shoulder and nodded towards the outside.

"They talk forever," whispered Kerké with a smile. "Come with me; I've got something to show you."

/***/

Kerké took Phoe out to a small stretch of dirt behind the rooms. It was still under the safe house's electrified roofing, but it was outside, and the sun beat down relentlessly. Phoe squinted hard, and Kerké opened a shed and grabbed a hat and some old newspapers from inside. She placed the newspapers on three stumps on the far end of the field and brought the hat back to Phoe.

"You still have beauty left to protect," said Kerké, handing Phoe the hat. "I lost my own beauty a long time ago."

Kerké stared at the sky and squinted.

"The sun took my skin and made it heavy and thick," she said. "Our kind is destined to burn, one way or another."

"*Our kind*," said Phoe. "You're like me."

"Yeah," said Kerké. "I'm a phoenix-class spanner, just like you."

Phoe didn't know what to say, but Kerké smiled.

"Phage should have told you about me, but I suppose he's got other things on his mind," said Kerké. "So does everyone nowadays, with the talk of destiny, Fountains, battles and whatnot. But Phage gave you your class name, and that's about it, right?"

"Yeah," said Phoe.

"Well, there's a lot more to our kind than the standard narrative," said Kerké. "We're all beautiful, or at least we once were, we fall in love, get heartsick and then get reborn in fire. You've heard that basic stuff, right?"

"Yes," said Phoe.

"Well, there's more," said Kerké. "In the rare cases when our kind don't die, odd things happen."

"It's our destiny to die young," said Phoe.

"Not mine," said Kerké, "though ninety-nine times out of a hundred that happens. But sometimes we live lives without love, and that protects us. Like in my case, a group rescued me as a child and told me the truth. They raised me with no access to anyone I could fall for, and soon my time had passed and they put me here, protecting these overgrown toddlers."

Kerké looked at Phoe again, and the old woman's eyes flashed orange.

"Your plight was a little less deliberate," said Kerké. "You grew up in a place where love wasn't an option, so your powers manifested themselves in a different way."

Kerké squinted at the sun once more and then smiled.

"You had a tough childhood, Phoe, I know this," said Kerké. "But there's an upside to it all. You didn't get to fall for some boy, but you didn't burst into fire when he took another girl to the roller rink either. You might end up like me, a bitter old woman with bad breath and a flamethrower, but there's a big upside to living a life without love."

"What is it?"

"I'll show you," said Kerké with a smile.

/***/

Kerké took three newspapers, rolled them up and put them on three posts in the distance. She walked back to Phoe and concentrated a moment before pointing her right hand at the rightmost post and exhaling quickly. The rightmost newspaper caught fire, and with another snap, Kerké put the flame out.

"Our emotions are strong," said Kerké, "and when we decide to stop feeling sorry for ourselves, we can push our feelings outwards. Phoenīcēs aren't born to fight, but when we do, we can do bad things. Do you want to learn?"

"Yes," said Phoe.

Kerké smiled and then brought another newspaper from the shed and replaced the paper she had burnt. She walked backwards to Phoe and pointed at the left post.

"Now, think back to a time when you felt a strong emotion," said Kerké, "but don't dwell too much on it. Whatever that feeling is, try to focus it on the paper I'm pointing at. Take your pain and put it there, and nowhere else."

Phoe nodded and then searched her mind for a particularly painful moment and didn't have to think back too far. She thought of a time when Bocephalus ordered her friend Porella out of her bed in the middle of the night two years ago. At the time, Phoe didn't know what he might have done to her, but she now had an idea, and it wasn't good. Phoe felt emotions rise within her and she began to frown. She became angry at herself for not stopping Bocephalus, she became resentful of Master Chergon for lying to them, and she became furious at fate for allowing the island to exist in the first place.

Phoe wanted to cry but held it in and instead chose to focus all her anger on the paper *on top of the left-hand post*. She closed her eyes and visualized her emotions *going inside the paper and tearing it to pieces*. She could tell it was working; the air now smelled of burning leaves, but Phoe didn't stop. She just kept focusing her rage into the small piece of newspaper until she heard a cracking sound and felt Kerké's hand on her shoulder.

"That's good!" said Kerké with a laugh.

Phoe opened her eyes and saw that all three posts were on fire, and the heat from the flames had reached them, causing Phoe to draw back and Kerké to sweat.

"You've got a lot of emotion, girl, and a *lot* of power," said Kerké. "You just have to learn how to manage it and focus so it hits your target and not everything else. I can give you a crash course over the next few days."

"Thank you," said Phoe.

"We've got a plane up here, and Phage, as much as I loathe him, is a damn good pilot," said Kerké. "The prodigies equipped it with some gadget to find Adam's group; it responds to the Fountain's energy, or some such thing. You'll fly north, and you'll get to where you need to go; the kids here know what's at stake, and you'll be where you need to be."

"Perfect," said Phoe.

"No, it's not perfect, not just yet," said Kerké. "What happens when you get there? There's a guy outside the compound walls who will track you down wherever you go, and he'll kidnap you unless you learn to protect yourself. Can you fight?"

"I'm good at running," said Phoe.

"The guy outside is a blur-class spanner, and he's a lot better at running than you," said Kerké. "Our final lesson will be dealing with him, head-on."

"You want me to fight him?"

"In a few days, after you've improved your skills," said Kerké. "I'll be there behind you, and we'll both let him know that you're a phoenix, but you aren't a victim any longer. He can run around all day, but we'll take your emotions and tear him right in half."

Kerké smiled and put an open hand towards the scorched posts. The fire died down for a moment, and then she pointed at them again and they all burst into an explosion of flames, cleaving the smoldering post in the center perfectly in two.

※ JON MAAS

A CITY OF SIBLINGS

Mayfly woke to hear the sound of Brogg snoring loudly. Two of the Treys were sleeping, one deeply and one restlessly. The restless Trey got up and nudged Brogg until the caveman turned over onto his stomach, and though it didn't help much, that Trey went back to bed. The sleeping Trey didn't wake up at all, and the third one was currently driving the RV. *I sleep an hour per night and they say it's efficient,* thought Mayfly, *but Trey is more efficient than I. He never rests and rests always.* Mayfly splashed some water on his face from the RV's sink and saw that Adam was also sleeping, but his hands were twitching. *And perhaps Adam rests the worst of us all,* thought Mayfly. *Though he sleeps soundly, his evenings are always filled with the same nightmare.*

Mayfly got up in the front of the RV and sat next to the driving Trey. It was still dark outside, but the clear sky cast pale moonlight over the snowy branches and Mayfly could see far into the night. Though the roads were well paved, they were in the middle of nowhere, and Mayfly wondered what would happen if they ran out of gasoline.

"The Wild Zone is a dark place," said Trey, eyeing Cattaga asleep in the back. "Cattaga's from Alaska, so she's used to the cold, but this place is more than just *cold*. This is a place most spanners choose to ignore, much like regular humans don't think about prisons."

"What exactly is it?" asked Mayfly.

"I don't quite know, other than legend," said Trey. "But yeah, all the really bad spanners are sent here. That part's true."

"The humans paved the roads?" asked Mayfly.

"Yeah, a few help manage this place," said Trey. "A very, very select few. A couple of them get together with guys like Adam every once in awhile to make sure spanners stay hidden and this place stays open."

"They send the crazy spanners here," said Mayfly.

"Not crazy like Juan," said Trey, "but *crazy and uncontrollable*, you know? Like if Brogg went nuts, what could you do? No prison can hold him, so they'd drug him and drop him off here, and he'd never get out."

"I've heard some spanners live here voluntarily," said Mayfly.

"Yep," said Trey, "and we're headed towards some of them to beg for fuel. There are spanners who don't want to live in normal society so they come up here, and this place takes them. No matter what you've done, as long as you can survive up here, you're okay."

They drove in silence for a while and Mayfly looked at the trees. It was quite desolate, but seemed pristine and beautiful; it didn't feel like the forest was filled with monsters.

"Tell me about the bad ones," said Mayfly, "the dangerous spanners that live here."

Trey smiled, thought for a moment and then nodded.

"Some of them are just like you and me but crazy and violent with random powers, and some are even animals," said Trey.

"Animals?"

"Well, legends say so," said Trey. "Spider-wolves."

"Spider-wolves," said Mayfly, his heart skipping a beat.

"Wolves with the lifespan of a spider, and rumor has it Juan's tamed a few," said Trey. "Breed fast, travel quick, and they can rip you open like a wolf, or poison you like a spider."

Mayfly tried to hide the chill that crawled up his back, but Trey picked up on it.

"It's not the spider-wolves that are really bad," said Trey. "They'll just kill you like all the other creatures out here, quickly and without too much pain. What really frightens me are the *berserkers*."

"Berserkers," said Mayfly, glad to be done talking about spiders. "I've heard of them, but I don't know much about them."

"No one does," said Trey, "and no one really knows what they are; some say they live two hundred years, some say longer. We do know they're like Brogg; they seem to devolve as they age, and get stronger too. But they're not entirely like Brogg; as they get stronger, they seem to lose their empathy and intelligence until they're just as much an animal as your average spider-wolf. So if, in normal society, there's a psychotically violent guy getting bigger and bigger, they find he's a berserker and drop him off here."

Trey pointed to the woods around him.

"They're out there, you know," said Trey. "They become feral and will eat anything they find, including you."

"Cannibalism," said Mayfly. "That's scary."

"Yeah," said Trey. "They'll hunt you in packs."

"Scary," said Mayfly with a smile.

"It's worse than you think," said Trey. "If they find you or me, they'll drag us away and gnaw on us for a few days. They've been known to keep their prey alive, and they love guys like Adam."

Mayfly looked back at Adam, who was asleep and twitching; still in the middle of a nightmare.

"Immortals," said Mayfly.

"Yep," said Trey. "The berserkers see his kind as an endless pantry. If they find Adam they'll take him, break his legs, put him in a tree and feast on him for a couple years at least."

Trey stared straight ahead at the road with a grim look on his face, and then moved the steering wheel as they entered a series of turns in the road.

"They say Adam's class of spanner fears only burial, but there are a lot worse things out there for him to be scared of, and many of them live in these woods. So when we make a pit stop for fuel, rest or whatever, don't wander too far off. This place is beautiful but there's always something out there waiting to get you, and if it does there'll be nothing we'll be able to do about it, because we're on our own."

Mayfly looked out the window and then rolled it down a bit, letting the cold bite against his face. Mayfly thought for a moment and then smiled.

"It's not all bad up here," said Mayfly.

"Why's that?" asked Trey.

"It's getting really cold, so cold that the Fountain doesn't need to live in the freezer anymore," said Mayfly. "We just need to open the window."

/***/

They drove for two more days straight, with Trey taking endless shifts; he wouldn't even stop to switch bodies and just did a quick maneuver where one of him would hold the wheel and the other would get out while holding down the gas until the other's foot was on it. But though they drove constantly and the roads were paved, it was slow going. The roads were winding and held endless switchbacks that often returned farther than where they started.

By the end of the second day, they realized that they needed more gasoline. Adam knew of an encampment with fuel to spare along the way and they stopped at it, got out of the RV and approached cautiously.

"I can't believe anyone lives out here," said Cattaga.

"They're not just anyone," said Adam. "These are *clone*-class spanners. They're not exactly dangerous, but they're ... eccentric."

"Eccentric?" asked Mayfly.

"Yeah," said Adam. "They're kind of stuck-up. We'll have to hide the Fountain from them; their attitude towards her might be unpredictable."

"*Stuck-up*," said Mayfly. "So stuck-up that they live up here?"

"They think they're better than everyone else," said Adam, "and the world doesn't understand that, so they live here."

"Do they have fuel?" asked Trey.

"They have everything," said Adam.

"Then let's go," said Trey.

"Yeah," said Mayfly. "They sound like fun."

/***/

Mayfly was shocked at how neat the village looked. It was surrounded by a heavy wall, but its front was wide open and it didn't seem like a rough place. There were two guards at the gate; one man and one woman, both unnaturally beautiful. As Mayfly walked through the village, he noticed everyone was part of a couple and that each couple looked just as beautiful as the guards they had first seen. The people in the village didn't all belong to one race or even reflect the current norms of beauty, but each couple seemed *perfect*, as if they belonged in a painting. Some were shorter, some were taller, some were dark skinned and some were light skinned, but all of them had flawless complexions, perfectly symmetrical faces and perfect teeth.

And though each couple is unique, the man and woman resemble one another, thought Mayfly, *and the children resemble their parents.*

Mayfly found them friendly and wondered how they could be considered *stuck-up*, but soon realized that they were shooting dark glances at Brogg, shaking their heads in disgust as they walked by.

"*Clone*-class spanners live their lifespans with perfect DNA," whispered Adam, "or at least they *consider* it perfect. They have no flaws; not a single mutation and not a single recessive gene that would bring disease or anything else."

"What's their spanner power?" whispered Mayfly.

"They don't consider themselves *spanners*," said Adam. "They consider themselves *perfect humans* and nothing more."

"Then why do they live up here?" asked Mayfly.

"They don't want to dilute their genetic perfection, so they inbreed," said Adam. "That doesn't fly in too many places."

"Inbreeding?" asked Mayfly. "Even in a perfect world that would cause bad things to happen."

"This is more than a perfect world," said Adam. "The couples are identical twins, but one is a girl and one is a boy. They have no flaws in their DNA, so when they reproduce it always comes out as two clones of themselves, one more boy and one more girl."

It makes sense in theory, thought Mayfly. *But there's something wrong with what they do, and I'll find it soon.*

The group walked towards a small building in the center of the village. A small, beautiful girl, about fourteen, walked outside the building with her brother.

"Our elders request to speak with you," they said in unison. "Leave the brute outside; he's an abomination."

Brogg grunted angrily and approached the two children, but Mayfly put up his hand to stop him and then bent down to whisper in the kids' ears.

"I wouldn't use the word 'abomination,'" said Mayfly to the young couple. "Not until your wedding night, at least."

/***/

The two children's parents were at the front of the hall, surrounded by ten other sets of twins, some young and some old.

"Adam, it is *interesting* that you stopped by," said the woman. "We've heard of you from our older selves."

"Indeed," said Adam. "I met your older self two generations back. I assume your couple name is still Fion and Fiona?"

"Time hasn't sharpened your intuition, Dr. Parr," said the woman. "We've done away with names. Our society runs perfectly and the lack of conflict obviates the need for possession, which in turn eliminates the need for names. We did away with this primitive form of self-identification years ago."

"I understand," said Adam.

"Now, what do you seek?" said a short, dark-skinned man from the far left of the hall. "Outside of the manipulator-class female you've brought, you can't hope to join us, so you've obviously come with some petty request in your own self-interest. Tell us what it is."

Mayfly looked at Cattaga; she clearly wasn't flattered by the clones' approval of her spanner class.

"We need fuel," said Adam, "pure and simple."

"Fuel?" scoffed a woman from the far right. "That begs the question: *What do you seek?*"

"I don't follow you," said Adam.

"It figures that a *tree* wouldn't be able to grasp this basic reasoning," said the woman, speaking deliberately slowly. "We ask what you *seek*. Why are you here in the Wild Zone, and where would you need ... *to go* ... with *our fuel*?"

Adam paused for a moment to think.

"Did you understand the question, Dr. Parr?" asked another man, in a mocking tone.

Mayfly tapped Adam on the shoulder and gave him a wink; Mayfly knew that Adam had a hard time lying under pressure and would need help. Adam gave Mayfly a relieved nod of approval, and Mayfly stepped forward to speak to the group.

"One of our own went missing in these woods," said Mayfly. "We're hoping to find her."

"One of your own is clearly dead, then," said a man in the center, "as you shall soon be, mayfly. Please leave before you perish right in front of us, as your kind are wont to do."

"Our missing friend is a scourge-class spanner," said Mayfly. "They fare quite well in these woods, and can even fell a berserker with a touch. And though your village is remote, the scourge might wander here, and I understand that their touch drains life from their victims ... and inadvertently *corrupts their victim's DNA.*"

The council looked at each other and some gasped. The woman at the front stood up, put her hands out and everyone calmed down.

"Threats are not heard here, especially from a terminally ill boy," said the woman. "You speak with the foresight of a man who will still draw breath one month hence. And furthermore—"

"This isn't a threat," said Mayfly. "All we want is to take our scourge home, and if you give us the fuel, you'll never see us or the scourge again."

The woman looked at Adam.

"Is this true, Dr. Parr?" she asked. "I understand you don't lie."

"We are hoping to bring a deadly spanner home," said Adam. "And if you give us fuel, the spanner won't harm your city."

"All right," said the woman. "What else can you give us?"

Adam had nothing to say, but once again Mayfly jumped in.

"I understand you aspire to be the purest form of humanity?" asked Mayfly.

"We *are* the purest," said the woman. "Humanity has reached its peak with us and has *no more need* to evolve. Furthermore—"

"You're anything *but* pure," said Mayfly. "I studied biology for a day and learned that ninety percent of your cells are nonhuman; they're other species of bacteria that live on you and in you. It's called the *human microbiome,* and it makes you quite dirty."

"State your point, boy," said the woman. "What will you give us?"

"One hour of my time," said Mayfly. "I have a photographic memory and know as much about human microbiome as anyone else on earth. I know that there are five tribes of bacteria on your inner elbow competing for space, you carry a kilogram of bacteria in your gut, and that every one of us is born completely free of these pathogens. I'll tell you everything I've learned, including how to get rid of all the foreign bodies inside your body; you have me for one hour, and then we get our fuel."

The council looked at each other and then at the woman.

"This is interesting indeed," she said.

"Yeah, it is," said Mayfly, smiling, "and make up your mind soon. I'm a 'terminally ill boy' and don't have much time."

/***/

Mayfly came out of the session smiling even more. They'd listened to every word he said but had only asked what they wanted to hear. *How do we clean ourselves of these vermin? How do we sterilize our insides and outsides? How do we become more pure, more human?* Mayfly felt obligated to warn them that they *shouldn't* sterilize themselves; it was impossible to clean themselves because the microbiome was just too ingrained to be extricated. *We have time to clean ourselves, unlike you, mayfly,* they had told him. Mayfly knew that stripping a body of its microbiome would lead to a slow death, but chose to let them learn that on their own.

Mayfly returned to the RV alone and saw a single clone helping Brogg load the fuel canisters. The clone was a female and looked different from the rest of them; she was sad, a bit weathered, and had no partner. She had a heavy jacket and a lot of camping equipment too.

"Get in," said Adam. "We're taking her with us."

/***/

Adam waited until the RV was out of the camp's range before making introductions.

"This is Davelia," said Adam. "She has a name and can be trusted; she's escaping this place."

"I'm not escaping," said Davelia. "They won't follow, or even notice that I'm gone."

Davelia looked at the crew in the RV and then hunched over, defeated.

"My husband-brother died two years ago, before we could have children," she said. "I'm useless to them, so I'm hoping to make it back and re-enter normal society."

"How are you going to get back?" asked Trey. "It's dangerous out here."

"It is," said Davelia. "But I've gotten good at hiding, and I have no other options. The roads north lead in a hundred different directions, but all the roads south lead out of the Wild Zone. It's not hard to escape this place if you can hide, as long as you keep moving south."

"You're welcome to come with us," said Mayfly.

"No," said Davelia. "You're going north, and I'd just get in the way of your mission."

Mayfly looked at Adam and he nodded back in understanding; this single clone knew a lot more than they had told the rest of the clones.

"What do you know about us?" asked Adam.

"I know little," said Davelia. "But I know you're not out hunting for a scourge. Rest assured, the other clones bought that white lie you told wholesale, but I know there's more to the story. Juan Ponce de León's been sending his spider-wolves north; we found them in the woods around our village, and he only sends spider-wolves when he's looking for something important."

Adam nodded.

"We have a different mission," he admitted.

"Tell me what it is, or part of it, and I'd be glad to help in any way I can," said Davelia. "Or tell me nothing and let me on my way; either one is fine with me."

Adam nodded at Cattaga; her eyes flashed for a moment, and she came up close to Davelia. Cattaga smelled the clone and nodded her approval at Adam.

Cattaga can smell the hormones released while lying, thought Mayfly, *and this clone isn't lying.*

Mayfly looked at Davelia and sensed that she was genuine and also sensed that she was lonely. She was an outcast from a village of outcasts, and even if she wanted to reveal their secrets, she wouldn't have anyone to reveal them to. Mayfly gave his own nod of approval and Adam pointed to the back where the Fountain was sleeping under her cold blankets.

"We have the Fountain," said Adam.

Davelia looked back behind the curtain and smiled.

"Interesting," said Davelia. "What would you like to know?"

"We're taking her north to Santos de León, also known as the Surgeon," said Adam. "Are we doing the right thing?"

"Yes," said Davelia.

"Go on," said Adam.

"We know of the Surgeon here," said Davelia. "Spanners come to him voluntarily because he takes away their weaknesses, albeit in painful ways. It's akin to visiting a doctor in the hopes of becoming taller and having him put screws in your leg bones for a year."

"They say the Surgeon will separate the Fountain's power into life and death and unleash them both," said Mayfly. "How will he do this?"

Davelia thought for a moment and then nodded.

"We've heard the legends about this in our city, of the Fountain, and of the battle for the Fountain," said Davelia. "We've always considered them legends and nothing else, but I knew they contained truth. They say that the Fountain is both life and death at once, much as a mule is both a horse and donkey at once. You can't split the mule back into the two creatures, and you can't split the Fountain back into life and death."

Davelia smiled a bit and looked down.

"This is only a legend of course, but there are also legends around the Surgeon, and the legend says that if you brought him a mule he'd find a way to split it back into a horse and a donkey. He lives in a dark place and many have met their end there, but he'll find a way to split her in two, something that no one else on earth can do."

Davelia looked behind the curtain, nodded and looked at Adam.

"The clones rejected me, but I'm glad they did," said Davelia. "They have their little kingdom here, but they won't expand, and one day they'll die out with no one to remember them. But all the legends surrounding this girl speak of her importance in history. Her power might make this world anew or might end it; I don't know, and all the myths I've heard are unclear as to her end. But if the choice is between bringing her to Santos de León or his brother Juan Ponce, I'd choose the former. The Surgeon will split her in two but has no desire to use her powers for his own gain. He has no intent, and Juan's intent is to put the world under his thumb. The results may end up the same, but from where we stand right now, you have no choice but to continue north."

Adam nodded, and then Davelia's gazed at the road ahead; Trey was driving towards a snowbound intersection.

"That's my stop," said Davelia. "Remember, if you ever get lost, just follow the roads south. It's dangerous, but they always lead out."

Trey parked the RV, and Davelia got out with her heavy winter gear and her backpack. She nodded goodbye to all of them and then walked down the road while the RV turned away from her. Mayfly envied Davelia; she was free from the destiny that had somehow trapped him, and if she were to survive the journey south, she'd be able to spend the rest of her days however she wished.

A few moments later, Davelia disappeared into the morning snow, and they resumed their journey north.

/***/

They hit a roadblock hours later, just after the sun had set; it was a large tree fallen over in the middle of the road. There was a deep ditch on either side of the path and Trey started to drive to the side to peek over, but Adam stopped him.

"Don't," said Adam. "The ditch is too deep and this tree's way too big to be from around here; it might be a trap."

"A trap," said Trey. "Who would set a—"

Adam put his hands up to his lips and Trey got quiet. Adam motioned for Mayfly to come out with him, and together they went out to inspect the obstruction.

They crept up to the tree quietly and could see it quite well with both the RV lights and the moon shining through the clear night.

"It's been ripped from the ground somehow," said Adam. "What else do you see?"

Mayfly jumped on the trunk and scurried over it. A few moments later, he came back to Adam and pointed to the curve of the path beneath and the dense forest around them.

"This tree is in the perfect place to block us," said Mayfly. "We won't be able to get around. And look at the missing bark on the trunk; it was like a bear pulled it up from the ground. Someone placed it here deliberately, someone *big*."

They heard a voice coming from the woods that was humming deeply. There was a pause and then it started again, and another voice joined it from another part of the woods. There was another moment of silence and then a third voice joined in; soon the forest came alive with humming from all around them.

"A bear didn't pull up this tree," said Adam. "It was a *berserker*, or rather a *group* of berserkers."

/***/

Back in the RV, Adam spoke to Trey and looked out the window.

"We need to go another way," said Adam.

"There is no other way," said Trey. "They only have one road."

"Then we leave and come back," said Adam. "Turn around."

"The road's too narrow and I can't turn," said Trey. "I can only put it in reverse."

Cattaga pointed ahead at the fallen tree in the middle of the road. There were two massive, muscular and pale-looking creatures on the tree looking back at them. They looked like they once were humans, but their faces had somehow been overgrown and distorted with time. They were twice the size of gorillas and were barking and growling at each other, and then one of them looked at the RV and started lumbering towards it. The one who stayed behind opened his mouth and hissed, showing two rows of sharp teeth.

Trey slipped the RV in reverse and backed away. He looked through the rear view mirror and the road seemed to be clear, but out of the blue the RV braked to a halt and everyone went flying backwards, including the Fountain. Trey floored the gas again, but it was to no avail; they were stuck. Another Trey had put his head out the window and looked outside.

"Two more of these things are behind us, holding us up," said the driving Trey.

The berserker that had first approached them was now right in front of the vehicle, staring forward with glowing white eyes. He jumped on top of the hood of the RV, blasted his fist through the metal beneath and came up with a fistful of wires from the engine, some of them pouring liquid over his hand. He then turned around on the hood and started to hum and was soon joined by his friend at the roadblock and the two berserkers who were holding up the RV from behind.

"We can't drive anymore," said Trey. "There's just no way."

"Can we use the Fountain?" asked Cattaga. "Perhaps her touch is still dangerous."

"She's not dangerous in this weather," said Adam. "It's too cold. But there's a way out of this, there's always a way—"

Adam was interrupted by the sound of the side door opening and the wind rushing in. Brogg had exited the RV and was angrily storming towards the berserker right in front of them.

/***/

Brogg's attack was crude, but somewhat effective. He didn't quite land his punches on the berserkers because they were surprisingly nimble, but even his glancing blows pushed them backwards.

They're as big as Brogg and more agile, thought Mayfly. *And there's four of them at least.* Mayfly also noticed that though the berserkers seemed to lack language skills, they fought in a coordinated way. The two that had stopped the RV from behind had now come up to join the fight and immediately surrounded Brogg in a circle.

One of them took a swipe at Brogg and he dodged it, and then another took a clumsy swing and Brogg ducked beneath it. Brogg grabbed a berserker and shoved him into the other three, but the group retained its structure and still hovered around Brogg.

"We need to do something," said Trey. "Maybe one of us can act as a distraction."

"No," said Adam. "Whoever does will be dead within moments; they're too fast."

"Make a fire," said Mayfly. "Fight them with that."

"That might work," said Adam. "They're animals, and animals hate fire."

/***/

Mayfly took one of the fuel canisters and snuck towards the felled tree. The berserkers were focused on Brogg and didn't notice when Mayfly crawled on the log and poured gasoline on it. After he had doused the wood with fuel, Mayfly looked to the left and saw that

Brogg was losing his fight. The caveman had bruises on his face and his left eye was almost completely swollen shut. One of the berserkers apparently had sharp nails too; Brogg had a huge gash across his stomach.

"Brogg!" yelled Mayfly. "Heads up!"

Mayfly dropped a match onto the log and it lit up. The berserkers jumped back, and Brogg used the time to create some space between himself and them. Brogg threw a berserker towards the fire and the creature fell on the flames, yelling a low-pitched cry of agony. The other berserkers continued to beat Brogg, indifferent to the fact that the tree was on fire and their friend was now burning with it.

They continued their assault, but Brogg could handle three berserkers a lot better than four, and he started to land his heavy punches. Mayfly took a flaming piece of wood and smashed it over one of their backs, but the creature barely noticed and continued to focus on defending himself against Brogg. Mayfly backed up and felt heat coming from behind him and turned around to duck just before a smoldering fist went over his head. He rolled towards the flaming logs and turned around to see that the berserker that had been thrown into the fire was attacking them, still partially aflame.

The other berserkers got out of the way and the smoldering creature assaulted Brogg quicker than before, catching the caveman off guard. The flaming berserker's punches would miss Brogg, but some embers would fall into the big man's hair and burn him. Sometimes Brogg would block a punch completely, but the blocked punch would still burn his arms.

This flaming berserker's going to tear Brogg in half, thought Mayfly. *I've got to distract them somehow. I can't fight them, and I can't outrun them. If only I could—*

Mayfly heard one of the other berserkers emit a loud, low-pitched growl, and the flaming one stopped fighting Brogg and turned to look to the left of the road. The enflamed berserker put his fists in the snow to cool them off and they shot off steam into the night air.

Mayfly turned and saw four other berserkers running up the hill towards the road, only they looked a bit healthier and a bit cleaner, as if they were tamed. The four berserkers also had ropes attached to holsters on their upper bodies, and they were all hauling a regular man on a sled behind them. The man was in his mid-fifties and was wearing a sleeveless vest, a leather cowboy hat, jeans and little else. *He's either immune to the cold,* thought Mayfly, *or he doesn't plan on staying here very long.*

"*Mwwwrooo-kai!*" said the man in a low voice.

His berserkers came to a halt and there was a standoff between his troop and the wild ones around Mayfly and Brogg. Mayfly nodded at Brogg and they both ducked out of the way towards the RV; none of the berserkers in the standoff even noticed.

"*Mwro-kai*-lo!" said the man, and he detached the line around his berserkers.

The tame berserkers rushed towards the wild ones and started to fight. Though the feral berserkers showed no fear, they were no match for their counterparts. The man's tame berserkers were disciplined, healthier and just fought better than the wild berserkers. Two of the tame berserkers would attack one wild one in a flurry, subdue him and then move on to the next one.

Within moments the tame berserkers had won and were tying up the wild berserkers and putting them in large rope sacks. The old man lit a cigarette and inspected his bounty, and by now, Adam, Cattaga and a Trey had come out to meet him.

"The name's Rajter," said the man in a slow, shaky voice with little eye contact. "Freeman Rajter. I'm a human, nothing more; my house is down yonder three hundred meters or so; you can roll your vehicle there. You can trust me ... and if you don't, that's fine. But if you do, you're welcome to spend the night, and I can promise you a fire, safety and whatever else you need."

Freeman Rajter attached leather straps to his berserkers and they each picked up one of the wild creatures in nets, got in formation and then faced down the hill.

"*Mwro-kai-mai!*" yelled the man.

His berserkers went down the hill and dragged his sled along with them, but this time they trudged down slowly.

Within a few moments they were gone, and Mayfly looked through the forest and saw lights in the distance from what appeared to be the man's homestead. Mayfly turned around and saw Adam shaking his head in disbelief.

"I've seen a lot in my lifetime," said Adam. "But I've never seen anything like that."

Brogg was tending to a burn wound on his upper left shoulder where the berserker had hit him.

"Next time Mayfly not use fire," said Brogg. "Mayfly not good with fire."

/***/

Brogg pushed the RV into Rajter's homestead, with the Fountain safely hidden in the back of the vehicle under her pile of blankets. She had been frightened by the fight with the berserkers, and Adam decided it was best to let her hide.

Inside Freeman Rajter's compound, Cattaga coughed up an aloe-like substance and rubbed it on Brogg's burns. Brogg sighed in relief as it covered his arm, and then nodded at her to put the substance on his other injuries.

"I secrete an antiseptic, so it's sterile," said Cattaga to Brogg. "Even if it wasn't we could still put it on you, because our diseases don't hurt you anymore. You've evolved into a different species entirely, as different from us as those berserkers."

Brogg put his head down and looked like he was about to cry. Cattaga realized she had hurt his feelings and went to console him.

"I'm sorry, Brogg," said Cattaga. "What I meant to say is that ... is that—"

"What she meant to say is that we're all different now," said Mayfly. "Each and every one of us is different, and all we have is each other."

Brogg nodded in understanding, and Mayfly patted him on the back before smiling at Cattaga.

"She might not have my way with words, Brogg," said Mayfly, "but if you ever get burned again, she's the one that's gonna cough up the aloe."

And if it wasn't for you, Brogg, thought Mayfly, *the berserkers would have gotten to us before Rajter did, and we'd all be stashed in a tree somewhere.*

Mayfly looked around at Rajter's homestead, which was primarily made of thick, uprooted logs from the forest implanted in the ground to form a surrounding barrier against the elements. Inside the barrier were prefabricated structures: houses and storage units made with plastic bought from an ordinary hardware store. One unit clearly served as a cookhouse; the smell of burnt meat was wafting towards them, and it smelled good.

"Hungry," said Brogg.

"Yeah," said Mayfly. "Hungry."

/***/

"You're lucky the *wild ones* only broke your fuel line," said Freeman Rajter, serving the group food. "You're even luckier they didn't kill you, or worse. I've not seen anyone survive an encounter with four wild ones, let alone escape with only a broken van. In any case, I've fixed your RV and you can go now, or in the morning if you prefer."

They ate stew indoors, and the source of the meat was visible through the window of their shed, strung out and frozen on wooden logs. Rajter had captured moose and bear and had stored them outside, meat, fur, entrails and all. Rajter would walk out of the shed, bring back a chunk of frozen meat and drop it in the stew. Mayfly guessed that he was currently eating a bear's liver.

"Food preserves here in the winter real good—just leave it outside and it keeps," said Freeman Rajter. "Finding food is easy, but you gotta eat the whole animal because there ain't any vegetables this far north. Eat the organs and you'll be fine; avoid the organs and you'll die of scurvy before spring."

Mayfly ate the bear's liver and then found a piece of meat in his stew, or perhaps another organ, that was greasy, rough and filled with sinews that tasted of rubber. Everyone ate except for Cattaga, who had gathered lichen from the forest.

"My body can digest plant material completely," she said. "And I'm a vegetarian."

Brogg wasn't. He couldn't get enough of Freeman Rajter's food and the old man seemed to like him a lot.

"Tell your brute he's welcome to stay with me any time," said Freeman Rajter. "All I ask is that I be allowed to tame him and brand him, like I've done the others."

Brogg put down his meat and growled in disagreement.

"I think that's a no," said Mayfly, but Rajter paid him no mind.

"I suppose you all wonder why a coot like me chooses to live out here."

The group nodded except for Brogg, who had forgotten about Rajter and instead focused on his meal again.

"You want to fill them in, Adam?"

"I know of you mostly through second-hand stories," said Adam. "So please, fill us all in."

Rajter took a ball of meat from the stew and put it in his mouth, taking his time to chew it. After he stopped chewing, he took a small flask tied to his belt and downed a shot of liquid inside, and then spat.

"I'm just a regular human, but I got cued in to what you spanners are and what you can do," said Freeman Rajter. "Only a select few humans are allowed to know about your kind, so the government tried to kill me."

"They tried to kill you?" asked Mayfly skeptically.

Freeman Rajter laughed in return.

"I know, I seem like some crazy old recluse," said Rajter, "and I *am* a recluse, but I ain't crazy. Tough little underground society you guys got going there, and a lot of people willing to kill to protect your secrets, ain't that right, Adam?"

"Yeah," said Adam, nodding. "You find out too much, bad things happen."

"I learned a lot about your kind," said Rajter. "So they sent a pretty little manipulator-class spanner much like your Cattaga to seduce me, but I smelt the poison on her lips and wouldn't have taken the bait anyway. I'm more into big, burly types with some facial hair, if you catch my drift."

Mayfly noticed that Brogg didn't *catch his drift* and was glad that the caveman didn't.

"Whatever the case, I did some study on the spanner mythos, and learned of this place," said Rajter. "I came for the freedom, stayed for the bear meat."

Mayfly took another bite and Freeman Rajter excused himself for a moment. Mayfly followed Rajter and saw that two of his trained berserkers were holding a wild one down so that the old man could put a red-hot brand to the creature's shoulder. Brogg grumbled, but Adam was entranced. When Freeman Rajter came back into their shelter, Adam smiled at him.

"You learned to train the berserkers," said Adam. "Impressive. I didn't think it possible."

"Everything's possible, Adam," said Rajter. "You of all people should know that. Every spanner has power, every spanner has a weakness, and every spanner can be controlled if you press the right buttons. You can even control your old nemesis, Juan Ponce de León."

"He can be controlled?" asked Adam.

"Of course," said Rajter. "You're controlling him right now. You brought the albino up and he's following you like a dog."

Adam didn't reveal anything, but Rajter broke the silence.

"Relax, Adam," said Rajter. "Everyone knows about you and this Fountain, this albino, or whatever she is, even me. I don't even own a phone, but the legends are pretty clear."

"Everyone talks about these legends," said Adam. "But no one has any answers."

"What have the legends told you?" asked Mayfly.

"They say that you're gonna bring the Fountain north to a cold place, a place *so cold that life grows*, whatever that means," said Rajter. "And there will be many battles, with a big one at the end."

"Many battles?" asked Adam.

"Yep, and that's the only way you beat a guy like Juan, because he's a persistent son-of-a-bitch, case in point the fact that you already buried him and he's here again," said Rajter. "You're gonna have to fight him, fight him, and fight him again until the final war. That's what happens when you got an immortal enemy."

"How do we know when it's *the* final battle?" asked Mayfly.

"You'll know," said Rajter. "But in the meantime, you've—"

Rajter stopped talking and pricked his ears up to hear a collective hum coming from his tame berserkers. The old man excused himself and went towards one of the far corners of the homestead. Adam quietly motioned for Mayfly to go with them, and Mayfly snuck behind Rajter as the old man approached a lookout post. The berserker on the post gestured outward and the old man peered into the woods beyond.

Mayfly took a small pair of night-vision binoculars from his pocket and looked in the direction of the forest. He saw a creature lurking in the distance; the creature had the shape of a wolf but crawled back and forth in an odd way, like an insect.

It looks like a large spider, thought Mayfly, *and I hate spiders.*

/***/

"I sent one of my berserkers to hunt the creature," said Freeman Rajter.

"Do you think it's Juan's crew?" asked Adam.

"Perhaps," said Freeman Rajter.

"Tell me where to look," said Cattaga, her eye already taking the shape of a cat's eye. "The moon's bright enough for me to see."

/***/

Cattaga couldn't find the spider-wolf in the forest, but looked back towards the road where their RV had once been and saw movement.

"I see a group of men," said Cattaga, "and no wolves."

"Men or spanners?" asked Freemen Rajter. "Juan might have sent just a few wolves to scout, but that means there's someone else lying in wait for us. Who do you think they are?"

"I can't tell," said Cattaga. "One of them's quite large, and that's about all I can see."

Mayfly looked at the group with his night-vision binoculars and saw that the big one was Juan's tweener-class spanner, Cannon, and he was as large as a shed. There was another big creature dead beneath him, and Mayfly zoomed in to see it was the berserker that had been sent out to scout. Mayfly saw Cannon throw a rock at their homestead, and saw that it was headed right towards Cattaga.

"Watch out!" said Mayfly.

Mayfly pushed Cattaga aside and the projectile just missed them, crashing into the wall behind him. Freeman Rajter looked up, speechless, and then went to the wall to pick up what was thrown.

It was the tamed berserker's head, and it was dried up.

"They've got a scourge on their side?" Rajter asked Adam.

"I believe so," said Adam.

"Scourges are pretty effective against my berserkers," said Rajter. "She's gonna pick 'em off one by one."

/***/

They found the remaining berserkers collapsed on the ground at the far end of the homestead. They weren't decapitated, but they had been drained of all life.

"Looks like we're on our own, kids," said Rajter. "The bad guys have stripped us of our guard dogs."

Mayfly looked at the far edges of the forest with his night-vision binoculars and saw that the scourge wasn't alone; she had Cannon and several humans with trucks by her side. Mayfly passed the binoculars to Adam and he looked in the wrong end before Mayfly corrected him. After Adam saw the group at the edge of the forest, he passed the binoculars to Freeman Rajter.

"The guys out there are gonna bust in, but they aren't looking to fight," said Freeman Rajter. "All they want is the Fountain. Where is she?"

"Hidden in the RV," said Adam.

"Adam, go to her and make sure that she stays in the RV and that she keeps quiet," said Rajter. "There's gonna be a lot of commotion, and she's gotta stay hidden. We'll fight whoever's out there and lead them away from the RV. While they're distracted, you'll drive the RV off and be far away before they know where you went, and we'll meet up with you later. Does this plan make sense?"

The group nodded.

"All right," said Freeman Rajter. "Now, you kids ever been in a battle before?"

"We've been in a riot," said Mayfly.

"Riots ain't the same thing, because you can hide 'til a riot blows over," said Freeman Rajter. "This is a battle, and two spanners or twenty, you won't be able to hide, so it's best to fight."

"We can do that," said Mayfly, eyeing Brogg.

"Good," said Freeman Rajter. "Now engage the enemy out there until the time is right; you'll have to gauge when that is. As for fighting, you all might be green, but I can help you get your feet wet."

Freeman Rajter walked over to another hut and opened it. It was filled with antique arms: swords, spears, slings and more; the old man had everything except for guns. Freeman Rajter went into the building and came out with two crossbows.

"These are mine," he said. "Take your pick of the rest, and get ready for a battle; it won't be your last."

/***/

Mayfly helped put the Fountain back in the RV, with Cattaga handling her and Mayfly speaking soothing Arawak words. The Fountain was frightened and Mayfly wanted to say more to calm her, but he had to rush out when he heard a vehicle crash through the far wall of the compound. Mayfly snuck over there and saw that it was a human guard who had driven his truck through the homestead's southern wall.

Here it is, thought Mayfly. *Our first battle is officially underway.*

One Trey jumped on top of the vehicle to distract the driver, and before the man had a chance to draw his weapon, the other Trey startled him by appearing on the right side of his car while the third Trey came on the left and dragged the man out. Brogg gave the guard a punch and was about to give him another strike, but Adam stopped him.

"Don't kill the humans unless it's absolutely necessary," said Adam. "We'll eventually need the moral high ground on our side."

There was one more crash and another part of the wall collapsed. It was Cannon, and he had pushed a patch of the homestead's outer barrier down with his bare hands, and then he looked up to stare at Mayfly with glowing eyes. Cannon was sweating profusely and smelled like sour ham, and though his body was covered with acne, his face was clear. Mayfly looked closer and saw that Cannon was wearing foundation to smooth his complexion. The pustules on his face had erupted and were beginning to bleed through the makeup.

"Humans are off limits for you, perhaps," said Freeman Rajter with a smile. "Spanners are never off limits for me."

Freeman Rajter took out his crossbow and started firing at Cannon. All of the shots hit, most lodging in his upper body, and one landed in his leg, making Cannon grimace as he ran towards the old man, undeterred by the injuries. Mayfly marveled at how fast Cannon was; even covered in arrows the kid shot forward like lightning, and when Cannon got to Rajter, he punched the old man in the stomach with a horrific *crack*. The old man lay incapacitated on the ground and Cannon picked him up as if he were a doll and threw him over a wooden fence. Cannon walked towards the wall Rajter was behind and prepared to punch through it, but before he did, Brogg's big forearm wrapped around Cannon's neck from behind and pulled him backwards. Mayfly ran in to help Brogg, but Adam held him back.

"They're out of your league," said Adam. "If you get in between them, you'll be crushed."

Adam started to speak in his own mother tongue; an extinct dialect of Chaldean. Adam only spoke to Mayfly in Chaldean when they didn't want to risk anyone else understanding them.

"If I don't make it out of here, you need to make sure the Fountain gets away safely. If they get me, just take her and go, ," said Adam.

"Go where?" asked Mayfly.

"I left a map in the RV's glove compartment detailing how to reach the Surgeon," said Adam. "I wrote the instructions in Chaldean; only you will be able to understand them."

"But—"

"This is too important," said Adam, his eyes glowing. "In fact, you should probably just go now. They're distracted, and this is the time to leave."

Mayfly ran just as Cannon had knocked Brogg out and was kicking the caveman's unconscious body.

/***/

Mayfly was pulled back into the fight before he reached the RV; the Treys were in a scrum with three of Juan's human guards. The Treys were quite graceful as they fought; they coordinated their attacks perfectly by ducking, punching, feinting and doubling-up on their opponents at just the right time. *The Treys are quite a team,* thought Mayfly, *but the humans have guns.* One of the guards pulled out a pistol and Trey was able to grapple with the guard to get out of the line of fire. Mayfly couldn't help it and jumped in the fight, disarmed the guard and used him as a human shield.

"You're on the wrong side, guys," said Mayfly, pointing his weapon at his new hostage's neck. "Drop your weapons."

Mayfly heard Cattaga yell and when the other guards' attention was drawn to the sound, Mayfly pushed his captive into them and gave three quick strikes, leaving them all unconscious.

"One-punch knockout," said Mayfly.

"Times three," said Trey, pointing away from the RV. "But you might need to give a few more."

Mayfly looked where Trey was pointing and saw that Cattaga was on the ground, about to be killed by the scourge.

/***/

Cattaga laid in the dirt and the scourge's eyes glowed as she held her outstretched fingers above Cattaga's neck and then glared at Mayfly and the Treys.

"My name's Drayne," said the girl. "If you want to see your girlfriend alive again, tell me where the Fountain is."

"Don't tell her—" wheezed Cattaga, dull blue veins glowing through her skin.

Drayne punched Cattaga with a gloved fist and looked at Mayfly and Trey again.

"Ten seconds to decide," said Drayne. "Tell me where the Fountain is, and the girl lives."

Cattaga's eyes glowed green and she first looked at Trey, and then Mayfly.

"We'll tell you," said Trey. "She's in—"

"No we won't," said Mayfly, holding his hand up. "Go ahead and kill her."

"Have it your way," said Drayne.

Drayne held Cattaga up like hostage, and then placed her hands on the girl's neck. Cattaga's life flowed into Drayne and then Cattaga started to seize. The seizure soon became so violent that Drayne could no longer hold her and Cattaga collapsed on the floor. Drayne backed up slowly before she started to frown and then she herself started to collapse. Soon Drayne was on the ground and Cattaga got up.

"Haven't had to fake a seizure before," said Cattaga.

Cattaga knelt down to look at Drayne, and then looked up at the Treys and Mayfly.

"She's still alive, but unconscious," said Cattaga. "Thank you, Mayfly."

All the Treys looked on cluelessly as Cattaga went past them to join Brogg in his fight.

"Cattaga's class is strong against scourge-class spanners," whispered Mayfly to Trey, "but Cattaga flooded her body with toxins nonetheless. When Drayne took Cattaga's lifespan, she also took the toxins, and that was the end of her."

"You know her well," said Trey.

"That I do," said Mayfly. "Now let's save Brogg and leave before we run out of tricks."

/***/

Cannon had an unconscious Brogg in a chokehold while Adam tried to negotiate his release.

"Just let him down, Cannon, and we can—" said Adam.

"No!" said Cannon. "If you come closer, I'll kill him!"

Mayfly heard the rumble of a helicopter in the distance; Juan's reinforcements were coming. Adam pointed at Mayfly to go, but he couldn't, not while Brogg was about to be strangled. Mayfly motioned to Adam that he wanted to speak, and Adam nodded at Mayfly to go ahead.

"Maybe we can just talk, bro," said Mayfly.

"Who are you?!" screamed Cannon.

"Someone who knows what it's like to be different," said Mayfly. "Someone who the world doesn't understand."

Cannon shook as he held Brogg's unconscious body in his hands; even though the boy was stronger and faster than anyone on earth, he was still terrified.

"You can do amazing things," said Mayfly. "We'd like to have you on our team. Be part of our club."

Cannon didn't let go of his grip on Brogg, but relaxed it just a little. His acne had completely bled through his makeup and now crusted over the side of his face. Mayfly smiled and then Cannon smiled just a bit too. Cannon was about to relax even more when Freeman Rajter came bursting through a hole in the homestead wall.

"Hey crater-face," said Freeman Rajter. "It's time to let the caveman go."

"What?!" screamed Cannon, his jaw quivering.

"You heard me," said Freeman Rajter. "You smell like a corpse and look like someone put your face in an ant pile. Now you want to fight me?"

"You shut up!" yelled Cannon.

Tears rolled down Cannon's face and soaked the dried blood that had come from his burst acne. He dropped Brogg with a thud and then ran at Freeman Rajter, who disappeared deep into the homestead, leaving the crew alone.

/***/

Adam went into the RV and opened the windows, letting the cool air dampen the Fountain's powers. The RV had become warm with her inside and the Fountain's unmuted power had weakened Adam, and when he got out of the vehicle he immediately collapsed to the ground. *She's radioactive,* thought Mayfly. *If that was me, I would have been killed.*

Mayfly rushed to Adam, but Adam wheezed at Mayfly to stay away; the RV would take a few more moments to cool off.

When the RV was cool, the Treys started it and the engine turned; it was loud but ran well. Freeman Rajter had only done a few hours' work on it, but it was enough and they would be able to get away.

Mayfly looked through the gate and saw that a blizzard had come in and a layer of snow was accumulating on the ground. One of the Treys went into the back of the RV and came out with tire chains. Two of him put the chains on the back tires, and the third backed up the RV. They did the same with the front tires, and in under a minute the RV was ready to drive through ice.

The Fountain was still hiding in the back, but she was no longer under the cold blankets. She was scared but sat compliantly as the group piled into the vehicle around her. Cattaga smiled at her; the Fountain smiled back nervously and then nodded to indicate that she was okay.

She trusts us, thought Mayfly. *She doesn't understand our language, and she doesn't know that the battle outside is over her, but she trusts us.*

As soon as they determined that the Fountain was secure and calm, they dragged Brogg into the vehicle. He was barely conscious and mostly dead weight, but they got him in. Adam went to unlock the gate, and in doing so had to step over the body of Freeman Rajter, who had been made unrecognizable by Cannon. They dragged the body of

Freeman Rajter into the RV as well, but Mayfly could tell at a glance that the old man was beyond help. Adam opened the gate and allowed the RV to roll through.

Several shots rang out, and Adam screamed in pain. He crumpled to the ground in agony, and the two human guards that had shot him were now rushing towards the RV, drawing their weapons. Adam rolled over on the ground and picked up one of Freeman Rajter's dropped crossbows and shot at the guards, hitting them both, but more guards were on the way. Mayfly went out to help Adam, but Adam yelled back with an anger he'd never shown before.

"Go!" Adam yelled. "I'll be fine. Go, or I'll kill you myself."

Mayfly knew this is what Adam wanted, so he ran into the RV and closed the door.

"Floor it," said Mayfly.

Trey accelerated as fast as he could, but the snowy ground slowed the vehicle. Shots rang out, but they didn't hit the RV or the RV's tires, and soon they had trudged into the mist and were out of the marksmen's range.

"Storms coming in," said Trey as he drove. "They won't get their helicopter up to follow us."

They drove in silence, and a few moments later Mayfly took his night-vision goggles and took one last look at the compound. He briefly saw Cannon ripping the crossbow out of Adam's hand and then punching him in his stomach.

"You did what needed to be done," said Cattaga to Mayfly.

"She's right. This is bigger than you and me both," said Trey. "This is even bigger than Adam."

THE INQUISITION

Adam woke up with a splitting headache and vomited soon thereafter. He had the wherewithal to aim away from himself, but the bile came slowly, and since he was tied to a chair, most of it ended up on his clothes. He looked around and noticed that he was in the room where his group had eaten the meat stew, but the room had been cleared out. There were no stray forks on the ground with which he could pry open the knots that bound his wrists, and there were no knives to cut the ropes or even to use as a weapon. He'd been captured like this before, and he knew when there was no escape. Adam had no recourse but to wait for his captors to come in and do whatever it was they wished to do with him.

Drayne soon came in and tried to hurt him, but she couldn't cause much damage. She started with blades and scalpels but couldn't get him to talk. Adam had been tortured with knives before, and they weren't effective against him; to Adam a knife through the stomach was like a needle from a doctor—unpleasant but tolerable. Drayne became frustrated and removed her gloves, and then Adam knew he had her. She put her hands on his neck and soon started to quiver, then fell to the ground unconscious. *Tree-class spanners are strong against scourges,* Adam thought. *We have more life than they can handle; it's like putting the power of a bomb into a small battery.*

Drayne had been debilitated from taking Adam's power, but she was still alive. Two gloved guards dragged her out of the shed, and Adam looked through the window and saw her twitching in the snow outside. Adam used the time to try to escape the chair, but it was no use; the ropes were too well tied.

Adam sat in the shed with vomit on his shirt and saw Cannon strutting outside, flexing his muscles. *This isn't going to be pretty,* thought Adam. *The boy won't get me to talk, but it'll be some time before he realizes it.*

They sent in Cannon after, and it wasn't good. The boy beat Adam senseless, and the kid's punches were like sledgehammers, relentless and without purpose. He broke Adam's nose and ribs, cracked his sternum and gave him so many bruises that they started to join one another, and soon Adam's body was a single discolored mess. Adam knew his injuries would heal, but in the meantime he had no choice but to take the blows, and soon he passed out again. When he woke up this time, he had a bigger headache and the vomit was still on his shirt.

How many times have I woken up like this? thought Adam.

Adam tried not to think of the times he'd been in similar situations, but the memories flooded his mind and he had to dwell on them. He had been chained and forgotten in a Spartan prison during a Helot revolt. A deranged commander had found him a year later, emaciated, and had beaten him for a week before he managed to escape.

Adam had been tortured for three days during the French Revolution, and pressed to death with large stones in Massachusetts after villagers had accused him of witchcraft. The Nazis thought he had knowledge of ammunition dumps during World War II, and he survived two weeks of their torment before their bunker was blown to pieces by Russian artillery, them along with it.

This is why I hide from the world, thought Adam. *Whenever I show myself, I end up in a place like this.*

"It's been some time, Adam," said a voice from the darkness.

The door to the shed was open, and Adam saw the thin figure of a man in the shadows; when the man walked forward Adam immediately recognized him as Balthasar, and he saw that he was carrying a metal case. Balthasar took a chair and table from the corner and placed it in front of Adam, and then sat down in the chair and opened the case to reveal a flask and two glasses. He poured two glasses and placed one near Adam, and it smelled like tequila.

"An immortal inevitably has a lasting relationship with all other immortals, don't you think, Adam?" asked Balthasar. "Friend, enemy or even stranger to one another, we're the only constants in each other's lives as the centuries pass."

Adam found truth in that statement but chose not to acknowledge it. *When tied to a chair you have but one weapon*, thought Adam, *and that's silence.*

"I know you're no stranger to sessions like these," said Balthasar, pushing the glass of tequila towards Adam. "So I'll assure you that I'm not trying to play psychological games; I like tequila, and would have brought cognac if I'd had the time. Drink if you so desire; I assure you it's not drugged."

Adam remained silent, and after a moment Balthasar sipped his own glass of tequila.

"I'll also be candid when I tell you your fate. Again, no mind games."

Balthasar took one more sip of the tequila and savored it. He was calm, but it sounded to Adam as if his speech had been rehearsed a hundred times over.

"You're in a bad place, Adam, and you know this," said Balthasar. "The only way out is to join our cause, and you'll do this by telling us where the Fountain is headed. I understand the chances of you assenting to this are slim, but allow me to rationally explain what we hope to achieve first. May I do this?"

Adam didn't respond.

"I'll explain, and you'll listen," said Balthasar, "and if I fail to persuade you that our goal is just, I'll have no recourse but to punish you, severely and permanently. I'll do this by bringing your class's persistent nightmare into being."

Adam's stomach became hollow and he started to sweat, but he averted his eyes and tried not to show his fear.

"But first, an argument on our behalf," said Balthasar. "I understand that you think Juan Ponce de León to be a mass murderer, and nothing more. I agree that if we have our way, a lot of people will die, but he's much more than a simple killer."

Balthasar took another sip from his tequila.

"Let's say we use the Fountain to kill ninety-nine percent of this earth; I'd say that's almost seven billion people. Tragic, hmm?"

Adam didn't respond.

"Perhaps," said Balthasar, "but perhaps *not*. Since you were born Adam, almost a hundred billion people have come and gone in this world ... a *hundred* billion born and now dead forever! Now, truthfully, answer me; does anyone mourn their deaths?"

Adam didn't answer.

"I'll not cover you with an avalanche of comparative statistics—a hundred and fifty-five thousand dying each day, five hundred dying since we started this conversation and so forth. But I'll tell you that death is part of life, and we only mourn those who are close to us, and once *we* are gone, there is no sadness to *their* deaths. The only thing that remains after death is what lasts, be it a poem, architecture, scientific progress or even a bizarre relic."

Balthasar gestured outside the shed's window at Drayne, who was still woozy but upright.

"She was in a brothel when I found her," said Balthasar. "Not the voluntary type, mind you, but the type where children are trafficked, bred, used and discarded against their will; that kind of thing. They're all around the world you know, in every country, operating around the clock while you hide in the shadows and do absolutely nothing to prevent it."

Balthasar took another drink of his tequila.

"Well *we're* doing something," said Balthasar. "We're not saving up to buy a girl from some predatory pimp, nor are we hoping to arrest a few traffickers in a daring midnight raid. We're *burning the brothel to the ground,* metaphorically speaking, of course. And if I could extend the metaphor, we'll burn every other brothel on earth to the ground and ensure that no others take their place."

Adam didn't respond.

"I understand you worked for Scotland Yard on and off for a century or two?" asked Balthasar. "All those arrests, using your experience to solve crimes ... and what of it? Did you ever once make a difference? You stemmed the bleeding perhaps, but you never fixed the wound. Solve a murder and another one comes; stop a robber and two more take his place elsewhere."

Balthasar got up and took another look at Drayne.

"We're creating a new world where brothels won't exist, and there will be no need for detectives. There will be no murder, no environmental destruction and no war caused by shortage of resources. Many will have to die to achieve this goal, but in a century they would have been dead anyway."

Balthasar walked around Adam twice and then knelt down and peered at him in the eye.

"We're creating a world with or without your help, Adam," said Balthasar. "It will be a small, *controlled* world with no room for sin, and no room for suffering. No one will mourn anyone who dies today, but humanity *will* know our society ten thousand years from now, because they'll still be living in the utopia we *will* create. All I ask from you is a little help telling me where your friends are headed. Tell us where the Fountain is, Adam, and help bring our new world into being."

Adam looked at Balthasar and then nodded his head towards the tequila. Balthasar brought the glass to his lips and Adam drank.

"You remind me of someone," said Adam. "A half century ago, I was tied to a chair in a freezing room just like this in the Gulag. They did brutal things there, which would have made a little sense if they'd been doing it to their enemies, but most of the prisoners were their own people, the ones for which they were trying to create a ... utopia.

"After one session much like this, I asked the guard *why* he was doing what he did. He responded just the same as you, that to create this utopia, bad things had to happen first. Stalin had to purge the elements that he had to purge, but the ends would justify the means; in a thousand years, the perfect world would make the pain we suffered now worth it."

With a nod, Adam asked for another draft of tequila, and Balthasar obliged.

"I've seen a lot over the years," said Adam. "Empires grown and crumbled and a thousand leaders come and gone with the same promise: *'Do whatever I ask, no matter how ignoble, and it will be worth it, for our way is the way that the world will remember.'*

Adam looked Balthasar in the eye.

"Your leader promises heaven if only you do horrible things," said Adam, "but heaven never comes from a frozen prison, and it never comes by force, with men tied to chairs and tortured. You know this to be true."

Balthasar didn't respond.

"Do what you need to do, because I'm not going to tell you where the Fountain is headed," said Adam. "But before you do away with me, think of what you've done, what you're doing now and what Juan will ask you to do next. Think of it and realize that utopia won't spring from your actions; you'll only be a cruel guard, torturing those beneath you because a man above you ordered it. That will be *your* utopia, Balthasar, and it's up to you to follow the path or not."

/***/

Balthasar had Cannon carry Adam outside, chair and all, and together they watched as the human guards sprayed hot water into the frozen ground twenty meters out, melting it just enough for Cannon to start digging.

"There's a wave of history coming, Adam," said Balthasar. "Right or wrong doesn't matter; the future will happen, and that will be that, just as when the asteroid cleared the dinosaurs out for us, the Romans cleared the Barbarians from their hovels, and we cleared the Indians away so that you and I could be here, at this point. It won't be 'right' or 'wrong'; it will be an event, and it will happen without judgment. Right now, you and your cadre are a minor roadblock to this event."

Adam took the words in, and shook his head in disbelief.

"You work for a monster, Balthasar," said Adam. "History always finds a way to rid itself of its monsters."

Balthasar looked at the hole Cannon had dug in the melted earth; it was shallow but still deep enough to keep Adam there forever.

"Perhaps we will be gotten rid of," said Balthasar, "but we will not be gotten rid of *now*, not before we achieve our goals. I'll give you one last chance Adam: Tell me, where you have taken the Fountain?"

"You're on the wrong side of history and the wrong side of morality, Balthasar," said Adam.

Balthasar smiled, nodded slowly and grabbed a shovel from the ground. He then nodded at Cannon, who picked up Adam's chair and leaned it over the hole for a few moments before returning him to Balthasar.

"Why, Adam?" asked Balthasar. "Just tell me *why* we're immoral."

"I can't argue from the basis of a higher power, and I can't argue from the basis of reason," said Adam, "because you've clearly abandoned both. All I'll say is that you're wrong because you *just are*, and you know it. I've been where you are right now before, and I've been where I am before, both a thousand times over. All I know is that morality exists within us, and for whatever reason, those who kill the innocent never bring a better society, and they *never* bring utopia. Look at where you are right now and realize that it won't end with me, Balthasar; it will only get worse."

Cannon approached Adam from behind and took hold of his chair, gripping it like he would a large trophy. Adam couldn't hold his fear any longer and started to hyperventilate. *Don't tell him anything,* he thought. *Mayfly will find you, somehow, Mayfly will find you.*

Cannon shoved Adam down into the muddy hole and Adam twisted himself around so that he fell on his back. The impact crushed his hands and he grimaced, but he didn't look up because he didn't want them to see his eyes glowing with fear. Adam felt a ball of warm mud fall on his legs and then a bit fell on his face; soon he was covered completely, and the mud started to harden in the cold night air. He couldn't see but heard the guards throwing more dirt on him, and then the soil was so heavy that he heard no more. The weight of the earth above got heavier and heavier, and then it stopped. Adam felt faint thuds from above and reasoned that it was the guards, smoothing out the ground. A minute passed and then he felt an enormous pressure, and then that too stopped.

That was their vehicle, thought Adam. *They ran over me and then left.*

Adam tried to move, but he was stuck. The pain of suffocation began, and within minutes he started to black out. He knew he'd wake up in an odd state; not quite dead, but conscious and still unable to move. He tried to kick his legs out, but it was no use; even if he could free himself from the chair, he was still buried by tons of dirt.

He would never get out of here by himself; there was simply no way.

Mayfly can save me, thought Adam before he blacked out. *He's the only hope I have, but he'll save me. He always finds a way.*

JON MAAS

THE REST HOME

They had taken a left fork in the road, another left, and then a right. At the next turn they took the center path of five roads, another left fork, and then a right turn that seemed to be taking them back where they came. The crew took on the quiet air of a group who were considering that they might be lost, but Mayfly was confident that they were going the correct way. Adam's instructions were dense but clear; their destination was impossible to find without a map, but with the map it was just a matter of time before they reached their goal.

Soon the road smoothed out into a long dirt road down a canyon, and it started to snow again. Adam's map indicated that there would be a colony just ahead and sure enough, there was another Wild Zone settlement on their left, precisely where Adam had said it would be. Mayfly couldn't figure out how anyone could live this far north, but the group was still happy to see the village because it confirmed the map's accuracy, and they relaxed a bit.

Mayfly relaxed too but didn't want them to stop. He told Trey that they couldn't risk running into trouble at this point; they had to reach their goal. Mayfly also argued that anyone living this far north in the Wild Zone was bound to be dangerous. *You have to be a predator to survive up here*, Mayfly had argued. *There is no other way.*

The truth was, Mayfly wanted desperately to return to Adam. He could tell what Juan's henchmen were going to do to him; he could see it in their eyes as the RV sped away.

Adam's buried right now, thought Mayfly. *As we drive, he's under the earth, screaming.*

Mayfly had never envied Adam's immortality; Mayfly considered it as sort of an odd burden, like getting a job that one would have to hold for forty years. Mayfly had often used his own mortality as a tool to bring him courage; whatever situation he faced, the worst that could happen would be his death. No one could torture or intimidate Mayfly, because fate had already dealt him a hand that he couldn't change.

But Mayfly felt fear for Adam; he knew Adam's nightmares, and so did everyone else. *I've got to get back there and save him,* thought Mayfly. *Somehow I've got to get back there and save him.*

Trey brought the RV to a halt, flipped on the parking brake and looked at the settlement in front of them, along with everyone else. Mayfly wanted to prod him to keep going, but it was no use; one Trey had already left the RV and was headed towards the colony's tall, imperious walls.

/***/

Mayfly found the walls high, but thin; he could probably smash through them with a rock.

"It's a village of *millennials*," said Mayfly.

They were definitely millennials; the settlement held all their trademarks: high logged walls and no windows for maximum privacy.

"Millennial-class spanners have almost no powers," explained Mayfly to the group, his face grim as he spoke. "Their class simply ages rapidly on the outside without aging on the inside, so by twenty they look like old men and women even though they're perfectly healthy. By forty they look like they're two hundred years old, and after that they're not fit to be seen in normal society."

Mayfly had heard legends of millennials but had never met one. He knew that they could pass in normal society while they were young and could hustle by challenging normal humans to fights or even footraces for cash. But millennials tended to disappear at age thirty due to their appearance; some became hermits or shut-ins, some lived as masked outcasts.

Some come up here to live freely, thought Mayfly. *This is the legendary "Rest Home" to which they retire. They're still shy and build high walls, even though no one lives up here to see them.*

"We should move on," said Mayfly. "You never know what'll happen here—"

"Millennials are harmless," said Cattaga as she walked into the village.

We should still be on guard, thought Mayfly. *Nothing this far north is harmless.*

/***/

Brogg was about to punch through the front wall when Mayfly stopped him and simply pulled a thin wood panel back and slipped through. Once inside, he opened the gate and let the crew through. Two Treys stayed on the lookout, but the third Trey, Cattaga and even the Fountain followed Brogg inside the village.

The settlement walls were tall from the outside, but seemed absolutely stifling from the inside because they leaned slightly inward and blocked out both horizon and sky. *This village isn't built to hide them from the outside,* thought Mayfly. *It's built to hide the outside from them.*

231

"It smells odd," said Cattaga.

"Increase your sensitivity," said Mayfly, "and tell us what it is."

Cattaga's eyes glowed, and she breathed in.

"It smells like death," she said.

/***/

They found the first millennial outside of his house. He was frozen and could have been dead anywhere from a few hours to a few months. Mayfly inspected him; he had the gnarled and thick skin of an old man but was probably only twenty years old himself. Mayfly knew that despite their elderly appearance millennials didn't just drop dead, so he looked closer and found the kid had two bite marks on his frozen arm, about four centimeters apart. The skin looked corroded around the marks, as if a scourge had touched him.

Brogg found a second millennial five minutes later; this one had been torn in half. It was an elderly woman, perhaps sixty, but the remaining part of her face looked to be ten times that age. Half of her was covered with frozen, sagging flesh and she had one remaining rheumy eye that stared lifelessly into the cold night. An unidentified carnivorous animal had gnawed the other half of her face, and it was a mess of bone and frozen blood.

"It takes something hungry to eat a face like that," said Trey.

"I didn't know berserkers came this far north," said Cattaga.

"It's not a berserker," said Trey. "Their kind find millennials repulsive."

Millennials are built to hide, not to defend, thought Mayfly, *but still, something vicious came here.*

"What do you sense it is, Cattaga?" asked Mayfly.

Cattaga put her hand to the frozen carcass of the millennial and then looked back at the first body. Brogg came out of another building carrying five more frozen millennials, which he dumped on the ground in front of them. Some had been mangled and some were mostly intact. One seemed completely untouched, save for two bite marks on his neck. No blood had come from the wound; like the first victim, there was simply a corroded area around the bite that spread out and faded over the rest of the body.

Cattaga concentrated on her hand and the nail on her smallest finger grew pointy and thick. She stabilized the finger with her other hand and dug out some frozen flesh around the body's bite wound. She tasted the frozen blood inside and then spat it out.

"They've been poisoned," said Cattaga. "At least some of them have, and—"

There was a rumbling from above, and a plane swooped over their heads. Mayfly ducked for a moment and then took a quick look at it before it disappeared. It was a simple propeller-driven bush plane with no weapons and didn't look like one of Juan's machines. Mayfly was wondering how a bush plane could get this far north when Trey turned around and gasped.

"The Fountain," said Trey. "She left."

Mayfly looked around and found that Trey was right; the Fountain was gone.

/***/

They found her at a tree about a hundred meters behind the settlement. The tree looked to be coated with ice, but upon a closer look it was covered with some sort of hanging silk. Though it was outwardly beautiful, something about the fibers gave Mayfly chills.

Mayfly caught eye contact with the Fountain, and she smiled at him.

"Do you know what this is?" she asked in Arawak.

"I don't know," said Mayfly in kind, *"but I don't like it."*

"This is from a creature," she said. "A creature that takes life."

"This is from whatever killed the old ones behind the walls?" asked Mayfly.

"Yes," said the Fountain. "The silk comes from deadly creatures to hold their children. Your friend is handling their young as we speak."

Mayfly looked at the tree and saw that two of the Treys were bringing what looked like a large, gelatinous sac of ostrich eggs to the ground. Mayfly looked up and saw that there were two more of these sacs hanging in the tree, and then found that almost all the trees surrounding them were covered in silk that held sacs.

"Check this out," said Trey, holding up his egg. "There's a wolf in here."

Mayfly looked at the eggs and shuddered; they were each filled with an eight-legged spider-wolf pup, pale and young but well developed and ready to hatch. Mayfly looked at the rest of the eggs hanging from the trees; they were all moving, and a few on the top were already breaking through their soft shells.

"Spider-wolves killed everyone in this village; either through biting them in half or leaving their poison. They're probably out hunting now, but they left their young here," said Mayfly. "That means they're coming back."

/***/

They heard the thin howl of adult spider-wolves in the distance, perhaps returning from a hunt, or perhaps returning to hunt them. Mayfly had a hard time seeing what was happening from within the millennial settlement; it was built for privacy and there were no towers to look out. Mayfly became worried; the village's thin doors wouldn't protect them against an onslaught, and its high walls wouldn't let them see the wolves coming.

"Brogg," said Mayfly, "build a few towers so we can look outwards. I don't care how you do it, just build some towers."

Brogg looked around and then destroyed one of their houses, revealing a dead millennial couple that looked to be ten thousand years old. Brogg took the materials from their house and built a makeshift tower, and then another one. Two Treys climbed each one and looked beyond the wall.

The team was snapping into action all around Mayfly, but he couldn't move. *Adam's fear is burial,* thought Mayfly. *Mine is spiders.*

"Mayfly, get up here!" said the Trey perched atop his tower. "Your vision is better than mine."

Mayfly couldn't move; he tried to remember that he was fighting for Adam, the Fountain and the mayflies trapped in Juan's asylum, but something within him told him to *run*; to run through the forest and never come back. *The wolves are trapping me,* thought Mayfly. *I'm trapped in their web just like—*

"Come here, Mayfly ... " said Cattaga, turning him around and pulling him back into a dark corner.

She put her lips to his for a long time, holding him firmly. Mayfly had kissed hundreds of girls before, but had never felt anything like this; it was as if time had stopped. Cattaga let go and smiled at him.

"I had my salivary glands release serotonin," she said. "It's a neurotransmitter that helps alleviate anxiety. You should have gotten enough of it."

"Almost enough," said Mayfly, and he kissed her again.

Mayfly indeed felt better; like there was an invisible barrier between him and the spider-wolves outside. He came out of the corner saw the Treys on Brogg's perches, looking outward. *It's a good thing he didn't see me kissing her,* thought Mayfly, *because she seemed to have enjoyed it.*

The Treys' ledges were spread out across the wall and they spread themselves so they could see a panorama. Mayfly felt bad; he had stolen women countless times before, but had never taken one from a friend, let alone someone who had saved his life before and was keeping him alive now. Brogg snapped him out of his thoughts by picking up Mayfly from behind and propping him on his shoulders and then walking to a low part of the wall where they could both see.

Mayfly saw that many of the eggs outside were breaking open, and some had already hatched. The spider-wolf pups crawling out of them were small but fully functional; they snapped their jaws, bounded about and made small howls. To make things worse, the adult spider-wolves had heard their children's howls and were coming out of the woods to return to them. The adults weren't particularly large, but their teeth were sharp and they were good at climbing; many had been staying in the trees and were descending the trunks facing forward. *If they decide to attack us,* thought Mayfly, *our walls will be useless.*

What was more, the spider-wolves acted *intelligently*. They spontaneously huddled in groups and one spider-wolf would howl and its troop would listen, and it soon became clear that they had some sort of a plan. Trey looked at Mayfly with a blank stare; he had no idea what to do if they were to attack. Mayfly went through twelve different scenarios in his head, came up with the best solution and then brought everyone around. One Trey got down and two stayed up on the wall.

"We can't run from them and we can't kill them," said Mayfly.

"These walls won't hold against the wolves," said Trey.

"Think of them as spiders," said Mayfly. "There's only one way to protect yourself from spiders: *don't let them in the house.*"

/***/

Brogg destroyed several of the buildings and they found more and more bodies; even the hidden underground bunkers were filled with dead millennials, either torn in half or discreetly bitten. *They exterminate their targets completely,* thought Mayfly. *We'll have to shut every single wolf out because we won't be able to hide.*

Mayfly opened one of the gates and then snuck out and brought the RV back inside the village; he could see the wolves peering at him from a distance, but Cattaga's serotonin was still running through him and he wasn't scared. They covered the RV with the materials Brogg had procured, and Trey worked to reinforce the inside of the vehicle. Another Trey found a cache of supplies; there was enough fuel, food and tools to last them a month. They agreed to stockpile food in the RV and save the fuel for later. *We won't be able to just make a run for it,* thought Mayfly. *These creatures are too smart and climb too well; we'll just have to lock ourselves in and wait them out.*

Mayfly climbed the perch and looked outwards; the spider-wolves had formed a perimeter around the village and looked like they had no plans to leave any time soon. The horizon was absolutely covered with them, and they didn't look like wolves scattered across a field so much as they resembled bugs smothering the skin of a carcass. Their numbers were endless, too many to count, and they surrounded the compound like a thick, furry carpet.

If all else fails we may have to make a break for it, thought Mayfly. *I don't know how, but we'll have to find a way.*

Mayfly and Trey propped up the RV's windows with boards, nailing them in and then carving out small viewing holes. *They'll attack at night,* thought Mayfly. *But we still need these holes; if not to see, then to breathe.*

Brogg built a crude fort around the RV and they did their best to nail it shut, but it wasn't perfect; there were too many cracks and openings. Night was approaching quickly, the wolves were beginning to howl and Mayfly's heart started to pound again. He nodded at Cattaga, and in another hidden moment they stole away behind a corner and she kissed him once more, only this time she lingered twice as long. He felt his pulse calm down and he gave her one more kiss in return before rejoining the group.

When he returned, he saw that the fortification of the RV was as good as it was going to get. He looked at the far corner and saw that one of the Treys was preparing a perch on the tallest building. *That Trey is going to get killed and he knows it,* thought Mayfly. *But we need him as a lookout.*

Mayfly walked up to the group and spoke but had a hard time looking any of the Treys in the eye.

"We've fortified our RV as much as we can," said Mayfly. "We need to spend the rest of the time situating ourselves in and preparing our weapons."

/***/

Night fell and the spider-wolves didn't attack immediately. The Trey inside the RV relayed the information from his bodies perched outside atop the towers and told them that the creatures had encircled the camp and were sending scouts forward. Adam had told Mayfly tales of the sieges he had endured in the Middle Ages, and some of them had lasted for months. *But this is no siege,* thought Mayfly. *These spider-wolves might be intelligent, but they're still wolves. They won't wait months.*

The wolves sent the first wave in two hours after nightfall. Mayfly had given his night-vision binoculars to one of the Treys on the outside and Cattaga had increased the amount of rods in her eyes and was peering out through their viewing hole.

"They've only sent five," said Cattaga. "Small ones."

"Are they small enough for us to kill easily?" asked Mayfly.

Cattaga peered through the viewing hole again and stared at the creatures. Mayfly could tell by the sound that the scouting wolves were right outside the RV, inspecting it.

"No," said Cattaga. "We won't be able to kill all five. Maybe one, but not all five."

They heard a faint creak as the RV buckled under the weight of the creatures crawling up the side. One of the creatures made it to the top and was walking back and forth. It made quick, faint sounds as its eight legs crawled over the roof, as if someone was nervously tapping their fingers on a table. Mayfly heard a soft howl from one of the creatures, and then there was silence. After a moment, Trey tapped Mayfly on the shoulder and nodded upwards. There was a hole in the roof of the RV that the group had overlooked, and one of the wolves had poked its head through it and was staring at them.

It wasn't a big creature, but its appearance was frightening. It had eight dull eyes laid over two rows, a long snout and an expressionless face covered with coarse black bristles. It snarled, and its teeth were long in the front and sharp in the back, built for both injecting poison and fighting.

Mayfly looked around and noticed that the others were just as frightened as he was, even the Fountain. She sat in the back of the RV, wrapped in the blanket, and Mayfly instinctively positioned himself in front of her. The animal made a strange snapping sound, and its jaw worked something like a mandible, biting both down and side to side.

In a flash, Brogg came from the darkness and grabbed the creature by its head. The spider-wolf struggled and whined, trying desperately to pull itself back, but couldn't break free of the caveman's grip. Brogg jerked it downwards, and the creature snapped desperately until the big man punched it in its head with such force that green liquid sprayed onto the floor. Brogg took the head and ripped it off, spraying more green liquid everywhere. The group paused to process what Brogg had done, and then Mayfly approached the creature's body and put his hand on the wound where its severed head had once been. The skin was armored but flexible; halfway between an insect's exoskeleton and a wolf's mane.

"If we can kill one," said Mayfly, "we can kill—"

In an instant the creature's headless body sprang to life and jumped at Mayfly. It grabbed onto him with surprisingly dexterous paws and wouldn't let go. At the same time its disembodied jaw started to snap, and Brogg dropped it out of sheer surprise. The headless creature pinned Mayfly with its last bit of strength and slammed him on the ground right next to the snapping head. The head was getting closer to Mayfly on the ground, but Trey picked it up deftly and put it in one of the RV's cabinets. Brogg peeled the creature's body off of Mayfly and beat it until it stopped moving. After ten hits it was dead again, and Trey put it in another cabinet for good measure.

"Thanks," said Mayfly.

"Anytime," said Trey.

Mayfly caught Cattaga's eye for a brief moment but soon the entire group looked up because the spider-wolves outside started to howl. It came through all four walls of the RV and was deafening; Brogg closed his ears and grimaced in pain, but the one that looked the most frightened was Trey, because he had a view from the outside. There was a pounding from the roof and the group seized up, but Trey relaxed them.

"It's me," he said, opening the roof to reveal the second Trey, who was covered in dirt but was physically okay.

"What do you see?" asked Mayfly.

"They're all around and they're coming," said Trey. "They're between my third body and the RV. They climb so well and—"

Both Treys started to wheeze violently and fell to the ground, and then one of them started to cough up blood. Cattaga rushed to him and tried to calm him, but he was seizing with too much force. She looked up and Mayfly shot her a look: *do whatever you need to do to save him.*

Cattaga rushed over to the seizing Trey and concentrated until her eyes began to glow. She held him down and kissed him deeply, and soon his spasming body stopped.

"That should relax you," she said.

Trey looked up at her and nodded, and then looked over at his other body.

"My third body has been killed," he said, pointing at his second self, "and this body here underwent shock because of it."

Trey got up and inspected his second body, and then looked at the group.

"We can't worry about that now though," said Trey, "because the wolves are coming."

Mayfly listened; the creatures outside had stopped howling, and all they heard was the tapping of little legs as the swarm of creatures approached the RV.

/***/

The spider-wolves started to howl again as they rushed over the van. The RV's shell buckled and it seemed like it would break from their collective weight, but it held; Brogg's reinforcements had worked. One more creature poked its head into the hole in the RV's roof and Brogg ripped it down, this time killing it thoroughly. They waited for another creature to come in through the small hole, but none did; it was as if they had learned that entering the hole meant their end.

"Spiders don't have a collective consciousness like ants," said Mayfly. "Both spiders and wolves are individuals, and individuals fear death. If we keep killing them, they'll stay away."

"If we keep killing them, we'll run out of space," said Trey as he tucked the smashed wolf's dead body in another compartment.

Mayfly nodded in agreement, but soon the creatures outside started to howl again. There was silence and then there was a guttural barking from what seemed like an alpha-wolf in the distance. The alpha-wolf barked twice, then a third time, and the RV shook violently. The creatures were rocking it back and forth, and the things inside the RV began to fall to the ground. Mayfly and the crew were thrown about, and Brogg fell against the ceiling with a smash, making a hole in the skylight window.

As they shook, a small spider-wolf pup snuck in through the new hole and latched onto the wall. Brogg went to get the creature, but the ground was too unstable. The young spider-wolf navigated through the rocking walls of the RV with agility and easily dodged Brogg's clumsy swipes. The creature finally managed to jump onto the unconscious Trey and sunk his small teeth into his neck before Brogg ripped the pup off and smashed it into the floor. The bitten Trey began to seize again, and a small wave of dead flesh started to spread from the bite. The healthy Trey started to cough in response and there was another violent trembling as the wolves outside assaulted the RV once more.

"It's going to tip over!" said Mayfly. "Hold on to something!"

The crew braced themselves, and the RV fell on its side. There was a crunch as the materials covering it broke down, and the hole near the RV's skylight shattered wide open. Mayfly scrambled to regain his balance and once he did, looked around to make sure everyone was still okay. The RV's interior was in pieces and the parts from the dead spider-wolves had flown from their cabinets, but everyone seemed intact. The Fountain was shaken, but maintained her composure as she stood back up and gathered her bearings. Brogg stood up too, and was about to fly into a rage, but Mayfly calmed him down and peered out of the broken skylight.

There was an endless flurry of spider wolves running over the skylight and peeking in; then there was a low, guttural bark from the alpha-wolf in the distance, and the other wolves dissipated. Soon it was quiet again, leaving the crew to listen as the poison continued to creep through Trey's second body.

Mayfly cautiously peeked out of the broken window and saw that thousands of spider-wolves still surrounded the RV, but had cleared a small path for the alpha.

The alpha spider-wolf approached the RV, but he maintained enough distance to be safe from Brogg. He was large, and his coarse black bristles were so long that they looked like they could cut through flesh. His eight spindly legs glided over the ground deftly and he crouched down to peer through the skylight, which was now touching the ground. He looked into the RV with his eight dull eyes and sniffed twice. He peered directly at the Fountain and sniffed three more times, and then howled. Mayfly was catching on to the language of their howls and could guess what the alpha-wolf was saying.

"Kill everyone but her," the wolf seemed to say. "Kill everyone but her."

The wolf walked back, and after a quick bark the swarm went over them again, trying to push their way in through the skylight. Brogg beat the first ones through the door and their bodies clogged the skylight, but Mayfly knew Brogg's defense wouldn't last long; there were too many creatures outside, and they were too fierce.

Some other spider-wolves were banging in through another skylight and soon were cracking it open. Cattaga and Trey were hitting the spider-wolves at that skylight, but they weren't as effective as Brogg. The spider-wolves were coming too fast and Mayfly considered that this could be the end.

Perhaps your destiny isn't to deliver this Fountain, nor to save Adam, nor to save the mayflies, he thought. *Perhaps your only destiny is to die.*

But Mayfly was snapped out of his thoughts by a high-pitched howl he had not yet heard, and soon he saw that all of the spider-wolves were retreating. Brogg even tried to hold one wolf back with his hands, but it squirmed out and ran into the darkness. There were a few moments of silence as the team realized that they were somehow safe, and then there was a deafening explosion of howls and shrieks from the spider-wolves outside. There were the sounds of snaps and pops and a dim light coming from outside, and it was warm.

Mayfly was the first to put his head out and saw fire burning through the droves of spider-wolves; each one was extremely flammable and as they ran about in agony, they would set fire to another.

"I don't know how, but we're safe for the moment," said Mayfly to the group. "But it's getting too hot for the Fountain, and we've got to get out of here before she kills us all."

The group went outside and couldn't help but smile, even Trey, who was carrying his own dying body. Brogg took the body from Trey and placed it over his shoulder as if it were a scarf, and the group scampered away from the fire until it was cold again. Trey walked cautiously, as if he had lost an eye, but he smiled and soon the group smiled with him because somehow, someway they had survived, and though the scene of burning animals was grotesque, they were alive.

They got to a safe distance and then watched the spider-wolves run into the forest in all directions, some on fire and some not. A few trees had been set ablaze because the spider-wolf silk was the most flammable substance of all, but after the webs burnt out, the surrounding snow largely kept the flames under control.

After twenty minutes nothing remained except for piles of smoking spider-wolf corpses. Many were still moving, but it was clear that they wouldn't be able to harm Mayfly's group anymore. In the distance, Mayfly saw two figures walking towards them and smiled when he saw the first one. It was Adam's sister, Phoe, and her hands were smoldering. But Mayfly's heart sank when he saw the other figure; it was Phage, and he looked angry.

"Stay away from the sickly looking one," said Mayfly to the group. "He's dangerous."

"They saved us though," said Cattaga.

"He's dangerous," said Mayfly.

"He saved us and—" said Cattaga.

"He tried to kill me once," said Mayfly, "and Phage has been known to save people's lives just so he can kill them personally."

Phage approached the group and started to laugh.

"If it isn't the Mayfly himself!" yelled Phage from a distance.

Mayfly smiled; he didn't fear Phage but was forever wary of him. *Phage somehow saved us, but he's a sociopath above all else,* thought Mayfly. *Everything he does comes at a price.*

Mayfly held the crew back, particularly the Fountain. Phage stopped walking and surprisingly held up his hands to show he was no threat.

"I understand why you want to stay away from me, kid," said Phage. "But I'm a changed man; ask Phoe."

Mayfly had a sharp sense of when someone was lying, and felt no evidence that Phage was being untruthful. Still, even if Phage was a *changed man* he was most likely carrying smallpox, so Mayfly held up his hand for Phage to keep his distance.

"I'll approach slowly," said Phage respectfully. "I only want to talk."

Trey was still traumatized at two thirds of his body being injured or dead, but Brogg looked healthy enough to fight, and Cattaga seemed eager to accept Phage as their momentary savior. Brogg positioned himself in front of the Fountain and Mayfly knew that he would smash Phage to bits if it was necessary, so Mayfly nodded at Phage to approach. Both Phage and Phoe walked up slowly and then knelt ten meters from them.

"Destiny has commissioned me to bring Phoe to Adam," said Phage. "I rescued her and took a bush plane north. The prodigious spanners that had sheltered us equipped it with technology to find you, so here we are."

"How did you save us?" asked Mayfly.

Phage nodded at Phoe and she spoke.

"I've taken my emotions and weaponized them," she said.

Mayfly had heard stories about Phoe from Adam, and they didn't quite describe the girl now before him. She had the thick golden hair, square jaw and soft skin that Adam had spoken of, but she didn't look quite as innocent as he had claimed. Her eyes were narrow and angry, and she walked deliberately towards them, leaving a trail of charred ground and steaming footsteps behind her in the snow. This wasn't the young girl who died with a broken heart; this was a killer.

"Thank you both for saving us," said Mayfly.

"Phoe was the one who saved you," said Phage. "She burned the spiders and their nests too, but since I brought her to the party, I guess that makes us even for all the stuff I've done to you, kid."

Mayfly knew he had to take what fate had given them, and nodded without making eye contact. He looked past Phage and saw that a few spider-wolves had relit part of the forest, in particular the trees that were covered with the spider-wolves' silk. The unhatched eggs were quite flammable; they were like small pyres, popping and snapping as the pups inside burned unhatched.

/***/

An hour later, Brogg knocked down an unburnt tree and cut it to pieces with an axe he had found in the village. Phoe set it alight with her hands to make a bonfire, and Mayfly made sure the Fountain kept her distance so her powers wouldn't kill them all from the warmth.

"Geryon's out there, in the forest," said Phage. "As you know, flames spook him. He'll join us soon."

Geryon once tried to strangle me with his chains, thought Mayfly. *This rescue party just gets better and better.*

"Where's Adam?" asked Phoe.

"He's south," said Mayfly. "Juan's crew got to him, and Adam sent us up north."

"Got to him *how?*" asked Phoe, accusingly.

"I don't know," said Mayfly.

He didn't want to tell her the whole truth, not now, but she was right to be angry. *Whatever danger we're in, Adam is in a worse place,* thought Mayfly. *He's in the worst place imaginable.*

"We don't know what happened to Adam," said Cattaga, "but Adam bound us to take the Fountain north, to Santos de León."

"The Surgeon," said Phage. "That guy scares me. But I hear you; you gotta do what you're bound to do, and there're a lot of words floating around concerning *destiny*, a *great battle*, and all that crap. We're all headed somewhere, and most of us are headed north for some reason."

Phage took a cigarette from his pocket, lit it in the bonfire with his bare hands and then took a few puffs. He looked over the group and then focused on Trey's dying body, still sick from the spider-wolf bite.

"That kid there is in bad shape," said Phage, looking at Trey. "You all won't survive another week in these woods yourselves, let alone be able to fight a battle against Juan's minions. He's probably sending another wave of spider-wolves up to fight you as we speak, and I'm here to help."

"Thank you," said Mayfly, meaning it. "But how?"

"We got a bush plane you can use to bring the blond boy along with the Fountain up to the Surgeon," said Phage. "Surgeon's a creepy dude, but if there's anyone on earth who can heal him, it's Santos de León. We'll fix the RV and take it down to rescue Adam."

"You're going to find Adam?" asked Mayfly.

"I'm bound by my atonement to bring Phoe to my brother," said Phage.

They looked at Phoe and she thought for a moment.

"I should go down to rescue Adam," said Phoe. "I don't remember him, but from what I understand he's been kind to me in the past, and above all else, he's my brother too."

"We'll bury my dead body here, and then fly my sick one up north," said the healthy Trey. "We'll bring the Fountain and that will be that."

"Sounds like a plan," said Phage. "Can any of you guys fly a plane?"

"I can," said Cattaga.

"You can?" asked Mayfly.

"I'm from Alaska," said Cattaga. "Everyone flies up there."

Mayfly looked at the group and wondered if this was the right move. He'd have a talk with Brogg and tell him to protect the Fountain against anyone who would do her harm, be it the elements or even Geryon. *But still*, thought Mayfly, *Adam bound me to bring the Fountain north, and no one else.*

Mayfly looked at the group that would ride in the plane: Cattaga, Brogg, Trey's invalid body, and Geryon, a tall mute who had once tried to kill him.

It's going to be okay, thought Mayfly. *Cattaga and Brogg will see this through. They'll bring the Fountain north and you'll fulfill your duty through them. You must go south because no one but you will free the mayflies, and no one but you can find Adam and dig him up.*

"All right," said Mayfly. "The plane gets Brogg, the Treys, the Fountain, Cattaga and Geryon. The rest of us go south to rescue Adam."

"I go where Phoe goes," said Phage, "and Geryon doesn't go anywhere without me, so he's coming down with us in the RV. The rest can go up north."

Mayfly thought for a moment and then nodded in agreement.

"Looks like you're headed south, Mayfly," said Phage, "and you're bringing a brand new crew."

"I guess I am," said Mayfly with a smile. "I guess I am."

/***/

They found the dead Trey an hour later; his body had been torn into three parts by the spider-wolves and then burnt to cinders by the fire after. They couldn't dig in the frozen ground, so Brogg found some more wood and they made a makeshift pyre for him. The healthy Trey couldn't watch; he later explained it was like watching one's own arm being cooked.

They said their goodbyes, and Mayfly whispered instructions into Brogg's ear: *"You must bring the Fountain to the Surgeon. I don't care if your plane crashes; make sure she gets there."*

Mayfly pulled Cattaga aside and gave her the map.

"I've translated it for you," said Mayfly. "Do you understand it?"

"Yes," said Cattaga. "We'll get there."

Cattaga pulled Mayfly in and gave him one more long kiss.

"Thanks," he said. "You give me courage."

"I didn't add anything to that one," she responded. "It was just me."

Mayfly smiled and they kissed again, and then it was time to leave.

"Make sure the Fountain gets north," said Mayfly. "She's more important than you or I, or anyone else here."

"I'll get her north," said Cattaga, "and I'll see you there shortly after I do."

/***/

The RV was easy to fix; it had been knocked about a bit, but once they turned it back over they found that the spider-wolves hadn't done any damage to the engine or any of the working parts. They patched up a tire, cleaned up the interior and then the vehicle was good to go. It looked beat to hell but was a tough old thing, and the engine sounded like it could run forever.

Mayfly drove south for an hour and began to miss his old crew; he felt unprotected without Brogg at his side, let alone Trey and Cattaga. Mayfly didn't fear Phage but didn't like driving with him in the back of the RV, out of his sight. Mayfly drove in silence, but felt Phage might reach out from the back of the RV at any moment and strangle him, even if out of habit. Each time Mayfly looked back though, Phage and Phoe were sleeping peacefully on opposite sides of the RV; just another brother and sister. Geryon somehow hid in the shadows; the man was twice Mayfly's height but still disappeared completely into the darkness, with the occasional round of clicks to let everyone know he was back there somewhere.

After an hour Phoe woke up and sat in the front seat soundlessly, lost in thought as they drove through the endless forest. Mayfly could sense that she didn't want to talk; she had a steely, cold look in her eyes absolutely unlike any description Adam had given of her. *She's emotionless,* thought Mayfly. *Perhaps that's why she's here with us and not burnt like she's supposed to be.*

They drove another hour in silence, and unlike their journey north, there were few forks in the road to navigate. *Like Davelia said, going north has a thousand paths,* thought Mayfly. *But the other way is easy; to leave this place, all you have to do is drive south.*

They passed some other settlements; most of them had been cleanly devastated by spider-wolves, as if an army of African ants had run through them. The structures remained intact, but nothing else lived. They even passed a dead berserker in the road, his throat ripped out by the wolves. When Mayfly tried to drive around him, there was movement in the forest and a living berserker approached the RV, injured by the wolves but still alive and eager to avenge his comrade. Mayfly was about to pull off the road to drive around the berserker when Phage's dirty hands appeared from the darkness and landed on Mayfly's shirt.

"He'll still fuck you up, kid," said Phage. "Stay right here."

Phage looked at Phoe and pointed at Mayfly.

"Make sure he stays right here," he commanded Phoe.

Phoe nodded and then Phage whistled at Geryon in back. The masked spanner came to the front of the RV and clicked twice before listening to the injured creature's movements. Geryon then got out of the vehicle and confronted the berserker head-on. The injured berserker was slow, but had Geryon's height and was nearly twice as broad. Geryon, blind and masked, started to click rapidly and dodged the charging berserker with ease.

Mayfly had fought Geryon once before and knew the berserker didn't stand a chance, but the berserker didn't understand that and became angry. The creature swung four times at Geryon and caught only air, and after a fifth miss, Geryon swung his arms together and generated a sonic boom that pushed the berserker off the road. Geryon approached the felled dead creature to do more work on him, but Phage called him back.

"We got to go, bro," said Phage. "You'll have plenty more opportunities to fight."

Geryon came back into the RV and Mayfly sped off, leaving the two unmoving berserkers behind them.

"He'll have plenty more opportunities, because like it or not, there's a war coming," said Phage.

"A man said the same thing," said Mayfly. "A human called Freeman Rajter told us that right before he died."

"Rajter, I heard of him … shame he passed. That coot was crazy," said Phage with a laugh. "I mean that in a good way; he was crazy for living in this frozen shithole but rational about everything else, and he was right about the war."

"I don't understand how a war will come," said Mayfly. "I mean, we've got a handful of spanners on our side, and so does Juan. Fight, sure, but battle? I don't see how."

"That's what the legend says, kid, so you gotta be ready for it, like it or not," said Phage. "And like it or not, Geryon, Phoe and I are on *your side*, kid. You're gonna have to learn to count on us, because when Juan's army comes, you're gonna have no one else."

/***/

Hours later, the sun came up and Phoe broke her silence.

"What do you know about Adam?" she asked Mayfly.

Mayfly smiled and then looked at Phage, who was sleeping loudly; he had a hacking cough that occasionally caused his body to spasm, but he was asleep.

"A lot," said Mayfly.

"Like what?"

"I don't know, but Adam once told me I knew him better than his siblings did," said Mayfly.

"Did I know him?" asked Phoe.

"Yeah," said Mayfly. "He sheltered you, but didn't reveal everything, like a father wouldn't. But he spoke of you all the time to me, and when we free him, he'll be really happy to see you."

"Why?" asked Phoe. "What have I done for him? Or for anyone?"

"I honestly don't know Adam's thinking," said Mayfly with a smile, "but I do know that he has a hard time connecting to people, even me. One way or another, he connected with you, sometimes as his sister, sometimes as his daughter, but for whatever reason, you reached him in a way that no one else could."

Phoe thought of that for a moment, watching the forest pass them by.

"Wouldn't it hurt, seeing your daughter die time and time again?" she asked.

"Yeah," said Mayfly, "but he told me it was worth it. You experienced everything in life for the first time, and that's the one part of life he couldn't experience for himself."

"But I died," said Phoe.

"And you always came back," said Mayfly, "to see everything for the first time, over and over again."

Phoe thought for a moment and then nodded. She was about to say something when Phage, now awake, interrupted from the back seat.

"That's a rosy picture of our brother Adam, but it's not the whole story," said Phage.

Mayfly didn't want to argue, so he let Phage speak.

"Adam gets bored with his own life, so he lives through you," said Phage, looking at Phoe. "Even though *he knows* it means you're gonna end up burning."

"She's a phoenix-class spanner, and that's what *she does*," said Mayfly. "*You* kill people, and she's reborn through fire; that's what your classes *do*."

"Bullshit," said Phage. "I don't kill anymore, at least not innocents, and she's avoided her destiny so far. You should have realized that when she was taking those wolves off your back."

Mayfly could easily beat Phage with rhetoric, but chose not to; Phage's argument held truth. Adam wasn't a bad man, but he wasn't without contradictions, and his treatment of Phoe left many questions unanswered. *We have bigger things to worry about than Adam's intentions, however,* thought Mayfly. *Whatever the case, don't worry about this, not here and not now.*

"It is what it is, Phage," said Mayfly, "but Adam's done a lot for us, and we need to rescue him. He's probably under the earth right now, because that's what Juan's people would do. He's buried and we need to find him as fast as we can. Everything else is secondary."

"Amen to that," said Phage with a smile.

They drove in silence for another ten minutes before Phoe spoke again.

"How did we begin?" asked Phoe. "How did our family begin?"

Phage laughed.

"Our beginning," said Phage. "That was a long time ago, and I'm a little hazy on the details. Why don't you field this one, Mayfly?"

"He didn't tell me much," said Mayfly. "He said he doesn't recall a childhood; his memory only goes back eight thousand years. As far as he knows, he's always been this way."

"Sounds like Adam," said Phage, shaking his head. "So much experience, but naïve to the hard truths of this world."

"The *hard truths*?" asked Phoe.

"Yep," said Phage. "Starting with his claim that he's *always been this way*. What was he, born full-grown? Or was he always here in the first place, even before the fucking universe began? What do you think, Mayfly, was he *always this way*? Me, was I always this way?"

"I don't know," said Mayfly, taking Phage's bait. "What do you think?"

"I think there's only one answer to his past, perhaps all our pasts," said Phage.

Phage took out a cigarette, lit it, took a drag and then coughed violently for a moment before taking another smoke.

"I don't remember that long ago, but my memory's never been that good. But our dear Adam's got a perfect memory; he's a tree-class spanner and they don't forget *shit*," said Phage. "And there's *one way* to make a tree-class spanner forget shit, and that's to erase their memory, and there's only *one way* to erase their memory."

"Burial," said Phoe.

"For a hundred fucking years," said Phage. "Bury a tree for a century and he emerges full grown, but anew. Juan Ponce ain't a tree, so he kept his memories when they buried him, but Adam's class? They come out like a baby, with no language, no nothin'."

Phage smoked a cigarette and let the empty morning road pass them by for a few minutes.

"So when a guy like Adam can't remember a childhood, what does that tell you?" asked Phage.

"Someone buried him once before," said Phoe.

"About eight thousand and one hundred years ago someone did just that," said Phage with a dry smile. "And eight thousand one hundred years later, our dear brother is right back where he started, under a ton of dirt."

Mayfly drove for a moment and then rolled down his window to let Phage's smoke clear.

"That's a scary story," said Mayfly, "but it doesn't affect us now."

Phage took another long drag off his cigarette, opened his window and blew the smoke outside.

"It absolutely affects us now," said Phage, "because Adam's our leader in this little quest, and he's currently living the nightmare that's addled his brain for the last 8,000 years. We'll find him and dig him up, but he won't be the same. He ain't gonna be the Adam you know and love; his memory won't be wiped, but he's gonna be a little crazy."

Mayfly looked straight ahead and saw in the mirror that Phage's eyes glowed a veiny red for a brief moment. *Phage is mortal now, but he's still a spanner,* thought Mayfly. *And he might be right about this.*

"We're all gonna help you in this upcoming war, kid, but you're gonna need Adam," said Phage. "We're gonna find a shell of a man under the ground, but we need Adam at full strength."

"How do we get him back to full strength?" asked Mayfly.

"You're the one with the three-hundred IQ, so you gotta figure it out," said Phage. "And do it quick, because you ain't got much time left. If your heart stops before Adam's fixed, we might as well leave him planted and turn the Fountain over to Juan Ponce right now."

Phage isn't politic with his words, but he's right. I've got to help Adam and I'm on borrowed time, thought Mayfly. *All of us are on borrowed time.*

/***/

They drove back to the ruins of Rajter's compound and it was covered with snow. Adam's mound wasn't too hard to find in daylight; there was a pile of smooth, frozen dirt near where they had left Adam. *Juan's crew has powers, but they always leave an opening for us,* thought Mayfly. *Maybe this legend is meant to be.*

Mayfly came up with a solution to dig in the frozen earth; they gathered wood from the wreckage of Freeman Rajter's compound and built a bonfire over the mound. Geryon fled into the forest immediately, preferring to deal with predatory creatures and the cold rather than face more flames.

After covering Adam's burial site completely, Phoe let her eyes glow and set the wood ablaze. The bonfire burned so hot that the fire was pure white and dazzled brightly, even against the noonday sun. They let it burn completely and then used some of Freeman Rajter's shovels to dig through the dirt as it was still smoldering.

The icy ground had softened and they found Adam after an hour, buried without a coffin, still tied to a chair, twitching but unable to speak.

"You're safe now," said Mayfly.

Phage took a stick and prodded Adam a couple of times, but he still didn't speak. Phoe knelt beside Adam and put her hand on his head, and Adam quivered slightly in response. His eyes focused on her and then glowed dimly in recognition.

"He's gonna be all right; it might take some rehab, but our dear brother's gonna be all right," said Phage. "I don't know what lies ahead of us, be it prophecy or war, but whatever it is, it's gonna happen. So stay alive, Mayfly, because whatever happens, it's gonna be *big*."

PART III

A BATTLE AT THE EDGE OF THE WORLD

JON MAAS

THE DEVIL'S ARMY

Balthasar had commanded a guard to whip him again, this time in private. The session lasted an hour, and by the end Balthasar couldn't move. He had ordered the guard to strike him until he became unresponsive, so the guard continued and Balthasar woke up eight hours later, sore and stiff, but healed. Juan, of course, was in his room when Balthasar awoke, and of course was drinking Malbec.

"I forbade you to self-flagellate, and yet you still do it," said Juan. "Tell me why."

Balthasar wouldn't speak.

"Perhaps you think you failed because the Fountain slipped through your fingers?"

Balthasar didn't respond, and after a moment Juan nodded.

"I'm disappointed, of course, but the Fountain was destined to escape you," said Juan. "And though I would have preferred that you would have brought me Adam in shackles, you made the only choice. Adam is craftier than you realize, and you wouldn't have made the journey back down here without him escaping. You did the only thing you could do with Adam."

Balthasar drank another swig of Malbec.

"We'll find him, wherever he is," said Juan. "If he's still buried, we'll ensure that he stays buried, and if he's escaped, we'll put him under such torment that he'll long for the dirt again."

Juan took out a bottle of tequila from under Balthasar's desk, a special bottle that Balthasar had hidden, telling no one. He offered Balthasar a glass, and Balthasar assented. He got past the initial bite of the drink, and then savored the taste for a moment before facing Juan.

"My self-pity is pointless," said Balthasar. "I understand this now."

"Do you?" asked Juan. "Because I don't think you do."

"Perhaps I don't," said Balthasar. "Please elucidate."

Juan drank his Malbec and smiled.

"It's all coming together," said Juan. "Our small failures aren't due to incompetence, but rather to destiny. Everything is leading us to war ... everything! Think of it: Our blur came back with heavy burns, beaten by a *phoenix-class* spanner! You let the Fountain slip away even though you were attacking a hovel! These things don't just happen to us, not with the means at our disposal."

Balthasar nodded.

"The Arawak legend appears to be coming true," said Juan. "Somehow, someway, we're destined for war and must prepare accordingly. No schemes, no legerdemain, no midnight kidnappings; we'll allow the spider-wolves to track the Fountain north, and we'll then bring our army to meet her. There will be a war, and that war will determine the world's future; there is no other way."

Juan walked around Balthasar and then looked down the back of his shirt to inspect the wounds from the whip, almost healed but still raw.

"*That* is why I want you to stop this pointless self-flagellation, Balthasar," said Juan. "There are conflicting demons within you that you care not to reveal, discuss or even *acknowledge,* but you must bring them out now and quash them. You are about to fight an *external and real* war with two sides, and there's no room for an emotional war within your soul. Can you quash the demons inside of you, whatever they may be?"

"Of course, sir," said Balthasar.

"Good," said Juan. "Now come with me; we're going to gauge the strength of the army that we have *now.*"

/***/

The guards had brought temporary walls to the compound's gymnasium and placed them on the floor until it turned into a gladiatorial pit. Juan and Balthasar sat in the upper edges of the gymnasium and waited for Cannon to enter, and when he came in he was grumpy, seemingly indifferent to the fact that he was about to fight for his life. Cannon usually slept until noon, so it had taken Blur some time to rouse him from his sleep, and the kid now rubbed his eyes with acne-covered hands.

"Now, Cannon, you're about to face quite a few opponents and they'll be angry; are you ready to fight them?" asked Juan from his perch in the gymnasium.

"Whatever," said Cannon, still rubbing his eyes.

Juan nodded to Balthasar, and Balthasar nodded to the guards on the gymnasium floor, who released a door to let the populous through. They spilled in through the makeshift gates towards Cannon with their usual zeal to swarm and beat anyone who was different than them.

They outnumbered Cannon fifty to one, but he was too strong to be cornered and too quick for them to grab onto him. Cannon was now half-awake and swung his fists clumsily, landing every third punch with devastating force. Each time his fists connected, a member of the populous went flying into a wall, with some body part being smashed so badly that they were unable to return.

The populous continued to swarm without fear, but Cannon was fully awake now and started to connect more punches, and soon he began to chip away at their collective psyche. After a minute they began to fight with a bit of caution. They finally managed to corner him in a coordinated attack, but Cannon wriggled and shook them off, ten bodies in all. *This is like a grown man being attacked by housecats,* thought Balthasar. *If he were outnumbered a thousand to one, they still wouldn't stand a chance.*

After twenty members of the populous were on the ground, writhing in agony with bones crushed and joints displaced, the thirty remaining members began to disperse, running desperately for an exit and finding none. Cannon chased a few down and pounded them until they were still, but the remaining populous were running too haphazardly and he was having a hard time focusing on one. The pit looked as if it held children playing a game of tag.

"Stop this farce immediately," whispered Juan.

Balthasar signaled the guards to end the melee and they nodded, obediently but cautiously walking onto the floor to tell Cannon that the fight was over. Cannon was too wrapped up in the moment to notice them, but after smashing two more members of the populous he saw the guards and knelt down, sweat soaking his cut-off shirt. The guards yelled at the surviving populous in the terse, commanding tongue to which they responded and ordered them to return to their holding cells. Cannon looked in the upper decks for Balthasar, seeking his approval. Balthasar shot down a quick nod and that was enough for Cannon, who left the pit while the guards set up a triage for his victims.

Balthasar looked to the side and found that Juan was gone; he had already retreated to his quarters.

/***/

As usual Juan was neither mad nor disappointed; he had expected this small failure and had a backup plan. They were about to go to war with an army that couldn't take down an overgrown teenager, but Juan didn't seem concerned. This time Juan drank tequila and offered a glass to Balthasar, who accepted without hesitation.

"When I was buried, my compatriot Hernán Cortés was conquering the land that yielded this drink," said Juan. "It was said that he *burned the boats*, do you know the story?"

Balthasar did, but allowed Juan to indulge in telling the tale.

"Cortés was an ambitious soldier of Spain much like myself, only his regiment happened to land south of Hispaniola, in the Yucatán. But unlike our party, he didn't meet an assortment of unrelated tribes; Cortés faced an *empire*.

"He approached the Aztec kingdom of three hundred thousand with only a few hundred men on his own side—starving, scurvied and mutinous men, no less. When his army refused to take on the Montezuma and threatened to hang him, Cortés burned his own ships so that his troops had only one option to survive: go forward and fight the Aztecs until they were conquered."

Juan sipped the tequila, pointed at the Aztec imagery on the bottle of tequila and laughed.

"Of course, this is a drastic oversimplification of what happened; perhaps the legend of boat burning is an outright lie. But the point is this: back then, all you needed to conquer an empire was a few weapons, some diseases, and in the case of Cortés, an environment of desperation. Legend of burning boats or not, his army of a few hundred men conquered the Aztecs, and now Montezuma's ziggurats grace only bottles of tequila."

Juan smiled and then sipped from his glass.

"Do you know what really allowed Cortés to conquer the Aztecs?"

"Please tell me, sir," said Balthasar.

"The same thing that allowed us to succeed," said Juan. "He was the first ashore."

Juan drained his glass and poured another.

"Cortés faced an empire, but Montezuma was prepared to fall to whoever fought them first. Cortés was not David fighting Goliath. The Aztec empire was surrounded by enemies waiting to turn the tables on their oppressors, and the Aztecs were inferior of weapon and had no protection against disease. If it were not Cortés, it would have been whoever came next.

"And if Hernán had been born a century later, or perhaps even a decade hence, he would have failed. Times changed quickly; the Aztecs fell, mixed their blood with the Europeans and centuries later, Mexico tore free from Spain. Life became too complex for a man to conquer a nation simply by burning his boats."

Juan took another sip of his tequila.

"The same is true for us," said Juan. "We're no longer the first ashore, and the plans that helped us five centuries ago would fail today; we can't achieve our goal simply by arriving at the battle with a horde of populous. The populous can't even conquer one of our own!"

"This is true," said Balthasar, not able to think of anything else to say in response.

Juan bid Balthasar to drink his tequila and he did so, after which Juan poured Balthasar another glass and then stared again at the Aztec ziggurat on the tequila bottle's label.

"But Cortés burned his boats and won," said Juan, his voice trailing off. "Perhaps he *might* have won ten years hence, a century hence, or even today. He was a crafty son-of-a-bitch, and maybe he would have found a way. Maybe we need to think like Cortés and burn our boats, metaphorically."

"Sir?" asked Balthasar.

"We need to raise an army, Balthasar," said Juan, "a *real* army; not just the populous. We must raise an army that will fight as fiercely as Cortés's army did when he destroyed his ships."

Balthasar had nothing to say to Juan in response.

"We will do this by raising the *Devil's army* from the ground," said Juan. "The Devil's army will have but two options: fight for us, or go back to Hell from whence they came. Their boats will already be burnt; do you understand this?"

Balthasar said nothing.

"Forgive me if I speak in strange metaphors," said Juan. "All will become understood as our plan progresses. But you must understand that I can't implement this plan without you, Balthasar. Would you like to know how we'll raise the Devil's army?"

"Of course, sir," said Balthasar.

"Splendid," said Juan. "Then come with me to our compound's basement."

/***/

They stood in front of an empty deep fryer in the basement that Balthasar had bought to cook meals for Cannon. It was a silver metal cylinder, about a meter in height and less than half that in width. Juan turned a switch at the bottom and a flame at the base began to heat the oil inside.

"When you buried Adam, how did it make you feel?" asked Juan.

"Sir?"

"How did it make you *feel*, Balthasar?" asked Juan. "Did you enjoy putting him under the ground and condemning him to a cruel fate? Be honest; I'll know if you're lying."

"No, sir," said Balthasar. "But I did what needed to be done."

"You acted bravely, much as Judas Iscariot did."

"Sir?"

Juan laughed and turned up the flame in the deep fryer.

"I apologize for yet another odd metaphor, but in these times, historical analogy is incredibly important," said Juan. "So I ask, and please be honest, what do you think of Judas Iscariot?"

"He betrayed our Savior and is a scoundrel, sir," said Balthasar. "I do not think him brave."

"I disagree," said Juan. "Judas Iscariot is a hero; think of it. For Jesus to become our Savior, he couldn't turn himself in; he *had to be betrayed*. So he chose his strongest disciple, Judas, to do it; Judas would help Jesus to the cross, and in exchange Judas would get a mere thirty pieces of silver, a hangman's noose, and a name that would be cursed for eternity. The other disciples did nothing and now enjoy noble places in history, but Judas did what *had to be* done and if he hadn't, we'd still be worshipping Jupiter and Apollo!"

"A fascinating viewpoint, sir," said Balthasar, wondering what this all had to do with the deep fryer in front of them.

"My point is this: if we're to win the battle, we must raise the Devil's army. And if we're to raise the Devil's army, you must be willing to go in league with Judas, and do such ignoble things that you'll become the fiercest punisher the world has ever known. Your burial of Adam is just the beginning, and you'll eventually do things that would cause Judas himself to shudder. Do you understand?"

"No, sir," said Balthasar.

Juan took the top off the deep fryer and listened to the oil bubble for a few moments. Part of the grease was popping out of the container and spackled Balthasar's pants, and he stepped back. Juan didn't step back, and didn't flinch as the droplets of oil fell on him. Instead, he focused on his hand, took two deep breaths and then plunged his arm into the oil. The grease sizzled around his arm, snapping and popping as they cooked his skin, but Juan clenched his jaw and kept his hand in the tank. After a few moments he withdrew and then presented his arm to Balthasar as if it were a piece of meat to be eaten.

Balthasar was aghast and couldn't intuit how Juan wanted him to respond. Juan's arm had already begun to heal, but it was still just a mass of raw, corroded flesh.

"Again, I speak, and even *act,* in metaphors," said Juan. "What needs to be done will become clear as we begin our journey. What I need from you is to know that you will continue to *do* what *needs* to be done to raise our army, even if it means plunging your hands into the ether of Hell itself. Will you do this?"

"Of course," said Balthasar.

"Martyrdom is easy," said Juan. "Will you plunge your hands into the fire to place *others* in Hell though? Not the purgatory of dull darkness to which you've sent Adam, but *Hell*?"

"I don't follow you, sir," said Balthasar, "but I'll do what needs to be done."

"I understand that I must be sounding like a whirling dervish of the apocalypse, spouting nonsense," said Juan, "but let me put it baldly: in order to raise our army, we must do some cruel, cruel things, and you are tasked with organizing this. You're going to create Hell in a microcosm, and when the souls we've trapped cry out for mercy, you must not waver. You must have the strength of Judas and the resolve of Cortés and be willing to punish these souls for a century, for a millennium, and for eternity if need be. Can you do this?"

"I will do this," said Balthasar.

"Good," said Juan, patting the fryer. "You'll create a place of cruelty not because you enjoy it, but because you must. You'll create a Hell so dark and unending that the demons of the earth will hear it and eventually come to our side."

/***/

The team drove west over the Arizona desert caravan style, with Blur taking over for Cannon, and then Drayne taking over for Blur. Cannon had been driving too erratically for the other vehicles to keep up, so Balthasar had radioed him to stop and then had Blur take over. Cannon was hurt by the switch, but after five minutes he calmed down, went into the backseat and took a nap.

After another hour, Blur radioed Balthasar and said that he needed a break himself; though he was recovering well from his fight with Phoe, his burns were deep and had taken away his energy. Balthasar instructed Drayne to take over and once again their caravan of trucks drove through the desert together.

Another guard chauffeured Juan because he hadn't yet learned to drive, and Balthasar drove his own truck alone, with the modified tank in the back. He had engineered the deep fryer to be much sturdier, and in addition to being able to cook he had given it the option to freeze, increase in pressure or become a vacuum at the press of a button. *This tank will be Hell in microcosm, but we won't need to run it for eternity, even if Juan thinks otherwise,* thought Balthasar. *This tank will be such a dark place that they'll relent in hours, obviating the need for extended punishment, let alone eternal suffering.*

/***/

They entered the Navajo nation just before noon, and Balthasar couldn't help but be bewildered by history's strange treatment of his former adversaries and their adjoining tribes. When Balthasar's people had set sail for the New World, they were out to conquer, but at least the conquistador's message was clear: *we're here to defeat you; if you should fight back and kill us, you will not be defeated.*

But religion added an odd twist to the advent of the conquistador; the presence of priests justified any and all brutal actions against the natives but also complicated things later. Killing a knife-wielding natural who didn't share your language was easy, but what happened when the natural put down his knife and became an obedient Christian? What happened when the natives began to intermarry and give birth to baptized children?

Balthasar had pondered these things for several decades and had even worked for the Bureau of Indian affairs back in the late 1800s, but never in his wildest dreams had he imagined the Indians would live such a paradoxical existence as they did now. They were marched from their homes to the worst lands on earth, and when the lands were found to have minerals they were told to move aside once more. Tribes cut in half by the Mexican border became a case study in extremes, with those to the north becoming rich off casinos but dying daily of diabetes mellitus, and those to the south being paragons of health but staying as a permanent underclass. *But the world is full of paradoxes just like this, due only to discordant cultures,* thought Balthasar. *After we take over, there will be one culture and the world will make more sense.*

They stopped at a rundown gas station in the middle of nowhere and saw a boy tending to a cage full of white doves.

"They're not Navajo, but this is where their kind resides," said Juan. "Do you remember him?"

Balthasar remembered the boy quite clearly; he had been tending to birds when they had first met. Five hundred years later, the boy was still tending to birds.

"They called him *Koriuaka*," said Balthasar. "*Parrot* in Arawak."

"*Koriuaka*," repeated Juan. "I remember; he served as our translator and though we treated him harshly, he still has his youth, so he can't be too bitter."

They surrounded the youngster, and he paid them no mind. Juan whispered the boy's name, and the kid looked up with eyes glowing faintly with fear, and they glowed again when he saw Juan's face. The kid froze for a moment and then tried to run, but he was caught by Cannon and held up with his feet dangling. *He's an immortal who's lived longer than we have,* thought Balthasar, *but right now he acts like a frightened child caught throwing stones through a church window.*

"We're not here to hurt you, Koriuaka," said Juan. "The past is the past. All I want to do is talk with your council. Can you call them in?"

The boy wouldn't speak.

"You're the mouthpiece, boy; this is what you were put on earth to do, so bring them in. If you don't do this, I'll find them all on *my* terms," said Juan. "Do you understand?"

The boy nodded and Cannon let him go. The boy paused to think for a moment, and then went back to tend to his birds.

"Give me four days," said the boy. "They can't make it here on short notice."

"You have two days," said Juan. "We're on a schedule, and if they're not here in two days, there will be consequences."

/***/

Two days later, Balthasar drove twenty kilometers south of Highway 160 to the Valu-7 motel on Highway 191. Blur had been managing his injuries well so Balthasar tasked him with implementing the plan, and most importantly, with keeping Cannon under control. If everything went haywire they would rely on Cannon to wrangle everyone by force, but until then, they needed stealth. Blur and Drayne would be all that was necessary; there were only five members of the council, six if you counted the boy with the white birds.

And we meet in a Valu-7 meeting room, rented for twenty dollars an hour, thought Balthasar. *This is an odd place to raise an army.*

Juan sensed Balthasar's reluctance to enter the dingy room and whispered in an old dialect of Spanish that only they could still understand.

"This place may be unassuming," said Juan, "but so were the Mount of Olives and the Bodhi tree that shaded Gautama Buddha. Humble places change the world; in fact, change comes from nowhere else."

Three men and two women were sitting at the tables, modestly dressed and dark-skinned from working sunny fields as day laborers. Balthasar knelt in the middle of the room facing the five council members who were seated; he thought he might remember them from five centuries ago but their faces were now rough, not from injury but from hard living. *They're immortal but choose the difficult life*, thought Balthasar. *It's been said they do this to hide; to stay "off the grid," as it were. They hide from the world like Adam, but more so.*

"*Esteemed Council of the Arawak nation,*" said Juan in Arawak. "*I am honored by your presence.*"

"*We doubt that,*" responded a man in Arawak, whom Balthasar now remembered to be their chief. "*We doubt that very much.*"

"Five hundred years of burial changes a man," said Juan with a smile.

"Indeed it does, and if it were up to me, you'd have been in the ground for another five centuries," said the chief, "and not just for the torture you committed on our kind. You broke our culture apart, and before that you destroyed a score of other cultures to reach us. Now I understand you've regained our jewel, the Fountain, and then you lost her, which is a good thing."

"We didn't *lose* her, she was *stolen* from us," said Juan, "and the man who has stolen her, Adam Parr, has made no effort to reach out to you. So it appears that we're both without the one thing that we want."

The council spoke amongst themselves in an obscure Arawak dialect that Balthasar couldn't understand.

"Adam is a friend of our people, and though he may not be on our side, he isn't actively out to *destroy* us either," said the chief. "We'd rather have the Fountain in his hands than in yours."

Juan smiled and then thought for a moment before speaking.

"I wouldn't be so sure," said Juan, "for though Adam is much more friendly than I, his vision for the future doesn't include you."

"He saved us from your cruelty five centuries ago," said the chief, "and though we need no more saving, at the very least Adam leaves us alone."

"That he does," said Juan, "and will continue to do so while you pick strawberries for a dollar per hour."

The chief once again commiserated with his compatriots in the unintelligible Arawak dialect; this time there was much hemming and hawing, and one member got up and tried to leave in a huff before being calmed down by one of the other members. *I wish Juan would end this pointless discourse,* thought Balthasar. *Our guards are at the door and the council's fate has already been sealed.*

"This is the life we choose," said the chief to Juan. "We live like ghosts and have taken a vow of freedom: no family, no property and no attachments of any kind."

"Sounds like most spanners," said Juan, "existing eternally but only in the shadows, living forever but without consequence."

"Did you call us here to insult us?" said the chief. "If so—"

"I called you here to grant you mercy!" yelled Juan.

There was a moment of stunned silence while the council absorbed what they had just heard, too shocked to laugh at Juan's apparent naiveté. They didn't fall back into their Arawak dialect, and merely looked at the chief to speak.

"*You* ... come to grant *us* mercy?" said the chief, still too shocked to make light of it.

"Yes," said Juan, "and you'll get only one opportunity. Kneel and swear your undying fealty to me right now, and I'll give you great rewards."

The council didn't speak and once again looked at the chief.

"We don't understand—" said the chief.

"I'm about to take over the world, with your Fountain as queen. There will be a place for her tribe as my personal detail, protecting me, fighting for me and doing my general bidding. If you bow to me right here, right now, *and swear to get the remaining members of your immortal tribe to do the same*, I'll allow you to exist under me. If you fail to do this, I'll punish you *immediately* and for eternity."

Two members of the council got up and stormed out but were greeted by Cannon, who took them both by their shirt collars and threw them back into their seats. The chief's eyes glowed dimly, and then he looked at Juan.

"Now it's *our* turn to give *you* one final warning, Conquistador," said the chief. "We've all taken vows of complete poverty, with no family, no property and no attachments of any kind. There's nothing with which you can threaten us and no one whom you can take hostage to make us bend. We're a loose collection of individuals who live forever, and nothing more. There's nothing that we want, and we have nothing for you to take away. If you continue to threaten us, we'll have no recourse but to bury you for a thousand years this time, not out of spite, but only so that we may continue our humble, hidden way of life."

Juan was unmoved by the threat and whispered to Balthasar in their old Spanish dialect.

"It's time," said Juan. *"Gather the troops."*

Balthasar coughed twice loudly, which was the signal to the guards waiting outside that no one should leave this place.

In a few moments Drayne will slip into this room and put them to sleep with a brush of her fingers, thought Balthasar. *If any try to escape, Cannon will put them to sleep with his fists. Then we'll take them far from here, bring out our hacksaws and begin our work in earnest.*

"I'll give you one last opportunity," said Juan to the council. "Swear fealty to me and you'll be rewarded. Disobey me, and four hours from now you'll experience an agony that no creature has ever experienced before, and your torment *will not end*."

Juan's eyes glowed and he looked at each member of the council, including the boy with the doves, who looked like he was about to run.

"Now," said Juan. "Will the immortal Arawak nation swear fealty to me, and swear that they'll fight for me in the upcoming battle? Will you spend an eternity under *me*, doing everything that I ask? Or will you choose an eternity in Hell, with no hope for salvation?"

/***/

Four hours and thirty minutes later, their trucks were a hundred kilometers north and twenty kilometers east into the desert. No human would ever see them, and no human would ever hear the screams from Koriuaka, the boy with the doves. He had been the most difficult to wrangle. The five members of the council stood to fight when Juan's crew attacked, but Cannon had made short work of them. The boy had run away and might have succeeded had they not found him by his birds, freeing the last one from its cage before Cannon grabbed him by the head and dragged him back to Juan.

They were far enough away from civilization that Koriuaka's screams couldn't be heard, but just in case an errant hiker was passing through, Drayne took enough of his life away so the boy could barely move. The boy's yells still came out, but they came out like faint wheezes, increasing in intensity each time Balthasar turned the heat up in his tank. The council's decapitated bodies writhed each time Balthasar increased the temperature, but they didn't make that much noise. After binding the five bodies with rope and putting them in a box, the only noise they made were faint thuds, persistent but not too distracting.

Juan told Balthasar to turn the flame off, and he did. It would take the oil an hour to cool down completely, so Drayne touched the boy lightly on the neck once more so that he still wouldn't yell. He was quiet, but the boy couldn't focus due to his pain, so she touched his severed wrist and it became black and deadened to pain signals. The boy calmed down but was still frightened and looked at Juan with glowing eyes.

"Now listen, *Koriuaka*," said Juan. "Five centuries ago you helped us, largely against your will, but here we are today and you'll do the same. Do you understand?"

The boy nodded faintly.

"Good," said Juan. "Now let me tell you the price of immortality. I paid a dear price at your hands: five centuries in a box. You, along with your council, are paying an even dearer price. The council's five living heads and your severed hand are now in a device that can do naught else but deliver pain. I don't know the mechanics of immortal biology, but I do know that an immortal's severed hand can still send pain signals to its detached body, even at great distances. Do you understand?"

The boy's eyes were watering up with tears, but he nodded.

"You're in a very dark place, Koriuaka," said Juan, "but the council is in a much worse place. A hand in boiling oil hurts, but their heads are *who they are*, and that hurts much more. We can of course choose to freeze the container, add pressure, or simply leave it boiling under the ground for a year if we so desire. Do you understand the power we have over you and the council? Do you understand that no one will ever find them?"

The boy nodded.

"Do you understand that one misstep, one lie, or one truth untold from you means that your head will be placed in this vessel next?"

More tears came from the boy's eyes and he started to shake; he eventually stopped and nodded.

"Good," said Juan. "Now I need information from you: a location that you've been sworn never to reveal; do you know the location of which I speak?"

The boy nodded and Juan stood up to address his crew.

"The time has come to raise our army," said Juan. "The immortal Arawaks punished me with burial, but I wasn't the only one. They gave many of their own this capital punishment, and though they saved such treatment for those amongst them that had committed the most grievous sins, over time the numbers under the earth swelled. This group is called the *imprisoned*, and the location of their graveyard is a secret. Koriuaka, like every member of the council, has been sworn to secrecy, but he will tell us where this burial site is, and we'll free the imprisoned so that they may fight for us."

Juan looked at Koriuaka and then turned his attention back to the group.

"The imprisoned are a tough folk, and their sins grievous, but Balthasar has a plan to heal them once they're exhumed and control them once they're active. We're going to raise these buried demons from the depths of Hell, breathe life into them and then unleash them at the final battle."

/***/

It took them three days to get to Florida, and another two days to travel far enough into the swamp to find the graveyard. It looked like just another area of the marsh, and Balthasar marveled at how the boy seemed so sure it was the right place. *He doesn't seem to be lying,* thought Balthasar. *I just pray for his sake that his memory has served him well.*

The boy's memory held true, and they found all the caskets in the area to which he had led them. A few of the bodies were bound in chained iron caskets much like the vessel that had trapped Juan, but most of the imprisoned had been buried before the Arawaks had discovered steel; these ancient victims had been placed in stone coffins. The work was dirty but they executed it efficiently; Juan's crew had no use for the heavy coffins, so they just opened them up underwater and brought the remaining bags of bones to the surface. It took them five days to exhume all the bodies; Balthasar counted 412 in all.

While the crew was resting, Juan spoke to Balthasar in private.

"If you remember, we used leeches on the Fountain when we became immortal," said Juan.

"I do," said Balthasar.

"Legends say that those leeches gained immortality themselves and have instinctively returned to these swamps, and they're as big as alligators and twice as deadly," said Juan.

"I've heard these legends too, sir."

Juan smiled.

"We need not fear giant leeches because we're making our own legends. Koriuaka has told me that there is one more prisoner a short way from here, one that was so bad that they had to bury him separately," said Juan to Balthasar. "He's been buried for fourteen hundred years; but perhaps we'll need his ferocity most of all."

"Of course, sir," said Balthasar.

"Four hundred and thirteen soldiers isn't a pretty number, but we won't have a pretty army," said Juan. "How long will it take to reanimate these creatures?"

"We'll use a new technique of rehabilitation that will have them up and running within a week," said Balthasar. "But it will be months before they look even remotely human."

"That's fine; they're an army of *ghouls*, as it were," said Juan, "and their necrotic appearance will bring fear to the enemy. But what of control? They owe us for their freedom, but will they *fight* for us?"

"I'll use the same technique on them that we perfected with the populous," said Balthasar. "It's a crude method of management; all we'll be able to do is tell them what they can destroy."

"That may be all we need to do."

Juan turned around and looked at the bag of bones they had collected on their boat; though there were more than four hundred bodies on the boat, their remains probably weighed less than ten men in total.

"When I was under the earth, I thought of them," said Juan. "There's no camaraderie in collective suffering, but there is *understanding*. I had many a dream of rising from the ground and leading my condemned brethren on a path of revenge."

"You'll do just that, sir," said Balthasar.

"Perhaps," said Juan. "But it's not that simple. Do you remember our second conquest in Hispaniola, when we were still mortals?"

"The mountainous island we named *El Carey*," said Balthasar. "I remember it vaguely, though please remind me of its importance, sir."

"El Carey was shaped like a giant turtle shell if you recall," said Juan, "and the naturals used that terrain to devastating effect, rooting in high ground that our artillery couldn't reach. Each run became a suicide mission and the soldiers refused to go, so I convinced my superiors to loose the prisons on Puerto Rico and let some inmates fight for their freedom. We used them and finally cleaned out the savages, but at a terrible cost; the inmates soon turned against the officers, and *that* became the true battle for the island."

"I remember, sir," said Balthasar.

"This army will be instrumental in reclaiming the Fountain, for they *are* from Hell," said Juan. "They've been buried by their own people for unspeakable sins, be it rape, serial murder, cannibalism or a score other worse things."

Juan pointed at the small bodies that Cannon was piling into storage containers. They would be formidable soon, but now they were just quivering bits of sinew and bone.

"But five centuries ago our prisoners took El Carey," said Juan, "and after they revolted, we killed them and then kept the island; we got what we wanted in the end. We may have to rely on you to do the same after the imprisoned take the Fountain for us."

"Sir?"

"Monstrous armies are needed to change history, but they'll have no place in the world we'll create. You've helped find this army, and you will be tasked with disposing of them once we're done."

"I don't understand, sir."

"You must build more tanks, Balthasar," said Juan, "more tanks for more heads. If we're to create Heaven, there must be a Hell, don't you think?"

Balthasar had no words.

"I plan to have a tank for my own captives of course," said Juan. "One that I'll place beneath my throne in which I can place Adam, so that I may bring his eternal punishment personally. But you, Balthasar, you'll be in charge of making sure Hell exists under our purview so that Heaven can exist everywhere else. Can you do this?"

Balthasar continued his silence.

"Don't worry," said Juan with a smile. "We're getting ahead of ourselves; the final war has not yet even begun."

There was a loud guffawing and commotion in the distance, and Balthasar saw that Cannon was bringing back the 413th imprisoned Arawak. Even though his body was nothing more than bones, he was larger than the rest—taller and almost as broad as Cannon. Cannon's face was bleeding, and Balthasar heard Cannon complain that the buried Arawak had bitten his ear while he was being rescued.

"Fourteen hundred years in a box and he still has enough energy to bite," said Juan. "This will be a fierce one; our army from Hell will all be fierce, and angrier than we can imagine."

PANTHERS IN THE SNOW

Adam woke to birds circling him far overhead; he thought they were vultures searching for carrion, but Phage told him otherwise.

"Vultures don't like the cold," said Phage, "and they don't come this far north."

"What are they?" said Adam.

"Something else," said Phage.

Adam still hadn't regained his form yet, but was improving. When they had first dug him out he was an absolute wreck; alternately lashing out violently and collapsing into a stupor, with little in between. They decided that it wasn't safe to drive him north at first; his violent episodes were paranoid and calculated. Mayfly feared he might get out of the ropes that they put him in and attack the driver, and Phoe feared that he might hurt himself. Adam gradually gained moments of lucidity and began to understand the triggers that caused his behavior; his violence was caused by the paranoia that someone might bury him again, and his depression was caused by the thought of them succeeding. Both feelings were worst after he woke. He had the same dreams of burial that he had always had, only this time there was no coffin; it was just him and the dirt.

Though his nightmares continued, his delusions passed and so did his times of catatonia, and within a few days he was functional enough to travel. They drove north slowly, lingering at each fork in the road and asking Adam twice which path to take. He still had the map in his head and they trusted him, but they were worried that the spell under the earth might have corrupted his memory.

They still followed Adam's instructions, taking lefts and rights, passing landmarks they had seen before and some of which they weren't so sure. They passed over open, frost-covered fields and traveled through forest so thick that snow couldn't touch the ground. They saw berserkers and other creatures pass by in the distance, but as they traveled north they noticed fewer and fewer signs of life.

"The birds are following us," said Phoe, pointing to the sky.

Adam looked up, and indeed she was correct; the flock of circling birds flew above them and seemed to be following their course north.

"Are they vultures?" asked Adam again.

"No, they're not," said Phoe. "They're doves—white doves."

I always taught Phoe that birds never fly towards the cold, and they don't. Am I wrong? thought Adam. *Maybe I'm wrong about this; maybe I'm wrong about a lot of things.*

"Tell me, Phoe," said Adam. "The childhood you just had without me—was it happy?"

Phoe shook her head *no*.

"I should have been there," said Adam. "I don't know how, but I should have—"

"Bad childhoods aren't the end of the world," said Phoe. "I'm here with you now."

Adam smiled and nodded. *Perhaps I should have let her go a long time ago, happy childhood or not,* thought Adam. *Though I failed to protect her, she can now protect herself.*

"Do you remember this, Adam?" said Phage from the backseat, pointing to the trees outside. "Because I don't; this looks different than the way we came down."

Adam considered that Phage might be right; their surroundings seemed somehow *off*. Adam considered that he might be wrong, but didn't show any trepidation. He remembered the path, and the Wild Zone had been known to do this to travelers before; strange things found a way to grow or die and disappear from day to day, making the scenery in the journey forward different than the journey back.

"We've got to continue north," said Adam. "We'll check our bearings in the morning."

"All right," said Phage with a smile, "you're the boss."

They drove on into the night, with Mayfly at the wheel. He only needed an hour of sleep, but his hour was coming up. Mayfly pulled over by the side of the road and told Adam that he needed to rest, perhaps until morning; they were deep in the forest and the road was difficult to see.

Adam looked back and saw Phoe and Phage sleeping in adjoining beds, with Geryon sleeping way in the back, darkness covering all but his feet. As Adam nodded off, he felt an odd sense of comfort from his family. *We might not all be friends*, thought Adam, *but we'll always find our way back to each other. One way or another, we'll always end up in moments like this.*

/***/

They woke up to find their keys missing, and a strange note by their door, etched into a slate of wood. Mayfly couldn't understand the language, but Adam recognized it as an ancient dialect of Norse and translated it for the group:

> YOU WILL NOT DEFEAT JUAN'S ARMY WITHOUT US
>
> FOLLOW THE PATH WE HAVE MADE FOR YOU
>
> FOLLOW THE CATS, FOLLOW THE GIRL
>
> WE ARE HERE TO HELP

The crew got outside and looked around in the night sky; they could barely see through the forest, and when Mayfly shined a flashlight into the woods they couldn't see much more. Still, it was quiet and no one felt any threat.

"I can hotwire the RV," said Mayfly. "Ten minutes and we're out of here."

"Maybe we should stay," said Phoe. "See where this note leads us."

"We don't have time," said Mayfly.

"We don't, and it's a dangerous area," said Adam. "Berserkers are about and—"

"There's nothing dangerous here, not this far north," said Phoe. "It's too cold for anything to live, even berserkers."

"Little sister's got a point," said Phage. "So far I haven't seen shit."

"We go into the forest, and then what?" asked Mayfly.

"What happens if you hotwire the car and we continue our drive?" asked Phage.

"We get to our destination," said Mayfly. "We find Santos de León and the Fountain."

"Ain't that simple," said Phage, taking a leaf from the tree in front of him. "My sense is that wherever we are, we're not on the right track."

"We're not lost," said Mayfly. "Adam knows the way."

"He *knew* the way," said Phage, "but a spell under the earth gives a mind different priorities."

There was a moment of silence; Mayfly shot Adam a look to see if Phage was right, and Adam averted his gaze. Phoe took Adam's hands in hers and looked into his eyes.

"Adam, are you one hundred percent positive we're on the right track?" asked Phoe.

After a moment, Adam shook his head *no*.

"We can't just run into the forest," said Mayfly. "It could be a trap."

"They crept in, took our keys and nothing else," said Phoe. "They could have slashed our tires or done something to *us*."

"Doesn't mean they're trustworthy," said Phage. "But yeah, if Juan Ponce was behind this, we wouldn't be here right now."

Mayfly thought for a moment and then nodded his head.

"We can follow this, whatever it is, but we have to maintain a clear path back to the RV at all times," said Mayfly. "In the meantime, was anyone here awake when our keys were stolen?"

The crew looked around and everyone shook their heads *no*—everyone except for Geryon, who clicked twice.

"He's a light sleeper," said Phage with a smile. "Geryon, did you sense anyone come in here in the last hour?"

Geryon was quiet and then clicked a few times, squealed and then stopped.

"He was out wandering the woods when he thought he heard someone come out of here, but he's not sure," said Phage. "The sound waves he put out spooked 'em and they ran away."

"What did he hear?" asked Adam.

Geryon clicked again while Phage nodded.

"Just like the note says," said Phage. "Geryon thought he heard a child and two creatures that sounded like lions."

/***/

They saw an eight-year-old girl at sunrise, barefoot and sandy blonde, with tan skin and angular features. She was beautiful and was wearing a moose pelt and little else. She shook their keys, giggled and then disappeared into the forest like a pixie spirit. Two creatures followed her; they looked like brown housecats but were as big as hyenas.

"Well," said Phage. "The note doesn't lie; shall we follow?"

"If we do," said Phoe, "we'll need someone to guard the RV."

"Geryon'll do it," said Phage. "I want to follow this little forest girl, because I am *officially* intrigued."

/***/

They followed the little girl through the forest, nipping at her heels but always slightly behind. Sometimes she stayed close and beckoned them forth with her hand, and sometimes she skipped ahead until she was just a speck of movement on the forest's horizon. But they followed her on and on, and though Adam was keeping track of their location as best he could, their surroundings were beginning to look the same to him. *You can't remember landmarks when there are no landmarks,* thought Adam, but he quashed the doubt inside and pressed on.

The girl eventually hung back long enough for Adam to get a better look at her. Though he pleaded with her in her note's Norse dialect to stop and tell them where they were headed, she just laughed and ran forward with her creatures.

"What are those cats?" asked Phage.

"Panthers," said Mayfly.

"Panthers don't live this far north," said Phage, "not even close."

"You could say the same for barefoot little girls," said Mayfly.

They followed the child for hours. Adam sensed that Mayfly was getting nervous due to the time, and Phage was winded by the travel. Phoe was having the time of her life though. *This is the Phoe that I remember,* thought Adam with a smile. *She won't want to leave this forest.*

They lost sight of the girl and were worried that she had gone too far ahead, but soon they heard a whistle and spotted her by a frozen stream. They approached her and she displayed a rock, thrust it through the ice and reached the rushing water below. She tossed the rock to Mayfly, and he caught it and did the same. Soon they all drank heartily; the water was bitterly freezing, but the group was thirsty and it soothed their palates. After quenching his thirst, Adam looked up to see the little girl down on all fours just like the cats next to her, lapping up the water with her tongue. She sat up, giggled and then climbed the tree behind her, as quick as a squirrel. She was gone for about five minutes, but came down with pockets full of nuts and berries. She ate a few in front of the group, and then approached them, giving them each a handful. She was quite small and they were close enough to grab her and demand that she tell them where they were headed, but nobody dared do it. *She's trustworthy, but we're also deep in the woods,* thought Adam. *If she were to run away, we'd be lost forever.*

The crew began to relax around her and her panthers. The nuts she had provided brought them a strange warmth, and though the panthers were fierce enough to maul any one of them, they seemed under complete control, as if they were sentient. She laughed twice and smiled, and then ran off deeper into the snowy woods. After a few moments she was gone, and they had only her cats to guide them.

They went deeper into the forest, and the cats kept pace with them much more consistently than the girl had. After another hour of walking, Adam realized that he hadn't seen her since the frozen river. Mayfly spotted her high in the tree canopy, jumping from branch to branch without making a sound.

"How long's she gonna do this?" asked Phage.

"We need a plan to get back if she runs much longer," said Mayfly.

The crew stopped and the panthers stopped with them.

"Kid's right," said Phage. "This trip gets weirder and weirder, all for a pair of keys and—"

Phoe stared straight ahead as if she had seen a ghost, and it distracted Phage. Adam looked ahead and saw a small clearing in the woods. Within the clearing was a stone homestead that had a low, circular wall around it. The stone buildings inside were large and covered with animal skins, but their corners were too square to be makeshift huts. The structure looked like it had been there for centuries.

"Looks like we're at our destination," said Phage. "And it's a poor man's castle."

"Close," said Adam. "It's a fortress; a Viking ring fortress."

/***/

The little girl greeted them at the gate, which swung to the side slowly in anticipation of their arrival. Adam was hesitant to enter, but trusted her enough to walk through. *Those with bad intentions generally take their first opportunity to employ them,* thought Adam.

They went into the interior of the fortress and found it to be a series of boxed houses covered with animal pelts, with each room connected to one another by a stone hallway. Most of the land inside was empty and frozen, and when the group entered the first building, it didn't get much warmer. The rooms were dimly lit and decorated with various artifacts, some Viking and some relics local to northern Canada. There were metal helmets and two-handed axes on one wall and Inuit totems on the next. The girl led them through a room that appeared to be filled with metal instruments of torment, but Adam soon recognized them as the traps of fur traders, covered in rust and no longer functional.

"A Viking castle that looks like a museum, in the land of the Eskimos," said Phage. "This is fucked up."

"I studied Viking culture for a day," said Mayfly. "They stopped building ring fortresses a thousand years ago."

"I can see why," said Phage. "Walls are low; this would be easy to invade."

"Easy to burn down, too," said Phoe, touching the wooden buttresses holding up the ceiling.

Adam looked around; the little girl had disappeared, and so had her cats.

"This fortress is creepin' me out," said Phage. "Adam, what kind of Vikings live here, anyway?"

Adam tried to remember, but his mind was hazy. He knew he had been in a ring fortress before but couldn't recall any of the details. *My class doesn't forget details,* thought Adam. *We remember everything.*

"It's okay, Phage," said Phoe.

"How do you know?" asked Phage.

"I sense it's okay," said Phoe. "Whoever's here is on our side; I just sense it."

"Well I guess we're in luck, then," said Phage with a smile, looking at the front of the hall.

Before them was a large, blond-bearded man, about the size of Brogg and dressed in animal pelts. Next to him was a dark-skinned woman with Indian features, and next to her was the girl; it was clear that the girl who had led them through the forest was their daughter. They had four panthers by their side, and when Adam focused on the Indian woman, her eyes glowed.

"My name is Leif the Bold, first of my king's Húskarlar, traveler, conqueror and warrior, and ruler of all you see before you," said the man in an old Viking dialect that Adam recognized. "This is my wife Yahíma and our daughter Dagmena. Welcome to our estate; we're no threat to you, but you're in great danger. Juan's forces have increased, and if you stay on your path, you'll face a quick and extraordinarily painful defeat. We're here to help you avoid that fate, and spare you an eternity of torture under Juan's throne."

Adam translated and Phage smiled.

"Looks like we made the right choice," said Phage. "Looks like we got a couple of new friends."

/***/

They ate reindeer meat and washed it down with a cloudy, sweet ale that Dagmena poured from a barrel in the corner. Leif took a piece of bread from a basket and then passed it on; when it got to Adam he realized that it was not bread but dried fish. *The streams here are frozen eight months out of the year,* thought Adam. *They must travel far from here to gather food, and they plan well.*

Dagmena gave Adam a jar of white paste and gestured that he should spread it on the fish, and he found that it tasted like butter and the dried salted fish tasted like a cracker. He nodded in approval, and Dagmena smiled and then ran away giggling.

"Before we tell you the truth of the danger you ... the danger we *face, allow me to tell you our tale,"* said Leif in his old Viking dialect.

"Speak, please, speak slow," said Mayfly, mirroring the Viking dialect. *"I translate."*

"Two speakers of our tongue!" said Leif with a hearty laugh. "This is rare indeed; even many of my fellow warriors who still live have forgotten this language."

"He learns fast," said Adam.

"Very well," said Leif, "my tale, slowly. I was a human Viking, working as the foreign Húskarlar bodyguard for Cnut the great, amongst others. I was a standard brute, drinking and fighting and whatnot, and one morning found myself conscripted on a longship headed towards what's now called Newfoundland; this was nigh on a thousand years ago. We met the natives; they killed some of ours and we some of theirs, but we didn't have the enormous impact that your conquistadors had five hundred years later.

"We were called back to the motherland, but I had nothing to return to," said Leif, "so I and two score other warriors stayed. We vowed to spend the rest of our days in exploration, and vowed to travel south until there was no more *south* beneath us. We journeyed down the continent, interacting with culture after culture, language after language, landscape after landscape. Some areas were friendly, most were dangerous, but we kept to our vows and traveled onwards.

"Five years later, and twenty of our comrades fallen, our remaining warriors reached an Arawak tribe with glowing eyes—the tribe of immortals. I met the wife you see before you and we decided to stay to serve as their guardians. After a few fierce battles with neighboring tribes, they took us in and decided to give us their gift of life. Two centuries later, my wife and I had a child and I wanted her to grow up in a different climate, in a land to call her own. So we came up here with a family of panthers to which they had also given the gift of immortality, and here we stay, two undying parents and a perpetually youthful daughter."

"Sounds idyllic," said Adam.

"It is," said Leif.

Leif nodded at his daughter, and she went to another room and came back with a white bird in her hand. She handed it to her father, and he took a small note attached to the bird's leg and handed it to Adam. It was written in an odd language neither he nor Mayfly could understand.

"We've largely split apart, and these doves are the immortal Arawak's only method of communication; the only thing that connects us all," said Leif. "And it says that Juan has the upper hand."

"How so?" said Adam.

"He's decapitated the Arawak council and unearthed the tribe's criminals to build his army," said Leif. "The criminals are bad men, and I should know; I buried a few of them myself."

Leif took a swig of the cloudy ale.

"As of right now, you'll reach your destination," said Leif, "but when Juan attacks with the imprisoned at his side, they'll run you over in a matter of moments."

"We will have Fountain on our side," said Mayfly, his Norse grammar now almost perfect.

"She can change the world, but she can't fight a war by herself," said Leif. "You'll need something stronger to break Juan's soldiers; an immortal army filled only with the desire to kill is hard to stop. You'll shoot them down and they'll come out of the ground that night and tear you in half. These are immortals without consciences, and they can't be broken, because they have no souls to break."

Mayfly translated, but Phage cut him off.

"Listen to me, King," said Phage. "I appreciate the warning, but I'm not gonna run from Juan or anyone else, and I don't know if you've heard but I've taken down a lot of people, *including* a few armies."

Mayfly translated for Leif, and the Viking spoke back to Mayfly directly.

"Tell him he hasn't seen an army like this," said Leif. "Tell him the imprisoned army doesn't respond to disease."

Mayfly translated, but Phage cut him off again.

"Tell *him* I don't give a shit," interrupted Phage. "If my bag of tricks doesn't work, fine, then ask him what will. I'm tired of being lectured about prophecies, invincible armies and whatnot. The future's what we make it, and *anyone* can be beaten, even Juan. Ask the Viking how to do it, and if he doesn't know, tell him to have his little brownie give us our keys back."

Mayfly translated, taking out Phage's vulgarity, but the king got his tone and started to laugh.

"I have heard of this one, even from my place here in the woods," said Leif. "They said he was a demon, and I see that in him. Demons aren't always bad, especially when they're on your side. The sick one will serve you well in the upcoming battle."

Leif sighed deeply and looked at his wife, who was downcast and sad.

"But the reality is that the other side has *four hundred* demons," said Leif. "You'll be crushed as it stands."

"Can you help us?" asked Adam, also becoming impatient.

"Yes; that's why I brought you here," said Leif. "I've already sent doves to both the remaining immortal Arawaks and my twenty immortal Viking compatriots. *This* will be your army, but it will take some time for them to reach the final battle place; my wife's tribe is now all around the world, mostly living without any sort of modern technology.

"As far as my compatriots, some are bankers in Oslo, some live much as I do, but I'll get word to them and they'll come. Though many of them have not picked up their axes in over three hundred years, I assure you they'll join this battle."

Leif sighed again, and then smiled.

"You're going to the Surgeon?" asked Leif.

"Do you know how to get there?" asked Mayfly.

"Yes," said Leif. "So does every Arawak and Viking. We'll get you there and get you an army, but this might not be enough."

"What is it that we need?" asked Mayfly. "Tell us, because we don't have much time."

"I don't know," said Leif. "You'll need an *edge*, something that I've not yet thought of, something that none of us aside from you can provide. All I can promise is that my troops and I will be there fighting for you and giving you time to think of this *edge*. We can't win the war for you; all we can do is provide protection until you figure out how to do it yourself."

/***/

They spent the night in the fortress; it was too dark and too cold outside to return to their RV.

"And there are some dangerous creatures about," said Leif's Indian wife Yahíma in heavily accented English. "Even up here there are dangerous things out at night."

Adam noticed that Mayfly couldn't sleep and was pacing the grounds endlessly, even venturing out into the bitter cold. *His time is short here, and is growing shorter still*, thought Adam. *I don't understand mortality like he does, but we're not on his time now, nor mine. We're on the time that fate has laid out for us, and we have no option but to follow it.*

Adam couldn't sleep either because of his nightmares; they were more intense than they had ever been. Now, as soon as he closed his eyes he was under the earth again, trapped and unable to move, and he would immediately wake up in a panic. If he did manage to sleep, the nightmare would get worse, with the dirt crushing him until he woke. The fourth time he screamed, he opened his eyes to see Yahíma's dark figure in the shadows.

"You are not right," she said. "Come with me if you want be right."

/***/

Her English was passable, but they found a better common language in French; she had spent some time with fur trappers in the 1600s and spoke an old, rough dialect, but they could communicate. She took him to another room and served him one more glass of the cloudy ale from a barrel that looked like it hadn't been touched in a century. Like all the rooms in the ring fortress, it was square, dark, and lit by a small fire in the corner.

"I feel something dark and heavy within you," said Yahíma. *"I sense you went through a traumatic experience?"*

"Of sorts," said Adam.

"I know of your burial, Adam; your mayfly told me of it."

Adam looked down.

"What's dark within you goes beyond that experience," said Yahíma. "Your recent burial only served to bring it out."

Adam nodded, but couldn't reply.

"Would you like to explore it further?"

"There's no time," said Adam.

"There's always time, even now," said Yahíma. "And broken men don't fare well in battle."

Adam didn't want to pursue the course she was laying before him but couldn't turn away from her. There was something about this woman that he couldn't quite grasp, and that was rare for him. *Perhaps she has some strange spanner power of hypnosis that I don't understand,* thought Adam. *Perhaps I'm broken and don't understand anything anymore.*

"Okay," said Adam. "I'd like you to help me."

Yahíma nodded and then went to the barrel of ale and brought out a wooden flask from behind it. She poured out thick, dark green liquid from the flask into a pot and bid that Adam sit on a chair in the center of the room. She then put the pot beneath Adam's chair and went to the fire in the corner and brought out some embers using tongs. She put the embers into the pot below Adam's feet, and the green liquid started to smoke. Yahíma then went to a far wall, picked up a leather flask and poured its liquid into two cups. The liquid was odorless and solid white, like milk.

"This is a technique I developed, half borne of the ancient Greek oracles, half of my people," said Yahíma. "Instead of divining the future, you divine your past. I'm about to send you to a dreamscape, and though none of it is real I warn you that it will feel real, as true as you are sitting in front of me now. It won't be pleasant; you'll feel pain and fear, perhaps more than anything you've ever felt, because we'll be traveling into the farthest depths of your being and you might not like what you find there. Do you wish to continue?"

"I do," said Adam.

"As you drink, stare at me and make sure that I'm the last thing that you see," said Yahíma. "This is so that I'll be there to help you in your dream. It won't be *me*, of course; it will be your mind's creation, but to you I'll be *there*."

"I understand," said Adam.

The smoke from under his chair was pouring out of its container and had expanded to fill the room. Adam could barely see Yahíma, but she eventually cut through the mist and handed him the cup of white liquid. He noticed that she had her own cup and her own chair, and they were both now covered in the thick vapor. Adam saw her holding up the cup to her lips, and soon her eyes glowed through the smoke.

"Now drink, Adam," she said. "And look straight ahead; make sure that I'm the last thing you see."

/***/

Her words entered his thoughts, and his thoughts slowly turned into dreams. Adam heard thousands of voices from all around him, as if he were in a crowd of people begging for his attention. The bewilderment passed and soon his mind was as lucid as Yahíma had said it would be.

He looked around and saw that he was floating over fog, and then realized that the fog was clouds made out of the smoke that Yahíma had brought from under his chair. He saw that he was on the inside of a large sphere seemingly the size of the Earth; he looked above and saw that the mist coated the inside completely. He flew outward to the edge of the sphere and peeked beneath the clouds and saw worlds on the edges below, and recognized them faintly.

He saw a grime-covered eighteenth-century London, followed by a stone wall patrolled by Roman soldiers. *This is Hadrian's Wall*, thought Adam. *This is the wall that demarcated the line between British Rome and the Barbarians beyond.*

He floated over a marble palace with gold-lined rooms and pathways covered with a hundred different types of animals on the inside. There were thousands of people walking within its walls, and Adam noticed that some of them appeared to be European; he even noticed himself. *This is when I accompanied Marco Polo*, thought Adam. *This is Kublai Khan's palace of Xanadu. What are all these places?*

"They're your memories, Adam," said a voice behind him as if it was answering his thoughts.

He turned around and saw Yahíma floating next to him, only she had the pale skin of the Fountain. Adam looked closer and saw that her skin was actually *translucent* and that a pure black heart beat within her chest.

"Choose one place, one of your memories, and we'll visit," said Yahíma.

"Which one?" asked Adam.

"It will come to you," said Yahíma.

Her beating black heart entranced Adam; it pumped rhythmically, spraying out glowing lights through her bloodstream that faded as they traveled outward. He was still lucid, so he turned his attention below to the dreamscape of his memories. He flew forward over Kublai Khan's gilded city and then passed the outer walls to find a dusty plain near a cave, where a blond boy was lying on the ground.

"That place," said Adam, not knowing why. "I want to go there."

"So be it," said Yahíma, and she flew down.

As she flew past Adam, he took a closer look at her dark heart and noticed that it had a small face of its own.

/***/

They landed on the ground near the blond boy and realized that he was dead. His body had been badly burnt by the sun, and from his severely bruised face, it looked like death might have been a welcome end for him.

"These are the Mines of Capua, second century BC," said Adam. "They sent slaves here to work for the rest of their lives."

"A tough place for anyone, but I understand that the fair-skinned Celtic peoples fared worst of all in this place," said Yahíma, kneeling by the blond boy.

"They would last a few months," said Adam. "The Romans would send them here as a death sentence."

"And why were you here, Adam? Weren't you a Roman soldier?"

"I was," said Adam.

"But you were sent here. Why?"

"I was sent with my cohort," said Adam. "One of our troop had refused an order to set fire to a village, so they condemned him for cowardice."

"The punishment for cowardice in the Roman army was cruel," said Yahíma.

"*Decimation*," said Adam. "In a sense, the cruelest punishment one can imagine."

Adam looked beyond the boy; a group of bound men were walking towards the mines, prodded and beaten as they walked. Adam recognized the men that he had once fought alongside, but only barely. They were bearded, dirty and rail-thin from months of malnutrition.

"Decimation," said Yahíma. "When one in your troop is condemned for cowardice, the cohort is split into groups of ten, and one in each ten is picked at random to die. He must be beaten to death by the other nine. He had nothing to do with the cowardice, and yet he dies at the hands of his friends."

"Yes," said Adam. "It was a cruel practice."

"But it turned Rome's army into a fearsome machine, did it not?"

"Perhaps."

"And Rome gave many gifts to the world," said Yahíma. "So perhaps the practice of decimation was worthwhile."

"No," said Adam, shaking his head. "No, it wasn't."

"Why not?"

"I don't know why not," said Adam. "It just wasn't."

There was a whip crack and then some yelling. A guard was beating one of Adam's cohorts with a club. Three other prisoners went to defend him, but they were ineffective; all three of them combined probably weighed less than the guard that wielded the club. Adam looked closer and found that one of the prisoners was his old self, bearded, thin and feigning weakness.

"Your group of ten is here, is this correct?" asked Yahíma.

"Yes," said Adam, "all ten."

"All ten?"

"We refused the order to kill one of our own," said Adam. "So we were sent here as a group."

"You fought nobly for Rome, battle after battle, and then you committed one more noble act, perhaps the most noble of all," said Yahíma. "And as a reward, you were sent here."

"Yes," said Adam.

"It was unjust, but once again, such actions built Rome," said Yahíma. "So perhaps it was worthwhile."

"No," Adam said, shaking his head more vehemently. "It was not."

Adam looked at Yahíma's heart; it had taken the shape of a small child and was now spreading its dark limbs outwards, emanating beads of light with every breath its host took.

/***/

Later that night it was pouring rain, and Adam was in an iron cage that held his old self and his cohorts. The prison guards had been instructed by Rome to place the cage outside in the event of rain, and the ten men slept under the downpour. Adam felt it too; though the men in the cage couldn't see him, this was more real than any dream he'd ever had.

Adam watched his own self, bearded and gaunt, wake up and look around with faintly glowing eyes. His past self took a small knife hidden in the cloths around his waist, and he proceeded to look for a weak part of the cage. Finding a bar thinner than the rest, he looked around to make sure no guards were on notice, and then proceeded to whittle away at the cage.

"Escape," said Yahíma. "Escape always holds salvation, regardless of the indignity around."

"No," said Adam, watching his past self knife through the bar. "That only works if you're successful. I led them out of the cage, but a week later we were caught."

"But you didn't give in to the indignity around you," said Yahíma. "History ultimately vindicated you and your cohorts."

"History did no such thing," said Adam. "It never vindicates those it kills."

/***/

Yahíma snapped her fingers and next thing he knew, he was in a dusty fighting pit, watching his old self battle a man twice his size.

"They caught you and sold you and your nine cohorts to the owner of an arena, on the condition that you all die in the gladiator pit within three months," said Yahíma.

"He accomplished that in two," said Adam.

"Except for you," said Yahíma.

Adam watched the crowd cheer half-heartedly as the bigger man pummeled his old self mercilessly. Adam's old self was clean-shaven, but not in much better shape than he had been as a prisoner of Capua.

"They billed you as the man who couldn't be killed," said Yahíma.

"But I ended up as the man who took endless beatings without fighting back," said Adam. "It didn't quite have the draw they wanted."

"Your dignity survived," said Yahíma.

"That, or I never learned how to fight," said Adam.

"Either way, you did the right thing," said Yahíma. "Of your limited options, you chose the best path."

"Did I?" asked Adam, looking grimly at Yahíma.

Adam knew where she was going, and this time snapped his fingers to move them forward. Right before the scene changed, he took one more look at her heart; the child inside her continued to shoot light through her body but was now crying. Its tears were deep red and just barely visible against its dark skin.

/***/

They next appeared a kilometer from the arena, and Adam's old self was tied and gagged on the ground. There were two other men there, one of them bound next to Adam, and both Adam and his old self looked on helplessly as the third man beat the second.

"The arena owner was given three months to kill all ten of you," said Yahíma. "This is month three, and Rome's emissary is set to arrive tomorrow."

"They were always on time," said Adam.

"The arena owner couldn't make money off you, so he tried to kill you," said Yahíma. "Failing that, he killed the man next to you in your stead. He killed an innocent man so that he could survive Rome's punishment."

They watched the owner of the arena beat the man until he stopped moving, then the owner drove him through with a lance and the victim was still. The arena owner then took a club and beat the dead man until his face was unrecognizable.

"Rome came and they thought it was me," said Adam. "I left the arena, but an innocent man had to die for that to happen."

Adam saw that the black child had been silently crying out in pain, and bloody tears now coursed through her host's veins, making her pale body glow bright red.

/***/

Yahíma snapped her fingers once more and they were in another cage, this one wooden and open-topped. They were being pulled on a horse's cart, and Adam saw that there was another woman in the cage with him; a woman with a mangled leg, holding a child. The woman was in a deep fever and barely conscious. Adam saw his old self walking by the cart with loosely bound feet, and then he stood up in the cart to see that he was in a caravan of thirty people. They were walking in the desert and the heat beat down on them more mercilessly than in either Capua or the arena; there was no one else around, not even animals.

"The owner of the arena sold you to a slaver, and the slaver took you on a yearlong journey across North Africa," said Yahíma. "Why?"

"To this day I have no idea," said Adam.

"Who was she?" asked Yahíma, pointing at the feverish woman with the child and the mangled leg.

"A prostitute from the fighting pit," said Adam. "She had been with one of my cohorts and became impregnated before he died. She was sold to the slaver to be his concubine, and he thought the child was his."

"She doesn't look well," said Yahíma.

"After she had the child, she fell off the cart and broke her leg; the fever that would kill her came soon thereafter."

"What happened to her child?"

"The slaver raised him until his face came in, and when he realized the child wasn't his, he sold the boy at the nearest village."

"And what happened to the boy?"

Adam crept closer to the mother holding her infant, smelling her sweat as she held onto the child with trembling arms, trying to suckle him.

"He grew up amongst thieves, and was later recruited by Carthage to fight in their Punic wars," said Adam. "He became a killer of Roman soldiers, known for slitting their throats while they slept."

"He did worse than that, Adam. Women, children, even villages—"

"But he was known for slitting Roman soldiers' throats in their sleep," said Adam. "That was his legacy."

"Misery begets misery, but it doesn't get in the way of progress," said Yahíma.

"Progress?" said Adam.

"Progress," said Yahíma, her voice shifting to a softer tone.

Adam realized that he was now alone with Yahíma in a graveyard, with cold grey mist all around them. The stone tombs were unmarked; the year, or even the century, was unknowable.

"Humanity continues, Adam," said Yahíma without moving her lips. "Society progresses, and the individual pays the cost for it to do so."

Adam realized that the dark child in Yahíma's chest was now speaking the words, and her outer body seemed to be in a trance.

"The cost is deep; it might take a thousand lives to end an inconsequential war," said the child within Yahíma. "It might take a million deaths to reveal a single truth."

"But why pay the cost?" asked Adam. "Why? What will it reveal?"

The child inside Yahíma's body began to glow, and it smiled. It spread out its arms and light poured out of its body into its host's bloodstream. The light became too bright and spilled outward, washing away the cemetery outside, until it was so white that Adam felt that he was flying through the air, bathed in warmth.

If being buried alive carries an opposite feeling, thought Adam, *this is it.*

Adam woke and he was in the room; there was no smoke, just him and Yahíma. This was no longer a dream, Yahíma was no longer pale, and she no longer had a child in place of her heart. He was awake, and it was real.

/***/

"Though it may have felt like it, I was not with you," said Yahíma. "So tell me what you saw, sparing no detail."

Adam told her everything and she thought for a few minutes.

"You've experienced suffering in your life," said Yahíma. "Is this true?"

"Not a great deal," said Adam. "I don't feel physical pain like others and don't think I've—"

"I said you've *experienced* suffering, not that you've suffered yourself," she said. "There's a difference."

"How so?"

"You watch others around you endure torment and experience it secondhand," said Yahíma. "You may enter a sacrificial pit with a group of martyrs, but you'll not experience their exact agony as the lances tear through your bodies; their wounds won't heal, but yours will. You'll not escape the pit unscathed though, for though your body might emerge intact, you'll forever hear their cries as they drew their last breaths, and you'll always remember the tears of those near to them."

Adam nodded; he'd seen countless atrocities and he'd remembered every single one.

"The rest of the world isn't burdened with this secondhand experience of humanity's anguish. When the realities of life get too great, people die and the new generation is there to take over, ever forgetful of the abominations that have come before.

"And that's how the world can function. There's been tremendous progress over the course of history, but humanity only sees what has been built, not the human cost to *have it built*. Only you have seen the *pain* behind the world's achievements, whether it's a slave killed to construct a pyramid or a hundred thousand families displaced by a war that yields a lasting peace."

Yahíma thought for a moment and then looked at Adam.

"Has your memory returned?" she asked.

Adam nodded; his memory had returned in even sharper detail.

"Yes," he said. "Completely."

"Think back to the woman in your dream state," said Yahíma. "When she died, did you feel anguish?"

"Yes," said Adam.

"Do you still feel anguish?"

"Yes."

Yahíma smiled, went up to the far corner and came back with two flasks of brown liquid. Adam drank and it tasted of ashes, but it relaxed him.

"Both humans and spanners have deep emotions, but the emotions have hard limits," said Yahíma. "If someone's parent or child dies, it's devastating, but if a thousand children died in a mudslide overseas they'd say *it's tragic* and then go about their day. If those children had perished a thousand years ago, even the most empathetic person in the world couldn't shed a tear."

Yahíma looked deeply into Adam's eyes.

"You're different, Adam; you still feel all the grief that has come before you, and your memory won't let it go. Every tragedy, every death, every bit of sadness ever experienced registers with you and doesn't leave. If I were to tell you a thousand children perished in a mudslide, let's say two millennia ago, what comes to mind?"

"Antioch," said Adam, not missing a beat. "I was in Emperor Trajan's troop and an earthquake destroyed the city, and we were near a school that collapsed."

Adam shuddered when he thought back to that time; he remembered the children's cries as they were trapped under the rubble, the parent's wails as the school eventually fell silent, and the overwhelming bleakness of the city the next day.

"There's a limit to human grief because it allows humanity to function in the wake of the surrounding chaos, but you are blessed with no such limitation. The collective pain of humanity is your burden, and every year it gets heavier."

Adam nodded in agreement and drank some more of the brown liquid. It continued relaxing him, but not in the blunt way that cognac helped him relax. The brown liquid seemed to bring the world into focus and didn't leave him exhausted; he felt as if he could keep drinking it in this room forever. His mouth had gotten used to the taste too; it no longer tasted of ashes and instead reminded him of the white tea that he'd drunk on the Sentinel islands.

"Why was I given this burden?" asked Adam.

Yahíma smiled as if he was asking just the question she had wanted to hear.

"You weren't given this burden just to suffer," said Yahíma. "Your burden and your powers are one and the same, and they were given to you for a much higher purpose than you'd ever considered."

Adam looked at the woman but didn't know what to say; in eight thousand years, he'd never considered the big questions surrounding his existence.

"You look lost, Adam," said Yahíma.

"I am," said Adam. "I've never given much thought to my own purpose."

"Nor does anyone until mortality starts to show itself," said Yahíma with a smile. "But let's speak of purpose; not of yours, but of everyone else's. Tell me, Adam, to what end is humanity headed? And what is the purpose of spanners? To what end is our kind headed?"

"I don't know," said Adam.

"Nor do I; nor does anyone else."

Yahíma looked at Adam as if he were supposed to take the next logical step by himself. He sipped the brown liquid, thought for a moment and then spoke.

"I am destined to understand everything," said Adam.

Yahíma smiled.

"You've experienced the entirety of human history and spanner mythos both, not just through study and hearsay, but you *have been here the whole time, and you remember everything*. One day, all the experience in your head will coalesce, and you'll realize the big answers to the big questions."

"Not me—I won't have the answers," said Adam with a laugh. "I can barely navigate a subway station by myself and—"

"*All* the answers are within you, Adam," said Yahíma, ignoring Adam's self-deprecation. "If you find a way to cut through the pain, it will be *you* who holds the answers to everything we've been asking, namely *why have spanners been brought to this earth, and to what end will they bring humanity?*"

Adam nodded and thought about that for a moment.

"So you're saying that I'll understand the answer to *why we are here*," said Adam, "spanner and human both?"

"Given enough time, you will understand just that," said Yahíma, "because at the end of time, both spanner and human histories will be one and the same."

Yahíma took another swig of her drink and thought for a moment.

"Though the answers lie within you, they'll not be answered now, because Juan is out to make his own path, a path that culminates in power for himself and nothing else," said Yahíma. "This makes him dangerous; Juan's not burdened by the past, and while you sit and wring your hands, he's bringing an army to put your head on a pike. He'll bring a blunt ignorance to this battle, and that's a strength, so don't underestimate him."

"I won't," said Adam. "I assure you of this."

"Good," said Yahíma. "And though your burden of knowledge is an unwieldy tool in the realm of battle, it can still be used."

"How so?"

"Adam, you must use it as motivation to *win*. If you fail this fight, Juan will find a way to destroy you, and the secrets to our purpose will find a way to die as well."

Adam nodded, and the weight of his experience seemed to shift, as if it was no longer a burden that weighed him down, but something important to be carried. *I've never considered the importance of purpose,* thought Adam. *Perhaps that's why I took care of Phoe, lifetime after lifetime; she gave me a purpose.*

"Thank you," said Adam.

"Of course," said Yahíma. "Is there any other way I can assist you?"

"Yes," said Adam. "Not me, though; there's someone else with whom I'd like you to speak."

"I hope he speaks French as well as you," said Yahíma.

"I'm sure he speaks it better," said Adam. "But even if not, he speaks your mother tongue of Arawak like a native."

/***/

Yahíma didn't have to give Mayfly the full oracle treatment. She simply took a draft of the brown liquid and offered Mayfly a glass. Mayfly drank it quickly and then asked for another, explaining his problems in Arawak. At first Mayfly translated what both he and Yahíma were saying for Adam, but being frustrated with that, Mayfly switched to the Old Norse dialect of her husband. Yahíma was surprised at his fluency.

"I understand mayflies learn languages within an hour," said Yahíma in Old Norse. *"But still, Adam, this is impressive."*

"He does a lot of things well," said Adam.

"Understood," said Yahíma, "and it's clear where his pain comes from."

"Where?" asked Mayfly.

"Mayflies don't live long, but this rarely concerns them, much as a twenty-year-old human doesn't overworry about his death sixty years hence," said Yahíma. "But you, Mayfly, have now been imbued with duty, perhaps too much. You want to win the war and free your brethren back home, both of which you could do if given enough time. You don't fear your own death, Mayfly; you fear leaving important things undone."

Mayfly's not been given enough time, thought Adam, *and I've been given too much.*

"How can I solve this?" asked Mayfly.

"You can be granted an *extension*, as it were," said Yahíma, "from the Surgeon."

"Santos de León?" asked Mayfly.

"Yes," said Yahíma, "though you may think there are more important things for him to do, all the characters have a role to play in this war, and him giving you more time is just as important as him splitting the Fountain in two."

Yahíma drank from her cup again and looked Mayfly in the eye.

"It won't be easy; the procedure Santos will do on you will be extraordinarily painful."

"I have no other choice," said Mayfly with a smile.

"Perhaps none of us have choices as the battle approaches," said Yahíma, now addressing them both, "but be assured that you're headed in the right direction, even though it might not seem like it when you enter the Surgeon's clutches."

"The legends surrounding the Surgeon are dark," said Adam. "Can we trust him completely?"

"Yes," said Yahíma, "because though Santos and Juan are cut from the same cloth, there's a fundamental difference in their motives: Juan seeks power, and Santos seeks knowledge. The Surgeon might not be friendly, but he's not out to harm anyone."

/***/

The next morning, Leif bid his daughter Dagmena to escort them back to their RV, with the instructions that she would guide them to the Surgeon's compound.

"My wife and I must stay here to send out more doves," he said. "Wrangling a distant Viking army takes patience, but we will be there."

And with that, Leif's daughter left the ring fortress, fearlessly venturing back into the woods with her two panthers.

/***/

They found the RV and Geryon was nearby, hiding in the forest. Phage yelled for Geryon to come out, and the big man emerged from the woods, his tall frame blending in with the trees that had concealed him.

Phage told Geryon what had happened, and Geryon clicked in apparent understanding.

They all got in the RV and drove north. Three days later they reached the compound, and from the outside it looked bleak. It had dull-grey towering walls that stretched endlessly to the horizon and leaned slightly outwards, making the walls impossible to climb. The fortress was covered with mist, and much of the fog rested in the open center of the structure. Adam looked closer, and it looked like the vapor was being produced from the middle of the compound and pushed outward through the open air. It was large, but the fog concealed its true size; from the outside the walls stretched on until they couldn't be seen.

"This land is a series of fortresses," said Phoe.

A gate at the front of the fortress opened up to reveal two strangely clean and good-looking men, who smiled and bid the group in with their RV.

"It's another fortress all right," said Phage, "but something tells me it's gonna be the last one we visit for a while."

A SURGEON'S WELCOME

They pulled the RV into the gate and it shut behind them with a thud. The two iridescently beautiful guards immediately went to the door of the RV and opened it for the crew. Mayfly got out and had to take off his grey hooded jacket; it was quite comfortable inside despite the fact that it was open air. Dagmena snuck past while giggling, running over the terrain as if she had been there before, and soon she disappeared behind a building in the far distance.

The architecture inside was clean, but held no charm beyond that. It was painted in solid greys and whites, made for protection and little else. *It's like a prison from the inside,* thought Mayfly. *So far it fits in with the dark legends surrounding the Surgeon.*

Mayfly noticed that the sky was beautiful from within the compound though; the mist that covered the fortress was thick enough to act as an atmosphere and formed a barrier against the elements above. It was not only warm inside but also *bright*; Mayfly looked up and saw that the mist diffused the sunlight perfectly and even held the blue tinge of a real sky.

Underneath the mist, the fortress was laid out more like a campus than a prison; though the buildings inside the walls were dull and imposing, there was land in between them and the land held strange trees and grasses. *I've never seen plants like this,* thought Mayfly, *not even in books, and definitely not this far north.*

Soon, everybody had gotten out of the RV and the others seemed as surprised and as cautious of the place as Mayfly, except for Phage who was smoking a cigarette and blowing the smoke upwards to join the mist above.

"My name is Skarr," announced the first guard. "We welcome you to our home at the end of the world."

"Thank you," said Adam. "We'd like to see our friends, and also speak with Santos de León."

"Your comrades are all safe, I assure you, and Santos is currently working. You will see them all in the morning," said Skarr. "We've prepared five rooms for you, and you must go to them."

"Five rooms?" asked Adam.

"Yes," said Skarr, "one for each of you."

"I'm sorry," said Adam, "but we'd like to make sure our friends are safe, and we'd like to speak with Santos now."

"I assure you, you'll see your comrades and Santos tomorrow morning," said Skarr. "Now you must retire to your rooms."

Mayfly was still hesitant, but Phage broke the silence with a smile and pointed in the direction of the buildings.

"This fortress is a little weird, Skarr," said Phage, "but I've slept in worse places, particularly in the last few days. I'm not gonna turn down my own room, 'specially if it's safe from berserkers, trolls and all the other shit up here."

"We're quite safe here in Santos's kingdom," said Skarr.

"Good enough for me," said Phage. "Now, take me to my private room."

Phage walked towards the buildings and the impetus prodded the group forward, with the guards walking along with them. Adam gave a quick shake of his head to Mayfly, signaling him to hang back.

"*What do you think of this place?*" whispered Adam in their private dialect.

"*I have no idea what to think,*" said Mayfly.

"*Nor do I,*" said Adam.

"*What should we do?*"

Adam and Mayfly stood at the base of the walls that now protected them. The slabs reached high into the mist and looked impenetrable, even to an invading army.

"We have no choice but to stay here and trust them, no matter how bizarre they might act," said Adam. "Juan's forces will be here soon, and we picked our side a long time ago."

Skarr was leading the group towards a building in the distance, and Adam headed to join them. Mayfly soon followed, and as he walked he heard the faint sound of a man screaming.

/***/

Skarr's fellow guard was an equally iridescently beautiful man, and he brought Mayfly to his quarters. Mayfly looked the guard over; there was something unsettling about his features. He was *too perfect*, as if he were airbrushed. The guard's crisp gait and unchanging smile disturbed Mayfly a bit as well. *Spanners are always a little odd,* thought Mayfly, *but they're odd because of their imperfections; this guard is like a machine with skin.*

"Here are your quarters," said the guard, holding a door open. "I apologize; what is your name?"

"I was born without a name," said Mayfly, "but they call me Mayfly."

The guard stared at Mayfly blankly, as if he didn't understand the answer.

"Here, we all have names that we give ourselves," said the guard. "We're not defined by our former classes, nor are we called by our former class names."

"Former classes?"

"Santos takes away our weaknesses," said the guard. "He makes us unique."

"I am unique," said Mayfly.

"Then he will make you more so," said the guard.

The guard gestured for Mayfly to enter his room; it was a comfortable cell, if sparse. Mayfly entered and turned around to face his guard.

"When will I get to see Santos?" asked Mayfly. "I want him to extend my—"

"You'll see him soon," said the guard as he shut the door. "He will make you unique."

/***/

In the evening Mayfly heard the faint sound of yelling, followed by a girl's cries. *I can barely hear it, but the yells are deeper than anything I've heard before,* thought Mayfly. *And the girl's cries are fainter still.*

Mayfly had left his room to explore the compound but found that the hallways always led to a locked door; the place was built for security and not comfort. *Juan and Santos are indeed cut from the same cloth,* thought Mayfly. *This place is every bit the prison that Juan's compound is.*

While he was planning his escape, there was a knock at Mayfly's door.

"Come in," said Mayfly, for lack of other options.

An old man and old woman, both elfin in appearance and small in stature, came in through the door. They both had strong, good-looking features and had aged gracefully. They were a lot easier to look at than the plastic guards that had escorted the group in.

The woman was carrying a tray of food and the man was carrying a pile of books.

"Good evening," said the woman, setting the tray of delicacies on the table. "Would you like something to eat?"

"If you take a bite out of it first," said Mayfly with a smile.

The man and the woman smiled at each other and then gave a quick nod. The man took a knife and fork from the tray and deftly cut a morsel from every bit of food, and the woman elegantly poured all the liquid into a separate cup. They both took a bite out of every piece of food and then drank some of the liquid, smiling gently the whole time. Mayfly sensed he could trust them, so he smiled and then took a bite out of the food; it was exquisite.

"Thank you," he said.

"We know your kind only sleeps an hour a night," said the woman. "So we brought you some books in case you get bored."

"I don't get bored," said Mayfly.

"I told you he's unique," said the man. "Left alone, the mayfly's mind is an active playground, an infinite library of thought. Placed in an empty room, a mayfly will write volumes of poetry in his head, solve impossible equations and invent a language. Is this correct?"

"Something like that," said Mayfly.

"Tell me," said the man, beaming at him. "How many languages have you made during your lifespan?"

"Six," said Mayfly, "and ten dialects."

The man and the woman looked at each other and smiled.

"I used to be like that," said the man. "Her too. I guess we aren't as sharp as we once were, but we can still marvel at you."

"You're mayflies," said Mayfly.

"We were," said the man.

"We still are," said the woman.

"We were and still are," said the man. "My name is Aedan and this is my wife Iona. We used to be like you until we found Santos, and we're still here, sixty years later."

"So it's true," said Mayfly. "He takes away our weakness."

"Yes, it's completely true," said Iona, smiling at him as if he were her child.

"How does he extend our lifespans?" asked Mayfly. "How can he extend mine?"

Aedan looked at his wife and she nodded at him to speak.

"Mayflies have a straightforward, if limited, biology," he said. "We don't get sick, and we tend not to die before our time. Our heart limits us; it beats strongly for our lifespan and then just stops one day."

"Can I get a new heart?"

"Our biology is so unique that the average human heart would last you a week at best," said Aedan.

He then opened his shirt to reveal a scar across his chest.

"But trust in the Surgeon and he'll give you a heart that lasts," said Aedan. "And though his methods are painful, if you accept his gifts you'll live to our age, perhaps twice as long if you take care of yourself."

Mayfly breathed a sigh of relief before realizing it wouldn't be that simple.

"In order for me to get a heart, someone has to give me one, perhaps a spanner," said Mayfly.

"Indeed," said Iona, smiling. "Both of ours are from others who are no longer with us."

"Who's going to give me a heart out here?" asked Mayfly.

"There is one of your party called Trey," said Aedan. "His second body is dying; you've heard his screams no doubt. His heart is still strong and he's agreed to donate it to you. You'll get the procedure in the morning."

"But—"

"This is all we're allowed to say at this hour," said Iona with a smile. "But come the morning, your friend Trey's second body will be dead, and his heart will beat within your chest. Our kind only needs an hour of sleep a night, so get that full hour; you'll need your rest for the procedure tomorrow."

And with a smile, they left and closed the door behind them, leaving Mayfly with the books and enough food to last him the night, possibly two.

/***/

Adam was awoken in the middle of the night by a soft knocking. He woke up feeling relaxed; Yahíma's treatment had worked, and he had been sleeping dreamlessly. He had no visions of being buried alive and woke with his heart calm and his breath normal.

He heard the knocking again and got up to open the door.

"I'm sorry," he said. "I'll be right there."

"Your door is unlocked," said a soft voice from the outside. "I'm just asking your permission to enter."

"Sure," said Adam. "Come on in."

The door opened to reveal a beautiful woman with dark features and a gentle face. She had clear green eyes and a shock of straight blonde hair that fell perfectly over her dark shoulders. *She's beautiful but I should be careful,* thought Adam. *Women that arrive in the small hours of the night never come without an agenda.*

"My name is Giselle," said the woman.

"Pleased to meet you, I'm—"

"I know who you are, Adam," said the woman. "May I enter?"

Adam almost said *no* out of habit but decided to let her in. He'd been feeling different ever since Yahíma had cleared his head, and he wanted to stop hiding and experience more.

He also sensed something genuine about this girl; she was a stranger, and the faint orange flickers in her eyes showed that she was a spanner, but she projected a feeling of trust and softness.

Giselle sat down at the small table in Adam's room and beckoned him to sit with her. He sat across from her and watched as she took out three candles and lit them. She brought out a jar of golden-brown liquid and two small snifters and then poured two glasses. Adam smelled the glass and smiled.

"Louis the Thirteenth Cognac," said Adam. "My favorite."

"Pardon the forwardness, and rest assured this isn't a trap," said Giselle, as if reading his thoughts. "They sent me here to welcome you, and to tell you of your importance."

"Everyone's been telling me of my importance," said Adam. "I assure you, when the fight comes, I'll be in the center of it all."

"I wasn't speaking of *your* importance, per se," said Giselle. "I'm speaking of your group's importance in the upcoming battle, in particular your family. And of your family I speak mostly of your sister, Phoe."

Adam nodded and then smelled the cognac one more time deeply and sipped it, savoring the taste.

"Do you recognize the vintage?" she asked.

"Precisely one hundred years old," he responded.

"Correct," said Giselle with a smile. "Where were you at the time?"

"Working a vineyard a few farms over from this one," said Adam. "I believe the *vigneron* of this bottle was a man named *Métivier*."

"Where was Phoe at the time?"

"Falling in love with Métivier's son," said Adam.

Adam took another sip of the cognac and smiled at Giselle. He was still suspicious; beautiful strangers had knocked on his door seventy-eight times before, and most of the times ended badly.

"How do you know about me?" asked Adam.

"Every spanner knows of you," said Giselle.

"How do you know about Phoe?" asked Adam. "I've largely kept her hidden."

Giselle smiled and the candlelight fell on her skin perfectly. Adam felt an odd kinship with her, as if he'd know her for years instead of moments.

"You're a phoenix-class spanner, aren't you?" asked Adam.

"I am," said Giselle. "Only Santos has taken away my weakness; I can still fall in love, I just don't die afterwards."

"Did they send you to—"

"I sent myself," said Giselle, placing her finger on Adam's lips. "I came to talk to you about Phoe, and tell you that in *this* lifespan she's headed towards her own destiny. I don't know what it is, but I know that she's going to play a great role in the upcoming battle. When that time comes you shouldn't protect her, no matter how much you want to; in other lifetimes part of her belongs to you, but in this one she belongs only to herself. So when the time comes you must let her go, even if it means her death—can you do that?"

"I can," said Adam.

"Good," said Giselle, sipping the cognac. "The sun will soon rise, and then we'll all be speaking of legends and battles."

Giselle put down her cognac, smiled at Adam and got up to leave.

"Stay," said Adam.

Giselle turned around and smiled slightly.

"Stay, please," said Adam. "Not to do anything untoward; I won't take advantage of your class's emotions. Just stay here with me, just to talk and keep each other company until tomorrow, when life becomes real."

"Okay," said Giselle, sitting down and opening up the cognac again.

"Thank you," said Adam. "I just want to talk, that's all."

"This is unlike everything they've said about you," said Giselle. "They say you're quiet, and you hide from the world."

"They were right, but I've changed," said Adam.

"What made you change?"

Adam took a sip of the cognac and thought about that for a moment.

"I realized that so much in life brings loss, but we should celebrate what we have now rather than mourn it when it's gone," said Adam. "For all we know, the upcoming battle might end our world, perhaps the whole world, but it won't end it today."

"It's still night," said Giselle.

"Then we have even more time," said Adam, drinking his cognac, "and whatever time we have, I'd like to spend it with you, talking about anything, as long as it's not legends or battles."

/***/

The next morning Phoe sat with Trey on top of the compound's eastern wall and watched the sun rise dimly over the distant forest. The walls were easy to climb from the inside but dropped steeply on the outside. *No one could survive a fall from the wall,* thought Phoe, *not even Adam.* Since the wall angled outwards, the fall looked endless and though the parapet was broad and built for walking, they proceeded cautiously.

She had heard the tales of Trey's sacrifices for the group and sat with him as his second body underwent surgery. Trey's healthy body next to her felt the pain as his second body died, and though he screamed she couldn't do anything but hold his hand and cry with him.

Phoe admired his resolve in the face of adversity; he seemed to *do what needed to be done*, regardless of his own state of mind. His second body was dying and Trey had immediately asked to donate the heart to Mayfly, a boy he had just met a few weeks ago. *We all have a part to play in the upcoming war,* Trey had said, *and Mayfly is no exception. If he dies, then the battle has been lost before it begins.*

Trey had wanted to stay near his second body during the surgery, but Phoe asked him to walk with her. She could tell that he was scared, and being apart from the surgery would help him forget about what he was about to lose. He wasn't one for self-pity, but she could tell that the deaths of his two bodies had disturbed him deeply. He seemed lost in thought, and as they traveled along the wall he walked close to the edge. *He's not being fearless,* thought Phoe. *He doesn't care.*

Phoe stopped walking, pulled him in and together they looked out at the frozen forest in the distance.

"It's beautiful up here," he said. "The mist and everything."

"It is," said Phoe.

"Santos developed the trees to exhale the fog," said Trey. "It acts as an atmosphere to keep everything warm inside and to keep it hidden from the outside. If Juan wasn't coming here, no one would find this place, not for a thousand years."

They looked through the mist and saw a speck in the distance. It seemed to move, and they waited for a moment and saw that it was approaching them, and that it was on foot and alone. Phoe squinted and saw that it was a rotund blond man, huffing and puffing as he trudged through the snow.

"It's one of the Vikings," said Trey with a smile. "The first wave of our reinforcements is here."

"It's going to be a fight all right," said Phoe. "But I've been in fights before, as have you."

Trey looked down, defeated. Phoe noticed that Trey had a tear in his eye and she wiped it away.

"What?" she asked.

"I'm just a normal human now," said Trey. "That's what most spanners want, but not me. I was special before; I could do things. I can't do anything now, and I won't be able to help this fight."

"You will," said Phoe.

"How do you know?"

"Because you said it yourself. You said *'we all have a part to play in the upcoming war.'* That includes both me and you."

"How?" asked Trey.

Phoe reached up and kissed Trey's lips. They lingered for a moment on the misty wall, and then she kissed him once more.

"I don't know," said Phoe. "But I know you're going to be an important piece, perhaps the most important piece of all, so stay away from this ledge. It's a long way down."

Trey smiled at her, looked over the wall and stepped back. They kissed some more and then she pulled back but kept her hand in his.

"Be careful with me," said Phoe with a smile. "You know my class is vulnerable."

"You're not vulnerable," said Trey. "At least not from what I've seen."

"I am vulnerable, so stay by my side," said Phoe, coming in close to Trey. "We have a part to play in the days to come, and we'll play it together."

/***/

Giselle and Adam stood outside the operating room, watching Mayfly breathe as the Surgeon operated on him. Next to Mayfly laid the dead body of Trey, his rib cage splayed open. In the other window they saw both Cattaga and Mayfly's two elderly handlers.

Santos de León, the Surgeon, closed up Mayfly's chest and then walked over to Adam and gave a nod, but no smile. *He hasn't changed one bit in the five hundred years since we parted ways,* thought Adam. *For all the legend surrounding him, he is today just as he was then: a grey-faced man with a permanent scowl.*

"He'll live," said the Surgeon dryly. "He's a lucky one, your Mayfly."

Adam looked at Mayfly, scarred in the chest but breathing calmly. *Mayfly makes his own luck,* thought Adam, *but not this time.*

"Adam, our first warrior has come in, and he brings some dark tidings," said Santos. "We need to speak with him now."

/***/

Adam, Giselle and Santos faced the round, red-faced man at the other end of the table. Adam recognized him as Harald Forkbeard, a cohort of Leif's and a feared Viking in his own right. Back in his day Harald's legend had spread throughout Europe, but now he was wheezing in front of them, tired from the journey, with his legendary beard now shaved. *He hasn't aged, though modern life has found a way to levy its toll,* thought Adam. *Yet still he's come to fight for us, and we'll need more of his kind, even if they come wheezing and red-faced.*

"I passed Juan's army en route up here," said Harald with a European businessman's English.

"How many are in his company?" asked Adam.

"A thousand? Maybe more," said Harald. "They had a bunch of different types with them, and some looked half-dead."

"How far away are they?"

"I can't tell for sure," said Harald. "They move slowly but they're traveling in vehicles, so I'd guess about three days."

"What kind of vehicles?" asked Adam.

"Some lorries with caged beds to transport the half-dead ones, and some equipment; I'm not an engineer, but it looks like cranes used to dig."

Adam thought about it for a moment and then nodded.

"Santos, do we have our own water supply here?" asked Adam.

"Food and water both," said Santos. "The water comes from a well underground, and the food will be provided by the plants that make the mist."

"Good," said Adam. "It looks like Juan might not just attack us; he might surround us and make a siege."

/***/

Santos had prepared a cell for Harald and soon the Viking was inside, snoring loudly.

"He laid down his sword centuries ago because the world demanded businessmen in lieu of warriors," said Santos, closing Harald's cell. "But my brother Juan will be coming with rough men, and we need rough men to fight back."

"They're not as rough as they once were," said Adam, "but they know what's at stake and they'll fight for it. When the battle begins, they'll be ready."

"Indeed," said Santos.

"The Viking warrior who sent us here was named Leif; do you know him?"

"I know of him, and he of me."

"He told me that we'll need an *edge* to defeat Juan," said Adam, "and that the warriors that come now can only provide *time* for us to gain that edge."

"I know of what he speaks," said Santos. "We have the edge in the Fountain, and her power will take time to come to fruition."

"We'll use the power of the Fountain against his army?" asked Adam.

"Not directly," said Santos. "If we were to place her amongst the battlefield, even with her full powers unleashed, my brother would find a way to capture her and all would be lost."

"What will you do then?" asked Adam.

Santos looked at Giselle and then back at Adam.

"They say I grant power to spanners, but I do no such thing," said Santos. "All I do is take away a spanner's weakness, such as extending Mayfly's lifespan or perhaps allowing Brogg to speak normally, if I were given the time. But after I separate the Fountain into her two selves, I'll be able to increase a spanner's power a hundredfold, maybe more. We'll use *this* power against my brother, and *this* will be our edge."

"When will you do this?" asked Adam.

"Once I have the Fountain's power of life and death in my hands, I need time to implement it; it could take hours, or perhaps days," said Santos. "But I can separate her powers soon. I'm going to try tonight."

/***/

Adam and Giselle stood atop one of the towers that evening and watched the endless stream of warriors come to their side. Some brought trucks and some came on foot; the majority were Arawak but Vikings came too, and not all were as rotund as Harald.

"They haven't fought for centuries," said Adam.

"Our fortress is built to withstand attacks," said Giselle. "They'll have some time to remember their old skills."

Adam realized she was right; the warriors looked rusty as they joked and swung swords at each other in the courtyard, but this castle was built for punishment. Juan would have all the time in the world once he surrounded the castle, but the Vikings and Arawaks had lived a long time. They weren't ready now, but they would be soon.

/***/

Later that evening, Adam sat with Giselle in the upper row of the operating room and noticed that she was shivering. He offered her his coat and she accepted; it was freezing in the room because Santos had funneled air in from the outside to mute the Fountain's powers.

The Fountain was lying on the operating table, conscious but comfortable. Though Santos had a suite of surgical instruments fanned out by her bedside table, she showed no fear. Perhaps Santos had spoken Arawak to her in preparation for the surgery, but whatever the case, this was no longer the frightened girl who didn't quite understand the commotion around her. This was a girl who was prepared to face the full truth of her destiny.

"When I separate her into her two selves, life and death, you must keep your distance," said Santos. "Her power of death will be able to harm you, even in the cold."

The operating room was clean and lit by candles, and most of the surfaces were hewn of wood. Santos's assistant Skarr brought a gloved hand over the Fountain's head and then placed a small canister on the floor. He placed a mask over her face, gently turned on the gas and then Santos went to work, slicing a hole in her abdomen. He was quite slow with his cuts, and it was a half hour before he took a step back and began the work in earnest. He then made small incision after small incision, cutting into her flesh with shallow movements, demanding a different instrument from Skarr with each cut. *This place is archaic,* thought Adam, *but the Surgeon knows what he's doing, and he keeps his own form of cleanliness. Perhaps that's the true nature of his castle; it's not dead, but rather 'sterile.'*

The Surgeon seemed to be cutting around something within the Fountain, and he sliced around it as gently as if he were slicing over the membrane of a bubble. Adam had witnessed surgeries before but had never seen someone so deft with a scalpel; Giselle later whispered to him that Santos only moved the knife in between his own heartbeats.

An hour later, the Surgeon was making visible progress; there was a small, black, slimy object within the Fountain's abdomen, and it appeared to be quivering. Adam looked closer; it was moving faintly, like a dying animal wriggling to get out of a hunter's net. The Surgeon nodded at Skarr, and the assistant brought over another machine and turned it on over the Fountain. It blew air on her body and was so cold that Adam felt the chill in the upper decks of the auditorium. *They're preparing to separate her two selves,* thought Adam. *She's about to become incredibly powerful and quite dangerous, like a living bomb.*

The Surgeon worked his way around the pulsating black mass for another hour, slowly trying to detach it from the body from whence it came. He cut and cauterized, sliced and then cut some more, gently bringing it out as if he was taking a baby from its womb. He bid Skarr to bring another machine and the assistant brought out a wheeled apparatus that looked like a tire pump. Skarr turned the machine on and it made a slow humming sound. The Surgeon then placed it inside of the black object's body, trying a few places with no success. The Surgeon eventually found the right spot, and soon the dark tissue was contracting and relaxing at a quick but consistent pace. *It's a living being, distinct from the Fountain,* thought Adam, *and Santos is helping it breathe on its own.*

Santos made a few more cuts and lifted the black object out and placed it on the table. There was a hush in the audience, and Skarr managed to genuflect quickly towards it before taking another large instrument out from the corner of the room: a container to place over the Fountain that had gloved holes to allow the Surgeon to operate on her from behind a barrier. He closed the Fountain's wounds relatively quickly; it was clear that he was nervous being around her separated form.

Santos completed his suturing on the Fountain and then turned around to face the black tissue, still breathing with the help of the machine.

"We have separated the two," said Santos. "Death and life."

"Death is the pale body on my left," said the Surgeon, "and the quivering black mass on my right ... is life."

/***/

"From her conception, the Fountain of Youth was *both* life and death," said Santos in a small room afterwards.

Skarr had placed the Fountain in her own frozen room and had placed the black tissue in a glass jar that would give it nutrients and help it grow. Santos was talking to Adam and Giselle alone. More Arawak and

Viking reinforcements were coming in outside, but Santos paid them no mind.

"The Fountain was a being sent from above, perhaps an angel sent to lead us to salvation," said Santos. "But whatever the case, in the womb she split into two beings, not just as a twin but as a *mirror* twin."

"The exact opposite," said Adam.

"Precisely," said Santos. "One held the power of life, and the other the power of death."

"Then why did they grow up as one?" asked Giselle.

"Death is more powerful than life, so in the womb the force of death *absorbed* the force of life, and forever after they lived in a parasitic fashion, with the force of life living as a digested twin, or a *bezoar*, if you will. You only saw the form of death in the pale girl that you have come to know, but they were both there the whole time, and now they'll live apart.

"Living as one, they largely cancelled each other out and only a glimpse of their powers came through; her outer self brought death to those who came near, and her inner blood granted the power of immortality. Now separated, their powers have increased by several orders of magnitude; the pale girl could kill others with her presence before, but now she could destroy a city if she so desired. Her inner self granted immortality before; now she can magnify a spanner's power by an untold amount, and perhaps one day bring the dead back to life."

They sat in silence and listened to the outside sounds of the Vikings sparring and clashing swords with each other. There was also the sound of gunfire as the Arawaks tested out their rifles.

"Both halves are innocent and don't mean anyone any harm," said Santos. "They're mere children with the powers of gods, and they can't help us defeat Juan by themselves. It's my role to take their power and win this war. Your role, Adam, is to help those out there hold Juan at bay until I figure out how to do just that."

A BATTLE AT THE EDGE OF THE WORLD

Brogg had a hard time digging into the frozen earth, which wasn't a bad thing overall. Adam had been on both sides of an extended siege, and knew that digging was much more important for the attacking party. The invaders would excavate trenches to hold catapults, hide troops and cut off supply lines from the outside. If the invader couldn't batter down a castle's gate, they would burrow under it; in general, frozen earth was a besieged castle's friend.

Geryon was nowhere to be seen; Cattaga had developed a high-pitched whistle that only he could hear, but she whistled and he didn't come.

"He ain't lazy; he'll help us dig when it's nighttime," said Phage, shoving a sharp stick into the ground. "Geryon doesn't like fire, and he doesn't care for the sunlight either, as weak as it is up here."

Phage was laying spiked traps in the small depressions between divots and then covering the traps with loose dirt and leaves. He had concocted a batch of deadly bacteria that could live in the cold, and he poured the liquid on the wooden spikes.

"These are what we call Punji sticks," said Phage. "They can kill a human, slow down an immortal. Wood pierces the skin, these bacteria do the rest."

"You fight dirty," said a bearded Viking named Erich, who was digging alongside Brogg.

Erich was wearing a dusty old helmet that had a guard to protect his eyes and nose, but it didn't fit well and he could barely see.

"I fight fair," said Phage. "If they don't want to get stuck, they shouldn't come."

The Viking Erich didn't quite understand Phage's reasoning, and Adam realized that therein lay a weakness in their army. The Vikings were looking forward to the battle but they were accustomed to invading, not defending. *Our Norse friends haven't fought in centuries,* thought Adam, *and they've never fought from behind a wall.*

Adam had lived through sieges before and knew that the main thing they needed was patience. He knew that the Vikings would be eager to scale down the walls and engage the enemy in hand-to-hand combat, perhaps dying nobly, but Adam knew that dying nobly never won a battle. Adam understood that he had to keep the Norse warriors on the wall; if the enemy scaled it, he'd need the Vikings to push them back down again.

Adam heard the sound of gunshots from far off and saw that the Arawaks were shooting at targets in the far distance. They had all brought rifles and Adam could see their sights peeking over the walls, ready to fire on command. *They'll keep Juan at bay, but we'll still need the Vikings,* thought Adam. *In a siege, ammunition runs out, but swords don't.*

Adam looked back at Santos's fortress; the walls were strong and high, and mostly stone. *Frozen ground will protect us on the outside,* thought Adam, *and the inside is invulnerable to fire.*

/***/

Adam and Phage went back to the castle and then walked along the parapet. Brogg had drilled holes into the stone for the Arawaks to shoot from, and Phage had Brogg drill more openings that led straight down.

"They call these *murder holes*," said Phage. "An army comes near you, you pour some nasty shit on them when they start to climb."

"It's a last line of defense," said Adam.

"Don't worry, I'll find something good to pour down there," said Phage. "I'll make it count."

/***/

Santos's guards did one more sweep around the fortress to make sure that no one had been trapped outside. Everyone was in except for two Vikings who hadn't arrived in the first place, so they closed the heavy doors, which shut so tightly that they all but disappeared into the outer wall. Adam went downstairs to see Mayfly, and Mayfly wasn't happy at the role Adam had given him.

"I should be out there fighting," said Mayfly. "If it's because of my heart—"

"It's not that," said Adam, and he pointed to the back rooms where the Surgeon kept the Fountain's two selves. "If this castle is breached, you need to be the last line of defense to keep them from kidnapping her."

"The best defense is for me to be up there fighting—"

"You need to be down here," interrupted Adam. "If Juan's crew sneaks in here, we'll depend on you."

"Depend on me to do what?"

"I don't know," said Adam. "You'll have to figure something out."

/***/

Adam saw the phalanx of Juan's troops approach the castle and stop a kilometer out. Adam looked at his troops' reaction to the enemy's arrival; the Arawaks held no expression, and the Vikings smiled and sang songs in their Old Norse dialect. Adam looked through his binoculars and saw that Juan's steward Balthasar was riding up to them on a horse, treading carefully and instinctively avoiding the patches of earth where Phage had buried his Punji sticks. Balthasar had an odd sack on the back of his horse and was yanking a walking boy behind him on a leash; upon closer look, Adam noticed that the boy was missing a hand.

Balthasar stopped twenty meters from the castle wall and then walked towards it, close enough that any of the Arawaks could have shot him.

"I was prepared to meet you halfway out, as war negotiations are wont to do," yelled Balthasar to the castle above. "But I want your army to hear what we can do for them if they surrender immediately, and what we'll do *to* them if they refuse."

The Vikings laughed at Balthasar's words, but he ignored them and pulled two containers from the bag on his horse. Adam saw that these containers were made of metal and looked like closed cooking pots, with three legs and small gas tanks underneath them. Balthasar got on the ground and lit a match under the pots; the flame under one vessel caught, and then the other, and as they heated up the boy started to yell in agony. The kid ran towards the containers, but his feet were bound and he tripped. The boy was now in too much pain and couldn't get up; he could only writhe on the ground and scream. It was enough to get the castle's attention, including the Vikings who had ceased their singing and were now staring grim-faced at Balthasar. One Viking was about to throw his axe at the steward, but Balthasar held up his hand and turned the flames on the pots down, and the boy stopped screaming, eventually settling on a small whimper.

"In the canister on the right is the head of one of the Arawak leaders, as well as the boy's hand, to give you a glimpse of the agony that we can inflict," said Balthasar. "The other container is filled with the head of one of your Viking compatriots; I believe his name is Ragnar."

The Norsemen were aghast; Ragnar was one of the Vikings that hadn't arrived at the fortress.

"You let them go!" yelled one of the Vikings from the roof. "I swear I'll—"

"We caught Ragnar with his friend Sweyn as they traveled up here, and we decapitated them both. We're now holding Sweyn well behind our front lines, along with four other Arawak chieftains," said Balthasar. "If you should try to harm me in any way, we'll spend the next day boiling the containers that we have."

The angry Viking spat and muttered something in Old Norse, but held himself back.

"This is our offer; hear it once, for I'll never give it again," said Balthasar. "Surrender now in aggregate, and we'll give these heads back to you. Whoever surrenders individually will be let go and not pursued. But if you should choose to fight, we'll kill your mortals in particularly harsh ways, and as for the immortals—"

Balthasar tapped the small containers by his feet.

"We have places for you in here," said Balthasar. "So either walk free now, or spend eternity roasting in a box."

Adam looked at his comrades; some of Santos's assistants looked nervous, but Balthasar's offer had only served to anger the Arawaks and Vikings. *The Arawaks loathe Juan and the Vikings don't understand the concept of surrender,* thought Adam. *Still, I must try to defray this a bit.*

"You say you'll create a new society?" yelled Adam.

"Yes," said Balthasar. "A new world, free of sin. There will only be ten thousand inhabitants of earth, no more, but there will be room for all of you if you surrender now. We'll have no war, crime or depravity, just peace and inhabitants with the power of gods. This is the future, and it's up to you to take your place in this world."

"Look at the tanks beneath your feet and the screaming boy at your leash," said Adam. "Is this the foundation from which a new world will be born?"

Balthasar looked down at the boy and the tanks, and though he seemed to understand what Adam had said, he shook it off.

"The time for philosophical discussion is over," said Balthasar.

"Then we'll not surrender," said Adam. "Again, all I ask is that you question what you're doing, Balthasar. Whoever wins this day, you'll fall on the wrong side of history."

"We'll win," said Balthasar. "And the winning side is always on the right side of history."

/***/

Adam took the binoculars and saw that Cannon had brought an actual cannon and was loading it with ammunition. The weapon had a semi-modern design and was most likely pilfered from a military depot. Adam told his crew to get down, and though the Arawaks did so immediately, the Vikings needed convincing. Adam saw Cannon fire the big gun, and Brogg had to tackle a stray Viking before the projectile hit the side of the fortress with a *crack*. Adam looked over and saw that though there was a mark where the cannonball had struck, there was no real damage. It had barely made a dent in the fortress.

There was a cheer amongst the warriors; the Norse started singing their strange songs again and one of the Vikings did a dance on the tower, making particularly obscene gestures towards Juan's army in the distance. The Vikings laughed at the display, and then Adam looked through his binoculars again and saw that Cannon was preparing another projectile to be fired. Adam tried to warn the Viking, but he was too late; the second cannonball reached the wall a split second before the sound of the blast did and careened through the top of the tower, spraying bricks and dust into the air. There were yells and screams in both Old Norse and Arawak, and when the dust settled, Adam noticed that the cannonball had torn the dancing Viking in two. The group gathered around him, and Adam instructed Brogg to check for more cannon fire.

The Viking's eyes glowed as he coughed up blood and smiled, vowing something in his old dialect, and the other Vikings listened intently as he spoke. His blood was all over the place and his midsection had been torn to shreds, but he held up his fist and soon his comrades were cheering for him. *He'll survive this,* thought Adam as the Vikings carried their compatriot's broken body down to the bowels of the fortress. *But he's out of this battle. We can't afford any more dancing Vikings.*

/***/

Juan's barrage lasted throughout the night. The cannon couldn't do much damage to the base of the fortress, but Juan's army had time on their side, and they shot projectiles towards the upper edges of the towers and into the courtyards. The defending army remained intact but the anticipation of the cannon blast unnerved them, particularly at night when all they could see was the flash of the cannon's muzzle. The group had to look on all four edges of the fortress too; though Juan's army had brought only a single cannon, they moved it from edge to edge, taking their time with each edge.

"How are you doing?" asked Adam of one of the Arawak chieftains.

"We've seen worse," said the Arawak, holding his rifle. "We may have to do a raid in the morning, to get a clear shot at that cannoneer."

"Let him shoot," said Adam. "Santos is working on unleashing the Fountain's power, and he needs time. These cannon shots may give Santos the time he needs."

/***/

By dawn the enemy troops had shifted to the east side of the castle, which caused great concern amongst the Vikings. Leif told Adam that this meant Juan's army was going to attack at sunrise.

"*It's a common tactic for a raid,*" he said in his old Viking dialect. "*Fight with the rising sun at your back so that your enemy is blinded.*"

They hastily prepared themselves for the morning battle as best they could; those with sunglasses put them on, and those with an extra pair shared them. Adam went downstairs and had Mayfly make sunglasses out of whatever he could; he found a cache of smoked plastic and hastily fashioned face shields out of them.

"Let me go upstairs," said Mayfly. "I'm wasting away down here."

"You'll waste away more up there," said Adam, pointing to the recovery room of the Viking who had taken a cannonball to the midsection.

The Viking was snoring loudly, but his body was mangled.

/***/

The sun rose and Juan sent the populous to attack the castle, flanked by a group of spider-wolves, running wild but still obedient enough to keep pace with their slower comrades. The endless mass of the populous became angry as they approached, and descended upon the castle with a yell. Some were equipped with makeshift armor, but most were not. The Arawak snipers did their best to shoot whoever they could, but they had a hard time shooting in the morning light and rarely connected. Some populous had fallen into Phage's traps, but they stayed down and the other members of the populous simply avoided them. *The Punji sticks slow the enemy down,* thought Adam, *but just barely. Of the thousand rushing towards us, perhaps twenty have been felled.*

The populous got closer to the walls, and Adam began to lose track of them in the sun but saw that many of them were carrying ladders, with the spider-wolves rushing between their feet. The Arawaks started to focus their fire on the populous with ladders, but they wouldn't be able to stop them completely; when the Arawaks' shots connected, another took the ladder and ran forward. The spider-wolves were too fast to shoot and would be scaling the fortress momentarily. *We can only slow them down,* thought Adam. *We can't stop them.*

"Vikings and marksmen!" yelled one of the Vikings. "Prepare yourselves, for they're coming over the walls!"

The Vikings rushed to the wall, axes in hand, and the Arawaks crept closer to Phage's murder holes. Brogg situated himself close to the edge and stretched his neck back and forth in anticipation of the invaders.

The first wave of the populous hit the fortress wall with a thud, climbing over each other to get on the ladders. Adam looked closer and couldn't help but be shocked at their appearance; they weren't warriors, but average-looking men, women and even children.

Brogg ripped one ladder up from under the populous and broke it in two over his knee. He then ran over to another ladder and tipped it backwards. The grounds of the castle were by now covered with the rioters, and they were beginning to climb each other as well as the ladders. The spider-wolves scurried up the wall between them with ease, but the Arawaks could hit them and each creature was deterred with a simple gunshot. Soon they were fighting off only the populous, and holding their own.

It shouldn't be this easy, thought Adam. *It shouldn't—*

Adam looked behind him at the west side of the wall and saw that spider-wolves were creaking over the edge, the sun glinting eerily off their eight eyes.

"It's a trick!" yelled one of the Arawaks, before turning around and firing at the other wall and taking down three spider-wolves. Six more took their place, and then twelve as the creatures began to flood over the western wall in droves, snarling and snapping their jaws. *They faked an attack on the east, and sent their wolves over the west. We're trapped in between them.*

"Keep your distance!" said Adam. "Fight the populous hand to hand and shoot the wolves from a distance!"

A few Vikings ran towards the spider-wolves out of habit but were held back by their comrades so that the Arawaks could have clearer shots. The Arawaks took the creatures down, one by one, but they kept coming. Adam saw that Phage had left his murder-hole and was firing a pistol at the approaching wolves, some of them at point-blank range. Phage wasn't a bad shot, but the mass of wolves was growing and would overwhelm him soon.

The spider-wolves kept their distance though, and instead of rushing at Phage they formed a mass on the western wall, slowly pushing the group back until they were pinned against the populous coming from the east.

"Adam, look," said Cattaga, pointing to the southern wall.

Adam saw that Cannon, Blur and Drayne were creeping over the southern wall, quietly climbing with ladders of their own. They weren't trying to fight the group and they weren't trying to support their fellow troops; they were trying to sneak into the fortress to steal the Fountain.

They sent a false attack to hide another false attack, thought Adam. *All to conceal what they wanted to do in the first place.*

"Get Brogg and go down to Santos's lair," said Adam. "Mayfly's there, but he can't fight them alone."

/***/

Mayfly heard creaks coming from upstairs and assumed they were from someone who wasn't supposed to be there. Mayfly double-checked the hidden door to Santos's room; he had been busying himself with covering it in case anyone came down. Mayfly knew that he didn't have time to reinforce the door, so he had concentrated on burying it behind pieces of equipment lying around. Whoever came down here might be able to find it, but not immediately.

Mayfly heard another noise and turned around to see a dark-skinned man moving quickly and looking fuzzy. The man stopped moving and slowed down his vibrations just enough so that Mayfly could see that the man had a burned face. *This must be the blur,* thought Mayfly.

"I've heard about you," said Blur with a smile.

"And I you," said Mayfly.

"I'm sure you have," said Blur. "That little blonde-haired girl might have gotten the best of me, but it won't happen twice."

Mayfly didn't respond; he just crouched in a fighting stance, which caused Blur to laugh.

"Mayfly-class spanners can do a lot of things," said Blur. "But there's no puzzle to solve here, no girl to charm, no computer to decode. There's just you—"

Blur ran twice around Mayfly, and then once through his legs before stopping behind him.

"And me," said Blur.

Mayfly turned around and resumed his fighting stance.

"All you have is charm, Mayfly," said Blur. "You have no physical powers, so give up now."

Mayfly dove at Blur, missing wildly but keeping his feet. He dove again and missed, and then dove once more, this time anticipating where Blur would dodge and meeting him there. Mayfly tried to grab him, but his vibrations were too slippery and he got away. Blur zoomed around Mayfly three times and stopped behind him, putting Mayfly in a chokehold.

"Where are your powers now, Mayfly?" asked Blur.

Mayfly instinctively dug his chin into Blur's arm and bit, and used his left hand to reach back and poke Blur's eye. Blur yelled and let go, and Mayfly used that moment to kick him in the groin and push him to the ground. Mayfly then took a chair leaning against the far wall and slammed it over Blur's head, causing the wooden chair to splinter into pieces.

"Where are *your* powers?" asked Mayfly. "Once you've stopped moving, you're nothing."

"Is that so?" said Blur, looking behind Mayfly.

Mayfly smelled something foul and turned around to see Cannon, followed by Drayne.

"I underestimated Phoe, and I'll no longer underestimate you," said Blur, motioning towards Cannon. "Maybe one-on-one combat isn't for me."

Cannon picked Mayfly up with his left hand and Drayne removed her gloves and placed them near Mayfly's neck.

"Why don't you tell us where you've hidden the Fountain, Mayfly?" asked Blur.

"Kill me if you want," said Mayfly with a calm smile. "I'd rather die than help you, so kill me. I mean it."

Blur started to vibrate again, and Mayfly could only see the white of his teeth as he smiled.

"We're on the right side, Mayfly. The right side's the one that's still around at the end of the day," said Blur. "Always has been, always will be."

"I hope you're right," said Mayfly with a smile, eyeing Brogg and Cattaga who had just come downstairs. "I really hope you're right."

/***/

The spider-wolves pushed over the western wall and were running amok in the courtyard of the fortress, but the Arawaks were containing them. They were easy to shoot from the high vantage point of the wall; though they were dangerous, from a distance they were just dogs. A few had overtaken the wall and jumped on their shooters, but the Arawaks' immortality had made them immune to their poison, so the spider-wolves landed a few bites and nothing more.

The populous were equally stymied, but their numbers were endless. The Vikings used their axes to hack the horde back, but their size was just too great, and two Vikings had been taken down, beaten mercilessly and then taken back to Juan's main camp. *Each Viking can take twenty populous,* thought Adam, *but they have far more than twenty times our numbers.*

While Adam was thinking about that, he heard the Arawak chatter and looked back at the eastern wall. In the distance, far behind the populous was a row of slow-moving fighters that looked like they had been assembled from spare parts. Adam took his binoculars and saw that they looked half-dead, and the ones who had their faces intact seemed angry. They were led by a big man nearly two meters tall, with big muscles half-covered by skin, and a mass of corroded tissue where his face should have been.

"Those are the criminals from our tribe we'd buried over the years," said the Arawak chieftain. "These are the *imprisoned.*"

The Arawaks began to panic and concentrated their fire away from the spider-wolves and onto the imprisoned in the distance. It was no use; the shots barely hit, and when they connected, the dead soldiers were not felled. The spider-wolves continued to pour over the western wall, and since the Arawaks weren't shooting them, they were amassing in the courtyard and would soon be able to overrun the group.

"We need someone firing on the wolves!" yelled Adam.

It was to no avail; the Arawaks couldn't focus on anyone but the imprisoned, and couldn't seem to grasp that their shots had no effect. A spider-wolf breached the wall and bit an Arawak shooter from behind and then dragged him away screaming. The other Arawaks turned around with their guns, but their comrade was still in the jaws of the wolf and no one could get a clear shot. A Viking approached the wolf and hacked it with his axe; it yelped and after two more strikes, it stopped moving. The Viking put his axe to two more wolves that had breached the wall and there was a moment of quiet.

"We'll take these imprisoned," said the Viking, looking at his comrades. "You keep the dogs away."

The Arawaks nodded in agreement and the Viking looked at his compatriots, who started to smile. They yelled some more words in Old Norse, threw a ladder over the edge of the wall and then tumbled down with their axes, hacking through the populous as they went forward. Soon they were in the open field, ambling towards the army of the imprisoned, which was twenty times their size.

They're built to fight unknown foes on the open range, not to defend castles, thought Adam. *But they're up against a horde, and each Viking needs to take down twenty immortals to make it even.*

/***/

Downstairs, Mayfly, Cattaga and Brogg broke into individual matchups as if they each had a personal vendetta against their counterpart. Mayfly kept fighting Blur but couldn't get a handle on him this time; Blur was too smart to grapple with Mayfly again. Cattaga fought Drayne and had made her own skin scaly, which gave her the look of a lizard but protected her against Drayne's touch.

The fight that dominated the scrum was between Cannon and Brogg. Each missed punch shattered some furniture or part of the wall, and each time they wrestled, one of them ended up being thrown into the other four. Drayne tried to help out by laying her hands on Brogg, but he kicked her with his boot and she flew into the wall, coughing up blood.

Concentrate on the foe in front of you, thought Mayfly, *and then help the others.*

Mayfly tried every move he knew, but couldn't get a hold on Blur; he was just too fast. Mayfly knew his only move was to lure Blur into a hand-to-hand grappling maneuver and then counterattack, but Blur wouldn't take the bait; he would just circle around Mayfly, slow down to punch him and then circle around him again.

Mayfly kept his distance and looked around at his comrades and realized they might end up losing this one; Juan's crew was trained to fight, and fight dirty. Drayne refused to be deterred by Brogg's kicks and broke free from Cattaga a few times to lay her hands on the big man while Cannon had him in a chokehold. Brogg's body was somewhat resistant to her powers, but her touch soon left necrotic patches on his skin and it started to slow him down. Cattaga tackled Drayne and eventually led her away from Brogg, but it was a struggle; Cattaga had many powers, but they hadn't equipped her for conflict.

Cannon eventually put Brogg in a solid chokehold, and Drayne freed herself from Cattaga and laid her hands on Brogg for a few moments. Brogg gave out a low, grating scream and then broke free from Cannon's grip, but Drayne had weakened him and he could no longer stand. Brogg fell to one knee and necrotic lesions pulsated over his body. Cannon gave him a punch and it was over; Brogg was out cold.

Cannon turned around to face Mayfly, his face covered with sweat. Cannon's acne had burst again, and his thick stench was causing Mayfly's eyes to water. He was easily four times Mayfly's size and almost as fast as Blur; Mayfly knew the skirmish was lost.

"Now, tell us where the Fountain is," said Drayne, "or we'll kill you all, beginning with the scaly girl."

Mayfly gave a look to Cattaga, but her eyes were already glowing and she was making a high-pitched whine that faded into nothingness.

"What's that?" asked Cannon, holding his ears. "Make her stop."

"Whatever the trick is, wolf-whistles won't help you now," said Drayne. "You have ten seconds to tell us where the Fountain is, before we kill you and search this rubble ourselves."

Cattaga continued her unheard whine and Blur stopped vibrating to stand right in front of Mayfly.

"What's she doing?" asked Blur.

"She's calling a friend," said Mayfly, eyeing Geryon who had appeared in the stairwell behind them.

Mayfly jumped up to grab the lights on the ceiling and yanked them down, leaving the room pitch-black. Mayfly heard Geryon's clicks in the darkness, and for the first time in his life, he was glad to hear them.

/***/

The Vikings fought nobly, but they were no match for the imprisoned. The Nordic warriors hacked and hacked at the revived men but couldn't do any lasting damage to the horde. The imprisoned were surprisingly agile at close range, and surprisingly strong. They would either dodge the Viking's attacks or take them in stride; and when they were hit they wouldn't receive anything more than superficial wounds because they didn't have much flesh to begin with. The imprisoned had their own weapons too: metal pikes that they handled clumsily but effectively, beating the Vikings back and even impaling two. The Vikings struck a few down, but those they felled soon got back up. The leader of the imprisoned grabbed a Viking, and in a single motion wrenched his head off cleanly. The ghoul threw the Viking's head to the ground and pounded the decapitated body into submission. The Arawaks began to shoot at the imprisoned's leader, landing shots in his body, but they didn't even slow him down. *Our side fights bravely,* thought Adam, *but bravery doesn't count for anything, not now.*

The imprisoned continued their steady assault on the eastern wall, dragging the Vikings deeper and deeper into the battlefield. Since the Arawak riflemen had shifted their focus, the populous and spider-wolves took advantage and were breaching the wall. Soon the populous started to overtake the Arawaks, ripping their guns from them and beating them down. The spider-wolves were fighting from the other end, and though the Arawaks were immune to their poison, the wolves' jaws were strong and they began to latch onto the Arawaks' bodies, pulling several of them down to the interior of the fortress.

Adam saw Mayfly creeping out of a hatch in the ground and yelled at him.

"Stay down!" yelled Adam. "Protect the Fountain!"

"The Fountain's ready to help us," said Mayfly.

Adam looked at their side; the Vikings were ineffective, the Arawak riflemen were now being torn apart by spider-wolves, and the imprisoned were steadily marching over the fortress's walls.

"How can the Fountain help us?" asked Adam.

"Santos unleashed her power of life and put it into one of our own," said Mayfly.

"Who?"

"The power of the Fountain of Youth is now within Trey," said Mayfly, "and he's coming to destroy Juan's army."

/***/

At that moment all doors in the castle opened up and an endless stream of Treys poured out, screaming and ready to fight. They plowed over the roof from every direction, climbing down the populous on the way to attack the invading army. Some engaged in fighting with the populous, some fought the spider-wolves and some ran forward to fight the imprisoned.

One Trey climbed the highest tower on the fortress and surveyed the battle from above; Adam could see his eyes glowing brightly. The spider-wolves tried to attack him, but four other Treys protected the base of the tower, and soon the Arawaks provided cover fire.

We're fighting an army of a thousand minds with an army of one mind and a thousand bodies, thought Adam.

The horde of the imprisoned held its own against the Treys but were pinned down; the Treys were attacking the crowd of half-dead warriors from all sides. The imprisoned impaled many Treys on their pikes, but more Treys came and each dead Trey made a wall that that pinned Juan's army down even more.

"Adam, look," said Mayfly, pointing to Phoe.

Phoe had now emerged from the basement and was perched upon the tower with Trey, tears streaming from her eyes.

"She's with him," said Mayfly. "She's fallen for him."

"Yes," said Adam grimly. "I've seen that look before."

"Does that mean she's going to, or he's going to ... ?"

"I don't know," said Adam, "but something big is about to happen."

Adam looked over the battlefield and saw that the Treys were beginning to lose their edge. They had no weapons and no training for the battlefield, so the imprisoned slaughtered them easily, much as the Arawaks had slaughtered the populous. Adam looked up at the Trey in the tower; he was bleeding from the nose and eyes, and bruises were forming on his body.

"The Fountain's power gave him thousands of bodies," said Adam. "But many are dying and the shock is too much for him."

"He knows this," said Mayfly. "He's setting the stage for something."

"The Treys are setting the stage for Phoe," said Adam. "She's about to meet her destiny."

Phoe kissed the Trey in the tower, and he fell to his knees as his other bodies were slaughtered on the battlefield. She kissed him once more and he fell again, unable to stand back up. She was crying, but Trey whispered words into her ears and then pointed to the battlefield. She cried for one more moment and then held it back in, turned around and climbed down the tower. She walked up to Adam and hugged him.

"Things go bad when I grow up alone," she said. "So please, find me in my next life."

Adam nodded and she walked off, tumbling over the side of the fortress, using the dead populous and dying Treys as a bridge. She walked into the battlefield towards the horde of the imprisoned, climbed the Treys surrounding the army and soon disappeared into the mass of soldiers.

There was a moment of silence and then smoke came from the center of the horde, and Adam heard the sound of roasting flesh. The fire grew and the imprisoned howled as they burnt, but there was nothing they could do; they were all trapped beneath an endless pile of Trey's dead bodies.

A few spider-wolves got hit with the flames and also caught fire; as they ran, the flames spread outwards. The creatures near the flames let out a high-pitched collective howl, and soon the spider-wolves in the courtyard heard it and scurried over the walls to run away.

A few flaming wolves ran into the populous, and that was enough to turn the mob's rage to fear, and soon they were fighting each other to flee. Inside the fortress, the Vikings who were still intact started to cheer and the Arawaks put their rifles down; there was nothing they could do that their enemy wasn't doing to themselves.

Santos had come up from the basement with Giselle and his two guards; all of them were covered in blood, and Adam reasoned that they must have all helped infuse Trey with the Fountain's power. *We all had a part to play in this war*, thought Adam, *though not all of us survived.*

Giselle came close to Adam and put her hand on his back, and together they watched as the flames surrounded their fortress. Santos looked upon the battlefield with a grim face for a few moments before speaking to Adam.

"We've won this battle, but it's not yet ended," said Santos. "We've knocked their army down but must make sure that they can't get up again; if we don't do this, everything will be lost."

/***/

The entire imprisoned army was reduced to a pile of smoldering ashes, but they were still intact and still alive. The Arawaks took them one by one and placed them in makeshift metal caskets that Santos had procured; no one yet knew what to do with their corpses, but the metal coffins would contain them indefinitely.

It was dirty, hectic work and they were racing the sunset; if night fell, Juan might come back to steal a few and turn them into a small but powerful militia. The Arawaks stood on the periphery of the pile with their guns as Brogg and the remaining Vikings separated the corpses of the imprisoned from those of the Treys.

"We must not fail in this difficult and odious task," said Santos. "Every single corpse must be accounted for."

Adam saw the work from afar; he was mainly concerned with cleaning up Geryon's handiwork in the bowels of the fortress. Geryon had handled his enemies brutally, but Adam wanted to be sure that none had escaped. Their bodies had been torn to pieces and cast around the room, and Adam had to count the torsos and limbs twice until he was assured that all had been killed. He was glad that Geryon had saved Mayfly and subsequently the Fountain, but he couldn't help but be horrified by Geryon's ability to kill. Drayne looked like someone had shoved a bomb in her midsection, and Blur looked as if he had been dragged through thorns for a week. Adam felt a pulse coming from Cannon's limp body, but didn't fear him any longer. *Even if he recovers,* thought Adam, *he'll not be the same, and he'll always fear the dark.*

Adam called down two guards and they put the remains of Blur and Drayne in one steel casket, and Cannon in another. Adam then walked upstairs with a bloody shirt, a bit embarrassed for it when he saw Giselle.

"Relax," she said with a faint smile, pointing towards the battlefield. "I've seen much worse."

"It's true; I should be grateful that at least the blood's not mine," said Adam, sending a grim smile back to her. "And besides, the battle's not over yet."

"It may be," she said. "There's a man on a horse in the distance, and he's waving a white flag."

/***/

The boy came before Balthasar, running desperately towards the Arawaks, holding his own severed hand and collapsing at their feet, crying and pleading for forgiveness in their native tongue. They embraced him immediately and started to cheer, but the boy was stricken with too many emotions and couldn't be consoled. Balthasar then came forward on his horse, carrying a large sack and looking stern. He stopped quite a distance from the group, telling them to stop.

"I have the heads of each of your chieftains in here," he yelled. "Come any further and I'll flee on my horse, and you shan't see them again. I demand negotiation, and I'll speak with Adam and no one else."

Both the Arawaks and the Vikings wanted to take their chances, but Adam held them back.

"His horse is swift, and the forest is only a stone's throw away," said Adam. "We won't be able to capture him if he flees."

"He must pay for what he's done," said the Arawak chieftain.

"He will," said Adam, "just not now. We must end this conflict."

"Perhaps," said the Arawak.

"Talk to him slowly," said one of the Vikings. "We'll spread wide so that we'll get him when he leaves, even if we're on foot."

"We need to end this," said Adam.

It was too late; as Adam walked towards Balthasar, the Vikings were already starting to spread out, hoping to hunt Balthasar down as soon as he relinquished the heads in the sack.

/***/

"Their bodies are stashed away in our compound, way down south," said Balthasar. "You'll find them eventually."

Adam counted the heads; all missing Arawaks and Vikings were accounted for, including some that had been lost at battle that day. Adam couldn't help but shudder; the heads had been boiled, burnt, mangled and skewered in every way conceivable. Adam couldn't avoid thinking what it would be like to be in the dark tank himself, disembodied and tormented for eternity under Juan's throne. Adam made a mental note to return these heads as soon as possible to their comrades so that they could be reattached to their respective bodies.

They didn't deserve to exist like this, and the sooner he could get them whole again, the better.

"I have one more for you," said Balthasar.

Balthasar took out another sack and gave it to Adam, and Adam opened it to see Juan's face peering back at him. It had a bullet hole through its head; Adam looked down to see that Balthasar's sword was bloodied from his former leader's decapitation, and he had a pistol by his side.

Balthasar peered up into the sky and thought for a moment before looking at Adam.

"He wanted to flee, form another army over the next few decades, take the lessons we've learned here and use them to defeat you," said Balthasar. "And we would have been successful too."

Adam went through several scenarios in his mind and realized that Balthasar was right; Juan had been defeated this day, but wouldn't have been defeated twice; he was too smart. If Juan had planned for a few more decades, his army would have been ten times stronger and perhaps a hundred times deadlier. *But that didn't happen*, thought Adam. *And now you're holding his head in your hands, and history is up to you.*

"Why did you do this?" asked Adam.

Balthasar thought for a moment, peering off into the distance, seeing the Vikings and Arawaks sneak into the forest, waiting to hunt him down as soon as he escaped.

"Juan always said that morality was what we make it, and nothing more," said Balthasar. "When you kill enough people, *so many that there are no survivors to mourn them, it's not a wrong act*. If Juan's world would have been made, you and your army would have been boiling under his throne, and it would have been right. What happens is what happens, and there's nothing else, whether an asteroid hits the earth or Juan slaughters the entire world to bring a better tomorrow."

The Vikings and Arawaks in the distance took notice that Balthasar had no more sacks to give, and they began to encroach inwards.

"But you ended Juan's history with your own hand," said Adam. "You made a *choice*."

"Precisely," said Balthasar. "Juan's worldview rests on the idea that morality doesn't exist outside of us and outside of what we make it, and I believe that. However, morality exists within us for a reason, and that's to prevent a worldview like Juan's from realization."

Adam looked outside and saw that his group was starting to get close; Balthasar had a minute left to flee at most, but still felt he needed to say the things that needed to be said.

"Both you and he spoke of *falling on the right and wrong side of history*," said Balthasar. "But that's not always the case; though history can run out of our control, it lays entirely within the hands of men. It can even land in the hands of small men, albeit for an instant only. For this brief moment, be it Napoleon's back turned to a soldier or the sympathetic guard choosing to release a young Genghis Khan from slavery, history isn't with the great but rather under control of secondary figures like myself. At that time, men like me have to make a choice. Judas Iscariot chose his path, and I followed mine."

Balthasar looked at Adam's bag and then looked at him with faintly glowing eyes. Adam nodded and then peered outwards; the Arawaks and Vikings were now running towards Balthasar.

"Life is what we make it, nothing more, so do whatever you want, Adam," said Balthasar, "but do not let Juan live again."

Balthasar turned his horse around and whipped it, causing it to flee towards the outlying forest. Within a few moments Balthasar was gone, but a score of Adam's compatriots followed him on foot.

Balthasar might get away for now, thought Adam. *But he'll be hunted for the rest of his days, and an immortal hunted by immortals will inevitably be caught.*

Adam looked down at the sack beside him and gave a grim smile; the battle was won. It was now up to them to ensure that the battle was won forever.

/***/

By the next morning the imprisoned were in their individual tanks. They had come alive and were pounding the inside of the caskets, but they were contained.

"What are we going to do with them?" asked Mayfly.

"I don't know," said Adam. "I was hoping that you'd come up with a solution to that."

"Keep them in there a few more months," said Mayfly. "I'll come up with something, but for now I've got to head south."

"To free your brethren," said Adam. "I understand. Will you be back?"

"Perhaps," said Mayfly. "The mayflies born in Juan's prisons won't be able to survive on the outside, so I'm hoping to make our own colony somewhere. Maybe I'll come back here."

"You could," said Adam with a smile, "but if it's too cold for you, I've got a friend with an island off the coast of India. No one will bother you there."

"I'll keep that in mind," said Mayfly.

Mayfly stood on the wall and surveyed the ground surrounding the castle; the mist had poured over the battlefield during the night, and the sunrise was burning it off to show unblemished land. It was as if the fog had washed away all memory of the war, and Adam was glad for it.

"What are you going to do?" asked Mayfly.

"I'll probably stick around," said Adam. "I don't quite know what we've done here, but perhaps I'll stay to see it through."

"And then what?" asked Mayfly, before laughing to himself.

"What's so funny?"

"I'm not used to asking *and then what*," said Mayfly. "I'm not used to seeing beyond the next month."

"Get used to it," said Adam, returning the smile. "You can't just live for the moment now."

Adam eyed Giselle walking along the other end of the fortress.

"I honestly don't know where I should be, or what I should do," said Adam. "None of my experience has prepared me for this day."

"What do you *want* to do?" asked Mayfly.

"Stay here. I don't know why, but something tells me to stay, at least for a little while."

/***/

Adam watched Mayfly walk with Cattaga and Brogg over the frozen fields towards the edge of the woods. Cattaga and Mayfly traveled lightly, and Brogg carried a pack as big as both of them. They lingered at the cusp of the forest for a moment, waved goodbye, and then they were gone.

"Will they be okay?" asked Giselle.

"They'll be fine," said Adam. "Brogg'll defend them against any creature that comes their way, and Mayfly'll do the rest. He'll probably find a way to hitch a ride, even all the way up here; he's got charm."

"What about your brothers Phage and Geryon?" asked Giselle. "They seem to be missing."

"That's their style," said Adam. "They're not ones to say goodbye. They disappear just as quickly as they show up."

Giselle smiled in response and put her hand on Adam's and it felt right; he didn't know why but it *felt* right. He took her hand in his and she stood a bit closer to him, and together they kissed, and then watched the noonday sun peek out from behind a cloud and bathe the ground in a cool grey light.

"Your sister Phoe will be born again," said Giselle.

"She will," said Adam.

"I think we should find her and raise her together," said Giselle. "She's my class and I'll be able to guide her."

Adam smiled and instead of speaking he just nodded and held her close to him, letting her know that he agreed.

Adam heard a commotion behind them and was shocked to see the Fountain coming up to the surface, walking through the Arawaks who were all kneeling in her presence; she was wearing a thick suit that Santos had made to ensure that she would do no harm. She blinked in the sun and smiled; she was deadly perhaps, but had no desire to be so. Underneath Santos's suit, she still looked like an innocent young girl.

A few moments later there was more commotion as Skarr brought up what looked to be a small child in his arms. The Arawaks continued to kneel and Adam looked closer to see that it was the other half of the Fountain, which upon closer inspection was something between a fetus and a small child, dark and not yet fully formed. It had small limbs and couldn't walk on its own, but it was now strong enough to live and breathe by itself.

"We're about to start something interesting," said Giselle. "Something important and real."

"We are," said Adam, bringing Giselle in close to him.

He looked across the endless field towards the forest and couldn't help but smile; he hadn't felt like this since he could remember, if ever. So much had been at stake in the last few days, and no one would ever know what had happened at this small, frozen stronghold at the edge of the earth. History wouldn't record what they had done, and there would be no statues to hold this day's memory. But Adam didn't mind; he was following what felt right, and that gave him the sense of purpose that had eluded him for so long. He wanted to stay awake and see the day, not hide in the shadows like he had always done.

"The future is what we make it and nothing more," he said, holding Giselle close as the sun crept fully out of the clouds. "I don't fully understand what's happened, nor what will happen, but I know that the future is up to us. It depends on what we do *today*, tomorrow, and every day thereafter. The only truth I know is that *right now*, the world is ours, and it belongs to no one else."

THE END

ABOUT THE AUTHOR

Jon Maas is a writer living in Los Angeles. He writes during his bus ride to and from work, and owes much of this novel to the traffic on Laurel Canyon. He is a fan of all types of literature, with his favorite writers being John Updike, Bernard Malamud, George R.R. Martin and Larry McMurtry.

Photo courtesy of Dustin Hamano

Other works by Jon Maas:
City of gods – *Hellenica*

This book was edited by Patty Smith. You can find her at www.foolproofcopyedit.com

The cover art is by LNC Art Studios.

Actor Shawn Christian met Jon on the set of the movie *Spanners*, a film in which he both starred and Executive Produced.

He now acts as an adviser on all *Spanners* projects.

Made in the USA
Lexington, KY
17 September 2016